BEST SELLERS

THE PAINTING OPPOSITE: *THE FOX HUNT* BY WINSLOW HOMER

BEST SELLERS

from Reader's Digest
Condensed Books

The Reader's Digest Association
Pleasantville, New York

READER'S DIGEST CONDENSED BOOKS

Editor: John T. Beaudouin

Executive Editor: Joseph W. Hotchkiss

Managing Editor: Anthony Wethered

Senior Editors: Ann Berryman, Doris E. Dewey (Copy Desk), Marcia Drennen,
Noel Rae, Robert L. Reynolds, Jane Siepmann, Jean N. Willcox, John S. Zinsser, Jr.

Associate Editors: Istar H. Dole, Barbara J. Morgan, Frances Travis,
Patricia Nell Warren

Art Editor: William Gregory

Associate Art Editors: Marion Davis, Thomas Von Der Linn

Art Research: George Calas, Jr., Katherine Kelleher

Senior Copy Editors: Olive Farmer, Anna H. Warren

Associate Copy Editors: Jean E. Aptakin, Catherine T. Brown, Estelle T. Dashman,
Alice Murtha

Assistant Copy Editors: Dorothy G. Flynn, Enid P. Leahy, Marian I. Murphy

Research Editor: Linn Carl

SPECIAL PROJECTS

Executive Editor: Stanley E. Chambers

Senior Editors: Marion C. Conger, Sherwood Harris, Herbert H. Lieberman

Associate Editors: Elizabeth Stille, John Walsh

Rights and Permissions: Elizabeth Thole

Reader's Digest Condensed Books are published five times a year at Pleasantville, N.Y.

The condensations in this volume have been created by The Reader's Digest
Association, Inc., and are used by permission of and special arrangement with
the publishers and the holders of the respective copyrights.

With the exception of actual personages identified as such, the characters and
incidents in the fictional selections in this volume are entirely the products of the
authors' imaginations and have no relation to any person or event in real life.

The original editions of the books in this volume are published and
copyrighted as follows:

Jaws, published at $6.95 by Doubleday & Company, Inc.
© 1974 by Peter Benchley

The Dogs of War, published at $7.95 by The Viking Press, Inc.
© 1974 by Danesbrook Productions Ltd.

© 1975 by The Reader's Digest Association, Inc.

CONTENTS

W S

As the little resort community
prepared for a gala summer,
there appeared offshore a monster
from the deep that would turn
the season into a nightmare

A CONDENSATION OF THE BOOK BY

Peter Benchley

ILLUSTRATED BY STANLEY GALLI

The great white shark lurked just beyond the shallows, raiding the beaches and seizing its victims at random. No one—not the marine experts, the fishermen or the Coast Guard—could explain why it had appeared off that particular Long Island town that summer. But there the huge predator was, making its sinister presence felt in more ways than one.

Police Chief Martin Brody saw his duty clearly: the beaches must be closed. Mayor Larry Vaughan disagreed: it must be business as usual or the resort community would be ruined. And to Brody's pretty, discontented wife the incident provided an unexpected opportunity for romance.

Then, as the death toll rose and the town remained sharply divided over what to do, the grim truth had to be faced. Somehow, the monster must be caught and killed. . . .

PART ONE

1

THE great fish moved silently through the night water, propelled by short sweeps of its crescent tail, the mouth open just enough to permit a rush of water over the gills. There was little other motion: an occasional correction of the apparently aimless course by the slight raising or lowering of a pectoral fin—as a bird changes direction by dipping one wing and lifting the other.

The senses transmitted nothing extraordinary to the small, primitive brain. The fish might have been asleep, save for the movement dictated by millions of years of instinctive continuity: lacking the flotation bladder common to other fish and the fluttering flaps to push oxygen-bearing water through its gills, it survived

11

only by moving. Once stopped, it would sink to the bottom and die of anoxia.

The land along the south shore of Long Island seemed almost as dark as the water, for there was no moon. All that separated sea from shore was a long, straight stretch of beach—so white that it shone. From a house behind the grass-splotched dunes, lights cast yellow glimmers on the sand.

The front door to the house opened, and a man and a woman stepped out onto the wooden porch. They stood for a moment staring at the sea, embraced quickly, then ran together to the beach.

"First a swim," said the woman, "to clear your head."

"Forget my head," said the man. Giggling, he fell backward onto the sand, pulling the woman down with him. Urgently they fumbled with each other's clothing.

Afterward the man lay back and closed his eyes. The woman looked at him and smiled. "Now, how about that swim?" she said.

"You go ahead. I'll wait for you here."

The woman rose and walked naked to where the gentle surf washed over her ankles. The water was colder than the night air, for it was only mid-June. She called back, "Sure you don't want to come in?" But there was no answer from the man, who had fallen asleep.

She backed up a few steps and ran at the water. At first her strides were long and graceful, but then a small wave crashed into her knees. She faltered, regained her footing and walked until the water covered her shoulders. Then she began to swim—with the jerky, head-above-water stroke of the untutored.

A hundred yards offshore the fish sensed a change in the sea's rhythm. It did not see the woman, nor yet did it smell her. Running within the length of its body were thin canals filled with mucus and dotted with nerve endings, and these nerves detected vibrations and signaled the brain. The fish turned toward shore.

The woman continued to swim away from the beach, stopping now and again to check her position by the lights shining from the house. The tide was slack, so she had not drifted. But she was tiring, so she rested for a moment, treading water, and then started for shore.

The vibrations were stronger now, and the fish recognized prey. The sweeps of its tail quickened, thrusting the giant body forward with a speed that agitated the tiny phosphorescent animals in the water and cast a mantle of sparks over the fish.

The fish closed on the woman and hurtled past, a dozen feet to the side and six feet below the surface. She felt only a wave of pressure that seemed to lift her up and ease her down again.

The fish smelled her now, and began to circle close to the surface. Its dorsal fin broke water, and its tail, thrashing back and forth, cut the glassy surface with a hiss.

For the first time the woman felt fear, though she did not know why. Adrenaline shot through her body, urging her to swim faster. She was about fifty yards from shore. She could see the lights in the house, and for a comforting moment she thought she saw someone pass by one of the windows.

The fish was about forty feet from the woman, off to the side, when it turned suddenly to the left, dropped entirely below the surface and, with two quick thrusts of its tail, was upon her.

There was no initial pain, only one violent tug on the woman's right leg. At first she thought she had snagged it on a rock. She reached down to touch her foot. She could not find it. She reached higher, and then she was overcome by a rush of nausea and dizziness. Her groping fingers had found a nub of bone and tattered flesh. She knew that the warm, pulsing flow over her fingers in the chill water was her own blood.

Pain and panic struck together. The woman threw her head back and screamed a guttural cry of terror.

Now the fish turned again, homing on the stream of blood from the woman's femoral artery. This time it attacked from below. The great conical head struck the woman like a locomotive, knocking her out of the water, and the gaping jaws snapped shut around her torso. The fish, with the woman's body in its mouth, smashed down on the water, spewing foam and blood and phosphorescence in a gaudy shower.

THE MAN AWOKE, shivering in the early morning cold. The sun had not yet risen, but a line of pink on the eastern horizon told him that daybreak was near. He stood and began to dress. He was annoyed that the woman had not wakened him when she went back to the house, and he found it curious that she had left her clothes on the beach. He picked them up and walked to the house.

He tiptoed across the porch and opened the screen door. The deserted living room was littered with glasses, ashtrays and dirty plates. He walked across it and turned right, down a hall, past two closed doors. The door to the room he shared with the woman was open, and a bedside light was on. Both beds were made. He tossed the woman's clothes on one of them.

There were two more bedrooms in the house. The owners slept in one. Two other houseguests occupied the other. As quietly as possible the man opened the door to the first bedroom. There were two beds, each containing only one person. He closed the door and moved to the next room. The host and hostess were asleep on either side of a king-size bed. The man closed the door and went to check the bathroom. It was unoccupied. Then he went back to his room to find his watch. It was nearly five o'clock.

He sat on one bed and stared at the bundle of clothes on the other. He was certain the woman wasn't in the house. He began to consider the possibility of an accident.

Very quickly the possibility became a certainty. He returned to the hosts' bedroom, hesitated for a moment beside the bed, and then placed his hand on a shoulder. "Jack," he said. "Hey, Jack."

The man sighed and opened his eyes. "What?"

"It's me. Tom. I hate like hell to wake you up, but have you seen Chrissie?"

"What do you mean? Isn't she with you?"

"No. And I can't find her."

Jack sat up and turned on a light. His wife stirred and covered her head with a sheet.

"I'm sorry," Tom said. "Do you remember when you saw her last?"

"Sure I remember. She said you were going for a swim, and

14

you both went out on the porch. When did *you* see her last?"

"On the beach. Then I fell asleep. Didn't she come back?"

"Not before we went to bed, and that was around one."

"I found her clothes on the beach."

"You looked in the living room?"

Tom nodded. "And in the Henkels' room. I checked the whole house."

"So what do you think?"

"What I'm beginning to think," said Tom, "is that maybe she had an accident. Maybe she drowned."

Jack looked at him for a moment, then glanced at his watch. "I don't know what time the police in this town go to work," he said, "but I guess this is as good a time as any to find out."

WHEN the phone rang Patrolman Leonard Hendricks was at his desk in the Amity police station reading a detective novel called *Deadly, I'm Yours.*

He picked up the phone. "Amity Police, Patrolman Hendricks," he said. "Can I help you?"

"This is Jack Foote, over on Old Mill Road. I want to report a missing person. Or at least I think she's missing."

"Say again, sir?" Hendricks had served in Vietnam as a radio-man, and he was fond of military terminology.

"One of my houseguests went for a swim at about one this morning," said Foote. "She hasn't come back yet. Her date found her clothes on the beach."

Hendricks scribbled on a pad. "What is her name?"

"Christine Watkins."

"Age?"

"I don't know. Say around twenty-five."

"Height and weight?"

"Wait a minute." There was a pause. "We think about five feet seven, between one twenty and one thirty pounds."

"Color of hair and eyes?"

"Listen, Officer, why do you need all this? If the woman's drowned, she's probably the only one tonight. Right?"

15

"Who said she drowned, Mr. Foote? Maybe she went for a walk."

"Stark-naked at one in the morning? Have you had any reports about a woman walking around naked?"

Hendricks relished the chance to be insufferably cool. "Not yet. But once the summer season starts you never know what to expect. Color of hair and eyes?"

"Her hair is . . . oh, dirty blond, I guess. I don't know what color her eyes are. Let's say hazel."

"Okay, Mr. Foote. As soon as we find out anything we'll contact you."

Hendricks hung up and looked at his watch. It was 5:10, and he wasn't anxious to wake the chief for something as vague as a missing-person report. But if she was washed up somewhere, Chief Brody would want the whole thing taken care of before the body was found by some nanny with a couple of young kids.

Judgment, that was what the chief kept telling him he needed; that was what made a good cop. The cerebral challenge of police work had played a part in Hendricks' decision to join the Amity force after he returned from Vietnam. He was convinced that as soon as he could get sprung from this midnight-to-eight shift, he would start to enjoy his work. But Chief Brody liked to break in his young men slowly—at a time of day when they wouldn't be overtaxed.

Eight a.m. to four p.m. was the business shift, and it called for experience and diplomacy. Six men worked that shift. One handled the traffic intersection at Main and Water streets. Two patrolled in squad cars. One manned the phones at the station house. One handled the clerical work. And the chief handled the public: ladies who complained that they hadn't been able to sleep because of the din coming from The Randy Bear or Saxon's, the town's two gin mills; homeowners who complained that bums were disturbing the peace; and the vacationing bankers or lawyers who stopped in to discuss their various plans for keeping Amity a pristine and exclusive summer colony.

Four to midnight was the trouble shift, when young studs from the nearby Hamptons would flock to The Randy Bear and get involved in a fight, or speed drunkenly along the Montauk Highway; when, very rarely, a couple of predators from Queens would lurk in the dark side streets and mug passersby; and when, about twice a month in the summer, the police would feel obliged to stage a pot bust at one of the huge waterfront homes. The six largest men on the force worked four to midnight.

Midnight to eight was usually quiet. Normally, during the summer, it was manned by three officers. One, however, young Dick Angelo, was taking his two weeks' leave before the season began to swing. The third was a thirty-year veteran named Henry Kimble, who held a daytime job as a bartender at Saxon's.

Hendricks tried to raise Kimble on the radio, but he knew the attempt was hopeless. As usual, Kimble would be asleep in a squad car parked behind the Amity Pharmacy. Hendricks picked up the phone and dialed Chief Brody's home number.

Martin Brody was in that fitful state of semiconsciousness before waking. On the second ring of the phone he rolled over and picked up the receiver. "Yeah?"

"Chief, this is Hendricks. I hate to bother you this early, but I think we've got a floater on our hands."

"A floater? What the hell is a floater?"

Hendricks had picked up the word from his night reading. "A drowning," he said, embarrassed. He told Brody about the call from Foote. "I didn't know if you'd want to check it out before people start swimming. It looks like it's going to be a nice day."

Brody heaved an exaggerated sigh. "Where's Kimble?" he said. "Oh, never mind. It was a stupid question. One of these days I'm going to fix that radio of his so he can't turn it off."

Hendricks said, "Like I said, Chief, I hate to bother—"

"Yeah, I know, Leonard. You were right to call. I'll take a look along the beach in front of Old Mill and Scotch, then I'll go out and talk to Foote and the girl's date. I'll see you later."

Brody hung up the phone and stretched. He looked at his wife, lying next to him in the double bed. She had stirred when the phone rang, but soon lapsed back into sleep.

17

Chief
Martin
Brody

Ellen
Brody

Matt
Hooper

Mayor
Lawrence P.
Vaughan

Quint

Harry
Meadows

Ellen Brody was thirty-six, five years younger than her husband. The fact that she looked barely thirty, though a source of pride to Brody, was also one of annoyance. She had been able, despite the strains of bearing three children, to keep her good looks, whereas Brody—though hardly fat at six feet one and two hundred pounds—was beginning to be concerned about his blood pressure and his thickening middle. Sometimes he would catch himself gazing with idle lust at the young, long-legged girls who pranced around town during the summer. But he never enjoyed the sensation, for it made him wonder if Ellen felt the same stirring when she looked at the tanned, slim young men.

Summers were bad times for Ellen Brody, for in summer she was tortured by thoughts of chances she had missed. She saw boarding-school classmates, now married to successful husbands, summering in Amity and wintering in New York, graceful women who stroked tennis balls and enlivened conversations with equal ease, women who (Ellen was convinced) joked among themselves about Ellen Shepherd marrying that policeman.

Ellen had been twenty-one when she met Brody. She had just finished her junior year at Wellesley and was spending the summer in Amity with her parents—as she had done for the previous eleven summers. Though she'd enjoyed the modest wealth her father had earned, she had not been eager to live a life like her parents'. The petty social problems had bored her.

Her first contact with Brody was professional. Late one night she was being driven home very fast by an extremely drunk young man. The car was stopped by a policeman who impressed Ellen with his youth, his looks and his civility. After issuing a summons he confiscated the car keys and drove Ellen and her date to their respective homes. The next morning Ellen wrote Brody a thank-you note, and also a note to the chief of police commending young Martin Brody. Brody telephoned to thank her.

When he asked her out to dinner and the movies on his night off, she accepted out of curiosity. She had scarcely ever talked to a policeman, let alone gone out with one. Brody was nervous, but Ellen seemed so interested in him and his work that he eventually calmed down enough to have a good time. Ellen found him delightful: strong, simple, kind—sincere. He had been a policeman for six years. He said his ambition was to be chief of the Amity force, to have sons to take duck shooting in the fall and enough money for a vacation every second or third year.

They were married that November.

There were some awkward moments during the first years. Ellen's friends would ask them to dinner, and Brody would feel ill at ease and patronized. When they got together with Brody's friends, Ellen's past seemed to stifle fun. Gradually, as new acquaintanceships developed, the awkwardness disappeared. But they never saw Ellen's old friends anymore.

Until about four years ago she had been too busy and too happy to let the estrangement bother her. But when her last child started school she found herself adrift, and she began to dwell on memories of how her mother had lived: shopping excursions (fun because there was money to spend), lunches with friends, tennis games, cocktail parties, weekend trips. What had

19

once seemed shallow and tedious now loomed in memory like paradise.

At first she tried to reestablish bonds with friends she hadn't seen in ten years, but all common interests had long since vanished. Ellen talked gaily about local politics, about her job as a volunteer at the Southampton Hospital. Her old friends talked about New York politics, about art galleries, painters and writers they knew. Most conversations ended with feeble pledges about getting together again.

Once in a while she would try to make friends among the summer people she hadn't known, but the associations were forced and brief. Ellen was self-conscious about her house and about her husband's job. She made sure that everyone she met knew she had started her Amity life on an entirely different plane. She was aware of what she was doing and hated herself for it, because in fact she loved her husband deeply, adored her children and—most of the year—was quite content with her lot. But somehow the resentments and the longings lingered.

Brody rolled over toward Ellen, raising himself on one elbow and resting his head on his hand. With his other hand he flicked away a strand of hair that was tickling her nose and making it twitch. He debated rousing her, but he knew her early morning moods were more cantankerous than romantic. Still, it would be fun. There had not been much sex in the Brody household recently. There seldom was when Ellen was in her summer moods.

Just then Ellen's mouth fell open and she began to snore. Brody got up and walked into the bathroom.

It was nearly 6:30 and the sun was well up when he turned onto Old Mill Road. From the road there was no view of the beach. All Brody could see were the tops of the dunes. So every hundred yards or so he had to stop the squad car and walk up a driveway to a point from which he could survey the shore.

There was no sign of a body. All he saw on the broad white expanse were pieces of driftwood, a can or two and a yard-wide belt of seaweed pushed ashore by the southerly breeze. There was practically no surf, so if a body had been floating on the surface it would have been visible.

By seven o'clock Brody had covered the whole beach along Old Mill and Scotch roads. He turned north toward town on Bayberry Lane and arrived at the station house at 7:10.

"No luck, Chief?" Hendricks said.

"That depends on what you mean by luck, Leonard. If you mean did I find a body, the answer is no."

Brody poured himself a cup of coffee, walked into his office and began to flip through the morning papers—the early edition of the New York *Daily News* and the Amity *Leader*.

Kimble arrived a little before eight o'clock, looking, aptly enough, as if he had been sleeping in his uniform, and had a cup of coffee with Hendricks while they waited for the day shift to appear. Hendricks' replacement came in at eight sharp, and Hendricks was about to leave when Brody came out of his office.

"I'm going out to see Foote, Leonard," Brody said. "You want to come along? I thought you might want to follow up on your . . . floater." He smiled.

"Sure, I guess so," said Hendricks. "I got nothing else going today, so I can sleep all afternoon."

At the Footes' house the door opened almost before Brody finished knocking. "I'm Tom Cassidy," said a young man. "Did you find her?"

"I'm Chief Brody. This is Officer Hendricks. No, Mr. Cassidy, we didn't find her. Can we come in?"

"Sure. Go on in the living room. I'll get the Footes."

Within five minutes Brody had learned everything he needed to know. Then, to be thorough, he looked through the missing woman's clothes. "She didn't have a bathing suit with her?"

"No," said Cassidy. "It's in the top drawer over there."

"I see," said Brody. "We'd better go down to the beach. You don't have to come. Hendricks and I can handle it."

"I'd like to come, if you don't mind."

On the beach Cassidy showed the policemen where he had fallen asleep—and where he had found Christine Watkins' clothes.

21

Brody looked up and down the mile-long stretch. For as far as he could see, clumps of seaweed were the only dark spots on the white sand. "Let's take a walk," he said. "Leonard, you go east as far as the point. Mr. Cassidy, let's you and I go west. You got your whistle, Leonard? Just in case."

"I've got it," said Hendricks. "You care if I take my shoes off? It's easier walking on the sand."

"I don't care," said Brody. "You can take your pants off if you want. Of course then I'll arrest you for indecent exposure."

Hendricks started eastward, the wet sand cool on his feet. He walked with his head down, looking at the tiny shells and tangles of seaweed. A few little black beetles skittered out of his path, and when the wave wash receded he saw minute bubbles pop above the holes made by sandworms. He enjoyed the walk. It was a funny thing, he thought, that when you lived in a place you almost never did the things that tourists did—like walk on the beach or go swimming in the ocean.

Once Hendricks turned around to see if Brody and Cassidy had found anything. He guessed that they were nearly half a mile away. As he started walking again, he saw ahead of him an unusually large clump of kelp. When he reached it he bent down to pull some of the weed away. Suddenly he stopped, frozen rigid. He fumbled in his pants pocket for his whistle, blew it weakly, then staggered back and fell to his knees, vomiting.

Snarled within the weed was a woman's head, still attached to her shoulders, part of an arm and about a third of her trunk.

HENDRICKS was still on his knees when Brody and Cassidy got to him. Brody was several steps ahead of Cassidy, and he said, "Mr. Cassidy, stay back there a second, will you?" He pulled apart some of the weeds, and when he saw what was inside he felt bile rise in his throat. He swallowed and closed his eyes. After a moment he said, "You might as well look now, Mr. Cassidy, and tell me if it's her or not."

Cassidy shuffled forward reluctantly. Brody held back a piece of weed, to give him a clear look at the gray and gaping face.

"Oh, my God!" said Cassidy, and he put a hand to his mouth.

"Is it her?"

Cassidy nodded. "What happened to her?"

"Offhand, I'd say she was attacked by a shark," said Brody.

Cassidy's knees buckled, and as he sank to the sand he said, "I think I'm going to be sick."

Brody knew instantly that he had lost his struggle for control. "Join the crowd," he said, and he vomited, too.

2

SEVERAL minutes passed before Brody felt well enough to stand, walk back to his car and call for an ambulance from the South-ampton Hospital. By eleven o'clock he was back in his office, filling out forms about the accident. He had completed everything but cause of death when the phone rang.

"Carl Santos, Martin," said the voice of the coroner.

"Yeah, Carl. What have you got for me?"

"Unless you have any reason to suspect a murder, I'd have to say shark."

"I don't think it's a murder, Carl. I've got no motive, no murder weapons and—unless I want to go off into left field—no suspect."

"Then it's a shark. A big one. Even the screw on an ocean liner wouldn't have done this. It might have cut her in two, but—"

"Okay, Carl," said Brody. "Spare me the gore."

"Sorry, Martin. Anyway, I'd say shark attack makes the most sense to put down, unless there are . . . other considerations."

"No. Not this time, Carl. Thanks for calling." He hung up, typed "shark attack" on the forms, and leaned back in his chair.

The possibility of other considerations hadn't occurred to Brody. Those considerations were the touchiest part of his job, forcing him constantly to assess the best means of protecting the common-weal without compromising either himself or the law.

It was the beginning of the summer season, and Brody knew that on the success or failure of those twelve brief weeks rested the fortunes of Amity for a whole year. The winter population of Amity was about a thousand; in a good summer the population jumped to nearly ten thousand. And those nine thousand summer visitors kept the thousand permanent residents alive for the rest of the year.

Local merchants—from the owners of the hardware store and the sporting-goods store and the two gas stations to the local pharmacist—needed a boom summer to support them through the lean winter. Charter fishermen needed every break they could get: good weather, good fishing and, above all, crowds.

Even after the best of summers Amity winters were rough. Three of every ten families went on relief. Dozens of men were forced to move for the winter to the north shore of Long Island, where they shucked scallops for a few dollars a day.

Brody knew that one bad summer would nearly double the relief rolls. And two or three bad summers in a row—a circumstance that fortunately hadn't occurred in more than two decades—could wreck the town. If people didn't have enough money to pay for clothes or food or repairs, then business firms would have to close down. The town would lose tax revenue, municipal services would deteriorate and people would begin to move away. So everyone was expected to do his bit to make sure that Amity remained a desirable summer community.

Generally, Brody's contribution—in addition to maintaining the rule of law—consisted of suppressing rumors and, in consultation with Harry Meadows, the editor of the Amity *Leader*, keeping a certain perspective on the rare unfortunate occurrences that qualified as news.

If one of the wealthier summer residents was arrested for drunken driving, Brody was willing to book him for driving without a license, and that charge would be duly reported in the *Leader*. But Brody made sure to warn the driver that the second time he would be booked and prosecuted for drunk driving.

When youngsters from the Hamptons caused trouble, Harry Meadows was handed every fact—names, ages and charges lodged. When Amity's own youth made too much noise at a party, the *Leader* usually ran a one-paragraph story without names.

But Brody wanted full disclosure of the shark incident. He intended to close the beaches for a couple of days, to give the shark time to travel far from the Amity shoreline.

He knew there would be a strong argument against publicizing the attack. So far Amity's summer was shaping up as a mediocre one. Rentals were up from last year, but they were not "good" rentals. Many were "groupers," bands of ten or fifteen young people who came from the city and split the rent on a big house. At least a dozen of the expensive shorefront properties had not yet been rented. Sensational reports of a shark attack might turn the season into a disaster.

Still, Brody thought, one death would certainly have less effect than three or four. The fish might have disappeared already, but Brody wasn't willing to gamble lives on the possibility. He dialed Meadows' number. "Free for lunch, Harry?" he said.

"Sure," said Meadows. "My place or yours?"

"Yours," he said. "Why don't we order out from Cy's?"

"Fine with me," said Meadows. "Cy's Thursday special okay?"

Suddenly Brody wished he hadn't called at mealtime. The thought of food nauseated him. "No, just egg salad, I guess, and a glass of milk. I'll be right there."

Harry Meadows was an immense man; the mere act of drawing breath caused perspiration to dot his forehead. He was in his late forties, ate too much, chain-smoked cheap cigars, drank bonded bourbon and was, in the words of his doctor, the Western world's leading candidate for a huge coronary infarction.

When Brody arrived Meadows was standing beside his desk, waving a towel at the open window. "In deference to what your lunch order tells me is a tender stomach," he said, "I am trying to clear the air of essence of White Owl."

"I appreciate that," said Brody. He glanced around the small, cluttered room and found a chair. He pulled it over to Meadows' desk and sat down.

Meadows rooted around in a large brown paper bag, pulled out a paper cup and a plastic-wrapped sandwich, and slid them across the desk to Brody. Then he began to unwrap his own lunch: a large meatball sandwich, a carton of fried potatoes and a quarter of a lemon meringue pie. He reached behind his chair and from a small refrigerator took a can of beer.

"Amazing," said Brody. "I must have had about a thousand meals with you, Harry, but I still can't get used to it."

"Everyone has his little quirks, my friend," Meadows said as he lifted his sandwich. "Some men chase other people's wives. Some lose themselves in whiskey. I find my solace in nature's own nourishment."

They ate in silence for a few moments. Brody finished his sandwich and lit a cigarette. Meadows was still eating, but Brody knew his appetite wouldn't be diminished by a discussion of Christine Watkins' death.

"About the Watkins thing," he said. "I have a couple of thoughts, if you want to hear them." Meadows nodded. "First, it seems to me that the cause of death is cut-and-dried. Santos thinks it was a shark attack, and if you'd seen the body, you'd agree."

"I did see it."

"So you agree?"

"Yes. I agree that's what killed her. But there are a few things I'm not so sure of."

"Like what?"

"Like why she was swimming at that time of night. Do you know what the temperature was around midnight? Sixty. And the water was about fifty. You'd have to be out of your mind to go swimming under those conditions."

"Or drunk," said Brody, "which she probably was."

"You're probably right. There's one other thing that bothered me, though. It seemed damn funny that we'd get a shark around here when the water's still this cold."

"Maybe there are sharks who like cold water. Who knows about sharks?"

"I know a lot more about them than I did this morning. After I saw what was left of Miss Watkins, I called a young guy I know up at the Woods Hole Oceanographic Institution. I described the body to him, and he said it's likely that only one kind of shark would do a job like that."

"What kind?"

"A great white. Others attack people, like tigers and hammerheads and maybe makos and blues, but this fellow, Matt Hooper, told me that to cut a woman in half you'd have to have a fish with a mouth like this"—he spread his hands about three feet apart—"and the only shark that grows that big *and* attacks people is the great white. There's another name for them—man-eaters."

"What did he say about the cold water?"

"That it's quite common for a great white to come into water this cold. Some years ago a boy was killed by one near San Francisco. The water temperature was fifty-seven."

Brody said, "You've really been checking into this, Harry."

"It seemed to me a matter of public interest to determine exactly what happened and the chances of it happening again."

"And did you determine those chances?"

"I did. They're almost nonexistent. From what I can gather, this was a real freak accident. According to Hooper, there's every reason to believe that the shark is long gone. There are no reefs around here. No fish-processing plant or slaughterhouse that dumps blood or guts into the water. So there's nothing at all to keep the shark interested." Meadows looked at Brody. "So it seems to me, Martin, there's no reason to get the public all upset over something that's almost sure not to happen again."

"That's one way to look at it, Harry. Another is that since it's not likely to happen again, there's no harm in telling people that it did happen this once."

Meadows sighed. "Journalistically, you may be right. But I don't think it would be in the public interest to spread this around. I'm not thinking about the townspeople; they'll know about it soon enough, the ones that don't know already. But what about the people who read the *Leader* in New York or Philadelphia or Cleveland? A lot of the summer people subscribe year-round. And you know what the real estate situation is like this season. If I run a story saying that a young woman was bitten in two by a monster shark off Amity, there won't be another house rented in this town. Sharks are like axe murderers, Martin. People react to them with their guts."

Brody nodded. "I can't argue with that, and I don't want to tell the people that there *is* a killer shark around. You're probably right. That shark has probably gone a hundred miles away and won't ever show up again. But suppose—just suppose—we don't say a word, and somebody else gets hit by that fish. What then? I want you to run the story, Harry. I want to close the beaches for a couple of days, just for insurance. If we tell people what happened and why we're doing it, I think we'll be way ahead."

Meadows sat back in his chair. "There won't be any story about the attack in the *Leader*, Martin."

"Just like that."

"Well, not exactly. I'm the editor of this paper and I own a piece of it, but not a big enough piece to buck certain pressures."

"Such as?"

"I've already gotten six phone calls. Five were from advertisers—a restaurant, a hotel, two real estate firms and an ice-cream shop. They were most anxious that we let the whole thing fade quietly away. The sixth call was from Mr. Coleman in New York, who owns fifty-five percent of the *Leader*. It seems Mr. Coleman had received a few phone calls himself. He told me there would be no story in the *Leader*."

"Well, Harry, where does that leave us? You're not going to run a story, so as far as the good readers of the *Leader* are concerned, nothing ever happened. I'm going to close the beaches and put up a few signs saying why."

TEN minutes after Brody returned to his office a voice on the intercom announced, "The mayor's here to see you, Chief."

Brody smiled. The mayor. Not Lawrence Vaughan of Vaughan & Penrose Real Estate; not Larry Vaughan, just calling to check in. But Mayor Lawrence P. Vaughan, the people's choice. "Send His Honor in," Brody said.

Larry Vaughan was a handsome man in his early fifties, with

a full head of salt-and-pepper hair and a body kept trim by exercise. A native of Amity, he had made a great deal of money in real estate speculation, and he was the senior partner (some thought the *only* partner) in the most successful agency in town. He dressed with elegant simplicity, in timeless British jackets, button-down shirts and Gucci loafers. Unlike Ellen Brody, who had descended from summer folk to winter folk, Vaughan had ascended smoothly from winter folk to summer folk. As a local merchant he was not one of them, so he was never asked to visit them in New York or Palm Beach. But in Amity he moved freely among all but the most aloof members of the summer community, which, of course, was very good for business.

Brody liked Vaughan. He didn't see much of him during the summer, but after Labor Day, Vaughan and his wife, Eleanor, would occasionally ask Brody and Ellen out to dinner at one of the better restaurants in the Hamptons. The evenings were special treats for Ellen, and that in itself was enough to make Brody happy. Vaughan seemed to understand Ellen. He always treated her as a club mate and comrade.

Vaughan walked into Brody's office and sat down. "I just talked to Harry Meadows," he said. "Where are you going to get the authority to close the beaches?"

Vaughan was obviously upset, which surprised Brody. "Officially, I'm not sure I have it," Brody said. "The code says I can take whatever actions I deem necessary in the event of an emergency, but I think the selectmen have to declare an emergency. I don't imagine you want to go through all that rigmarole."

"Not a chance. But I don't want you to close the beaches. The Fourth of July isn't far off, and that's the make-or-break weekend. We'd be cutting our own throats."

"I know the argument, and I'm sure you know my reasons. It's not as if I have anything to gain by closing the beaches."

"No. I'd say quite the opposite is true. Look, Martin, this town doesn't need that kind of publicity."

"It doesn't need any more people killed, either."

"Nobody else is going to get killed. All you'd be doing by

29

closing the beaches is inviting a lot of reporters to come snooping around where they don't have any business."

"So? They'd come out here, and when they didn't find anything worth reporting, they'd go home again."

"Suppose they did find something. There'd be a big to-do that couldn't do anybody any good."

"Like what, Larry? What could they find out? I don't have anything to hide. Do you?"

"No, of course not. Look, if you won't listen to reason, will you listen to me as a friend? I'm under a lot of pressure from my partners. Something like this could be very bad for us."

Brody laughed. "That's the first time I've heard you admit you *had* partners, Larry. I thought you ran that shop like an emperor."

Vaughan was embarrassed, as if he felt he had said too much. "My business is complicated," he said. "There are times I'm not sure *I* understand what's going on. Do me a favor. This once."

Brody looked at Vaughan, trying to fathom his motives. "I'm sorry, Larry, I have to do my job."

"If you don't listen to me," said Vaughan, "you may not have your job much longer."

"You haven't got any control over me. You can't fire any cop in this town."

"Not off the force, no. But believe it or not, I do have discretion over the job of chief of police." From his jacket pocket he took a copy of Amity's corporate charter. He found the page he sought and handed the pamphlet to Brody. "What it says, in effect, is that even though you were elected by the people, the selectmen have the power to remove you."

Brody read the paragraph Vaughan had indicated. "You're right," he said. "But I'd love to see what you put down for 'good and sufficient cause.'"

"I dearly hope it doesn't come to that, Martin. I had hoped you'd go along, once you knew how I and the selectmen felt."

"All the selectmen?"

"A majority."

"Like who?"

"I'm not going to sit here and name names for you. All you have to know is that I have the board behind me, and if you won't do what's right, we'll put someone in your job who will."

Brody had never seen Vaughan in a mood so aggressively ugly. He was fascinated, but he was also slightly shaken. "You really want this, don't you, Larry?"

"I do." Sensing victory, Vaughan said evenly, "Trust me, Martin. You won't be sorry."

Brody sighed. "I don't like it," he said. "It doesn't smell good. But okay, if it's that important."

"It's that important." Vaughan smiled. "Thanks, Martin."

BRODY arrived home a little before five o'clock. His stomach had settled down enough to permit him a beer or two before dinner. Ellen was in the kitchen, still dressed in the uniform of a hospital volunteer. Her hands were busy, making a meat loaf.

"Hello," she said, turning her head so Brody could plant a kiss on her cheek. "What was the crisis?"

"You were at the hospital. You didn't hear?"

"No. I was stuck in the Ferguson wing."

"A girl got killed off Old Mill. By a shark." He reached into the refrigerator for a beer.

Ellen stopped kneading meat and looked at him. "A shark! I've never heard of that around here. You see one once in a while, but they never do anything."

"Yeah, I know. It's a first for me, too."

"So what are you going to do?"

"Nothing."

"Really? Is that sensible? Isn't there anything you can do?"

"Sure, there are some things I could do. Technically. But the powers that be are worried that it won't look nice if we get all excited just because one stranger got killed by a fish. They're willing to take the chance that it won't happen again."

"What do you mean, the powers that be?"

"Larry Vaughan, for one. He said he'd have my job if I closed the beaches."

"I can't believe that, Martin. Larry isn't like that."

"I didn't think so, either. Hey, what do you know about his partners?"

"In the business? I didn't think there were any. I thought he owned the whole thing."

"Apparently not."

"Well, it makes me feel better to know you talked to Larry. He tends to take a wider, more overall view of things than most people. He probably does know what's best."

Brody felt the blood rise in his neck. He tore the metal tab off his beer can, flipped it into the garbage, and walked into the living room to turn on the evening news.

3

FOR the next few days the weather remained clear. A gentle breeze rippled the surface of the sea but made no whitecaps. Only at night was there a crispness to the air, and after days of constant sun the earth and sand had warmed.

Sunday was the twentieth of June. About noon, on the beach in front of Scotch and Old Mill roads, a boy of six was skimming flat stones into the water. He stopped, walked up to where his mother lay dozing, and flopped down next to her. "Hey, Mom," he said. "I don't have anything to do."

"Why don't you go throw a ball?"

"With who? There's nobody here. Can I go swimming?"

"No. It's too cold. Besides, you know you can't go alone."

"Will you come with me?"

"Alex, Mom is pooped, absolutely exhausted. Can't you find anything else to do?"

"Can I go out on my raft? I won't go swimming. I'll just lie on my raft."

His mother sat up and looked along the beach. A few dozen yards away a man stood in waist-deep water with a child on his shoulders. She looked in the other direction. Except for a few couples in the distance, the beach was empty. "Oh, all right," she said. "But don't go too far out." To show she was serious she lowered her sunglasses so the boy could see her eyes.

"Okay," he said. He grabbed his rubber raft and dragged it down to the water. When the water reached his waist, he held the raft in front of him and leaned forward. A swell lifted it, with the boy aboard. He paddled smoothly, with both arms, his feet hanging over the rear of the raft. He moved out a few yards, then began to paddle up and down, parallel to the beach. Though he didn't notice it, a gentle current carried him slowly offshore.

Fifty yards farther out, the ocean floor sloped precipitously. The depth of the water increased from fifteen feet to twenty-five, then forty, then fifty, leveling off at about a hundred feet until the true ocean depths began.

IN THIRTY-FIVE feet of water the great fish swam slowly, its tail waving just enough to maintain motion. It saw nothing, for the water was murky with motes of vegetation. The fish had been moving parallel to the shoreline, too. Now it turned and followed the bottom upward.

The boy was resting, his arms dangling down, his feet and ankles dipping in and out of the water with each small swell. His head was turned toward shore, and he noticed that he had been carried out beyond what his mother would consider safe. He could see her lying on her towel, and the man and child playing in the wave wash. He began to kick and paddle toward shore. His arms displaced water almost silently, but his kicking feet made erratic splashes and left swirls of bubbles in his wake.

The fish did not hear the sound but rather registered the sharp and jerky impulses emitted by the kicks. It rose, slowly at first, then gaining speed as the signals grew stronger.

The boy stopped for a moment to rest, and the signals ceased. The fish slowed, turning its head from side to side, trying to recover them. The boy lay perfectly still, and the fish passed beneath him, skimming the sandy bottom. Again it turned.

The boy resumed paddling. He kicked only every third or fourth stroke, but the occasional kicks sent new signals to the fish. This time it needed to lock on them only an instant, for it was almost directly below the boy.

The fish rose. Nearly vertical, it now saw the commotion on the surface. There was no conviction that what thrashed above was food, but the fish was impelled to attack. If what it swallowed was not digestible, it would be regurgitated. The mouth opened, and with a final sweep of the sickle tail the fish struck.

The boy had no time to cry out. The fish's head drove the raft out of the water. The jaws smashed together, engulfing head, arms, shoulders, trunk, pelvis and most of the raft.

On the beach the man with the child shouted, "Hey!" He was not sure what he had seen. He had been looking toward the sea, then started to turn his head when an uproar caught his eye. He jerked his head back seaward again, but by then there was nothing to see but the waves made by the splash. "Did you see that?" he cried. "Did you see that?"

"What, Daddy, what?" His child stared up at him, excited.

"Out there! A shark or a whale or something! Something huge!"

He ran toward the boy's mother, who was half asleep on her towel. She opened her eyes and squinted at the man. She didn't understand what he was saying, but he was pointing at the water, so she sat up and looked out to sea. At first the fact that she saw nothing didn't strike her as odd. Then she said, "Alex."

BRODY was having lunch at home when the phone rang.

"Bixby, Chief," said the voice from the station house. "I think you'd better come down here. I've got this hysterical woman on my hands."

"What's she hysterical about?"

"Her kid. Out by the beach."

A twinge of unease shot through Brody's stomach. "What happened?"

"It's . . ." Bixby faltered, then said quickly, "Thursday."

Brody understood. "I'll be right there." He hung up the phone. Fear and guilt and fury blended in a thrust of gut-wrenching pain. He felt at once betrayed and betrayer, a criminal forced into a crime. He had wanted to do the right thing; Larry Vaughan had forced him not to. But if he couldn't stand up to Vaughan, what kind of cop was he? He should have closed the beaches.

"What is it?" asked Ellen.

"A kid just got killed."

"How?"

"By a goddam shark."

"Oh, no! If you had closed the beaches—"

"Yeah, I know."

HARRY Meadows was waiting for Brody in the parking lot behind the station house. "So much for the odds," he said.

"Yeah. Who's in there, Harry?"

"A man from the *Times*, two from *Newsday*. And the woman. And the man who says he saw it happen."

"How did the *Times* get hold of it?"

"Bad luck. He was on the beach. So was one of the *Newsday* guys. They're both staying with people for the weekend. They were on to it within two minutes."

"Do they know about the Watkins thing?"

"I doubt it. They haven't had any digging time."

"They'll get on to it, sooner or later."

"I know," said Meadows. "It puts me in a difficult position."

"*You!* Don't make me laugh."

"Seriously, Martin. If the *Times* prints that Watkins story in tomorrow's paper, along with today's attack, the *Leader* will look like hell. I'm going to have to use it, to cover myself, even if the others don't."

"Who are you going to say ordered it hushed up? Vaughan?"

"I'm not going to say anybody ordered it hushed up. There was no conspiracy. I'm going to talk to Carl Santos. If I can put the right words in his mouth, we may all be spared a lot of grief."

"What about telling the truth? Say that I wanted to close the beaches and warn people, but the selectmen disagreed. And say that because I was too much of a chicken to fight and put my job on the line, I went along with them."

35

"Come on, Martin, it wasn't your fault. It wasn't anybody's. We took a gamble and lost. That's all there is to it."

"Terrific. Now I'll just go tell the kid's mother that we're terribly sorry we had to use her son for chips."

Brody entered his office through a side door. The boy's mother was sitting in front of the desk, clutching a handkerchief. She was wearing a short robe over her bathing suit. Her feet were bare. Brody looked at her nervously, once again feeling the rush of guilt. He couldn't tell if she was crying, for her eyes were masked by large, round sunglasses.

A man was standing by the back wall. Brody assumed he was the one who claimed to have witnessed the accident.

Brody had never been adept at consoling people, so he simply introduced himself and started asking questions. The woman said she had seen nothing: one moment the boy was there, the next he was gone, "and all I saw were pieces of his raft." Her voice was weak but steady. The man described what he thought he had seen.

"So no one actually saw this shark," Brody said, courting a faint hope in the back of his mind.

"No," said the man. "But what else could it have been?"

"Any number of things." Brody was lying to himself as well as to them, testing to see if he could believe his own lies. "The raft could have gone flat and the boy could have drowned."

"Alex is a good swimmer," the woman protested. "Or . . . was."

"And what about the splash?" said the man.

Brody realized that the exercise was futile. "Okay," he said. "We'll probably know soon enough, anyway."

"What do you mean?" said the man.

"One way or another, people who die in the water usually wash up somewhere. If it was a shark, there'll be no mistaking it." The woman's shoulders hunched forward, and Brody cursed himself for being a clumsy fool. "I'm sorry," he said. The woman shook her head and wept.

Telling them both to wait in his office, Brody walked out into the front of the station house. Meadows was by the outer door, leaning against the wall. A young man in swim trunks and a short-

sleeved shirt was gesturing at Meadows and seemed to be asking questions. Two men were sitting on a bench. One wore swim trunks, the other a blazer and slacks.

"What can I do for you?" Brody said.

The young man next to Meadows stepped forward and said, "I'm Bill Whitman, from *The New York Times*. I was on the beach."

"What did you see?"

One of the others—obviously from *Newsday*—answered. "Nothing. I was there, too. Nobody saw anything. Except maybe the guy in your office."

The *Times* man said, "Are you prepared to list this as a shark attack?"

"I'm not prepared to list this as anything, and I'd suggest you don't either, until you know a lot more about it."

The *Times* man smiled. "Come on, Chief, what do you want us to do? Call it a mysterious disappearance? Boy lost at sea?"

Brody said, "Listen, Mr. Whitman. We have no witnesses who

saw anything but a splash. The man inside thinks he saw a big silver-colored thing that may have been a shark, but he says he has never previously seen a live shark, so that's not what you'd call expert testimony. We have no body, no real evidence that anything violent happened to the boy—"

Brody stopped at the sound of tires grinding on gravel. A car door slammed, and Hendricks charged into the station house, wearing swim trunks. "Chief, there's been another attack!" he said.

The *Times* man quickly asked, "When was the first one?"

Before Hendricks could answer, Brody said, "We were just discussing it, Leonard. I don't want you or anyone else jumping to conclusions. After all, the boy could have drowned."

"Boy?" said Hendricks. "What boy? This was a man, an old man. Five minutes ago. He was just beyond the surf, and suddenly he screamed bloody murder and his head went underwater and it came up again and he screamed something else and then he went down again. There was all this splashing around, and the fish kept coming back and hitting him again and again. That's the biggest fish I ever saw, big as a station wagon. I went in and tried to get to the guy, but the fish kept hitting him."

Hendricks paused, staring at the floor. His breath squeezed out of his chest in short bursts. "Then the fish quit," he said. "Maybe it went away, I don't know. I waded out to where the guy was floating. His face was in the water. I took hold of one of his arms and pulled. . . . It came off in my hand." Hendricks looked up, his eyes red and filling with tears of exhaustion and fright.

"Did you call the ambulance?"

Hendricks shook his head.

Brody said, "Bixby, call the hospital. Leonard, are you up to doing some work?" Hendricks nodded. "Then go put on some clothes and find some notices that close the beaches."

WHEN Brody arrived at his office in the station house on Monday morning *The New York Times* lay in the center of his desk. About three-quarters of the way down the right-hand side of page one he saw the headline and began to read:

SHARK KILLS TWO ON LONG ISLAND

BY WILLIAM F. WHITMAN

Special to The New York Times

AMITY, L.I., June 20—A 6-year-old boy and a 65-year-old man were killed today in separate shark attacks that occurred within an hour of each other near the beaches of this resort community on the south shore of Long Island.

Though the body of the boy, Alexander Kintner, was not found, officials said there was no question that he was killed by a shark. A witness, Thomas Daguerre, of New York, said he saw a large silver-colored object rise out of the water and seize the boy and his rubber raft and disappear into the water with a splash.

Amity coroner Carl Santos reported that traces of blood found on shreds of rubber recovered later left no doubt that the boy had died a violent death.

At least 15 persons witnessed the attack on Morris Cater, 65, which took place at approximately 2 P.M. a quarter of a mile down the beach from where young Kintner was attacked. Mr. Cater called out for help, but all attempts to rescue him were in vain.

These incidents are the first documented cases of shark attacks on bathers on the Eastern Seaboard in more than two decades.

According to Dr. David Dieter, an ichthyologist at the New York Aquarium at Coney Island, it is logical to assume—but by no means a certainty—that both attacks were the work of one shark.

Dr. Dieter said the shark was probably a "great white" (*Carcharodon carcharias*), a species known throughout the world for its voraciousness and aggressiveness.

In 1916, he said, a great white killed four bathers in New Jersey on one day—the only other recorded instance of multiple shark-attack fatalities in the United States in this century.

Brody finished reading the article and put down the paper. There were three people dead now, and two of them could still be alive, if only Brody had . . .

Meadows was standing in the doorway. "You've seen the *Times*," he said.

"Yeah, I've seen it. They didn't pick up the Watkins thing."

"I know. Kind of curious, especially after Leonard's little slip of the tongue."

"But you did use it."

"I had to. Here." Meadows handed Brody a copy of the Amity *Leader*.

The banner headline ran across all six columns of page one: TWO KILLED BY MONSTER SHARK OFF AMITY BEACH. Below that, in smaller type, a subhead: NUMBER OF VICTIMS OF KILLER FISH RISES TO THREE.

The victims were Alexander Kintner, age 6, who lived with his mother in the Goose Neck Lane house owned by Mr. and Mrs. Richard Packer, and Morris Cater, 65, who was spending the weekend at the Abelard Arms Inn. Patrolman Leonard Hendricks, who by sheer coincidence was taking his first swim in five years, made a valiant attempt to rescue the struggling Mr. Cater, but the fish gave no quarter. Mr. Cater was dead by the time he was pulled clear of the water.

The *Leader*'s account of the killings continued:

Last Wednesday night, Miss Christine Watkins, a guest of Mr. and Mrs. John Foote of Old Mill Road, went for a swim and vanished.

Thursday morning, Police Chief Martin Brody and Officer Hendricks recovered her body. According to coroner Carl Santos, the cause of death was "definitely and incontrovertibly shark attack." Asked why the cause of death was not made public, Mr. Santos declined to comment.

Brody looked up from the paper and said, "What about the beaches not being closed? Did you go into that?"

"*You* did. Read on."

Asked why he had not ordered the beaches closed until the marauding shark was apprehended, Chief Brody said, "The Atlantic Ocean is huge. Fish don't always stay in one area, especially an area like this where there is no food source. What were we going to do? Close our beaches, and people would just drive up to East Hampton and go swimming there. And there's just as good a chance that they'd get killed in East Hampton as in Amity."

After yesterday's attacks, however, Chief Brody did order the beaches closed until further notice.

"My God, Harry," said Brody. "You really put it to me. You've got me arguing a case I don't believe, then being proved wrong and *forced* to do what I wanted to do all along. That's a pretty dirty trick."

"It wasn't a trick. I had to have someone give the official line. I tried to get hold of Larry Vaughan, but he was away for the weekend. So you were the logical one. You admit you agreed to go along with the decision, so—reluctantly or not—you supported it."

"I suppose. Anyway, it's done. Is there anything else I should read in this?"

"No. I just quote Matt Hooper, that fellow from Woods Hole. He says it would be remarkable if we ever have another attack. But he's a little less sure than he was the last time."

"Does he think one fish is doing all this?"

"He doesn't know, of course, but offhand, yes. He thinks it's a big white."

"I do, too. I mean, I think it's one shark."

"Why?"

"I'm not sure, exactly. Yesterday afternoon I called the Coast Guard out at Montauk. I asked them if they'd noticed a lot of sharks around here recently, and they said they hadn't seen a one so far this spring. They said they'd send a boat down this way later on and give me a call if they saw anything. I finally called them back. They said they had cruised up and down this area for two hours and hadn't seen a thing. So there sure aren't many sharks around."

"Hooper said there was one thing we could do," Meadows said. "We could chum. You know, spread fish guts and goodies like that around in the water. If there's a shark around, he said, that will bring him running."

41

"Oh, great. And what if he shows up? What do we do then?"

"Harpoon him."

"Harry, I don't even have a police boat, let alone a boat with harpoons on it."

"There are fishermen around. It seems to me—" A commotion out in the hall stopped Meadows in midsentence.

They heard Bixby say, "I told you, ma'am, he's in conference."

Then a woman's voice said, "I don't care! I'm going in there."

The door to Brody's office flew open, and standing there clutching a newspaper, tears streaming down her face, was Alexander Kintner's mother.

Meadows offered her a chair, but she ignored him and walked up to Brody.

"What can I do—"

The woman slapped the newspaper across his face. It made a sharp report that rang deep into his left ear. "What about this?" Mrs. Kintner screamed. "What about it?"

"What about what?" said Brody.

"What they say here. That you knew it was dangerous to swim. That somebody had already been killed by that shark. That you kept it a secret."

Brody couldn't deny it. "Sort of," he said. "I mean yes, it's true, but it's . . . Look, Mrs. Kintner—"

"You killed Alex!" She shrieked the words, and Brody was sure they were heard all over Amity. He was sure his wife heard them, and his children.

He thought, Stop her before she says anything else. But all he could say was, "Sssshhh!"

"You did! You killed him!" Her fists were clenched at her sides, and her head snapped forward as she screamed, "You won't get away with it!"

"Please, Mrs. Kintner," said Brody. "Calm down. Let me explain." He reached to touch her shoulder and help her to a chair, but she jerked away.

"Keep your hands off me!" she cried. "You knew! You knew all along, but you wouldn't say. And now a six-year-old boy, a beautiful six-year-old boy, my boy . . ." Tears seemed to pulse from her eyes. "You knew! Why didn't you tell? Why?"

"Because we didn't think it could happen again." Brody was surprised by his brevity. That was it, really, wasn't it?

The woman was silent for a moment, letting the words register in her muddled mind. She said, "Oh," then slumped into the chair next to Meadows and began to weep in gasping, choking sobs.

Meadows tried to calm her, but she didn't hear him. She didn't hear Brody tell Bixby to call a doctor. And she saw, heard and felt nothing when the doctor came into the office, gave her a sedative, led her to his car and drove her to the hospital.

When she had left, Brody said, "I could use a drink."

"I have some bourbon in my office," said Meadows.

Brody smiled. "No. If this was any indication of how the day's going to go, I better not louse up my head."

The phone rang. It was answered in the other room, and a voice on the intercom said, "It's Mr. Vaughan."

Brody pushed the lighted button, picked up the receiver and said, "Hi, Larry. Did you have a nice weekend?"

"Until about eleven o'clock last night," said Vaughan, "when I turned on my car radio driving home. I was tempted to call you, but I figured you had had a rough enough day without being bothered at that hour."

"That's one decision I agree with."

"Don't rub it in, Martin. I feel bad enough."

Brody wanted to scrape the wound raw, to unload some of the anguish onto someone else, but he knew it was impossible, so all he said was, "Sure."

"I had two cancellations already this morning. Big leases. Good people. I'm scared to answer the phone. I still have twenty houses that aren't rented for August."

"I wish I could tell you different, Larry, but it's going to get worse with the beaches closed."

"You know that next weekend is the Fourth of July. It's already too late to hope for a good summer, but we may be able to salvage something—if the Fourth is good."

Brody couldn't read the tone in Vaughan's voice. "Are you arguing with me, Larry?"

"No. I guess I was thinking out loud. Anyway, you plan to keep the beaches closed until when? Indefinitely?"

"I haven't had time to think that far ahead. Let me ask you something, Larry. Just out of curiosity."

"What?"

"Who are your partners?"

It was a long moment before Vaughan said, "Why do you want to know? What does that have to do with anything?"

"Like I said, just curiosity."

"You keep your curiosity for your job, Martin. Let me worry about my business."

"Sure, Larry. No offense."

"So what are you going to do? We can't just sit around and hope the thing will go away."

"I know. A fish expert, friend of Harry's, says we could try to catch the fish. How about getting up a couple of hundred dollars to charter Ben Gardner's boat for a day or two? I don't know that he's ever caught any sharks, but it might be worth a try."

"Anything's worth a try, just so we get rid of that thing and go back to making a living. Go ahead. Tell him I'll get the money from somewhere."

Brody hung up the phone and said to Meadows, "I'd give a lot to know more about Mr. Vaughan's business affairs."

"Why?"

"He's a very rich man. No matter how long this shark thing goes on, he won't be badly hurt. But he's taking all this as if it was life and death—and I don't mean just the town's. His."

4

THURSDAY afternoon Brody sat on the beach, his elbows resting on his knees to steady the binoculars in his hands. When he lowered the glasses he could barely see the boat—a white speck that disappeared and reappeared in the ocean swells.

"Hey, Chief," Hendricks said, walking up to Brody. "I was just passing by and I saw your car. What are you doing?"

"Trying to figure out what the hell Ben Gardner's doing."

"Fishing, don't you think?"

"That's what he's being paid to do, but I've been here an hour, and I haven't seen anything move on that boat."

"Can I take a look?" Brody handed him the glasses. Hendricks raised them and looked out to sea. "Nope, you're right. How long has he been out there?"

"All day, I think. He said he'd be taking off at six this morning."

"You want to go see? We've got at least two more hours of daylight. I'll borrow Chickering's boat."

Brody felt a shimmy of fear skitter up his back. He was a very poor swimmer, and the prospect of being on top of—let alone in—water above his head gave him what his mother used to call the whim-whams: sweaty palms, a persistent need to swallow and an ache in his stomach—essentially the sensation some people feel about flying. "Okay," he said. "I guess we should. Maybe by the time we get to the dock he'll already have started in. You go get the boat ready. I'll telephone his wife to see if he's called in on the radio."

Hendricks was standing in Chickering's Aquasport, the engine running, when Brody came along the town dock and climbed down into the boat.

"What did she say?" asked Hendricks.

"She hasn't heard a word. She's been trying to raise him for half an hour, but she figures he must have turned off the radio."

"Is he alone?"

"As far as she knows. His mate had an impacted wisdom tooth that had to be taken out today."

Hendricks cast off the hawser at the bow, walked to the stern, uncleated the stern line and tossed it onto the deck. He moved to the control console and pushed a knobbed handle forward. The boat lurched ahead, chugging.

Brody grabbed a steel handle on the side of the console. "Are there any life jackets?" he asked.

"Just the cushions," said Hendricks. "They'd hold you up all right, if you were an eight-year-old boy."

"Thanks."

The breeze had died, but there were small swells, and the boat took them roughly, smacking its prow into each one, recovering with a shudder that unnerved Brody. "This thing's gonna break apart if you don't slow down," he said.

Hendricks smiled. "No worry, Chief. If I slow down, it'll take us a week to get out there."

Gardner's boat was anchored about three-quarters of a mile from shore, its stern toward them. As they drew nearer, Brody could make out the black letters on the flat wooden transom: *FLICKA.*

Fifty yards from the *Flicka,* Hendricks throttled down, and the boat settled into a slow roll. They saw no signs of life. There were no rods in the rod holders. "Hey, Ben!" Brody called. There was no reply.

"Maybe he's below," said Hendricks.

When the bow of the Aquasport was only a few feet from the *Flicka's* port quarter, Hendricks pushed the handle into neutral, then gave it a quick burst of reverse. The Aquasport stopped and, on the next swell, Brody grabbed the gunwale.

Hendricks made a line fast to the other boat, then both men climbed into the *Flicka's* cockpit. Brody poked his head through the forward hatch. "You in there, Ben?" He looked around, withdrew his head and said to Hendricks, "He's not on board. No two ways about it."

"What's that stuff?" said Hendricks, pointing to a bucket in one corner of the stern.

Brody walked to the bucket and bent down. A stench of fish and oil filled his nose. "Must be chum—fish guts," he said. "You spread it around in the water and it's supposed to attract sharks. He didn't use much of it. The bucket's almost full."

Suddenly a voice crackled over the radio. "This is the *Pretty Belle.* You there, Jake?"

"He never turned off his radio," said Brody.

"I don't get it, Chief. He didn't carry a dinghy, so he couldn't have rowed away. He swam like a fish, so if he fell overboard he would've just climbed back on."

Brody was standing at the starboard gunwale when the boat moved slightly, and he steadied himself with his right hand. He felt something strange and looked down. There were four ragged screw holes where a cleat had been. The wood around the holes was torn. "Look at this, Leonard."

Hendricks ran his hand over the holes. He looked to the port side, where a ten-inch steel cleat still sat securely on the wood. "What would it take to pull a thing as big as that out?" he said.

"Look here, Leonard." There was an eight-inch scar on the gunwale. "It looks like someone took a file to this wood."

Brody walked to the stern and leaned on his elbows on the gunwale. As he gazed down at the transom a pattern began to take shape, a pattern of holes, deep gouges in the wood, forming a rough semicircle more than three feet across. Next to it was another, similar pattern. And at the bottom of the transom, just at the waterline, were three short smears of blood. Please, God, thought Brody, not another one. "Come here, Leonard," he said.

Hendricks walked to the stern and looked over. "What?"

"If I hold your legs, you think you can lean over and take a look at those holes and try to figure out what made them?"

"I guess so." Hendricks lay on the top of the transom. Brody took one of his legs under each arm and lifted.

"Okay?" said Brody.

"A little more. Not too much! You just dipped my head in the water."

"Sorry. How's that?" Brody said.

"Okay, that's it." Hendricks began to examine the holes. "If some shark came along he could grab me right out of your hands."

"Don't think about it. Just look."

In a moment Hendricks said, "Hey, pull me up. I need my pocketknife."

"What is it?" Brody asked when Hendricks was back aboard.

"There's a white chip or something stuck into one of the holes," Hendricks replied. Knife in hand, he allowed himself to be lowered over the rail again. He worked briefly, his body twisting from the effort. Then he called, "Okay. I've got it. Pull."

Brody hoisted Hendricks over the transom. "Let's see," he said, and Hendricks dropped a triangle of glistening white denticle into his hand. It was nearly two inches long. The sides were tiny saws. Brody scraped the tooth against the gunwale, and it cut the wood.

"It's a tooth, isn't it?" said Hendricks. "My God! You think the shark got Ben?"

"I don't know what else to think," said Brody. He dropped the tooth into his pocket. "We might as well go. There's nothing we can do here."

"What do you want to do with Ben's boat?"

"It's getting dark. We'll leave it here. No one's going to need this boat before tomorrow, especially not Ben Gardner."

THEY arrived at the dock in late twilight. Harry Meadows and another man, unknown to Brody, were waiting for them. As Brody climbed the ladder onto the dock Meadows gestured toward the man beside him. "This is Matt Hooper. Matt Hooper, Chief Brody."

The two men shook hands. "You're the fellow from Woods Hole," Brody said, trying to get a look at him in the fading light. He was young—mid-twenties, Brody thought—and handsome: tanned, hair bleached by the sun. He was about as tall as Brody, an inch over six feet, but leaner.

"That's right," said Hooper.

Meadows said, "I called him. I thought he might be able to figure out what's going on."

Brody sensed resentment in himself at the intrusion, the complication that Hooper's expertise was bound to add, the implicit division of authority that Hooper's arrival had created. And he recognized the resentment as stupid. "Sure, Harry," he said.

"What did you find out there?" Meadows asked.

Brody started to reach in his pocket for the tooth, but he stopped. "I'm not sure," he said. "Come on back to the station house and I'll fill you in."

"Is Ben going to stay out there all night?"

"It looks that way, Harry." Brody turned to Hendricks, who had finished tying up the boat. "You going home, Leonard?"

"Yeah. I want to clean up before I go to work."

Brody arrived at police headquarters before Meadows and Hooper. It was almost eight o'clock. He had two phone calls to make—to Ellen, to see if there were any dinner leftovers, and, the call he dreaded, to Sally Gardner. He called Ellen first; the pot roast could be reheated. It might taste like a sneaker, but it would be warm. He hung up, checked the phone book for the Gardner number and dialed it.

"Sally? This is Martin Brody." Suddenly he regretted having called without thinking about what he should tell her.

"Where's Ben, Martin?" The voice was calm, but pitched slightly higher than normal.

"I don't know, Sally. He wasn't on the boat."

"You went on board? You looked all over it? Even below?"

"Yes." Then a tiny hope. "Ben didn't carry a dinghy, did he?"

"No. How could he not be there?" The voice was shriller now.

Brody wished he had gone to the house in person. "Are you alone, Sally?"

"No. The kids are here."

Brody dug at his memory for the ages of the Gardner children. Twelve, maybe; then nine, then about six. Who was the nearest neighbor? The Finleys. "Just a second, Sally." He called to the officer at the front desk. "Clements, call Grace Finley and tell her to get over to Sally Gardner's house. Tell her I'll explain later." As he turned back to the phone Meadows and Hooper walked into the office. He motioned them to chairs.

"But where could he be?" said Sally Gardner. "You don't just get off a boat in the middle of the ocean."

"No."

"Maybe someone came and took him off in another boat. Maybe the engine wouldn't start. Did you check the engine?"

"No," Brody said, embarrassed.

"That's probably it, then." The voice was subtly lighter, almost girlish, coated with a veneer of hope that, when it broke, would

49

shatter like iced crystal. "And if the battery was dead, that would explain why he couldn't call on the radio."

"The radio was working, Sally."

"Wait a minute. . . . Who's there? Oh, it's you." Brody heard Sally talking to Grace Finley. Then Sally came back on the line. "Grace says you told her to come over here. Why?"

"I thought—"

"You think he's dead, don't you?" She began to sob.

"I'm afraid so, Sally. That's all we can think at the moment. Let me talk to Grace, will you please?"

A couple of seconds later Grace's voice said, "Yes, Martin?"

"Can you stay with her for a while?"

"Yes. All night."

"That might be a good idea."

"Is it that . . . *thing* again?"

"Maybe. That's what we're trying to figure out. But do me a favor, Grace. Don't say anything about a shark to Sally. It's bad enough as it is." He replaced the phone and looked at Meadows. "You heard."

"I gather that Ben Gardner has become victim number four."

Brody nodded. "I think so." He told Meadows and Hooper about his trip with Hendricks. Once or twice Meadows interrupted with a question. Hooper listened, his angular face placid and his eyes— a light, powder blue—fixed on Brody. At the end of his tale Brody reached into his pants pocket. "We found this," he said. "Leonard dug it out of the wood." He flipped the tooth to Hooper, who turned it over in his hand.

"What do you think, Matt?" said Meadows.

"It's a great white."

"How big?"

"Fifteen, twenty feet. That's some fantastic fish." He looked at Meadows. "Thanks for calling me. I could spend a whole lifetime around sharks and never see a fish like that."

Brody asked, "How much would a fish like that weigh?"

"Five or six thousand pounds."

Brody whistled. "Three tons."

"Do you have any thoughts about what happened?" Meadows asked Hooper.

"From what the chief says, it sounds like the fish killed Mr. Gardner."

"How?" said Brody.

"Any number of ways. Gardner might have fallen overboard. More likely, he was pulled over. His leg may have gotten tangled in a harpoon line. He could even have been taken while he was leaning over the stern."

"How do you account for the teeth in the stern?"

"The fish attacked the boat."

"What the hell for?"

"Sharks aren't very bright, Chief. They exist on instinct and impulse. The impulse to feed is powerful."

"But a thirty-foot boat—"

"To him it wasn't a boat. It was just something large."

"And inedible."

"Not till he'd tried it. You have to understand. There's nothing in the sea this fish would fear. Other fish run from bigger things. That's their instinct. But this fish doesn't run from anything."

"Do you have any idea why he's hung around so long?" said Brody. "I don't know how much you know about the water here, but—"

"I grew up here."

"You did? In Amity?"

"No, Southampton. I spent all my summers there."

"*Summers.* So you didn't really grow up there." Brody was groping for something with which to reestablish his parity with, if not superiority to, the younger man, and what he settled for was reverse snobbism, a defensive attitude not uncommon to year-round residents of resort communities. It was an attitude that, in general, Brody found both repugnant and silly. But he felt somehow threatened by the younger man.

"Okay," Hooper said testily, "so I wasn't born here. But I've spent a lot of time in these waters, and I wrote a paper on this coastline. Anyway, you're right. This isn't an environment that would normally support a long stay by a shark. On the other hand, anyone who'd risk money—not to mention his life—on a prediction about what a shark will do is a fool. There are things that could cause him to stay here—natural factors, caprices."

"Like what?"

"Changes in water temperature or current flow or feeding patterns. As food supplies move, so do the predators. Last summer, for example, off Connecticut and Rhode Island, the coastline was suddenly inundated with menhaden—fishermen call them bunker. They coated the water like an oil slick. Bluefish and bass feed on menhaden, so all of a sudden there were masses of bluefish right off the beaches. Then the big predators came—tuna, four, five, six hundred pounds. Deep-sea fishing boats were catching bluefin tuna within a hundred yards of the shore. Then suddenly it stopped. The menhaden went away, and so did the other fish. I spent three weeks up there trying to figure out what was going on. I still don't know."

"But this is even weirder," said Brody. "This fish has stayed in one chunk of water only a mile or two square for over a week. He hasn't touched anybody in East Hampton or Southampton. What is it about Amity?"

"I don't know. I doubt that anyone could give you an answer."

Meadows said, "Minnie Eldridge has the answer."

"Who's Minnie Eldridge?" asked Hooper.

"The postmistress," said Brody. "She says it's God's will, or something like that. We're being punished for our sins."

Hooper smiled. "Right now, anyway, that's as good an answer as I've got."

"That's encouraging," said Brody. "Is there anything you plan to do to *get* an answer?"

"There are a few things. I'll take water samples here and in East Hampton. I'll find out how other fish are behaving—and I'll try to find that shark. Which reminds me, is there a boat available?"

"Yes, I'm sorry to say," said Brody. "Ben Gardner's. Do you really think you can catch that fish, after what happened to him?"

"I don't think I'd want to try to catch it. Not alone, anyway."

Brody looked into Hooper's eyes and said, "I want that fish killed. If you can't do it, we'll find someone who can."

Hooper laughed. "You sound like a mobster. 'I want that fish killed.' So go get a contract out on him. Who are you going to get to do the job?"

"I don't know. What about it, Harry? You're supposed to know everything that goes on around here. Isn't there any fisherman on this whole damn island equipped to catch big sharks?"

Meadows thought for a moment before he spoke. "There may be one. I don't know much about him, but I think his name is Quint, and I think he operates out of a private pier somewhere around Promised Land. I can find out a little more about him if you like."

"Why not?" said Brody. "He sounds like a possible."

Hooper said, "Look, Chief, that shark isn't evil. It's not a murderer. It's just obeying its instincts. Trying to get retribution against a fish is crazy."

"Listen, you . . ." Brody was growing angry—an anger born of frustration and humiliation. He knew Hooper was right, but he felt that right and wrong were irrelevant to the situation. The fish was an enemy. It had come upon the community and killed two men, a woman and a child. The people of Amity would demand the death of the fish. They would need to see it dead before they could feel secure enough to resume their normal lives. Most of all, Brody needed it dead, for the death of the fish would be a catharsis for him. But he swallowed his rage and said, "Forget it."

The phone rang. "Mr. Vaughan, Chief," Clements called.

"Oh, swell. That's just what I need." Brody picked up the receiver. "Yeah, Larry."

"Hello, Martin. How are you?" Vaughan was friendly, almost effusive. Brody thought, He's probably had a couple of belts.

"As well as can be expected, Larry."

"I heard about Ben Gardner. Are you sure it was the shark?"

"Yeah, I guess so. Nothing else seems to make any sense."

"Martin, what are we going to *do?* I'm getting cancellations every day. I haven't had a new customer in here since Sunday."

"So what do you want *me* to do?"

"Well, I thought . . . I mean, what I'm wondering is, maybe we're overreacting to this whole thing."

"You're kidding. Tell me you're kidding."

There was a moment of silence, and then Vaughan said, "What would you say to opening the beaches, just for the Fourth of July weekend?"

"Not a chance."

"Now listen—"

"No, you listen, Larry. The last time I listened to you we had two people killed. If we catch that fish, if we kill him, then we'll open the beaches. Until then, forget it."

"What about patrols? We could hire people to patrol up and down the beaches in boats."

"That's not good enough, Larry. What is it with you, anyway? Are your partners on you again?"

"That's none of your business, Martin. For God's sake, man, this town is dying!"

"I know it, Larry," Brody said softly. "And as far as I know, there's not a damn thing we can do about it. Good night." He hung up the phone.

Meadows and Hooper rose to leave. Brody walked them to the front door of the station house. As they started out Brody said to Meadows, "Hey, Harry, you left your lighter inside. Come on back and I'll give it to you." He waved to Hooper. "See you."

When they were back in Brody's office Meadows took his lighter from his pocket and said, "I trust you had something to say."

Brody shut the door. "You think you can find out something about Larry's partners?"

"I guess so. Why?"

"Ever since this thing began Larry has been after me to keep the beaches open. And now, after all that's just happened, he says he wants them open for the Fourth. The other day he said he was under heavy pressure from his partners. I told you about it."

"And?"

"I think we should know who it is who has enough clout to drive Larry crazy. He's the mayor of this town, and if there are people

54

telling him what to do, I think I ought to know who they are."

Meadows sighed. "Okay, Martin. I'll do what I can. But digging around in Larry Vaughan's affairs isn't my idea of fun."

Brody walked Meadows to the door, then went back to his desk and sat down. Vaughan had been right about one thing, he thought: Amity was showing all the signs of imminent death. And it wasn't just the real estate market.

Two new boutiques that had been scheduled to open the next day had had to put off their debuts until July third. The sporting-goods store had advertised a clearance sale—a sale that normally took place over the Labor Day weekend. The only good thing about the Amity economy, as far as Brody was concerned, was that Saxon's was doing so badly that it had laid off Henry Kimble. Now that he didn't have his bartending job, he could occasionally get through a shift of police work without a nap.

Beginning on Monday morning—the first day the beaches had been closed—Brody had posted men on them. Since then there had been four reports of shark sightings by members of the public. One had turned out to be a floating log. Two, according to fishermen, were schools of jumping baitfish. And one, as far as anyone could tell, was a flat nothing.

On Tuesday evening at dusk Brody had received an anonymous phone call telling him that a man was dumping shark bait into the water off the beach. It turned out to be not a man, but a woman in a man's raincoat—Jessie Parker, one of the clerks at Walden's Stationery Store. She admitted she had tossed a paper bag into the surf. It contained three empty vermouth bottles.

"Why didn't you throw them in the garbage?" Brody had asked.

"I didn't want the garbage man to think I'm a heavy drinker."

"Then why didn't you throw them in someone else's garbage?"

"That wouldn't be nice," she had said. "Garbage is . . . sort of private, don't you think?"

Brody had told her that from now on she should take her empty bottles, put them in a plastic bag, put that bag in a brown paper bag, then smash the bottles with a hammer until they were ground up. Nobody would ever know they had been bottles.

Brody looked at his watch. It was after nine o'clock. Before he left the office he called the Coast Guard station at Montauk and told the duty officer about Ben Gardner. The officer said he would dispatch a patrol boat at first light to search for the body.

"Thanks," said Brody. "I hope you find it before it washes up." He was suddenly appalled at himself. "It" was Ben Gardner, a friend.

"We'll try," said the officer. "Boy, I feel for you guys. You're having some summer."

"I only hope it isn't our last," said Brody. He hung up, turned out the light in his office and walked out to his car.

As HE turned into his driveway Brody saw the familiar blue-gray light of television shining from the windows. He walked through the front door and poked his head into the living room. His oldest boy, Billy, fourteen, lay on the couch. Martin, age twelve, lounged in an easy chair. Eight-year-old Sean sat on the floor, his back against the couch. "How goes it?" said Brody.

"Good, Dad," said Bill, without shifting his gaze from the tube.

"Where's your mom?"

"Upstairs. She said to tell you your dinner's in the kitchen."

"Okay. Not too late, Sean, huh? It's almost nine thirty."

Brody went into the kitchen and got a beer from the refrigerator. The remains of the pot roast sat on the counter in a roasting pan. He sliced a thick slab of meat and made a sandwich. He put it on a plate, picked up his beer and climbed the stairs to his bedroom.

Ellen was sitting up in bed, reading a magazine. "Hello," she said. "A tough day? You didn't say anything on the phone."

"You heard about Ben Gardner? I wasn't positive when I talked to you." He put the plate and the beer on the dresser and sat down to remove his shoes.

"Yes. I got a call from Grace Finley asking if I knew where Dr. Craig was. She wanted to give Sally a sedative."

"Did you find him?"

"No. But I had one of the boys take some Seconal over to her."

"I didn't know you were taking sleeping pills."

"I don't often. Just every now and then. I got them from Dr. Craig, when I went to him last time about my nerves. I told you."

"Oh." Brody began to eat his sandwich.

Ellen said, "It's so horrible about Ben. What will Sally do?"

"I don't know," said Brody. "Have you ever talked money with her?"

"There can't be much. She's always saying she'd give anything to be able to afford meat more than once a week, instead of having to eat the fish Ben catches. Will she get Social Security?"

"I'd think so, but it won't amount to much. There may be something the town can do. I'll talk to Vaughan about it."

"Have you made any progress?"

"You mean about catching that damn thing? No. Meadows called that friend of his down from Woods Hole, so he's here."

"What's he like?"

"He's all right, I guess. A bit of a know-it-all, but he seems to know the area. As a kid he spent his summers in Southampton."

"Working?"

"I don't know, living with the parents probably." He finished his sandwich in silence as Ellen aimlessly turned the pages of her magazine.

"You know," she said, "we should give the boys tennis lessons."

"What for? Have they said they want to play tennis?" Brody rose, undressed, and went to find his pajamas in the closet.

"No. Not in so many words. But it's a good sport for them to know. It will help them when they're grown-up."

"Where are they going to get lessons?"

"I was thinking of the Field Club. I think we could get in. I still know a few members."

"Forget it. We can't afford it. I bet it costs a thousand bucks to join, and then it's at least a few hundred a year."

"We have savings."

"Not for tennis lessons! Come on, let's drop it." He walked to the dresser to turn out the light.

"It would be good for the boys."

Brody let his hand fall to the top of the dresser. "Look, we're not tennis people. We wouldn't feel right there. *I* wouldn't feel right there." He switched off the light, walked over to the bed and slid in next to Ellen. "Besides," he said, nuzzling her neck, "there's another sport I'm better at."

Ellen yawned. "I'm so sleepy," she said. "I took a pill before you came home."

"What for?" Brody asked.

"I didn't sleep well last night, and I didn't want to wake up if you came home late."

"I'm going to throw those pills away." He kissed her cheek, then tried to kiss her mouth.

"I'm sorry," she said. "I'm afraid it won't work."

Brody turned onto his back and lay staring at the ceiling.

In a moment Ellen said, "What's Harry's friend's name?"

"Hooper."

"Not David Hooper."

"No. I think his name is Matt."

"Oh. I went out with a David Hooper a long, long time ago. I remember . . ." Before she could finish the sentence her eyes shut, and soon she slipped into the deep breathing of sleep.

PART TWO

5

ON HER way home Friday noon, after a morning of volunteer work at the Southampton Hospital, Ellen stopped at the post office to buy a roll of stamps and get the mail. There was no home delivery in Amity.

The post office, just off Main Street, had 500 mailboxes, 340 of which were rented to permanent residents. The other 160 were allotted to summer people according to the whims of the postmistress, Minnie Eldridge. Those she liked were permitted to rent boxes for the summer. Those she didn't like had to wait in line at the counter.

It was generally assumed that Minnie Eldridge was in her early seventies and that she had somehow convinced the authorities in Washington that she was well under compulsory retirement age. She was small and frail-looking, but able to hustle packages and cartons nearly as quickly as the two young men who worked with her. She never spoke about her past. The only common knowledge about her was that she had been born on Nantucket Island. But she had been in Amity for as long as anyone could remember.

Ellen sensed that Minnie didn't like her, and she was right. Minnie felt uneasy with Ellen because she was neither summer folk nor winter folk. She hadn't earned her year-round mailbox, she had married it.

Minnie was sorting mail when Ellen arrived.

"Morning, Minnie," Ellen said.

Minnie looked up at the clock and said, "Afternoon."

"Could I have a roll of eights, please?" Ellen put a five-dollar bill and three ones on the counter.

Minnie gave Ellen a roll of stamps and dropped the bills into a drawer. "What's Martin going to do about that shark?" she said.

"I don't know. I guess they'll try to catch it."

"*Canst thou draw out leviathan with an hook?*"

"I beg your pardon?"

"Book of Job," said Minnie. "No mortal man's going to catch that fish."

"Why do you say that?"

"We're not meant to catch it, that's why."

"I see." Ellen put the stamps in her purse. "Well, maybe you're right. Thanks, Minnie."

Ellen walked to Main Street and stopped at Amity Hardware. There was no immediate response to the tinkle of the bell as she opened the door.

She walked to the back of the store, to an open door that led to the basement. She heard two men talking below.

"I'll be right up," called the voice of Albert Morris. "Here's a whole box of them," Morris said to the other man. "Look through and see if you find what you want."

"Cleats," Morris said as he climbed to the top of the stairs.

"What?" said Ellen.

"Cleats. Fella wants cleats for a boat. Size he's looking for, he must be captain of a battleship. What can I do for you?"

"I want a rubber nozzle for my kitchen sink."

"Up this way." Morris led Ellen to a cabinet in the middle of the store. "This what you had in mind?" He held up a rubber nozzle.

"Perfect."

As he rang up the sale Morris said, "Lots of people upset about this shark thing. Maybe this fish expert can help us out."

"Oh, yes. I heard he was in town."

"He's down cellar. He's the one wants the cleats."

Just then Ellen heard footsteps on the stairs. She saw Hooper coming through the door and felt a surge of girlish nervousness, as if she were seeing a beau she hadn't seen in years.

"I found them," said Hooper, holding up two large stainless-steel cleats. He smiled politely at Ellen, and said to Morris, "These'll do fine." He handed Morris a twenty-dollar bill.

Ellen hoped Albert Morris would introduce them, but he seemed to have no intention of doing so. "Excuse me," she said to Hooper, "but I have to ask you something."

Hooper looked at her and smiled again—a pleasant, friendly smile. "Sure," he said. "Ask away."

"You aren't by any chance related to David Hooper, are you?"

"He's my older brother. Do you know David?"

"Yes," said Ellen. "Or rather, I used to. I went out with him a long time ago. I'm Ellen Brody. I used to be Ellen Shepherd."

"Oh, sure. I remember you."

"You don't."

"I do. No kidding. Let me see. . . . You wore your hair shorter then, sort of a pageboy. You always wore a charm bracelet. It had a big charm that looked like the Eiffel Tower. And you always used to sing that song—what was it called?—'Sh-boom,' right?"

Ellen laughed. "My heavens, you have quite a memory."

"It's screwy the things that impress kids. You went out with David for what—two years?"

"Two summers," Ellen said. "They were fun."

"Do you remember me?"

"Vaguely. You must have been about nine or ten then."

"About that; David's ten years older than I am. Another thing I remember: everybody called me Matt, but you called me Matthew. You said it sounded more dignified. I was probably in love with you."

"Oh?" Ellen reddened, and Albert Morris laughed.

Morris handed Hooper his change, and Hooper said to Ellen, "I'm going down to the dock. Can I drop you anywhere?"

"Thank you. I have a car. So now you're a scientist," she said as they walked out together.

"Kind of by accident. I started out as an English major. But then I took a course in marine biology to satisfy my science requirement, and—bingo!—I was hooked."

"On what? The ocean?"

"Yes and no. I was always crazy about the ocean. But what I got hooked on was fish, or, to be really specific, sharks."

Ellen laughed. "It's like having a passion for rats."

"That's what most people think," said Hooper. "But they're wrong. Sharks are beautiful. They're like an impossibly perfect piece of machinery. They're as graceful as any bird. They're as mysterious as any animal on earth. No one knows for sure how long they live or what impulses—except for hunger—they respond to. There are more than two hundred and fifty species of shark, and every one is different from every other." He stopped, looked at Ellen and smiled. "I'm sorry. I don't mean to lecture."

"You must be the world's greatest living shark expert."

"Hardly," Hooper said with a laugh. "But after graduate school I spent a couple of years chasing sharks around the world. I tagged them in the Red Sea and dove with them off Australia."

"You dove with them?"

Hooper nodded. "In a cage mostly, but sometimes not. I know what you must think. A lot of people think I've got a death wish, but if you know what you're doing, you can reduce the danger to almost nil."

"Tell me about David," Ellen said. "How is he?"

61

Jaws

"He's okay. He's a broker in San Francisco. He's been married twice. His first wife was—maybe you know this—Patty Fremont."

"Sure. I used to play tennis with her."

"That lasted three years, until she latched on to someone else. So David found himself a girl whose father owns most of an oil company. She's nice, but she's got the IQ of an artichoke. If David had had any sense he would have held on to you."

Ellen blushed and said softly, "You're nice to say it."

"I'm serious. That's what I'd have done."

"What did you do? What lucky girl finally got you?"

"None, so far. I guess there are girls around who just don't know how lucky they could be." Hooper laughed. "Tell me about yourself. No, don't. Let me guess. Three children. Right?"

"Right. I didn't realize it showed that much."

"No, no. I don't mean that. It doesn't show at all. Not at all. Your husband is—let's see—a lawyer. You have an apartment in town and a house on the beach in Amity."

Ellen shook her head, smiling. "Not quite. My husband is the police chief in Amity."

Hooper let his surprise show for only an instant. Then he said, "Of course—Brody. I never made the connection. Your husband seems like quite a guy."

Ellen thought she detected a flicker of irony in Hooper's voice, but then she told herself, Don't be stupid. You're making things up. "Do you live in Woods Hole?" she said.

"No. In Hyannis Port. In a little house on the water. I have a thing about being near the water. Say, do you still dance?"

"Dance?"

"Yeah. David used to say you were the best dancer he ever went out with. You won a contest, didn't you?"

The past was suddenly swirling around in her head, showering her with longing. "A samba contest," she said. "At the Beach Club. I'd forgotten. No, I don't dance anymore. Martin doesn't dance, and even if he did, nobody plays that kind of music anymore."

"That's too bad. Well, I should get down to the dock. You're sure I can't drop you anywhere?"

"Positive, thank you. My car's just across the street."

"Okay." Hooper held out his hand. "I don't suppose I could get you out on a tennis court late some afternoon."

Ellen laughed. "Oh, my. I haven't held a tennis racquet in my hand since I can't remember when. But thanks for asking."

"Okay. Well, see you." Hooper hurried off to his car. As he pulled out into the street and drove past her she raised her hand and waved, tentatively, shyly. Hooper waved back. Then he turned the corner and was gone.

A terrible sadness clutched at Ellen. More than ever before she felt that her life—the best part of it, at least—was behind her. Recognizing the sensation made her feel guilty, for she read it as proof that she was an unsatisfactory mother, an unsatisfied wife. She thought of a line from a song Billy played on the stereo. *I'd trade all my tomorrows for a single yesterday.* Would she make a deal like that? She wondered.

A vision of Hooper's smiling face flashed across her mind. Forget it, she told herself.

WITH the beaches closed, Amity was practically deserted on the weekend. Hooper cruised up and down offshore in Ben Gardner's boat, but the only signs of life he saw in the water were a few schools of baitfish and one small school of bluefish. By Sunday night he told Brody he was ready to conclude that the shark had gone back to the deep.

"What makes you think so?" Brody had asked.

"There's not a sign of him," said Hooper. "And there are other fish. If there was a big white in the neighborhood, everything else would vanish. That's one thing divers say about whites. When they're around there's an awful stillness in the water."

"I'm not convinced," said Brody. "At least not enough to open the beaches. Not yet." He almost wished Hooper had seen the fish. This was nothing but negative evidence, and to his policeman's mind that was not enough.

On Monday afternoon Brody was sitting in his office when Ellen phoned. "I'm sorry to bother you," she said. "But what would you

63

think about giving a dinner party? I can't even remember when our last one was."

"Neither can I," said Brody. But it was a lie. He remembered their last dinner party all too well. Three years ago, when Ellen was in the midst of a crusade to reestablish her ties with the summer community, she had asked three summer couples. They were nice enough people, Brody recalled, but the conversations had been stiff and uncomfortable. Brody and the guests had few common interests, and after a while the guests had fallen back on talking among themselves. When they had left, and after Ellen had done the dishes, she said twice to Brody, "*Wasn't* that a nice evening!" Then she shut herself in the bathroom and wept.

"Well, what do you think?" said Ellen.

"I guess it's all right. Who are you going to invite?"

"First of all, I think we should have Matt Hooper."

"What for? He eats over at the Abelard, doesn't he? It's all included in the price of the room."

"That's not the point. He's alone in town, and he's very nice."

"I didn't think you knew him."

"I ran into him in Morris's on Friday. I'm *sure* I mentioned it to you, because it turns out he's the brother of the Hooper I used to know."

"Uh-huh. When are you planning this shindig for?"

"I was thinking about tomorrow night. And it's not going to be a shindig. I simply thought we could have a nice, small party with a few couples. What about the Baxters? Would they be fun?"

"I don't think I know them."

"Yes, you do. Clem and Cici Baxter. She was Cici Davenport. They live out on Scotch. He's taking some vacation now."

"Okay. Try them if you want. How about the Meadowses?"

"But Matt Hooper already knows Harry."

"He doesn't know Dorothy."

"All right," said Ellen. "I guess a little local color won't hurt."

"I wasn't thinking about local color," Brody said sharply. "They're our friends."

"I know. I didn't mean anything."

64

"If you want local color, all you have to do is look on the other side of your bed."

"I *know*. I said I was sorry."

"What about a girl?" said Brody. "I think you should try to find some nice young thing for Hooper."

There was a pause before Ellen said, "All right. I'll see if I can think of somebody who'd be fun for him."

WHEN Brody arrived home the next evening Ellen was setting the dinner table. He kissed her and said, "It's been a long time since I've seen that silver." It was Ellen's wedding silver, a gift from her parents.

"I know. It took me hours to polish it."

"And will you look at this?" Brody picked up a tulip wineglass. "Where did you get these?"

"I bought them at The Lure."

"How much?" Brody set the glass down on the table.

"Twenty dollars. But that was for a whole dozen."

"You don't kid around when you throw a party."

"We didn't have any decent wineglasses," she said defensively.

Brody counted the places set. "Only six?" he said.

"The Baxters couldn't make it. Clem had to go into town on business, and Cici thought she'd go with him. They're spending the night." There was a fragile lilt to her voice, a false insouciance.

"Oh," said Brody. "Too bad." He dared not show that he was pleased. "Who'd you get for Hooper, some nice young chick?"

"Daisy Wicker. She works at The Bibelot. She's a nice girl."

"What time are people coming?"

"The Meadowses and Daisy at seven thirty. I asked Matthew for seven. I wanted him to come early so the kids could get to know him. I think they'll be fascinated."

Brody looked at his watch. "If people aren't coming till seven thirty, we won't be eating till eight thirty or nine. I think I'll grab a sandwich." He started for the kitchen.

"Don't stuff yourself," said Ellen. "I've got a delicious dinner coming."

65

Brody sniffed the kitchen aromas, eyed the clutter of pots and packages and said, "What are you cooking?"

"It's called butterfly lamb. I hope I don't botch it."

"Smells good," said Brody. "What's this stuff in the pot by the sink? Should I throw it out?"

Ellen hurried into the kitchen. "Don't you dare—" She saw the smile on Brody's face. "Oh, you rat." She slapped him on the rear. "That's gazpacho. Soup."

Brody shook his head. "Old Hooper's going to wish he ate at the Abelard," he said.

"You're a beast," she said. "Wait till you taste it. You'll change your tune."

At 7:05 the doorbell rang, and Brody answered it. He was wearing a blue madras shirt, blue uniform slacks and black cordovans. He felt crisp and clean. But when he opened the door for Hooper, he felt outclassed. Hooper wore bell-bottom blue jeans and Weejun loafers with no socks. It was the uniform of the young and rich in Amity.

"Hi," said Brody. "Come in."

"Hi," said Hooper. He extended his hand, and Brody shook it.

Ellen came from the kitchen in a long batik skirt and a silk blouse. She wore the cultured pearls Brody had given her as a wedding present. "Matthew," she said. "I'm glad you could come."

"I'm glad you asked me," Hooper said, shaking Ellen's hand. He turned and said to Brody, "Do you mind if I give Ellen something?"

"What do you mean?" Brody said. He thought, Give her what? A kiss? A box of chocolates? A punch in the nose?

"A present. Nothing, really. Just something I picked up."

"No, I don't mind," said Brody.

Hooper dug into the pocket of his jeans and handed Ellen a small package wrapped in tissue. "For the hostess," he said.

Ellen tittered and carefully unwrapped the paper. Inside was what seemed to be a pendant, an inch or so across.

"It's a tiger-shark tooth," said Hooper. "The casing's silver."

"Where did you get it?"

"In Macao. I passed through there a couple of years ago on a

66

project. There's a superstition that if you keep it with you, you'll be safe from shark bite. Under the present circumstances, I thought it would be appropriate."

"Completely," said Ellen. "Do you have one?"

"I have one," said Hooper, "but I don't know how to carry it. I don't like to wear things around my neck, and if you carry a shark tooth in your pants pocket, you end up with a gash in your pants."

Ellen laughed and said to Brody, "Martin, could I ask a huge favor? Would you run upstairs and get that silver chain out of my jewelry box? I'll put Matthew's shark tooth on right now."

Brody started up the stairs, and Ellen said, "Oh, and Martin, tell the boys to come down."

As he rounded the corner at the top of the stairs Brody heard Ellen say, "It *is* such fun to see you again."

Brody walked into the bedroom and sat down on the edge of the bed, clenching and unclenching his right fist. He felt as if an intruder had come into his home, possessing subtle weapons he could not cope with: looks and youth and sophistication and, above all, a communion with Ellen born in a time which, Brody knew, Ellen wished had never ended. He felt that Ellen was trying to impress Hooper. He didn't know why. It demeaned her, Brody thought; and it demeaned Brody that she should try, by posturing, to deny her life with him.

"To hell with it," he said aloud. He stood up, opened Ellen's jewelry box and took out the silver chain. Before going downstairs he poked his head into the boys' rooms and said, "Let's go, troops."

Ellen and Hooper were sitting on the couch, and as Brody walked into the room he heard Ellen say, "Would you rather that I not call you Matthew?"

Hooper laughed. "I don't mind. It sort of brings back memories."

"Here," Brody said to Ellen, handing her the chain.

"Thank you." She unclasped the pearls and tossed them onto the coffee table. "Now, Matthew, show me how this should go."

Brody went into the kitchen to make drinks. Ellen had asked for vermouth on the rocks, Hooper for a gin and tonic. He poured the vermouth and mixed Hooper's drink, then started to make a rye

67

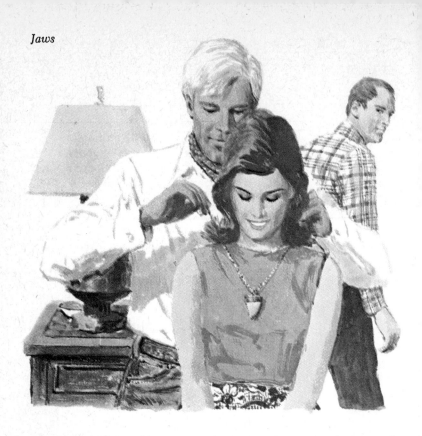

and ginger for himself. By habit he began to measure the rye with a shot glass, but then he changed his mind and poured until the glass was a third full. He topped it off with ginger ale, dropped in a few ice cubes and reached for the two other glasses. The only convenient way to carry them in one hand seemed to involve sticking his index finger down inside one glass.

The boys, neatly dressed in sport shirts and slacks, had joined Ellen and Hooper in the living room. Billy and Martin were crowded onto the couch with them and Sean was sitting on the floor. Brody heard Hooper say something about a pig, and Martin said, "Wow!"

"Here," said Brody, handing Ellen the glass with his finger in it.

"No tip for you, my man," she said. "It's a good thing you decided against a career as a waiter."

Brody looked at her, considered a rude remark and settled for, "Forgive me, Duchess." He handed the other glass to Hooper.

"Matt was just telling us about a shark he caught," said Ellen. "It had almost a whole pig in it."

"No kidding," said Brody. He took a long swallow of his drink.

"And that's not all, Dad," said Martin. "There was a roll of tar paper, too."

"And a human bone," said Sean.

"I said it looked like a human bone," said Hooper. "There was no way to be sure at the time. It might have been a beef rib."

"Hey, Dad," said Billy. "You know how a porpoise kills a shark?"

"With a gun?"

"No, man. It butts him to death. That's what Mr. Hooper says."

"Terrific," said Brody, and he drained his glass. "I'm going to have another drink. Anybody else ready?"

"On a weeknight?" said Ellen. "My!"

"Why not? It's not every night we throw a no-kidding, go-to-hell dinner party." Brody started for the kitchen but was stopped by the doorbell. He opened the door and saw Dorothy Meadows, wearing a dark blue dress and a single strand of pearls. Behind her was a girl Brody assumed was Daisy Wicker—a tall, slim girl with long, straight hair. She wore slacks and sandals and no makeup. Behind her was the unmistakable bulk of Harry Meadows.

"Hello, there," said Brody. "Come on in."

"Good evening, Martin," said Dorothy Meadows. "We met Miss Wicker as we came into the driveway."

"I walked," said Daisy Wicker. "It was nice."

"Good, good. Come on in." Brody led them into the living room and turned them over to Ellen for introduction to Hooper. He took drink orders, but before fixing them he made a fresh one for himself and sipped it while preparing the others. By the time they were ready he had finished half his drink, so he poured in a generous splash of rye and a dash more ginger ale.

Brody took Dorothy's and Daisy's drinks first, and returned to the kitchen for Meadows' and his own. He was taking one last swallow before rejoining the company when Ellen came in.

"Don't you think you better slow down?" she said.

"I'm fine," he said. "Don't worry about me." As he spoke he realized she was right: he had better slow down. He walked into the living room.

The children had gone upstairs. Dorothy Meadows was chatting with Hooper about his work, while Harry listened. Daisy Wicker was standing alone, on the other side of the room, gazing about with a subdued smile on her face. Brody strolled over to her.

"You're smiling," he said.

"Am I? I guess I was just interested. I've never been in a policeman's house before."

"And what have you decided? It looks just like a normal person's house, doesn't it?"

"I guess so." She took a sip of her drink and said, "Do you like being a policeman?"

Brody couldn't tell whether or not there was hostility in the question. "Yes. It's a good job, and it has a purpose to it."

"What's the purpose?"

"What do you think?" he said, slightly irritated. "To uphold the law."

"Don't you feel alienated?"

"Why the hell should I feel alienated? Alienated from what?"

"From the people. I mean, the only thing that justifies your existence is telling people what not to do. Doesn't that make you feel freaky?"

For a moment Brody thought he was being put on, but the girl never smiled or shifted her eyes from his. "No, I don't feel freaky," he said. "I don't see why I should feel any more freaky than you do, working at the whatchamacallit."

"The Bibelot."

"Yeah. What do you sell there, anyway?"

"We sell people their past. It gives them comfort."

"What do you mean, their past?"

"Antiques. They're bought by people who hate their present

and need the security of their past. If not theirs, someone else's. I bet that's important to you, too."

"What, the past?"

"No, security. Isn't that supposed to be one of the heavy things about being a cop?"

Brody glanced across the room and noticed that Harry Meadows' glass was empty. "Excuse me," he said. "I have to tend to the other guests."

Brody took Meadows' glass and his own into the kitchen. Ellen was checking the meat in the broiler.

"Where the hell did you find that girl?" he said. "She's a spook. She's just like some of the kids we bust who start smart-mouthing us in the station." He made a drink for Meadows, then poured another for himself. He looked up and saw Ellen staring at him.

"What's the matter with you?" she said.

"I guess I don't like people coming into my house and insulting me." He picked up the two drinks and started for the door.

Ellen said, "Martin . . ." and he stopped. "For my sake . . . please."

"Calm *down*," he said. "Everything'll be fine."

He refilled Hooper's glass and Daisy Wicker's. Then he sat down and nursed his drink through a long story Meadows was telling Daisy. Brody felt all right—pretty good, in fact—and he knew that if he didn't have anything more to drink before dinner, he'd be fine.

At 8:30 Ellen brought the soup plates out from the kitchen and set them around the table. "Martin," she said, "would you open the wine for me while I get everyone seated? There's a bottle of white in the refrigerator and there are two reds on the counter. You may as well open them all. The red will need time to breathe."

"Of course it will," Brody said as he stood up. "Who doesn't?"

In the kitchen he found the corkscrew and went to work on the two bottles of red wine. He pulled one cork cleanly, but the other crumbled, and pieces slipped into the bottle. He took the bottle of white out of the refrigerator, uncorked it and took it into the dining room.

Ellen was seated at the end of the table nearest the kitchen. Hooper was at her left, Meadows at her right. Next to Meadows, Daisy Wicker, then an empty space for Brody at the far end of the table, and, opposite Daisy, Dorothy Meadows.

When he had poured the wine Brody sat down and took a spoonful of the soup in front of him. It was cold, and it didn't taste anything like soup, but it wasn't bad.

"I love gazpacho," said Daisy, "but it's such a pain to make that I don't have it very often."

"Mmmm," said Brody, spooning another mouthful.

"Have you ever tried a G and G?"

"Can't say as I have."

"You ought to try one. Of course, you might not enjoy it since it's breaking the law."

"What is it?"

"Grass and gazpacho. Instead of herbs, you sprinkle a little marijuana over the top. It's really wild."

Brody didn't answer right away. He scooped out the last little bit of his soup, drained his wineglass in one draft and looked at Daisy, who was smiling sweetly at him. "You know," he said, "I don't find—"

"I bet Matt's tried one." Daisy raised her voice and said, "Matt, excuse me." The conversation at the other end of the table stopped. "I was just curious. Have you ever tried a G and G? By the way, Mrs. Brody, this is terrific gazpacho."

"Thank you," said Ellen. "But what's a G and G?"

"I tried one once," said Hooper. "But I was never really into that."

"Matt'll tell you," said Daisy to Ellen, and she turned to talk to Meadows.

Brody cleared away the soup bowls and Ellen followed him into the kitchen. "I'll need some help carving," she said.

"Okeydoke," said Brody, and Ellen hefted the lamb onto the carving board.

"Slices about three-quarters of an inch thick, the way you'd slice a steak," she said.

Brody searched through a drawer for a carving knife and fork. That Wicker dame was right about one thing, he thought as he slashed the meat: I sure feel alienated right now. A slab of meat fell away, and he said, "Hey, I thought you told me this was lamb."

"It is."

"It isn't even done. Look at that." He held up a piece he had sliced. It was pink and, toward the middle, almost red.

"That's the way it's supposed to be."

"Not if it's lamb, it isn't. Lamb's supposed to be well-done."

"Martin, believe me. It's all right to cook butterfly lamb sort of medium. I promise you."

Brody raised his voice. "I'm not gonna eat raw lamb!"

"Ssshhh!" said Ellen. "It's done! If you don't want to eat it, don't eat it, but that's the way I'm going to serve it."

"Then cut it yourself." He dropped the knife and fork on the board, picked up the two bottles of red wine and left the kitchen.

"There'll be a short delay," he said as he approached the table, "while the cook kills our dinner. She tried to serve it as it was, but it bit her on the leg."

Brody filled the wineglasses and sat down. He took a sip of his wine, said, "Good," then took another.

Ellen came in with the lamb. She returned to the kitchen, and came back carrying two vegetable dishes. "I hope it's good," she said. "I haven't tried it before."

"What is it?" asked Dorothy Meadows. "It smells delicious."

"Butterfly lamb. Marinated."

"Really? What's in the marinade?"

"Ginger, soy sauce, a whole bunch of things." She put a slice of lamb, some asparagus and some summer squash on each plate.

When everyone had been served and Ellen had sat down, Hooper raised his glass and said, "A toast to the chef."

The others lifted their glasses, and Brody said, "Good luck."

Meadows took a bite of meat and said, "Fantastic. It's like a very tender sirloin, only better. What a flavor!"

"From you, Harry," said Ellen, "that's a special compliment."

"It's delicious," said Dorothy. "Will you promise to give me the

73

recipe? Harry will never forgive me if I don't give this to him at least once a week."

"He better rob a bank," said Brody.

"But it is delicious, Martin, don't you think?"

Brody didn't answer. He had started to chew a piece of meat when a wave of nausea hit him. He felt detached, as if his body were controlled by someone else. His fork felt heavy, and for a moment he feared it might slip from his fingers. It was the wine. It had to be. With exaggerated precision he reached forward to push his wineglass away from him. He sat back and took a deep breath. His vision blurred. He tried to focus his eyes on a painting above Ellen's head, but he was distracted by the image of Ellen talking to Hooper. Every time she spoke she touched Hooper's arm—lightly, but, Brody thought, intimately, as if they were sharing secrets. He didn't hear what anyone was saying. The last thing he remembered hearing was, "Don't you think?" Who had said it? He looked at Meadows, who was talking to Daisy. Then he looked at Dorothy and said thickly, "Yes."

She looked up at him. "What did you say, Martin?"

He couldn't speak. He wanted to stand and walk out to the kitchen, but he didn't trust his legs. Just sit still, he told himself. It'll pass.

And it did. His head began to clear, and by the time dessert was served he was feeling well. He had two helpings of the coffee ice cream in a pool of crème de cacao and chatted amiably with Dorothy.

They had coffee in the living room, and Brody offered drinks, but only Meadows accepted. "A tiny brandy, if you have it," he said.

Brody poured Meadows' drink and thought briefly of having one, too. But he resisted, telling himself, Don't press your luck.

At a little after ten o'clock Meadows yawned and said, "Dorothy, I think we had best take our leave."

"I should go, too," said Daisy. "I have to be at work at eight. Not that we're selling very much these days."

Meadows stood up. "Well, let's hope the worst is over," he said.

"From what I gather from our expert here, there's a good chance the leviathan has left."

"A chance," said Hooper. "I hope so." He rose. "I should be on my way, too."

"Oh, don't go!" Ellen said. The words came out much stronger than she intended, and she added quickly, "I mean, it's only ten."

"I know," said Hooper. "But if the weather's good, I want to get out on the water early. I can drop Daisy off on my way home."

Daisy said, "That would be fun."

"The Meadowses can drop her," Ellen said.

"True," said Hooper, "but I really should go so I can get up early. But thanks for the thought."

They said their good-bys at the front door. Hooper and Daisy were the last to leave, and when he extended his hand to Ellen she took it in both of hers and said, "Thank you *so* much for my shark tooth."

"You're welcome. I'm glad you like it."

"We'll see you again before you go?"

"Count on it."

"Wonderful." She released his hand. He said a quick goodnight to Brody and walked to his car.

Ellen waited at the door until both cars had pulled out of the driveway, then she turned off the outside light. Without a word she began to pick up the glasses, cups and ashtrays.

Brody carried a stack of dessert dishes into the kitchen, set them on the sink and said, "Well, that was all right."

"No thanks to you," said Ellen. "You were awful."

He was surprised at the ferocity of her attack. "What are you talking about?"

"I don't want to talk about it."

"Just like that. You don't want to talk about it. Look . . . okay, I was wrong about the damn meat. I'm sorry. Now—"

"I said I don't want to talk about it!"

Brody was ready for a fight, but he said only, "Well, I'm sorry about that." He walked out of the kitchen and climbed the stairs.

As he was undressing, the thought occurred to him that the

cause of all the unpleasantness was a fish: a mindless beast that he had never seen. The ludicrousness of it made him smile.

He crawled into bed and fell into a dreamless sleep.

6

BRODY awoke with a start, jolted by a signal that told him something was wrong. He threw his arm across the bed to touch Ellen. She wasn't there. He sat up and saw her sitting in a chair by the window. Rain splashed against the panes, and he heard the wind whipping through the trees.

"Lousy day, huh?" he said. She didn't answer, continuing to stare fixedly at the drops sliding down the glass. "How come you're up so early?"

"I couldn't sleep." She seemed subdued, sad.

"What's the matter?"

"Nothing."

"Whatever you say." Brody got out of bed.

When he had shaved and dressed he went down to the kitchen. The boys were finishing breakfast, and Ellen was frying his egg. "What are you guys gonna do on this crummy day?" he said.

"Clean lawnmowers," said Billy, who worked during the summer for a local gardener. "Boy, do I hate rainy days."

"And what about you two?" Brody said to Martin and Sean.

"Martin's going to the Boys Club," said Ellen, "and Sean's spending the day at the Santoses'."

"And you?"

"I've got a full day at the hospital. Which reminds me: I won't be home for lunch. Can you get something downtown?"

"Sure. I didn't know you worked a full day Wednesdays."

"I don't, usually. But one of the girls is sick, and I said I'd fill in. Could you drop Sean and Martin off on your way to work? I want to do a little shopping on my way to the hospital."

"No problem."

After they had left, Ellen looked at the kitchen clock. It was a few minutes to eight. Too early? Maybe. But better to catch him now, before he went off somewhere. She held out her right hand and tried to steady the fingers, but they quivered uncontrollably. She went upstairs to the bedroom and picked up the green phone book. She found the number for the Abelard Arms Inn, hesitated for a moment, then dialed.

"Abelard Arms."

"Mr. Hooper's room, please."

Ellen heard the phone ring once, then again. She could hear her heart beating, and she saw the pulse throb in her right wrist. Hang up, she told herself. Hang up. There's time.

"Hello?" said Hooper's voice.

Ellen swallowed and said, "Hi. It's me . . . I mean it's Ellen."

"Oh, hi."

"I hope I didn't wake you."

"No. I was just going for breakfast."

"Good. It's not a very nice day. Will you be able to work?"

"I don't know. I was trying to figure that out."

"Oh." She paused, fighting the dizziness that was creeping up on her. Do it, she said to herself. The words spilled from her mouth. "I was wondering, if you can't work today . . . if there was any chance you'd like to . . . if you're free for lunch."

"Lunch?"

"Yes. You know, if you have nothing else to do."

"You mean you and the chief and I?"

"No, just you and I. Martin usually has lunch at his desk. I don't want to interfere with your plans or anything. . . ."

"No, no. That's okay. What did you have in mind?"

"There's a wonderful place up in Sag Harbor. Banner's. Do you know it?" She hoped he didn't. She didn't know it, but she had heard that it was good and quiet and dark.

"Sag Harbor," said Hooper. "That's quite a hike for lunch."

"It's only about fifteen or twenty minutes. I could meet you there whenever you like."

"Anytime's all right with me."

"Around twelve thirty, then?"

"Twelve thirty it is. See you then."

77

Ellen hung up the phone. Her hands were still shaking, but she felt elated, excited. Her senses seemed alive and incredibly keen. She felt more intensely feminine than she had in years.

She took a shower. Then she stood before the full-length mirror examining herself. Would the offering be accepted? She had worked to keep in shape, to preserve the smoothness and sinuousness of youth. She could not bear the thought of rejection.

She dressed in her hospital clothes. From the back of her closet she took a plastic shopping bag, into which she put fresh underthings, a lavender summer dress and a pair of low-heeled pumps. She carried the bag to the garage, tossed it into her Volkswagen and drove to the Southampton Hospital.

She didn't know exactly when she had decided on this rash, dangerous plan. She had been thinking about it—and trying not to think about it—since the day she first met Hooper. She had weighed the risks and somehow calculated that they were worth taking. She wanted to be reassured that she was desirable—not just to her husband, but to the people she saw as her real peers, the people among whom she still numbered herself. The thought of love never entered her mind. Nor did she want a relationship either profound or enduring. She sought only to be restored.

Ellen was grateful that her work at the hospital demanded concentration and conversation, for it prevented her from thinking. At 11:45 she told the supervisor of volunteers that she didn't feel well. Her thyroid was acting up again, she said, and she thought she'd probably go home and lie down.

SHE drove most of the way to Sag Harbor, then stopped at a gas station. When the tank was full and the gas paid for, she used the ladies' room to change her clothes.

It was 12:20 when she arrived at Banner's, a small steak-and-seafood restaurant on the water. The parking lot was concealed from the street, for which she was grateful; someone she knew might drive by, and she didn't want her car in plain view.

The restaurant was dark, with a bar on the right as she walked in. The bartender, a young man with a Vandyke beard and a button-down shirt, sat by the cash register, reading the New York *Daily News,* and a waitress stood at the bar, folding napkins. Apart from one couple at a table, they were the only people in the room. Ellen looked at her watch. Almost 12:30.

The waitress saw Ellen and said, "Hello. May I help you?"

"Yes. I'd like a table for two, please. That corner booth, if you don't mind."

"Sure," said the waitress. "Anywhere you like." She led Ellen to the booth, and Ellen slipped in with her back to the door. Hooper would be able to find her. "Can I get you a drink?"

"Yes. A gin and tonic, please."

The waitress brought the drink, and Ellen drank half of it immediately, eager to feel the relaxing warmth of alcohol. It was the first time since her wedding that Ellen had had a drink during the day. Every few seconds she checked the door and looked at her watch. It was almost 12:45. He's not going to come, she thought. What will I do if he doesn't come?

"Hello." Hooper slid into the seat opposite her and said, "I'm sorry I'm late. I had to stop for gas, and the station was jammed." He looked into her eyes and smiled.

Ellen looked down at her glass. "You don't have to apologize. I was late myself."

The waitress came over, and Hooper, noticing Ellen's glass, ordered a gin and tonic.

"I'll have another," said Ellen. "This one's almost finished."

The waitress left, and Hooper said, "I don't normally drink at lunch."

"Neither do I."

"After about three drinks I say stupid things. I never did hold my liquor very well."

Ellen nodded. "I know the feeling. I tend to get sort of . . ."

"Impetuous? So do I."

"Really? I thought scientists weren't ever impetuous."

Hooper smiled. "Beneath our icy exteriors," he said, "we are some of the raunchiest people in the world."

They chatted about old times, about people they had known,

about Hooper's ambitions in ichthyology. They never mentioned the shark or Brody or Ellen's children. It was an easy, rambling conversation, which suited Ellen. Her second drink loosened her up, and she felt happy and in command of herself.

She wanted Hooper to have another drink, and she knew he was not likely to take the initiative and order one. She picked up a menu and said, "Let me see. What looks good?"

Hooper picked up the other menu, and after a minute the waitress strolled over to the table. "Are you ready to order?"

"Not quite yet," said Ellen. "Why don't we have one more drink while we're looking?"

Hooper pondered for a moment. Then he nodded his head and said, "Sure. A special occasion."

The waitress brought their drinks and said, "Ready?"

"Yes," said Ellen. "I'll have the shrimp cocktail and the chicken."

Hooper said, "Are these really bay scallops?"

"I guess so," said the waitress. "If that's what it says."

"All right. I'll have the scallops."

"Anything to start?"

"No," said Hooper, raising his glass. "This'll be fine."

In a few minutes the waitress brought Ellen's shrimp. When she had left, Ellen said, "Do you know what I'd love? Some wine."

"That's a very good idea," Hooper said, looking at her. "But remember what I said about impetuousness. I may become irresponsible."

"I'm not worried." Ellen felt a blush crawl up her cheeks.

"Okay," Hooper said, "but first I'd better check the treasury." He reached in his back pocket for his wallet.

"Oh, no. This is my treat."

"Don't be silly."

"No, really. I asked you to lunch." She began to panic. She didn't want to annoy him by sticking him with a big bill.

"I know," he said. "But I'd like to take *you* to lunch."

She toyed with the one shrimp left on her plate. "Well . . ."

"I know you're only being thoughtful," Hooper said, "but don't be. Didn't David ever tell you about our grandfather?"

"Not that I remember. What about him?"

"Old Matt was known—and not very affectionately—as the Bandit. If he were alive today, I'd probably be at the head of the pack calling for his scalp. But he isn't, so all I've had to worry about was whether to keep the bundle of money he left me or give it away."

"What did your grandfather do?"

"Railroads and mining. Technically, that is. Basically he was a robber baron. At one point he owned most of Denver. He was the landlord of the red-light district." Hooper laughed. "And from what I hear, he liked to collect his rent in trade."

"That's supposed to be every schoolgirl's fantasy," Ellen ventured playfully.

"What is?"

"To be a . . . you know . . . to sleep with a whole lot of different men."

"Was it yours?"

Ellen laughed to cover her blush. "I don't remember if it was exactly that," she said. "But I guess we all have fantasies of one kind or another."

Hooper smiled and called the waitress. "Bring us a bottle of cold Chablis, would you, please?"

Something's happened, Ellen thought. She wondered if he could sense the invitation she had extended. Anyhow, he had taken the offensive. All she had to do was avoid discouraging him.

Their entrées came, followed a moment later by the wine. Hooper's scallops were the size of marshmallows. "Flounder," he said after the waitress had left.

"How can you tell?" Ellen asked.

"They're too big, for one thing. And the edges are too perfect. They were obviously cut."

"I suppose you could send them back." She hoped he wouldn't; a quarrel with the waitress could spoil their mood.

"I might," said Hooper, and he grinned at Ellen. "Under different circumstances." He poured her a glass of wine, then filled his own and raised it. "To fantasies," he said. He leaned forward

81

until his face was only a foot from hers. His eyes were a bright, liquid blue and his lips were parted in a half smile.

Impulsively, Ellen said, "Let's make our own fantasy."

"Okay. How do you want to start?"

"What would we do if we were going to . . . you know."

"That's a very interesting question," he said with mock gravity. "Before considering the what, however, we'd have to consider the where. I suppose there's always my room."

"Too dangerous. Everybody knows me at the Abelard. Anywhere in Amity would be too dangerous."

"There must be motels between here and Montauk."

"All right. That's settled."

ELLEN arrived home a little before 4:30. She went upstairs, into the bathroom, and turned on the water in the tub. After her bath she put on a nightgown and climbed into bed. She closed her eyes and gave in to her fatigue.

Almost instantly, it seemed, she was awakened by Brody saying, "Hey, there, are you okay?"

She yawned. "What time is it?"

"Almost six."

"Oh-oh. I've got to pick up Sean. Phyllis Santos must be having a fit."

"I got him," said Brody. "I figured I'd better, once I couldn't reach you."

"You tried to reach me?"

"A couple of times. I tried you at the hospital at around two. They thought you'd come home. Then I tried to reach you here."

"My, it must have been important."

"No. If you must know, I was calling to apologize for whatever I did that got you upset last night."

A twinge of shame struck Ellen, and she said, "You're sweet, but don't worry. I'd already forgotten about it."

"Oh," said Brody. "So where were you?"

"I came home and went to bed. My thyroid pills aren't doing what they should."

"And you didn't hear the phone? It's right there." Brody pointed to the table near the other side of the bed.

"No, I . . . I took a sleeping pill. The moaning of the damned won't wake me after I've taken one of them."

Brody shook his head. "I really am going to throw those things down the john. You're turning into a junkie." He went into the bathroom. "Have you heard from Hooper?" he called to her.

Ellen thought for a moment about her response, then said, "He called this morning to say thank you. Why?"

"I tried to get hold of him today. The hotel said they didn't know where he was. What time did he call here?"

"Just after you left for work."

"Did he say what he was going to be doing?"

"He said . . . he said he might try to work on the boat, I think. I really don't remember."

"Oh? That's funny."

"What is?"

"I stopped by the dock on my way home. The harbor master said he hadn't seen Hooper all day."

On Thursday morning Brody got a call summoning him to Vaughan's office for a noon meeting of the board of selectmen. He knew what the subject of the meeting was: opening the beaches for the weekend—the Fourth of July weekend. Brody was convinced that opening the beaches would be a gamble. They would never know for certain that the shark had gone away.

The town hall was an imposing, pseudo-Georgian affair—red brick with white trim and two white columns framing the entrance. The rooms inside were as preposterously grandiose as the exterior: huge and high-ceilinged, each with its own elaborate chandelier. Mayor Vaughan's office was on the southeast corner of the second floor, overlooking most of the town.

Vaughan's secretary, a wholesome, pretty woman named Janet Sumner, sat at a desk outside his office. Brody was paternally fond of Janet, and he was idly mystified that—at age twenty-six—she was still unmarried. He usually made a point of inquiring about her love life, but today he said simply, "Are they all inside?"

"All that's coming." Brody started into the office, and Janet said, "Don't you want to know who I'm going out with?"

He stopped, smiled and said, "Who is it?"

"Nobody. I'm in temporary retirement. But I'll tell you one thing." She lowered her voice and leaned forward. "I wouldn't mind playing footsie with that Mr. Hooper."

"Is he in there?"

Janet nodded.

"I wonder when he was elected selectman."

"I don't know," she said. "But he sure is cute."

As soon as he was inside the office Brody knew he would be fighting alone. The only selectmen present were longtime allies of Vaughan's: Tony Catsoulis, a contractor who was built like a fire hydrant; Ned Thatcher, a frail old man whose family owned the Abelard Arms Inn; Paul Conover, owner of Amity Liquors; and Rafe Lopez (pronounced Loaps), a dark-skinned Portuguese elected to the board by the town's black community.

The selectmen sat around a coffee table at one end of the room. Hooper stood at a southerly window, staring out at the sea.

"Where's Albert Morris?" Brody said to Vaughan after greeting the others.

"He couldn't make it," said Vaughan. "I don't think he felt well."

"And Fred Potter?"

"Same thing. There must be a bug going around." Vaughan stood up. "Well, I guess we're all here. Grab a chair and pull it over by the coffee table."

He looks awful, Brody thought. Vaughan's eyes were sunken and dark. His skin looked like mayonnaise.

When everyone was seated Vaughan said, "You all know why we're here. And I guess it's safe to say that there's only one of us that needs convincing about what we should do."

"You mean me," said Brody.

Vaughan nodded. "Look at it from our point of view, Martin. The town is dying. People are out of work. Stores that were going

to open aren't. People aren't renting houses, let alone buying them. And every day we keep the beaches closed, we drive another nail into our own coffin."

"Suppose you do open the beaches for the Fourth, Larry," said Brody. "And suppose someone gets killed."

"It's a calculated risk, but I think—we think—it's worth taking."

"Why?"

Vaughan said, "Mr. Hooper?"

"Several reasons," said Hooper. "First of all, nobody's seen the fish in a week."

"Nobody's been in the water, either."

"That's true. But I've been on the boat looking for him every day—every day but one."

"I meant to ask you about that. Where were you yesterday?"

"It rained," said Hooper. "Remember?"

"So what did you do?"

"I just . . ." He paused, then said, "I studied some water samples. And read."

"Where? In your hotel room?"

"Part of the time, yeah. What are you driving at?"

"I called your hotel. They said you were out all afternoon."

"So I was out!" Hooper said angrily. "I don't have to report in every five minutes, do I? You're not even paying me!"

Vaughan broke in. "Come on. This isn't getting us anywhere."

"Anyway," said Hooper, "I haven't seen a trace of that fish. Not a sign. And the water's getting warmer every day. It's almost seventy now. As a rule great whites prefer cooler water."

"So you think he's gone farther north?"

"Or out deeper, into colder water. He could even have gone south. You can't predict what these things are going to do."

"That's my point," said Brody. "All you're doing is guessing."

Vaughan said, "You can't ask for a guarantee, Martin."

"Tell that to Christine Watkins. Or the Kintner boy's mother."

"I know, I know," Vaughan said. "But we have to do something. God isn't going to scribble across the sky, 'The shark is gone.' We have to weigh the evidence and make a decision."

"The decision's already been made," said Brody.

"You could say that, yes."

"And when someone else gets killed? Who's taking the blame? Who's going to talk to the husband or the mother or the wife and tell them, 'We were just playing the odds, and we lost'?"

"Wait a minute, Martin."

"If you want the authority for opening the beaches, then you take the responsibility, too."

"What are you saying?"

"I'm saying that as long as I'm chief of police in this town those beaches will not be open."

"I'll tell you this, Martin," said Vaughan. "If those beaches stay closed over Fourth of July weekend, you won't have your job very long. Twenty minutes after they hear you won't open the beaches the people of this town will impeach you, or find a rail and run you out on it. Do you agree, gentlemen?"

"I'll give 'em the rail myself," said Catsoulis.

"My people got no work," said Lopez. "You don't let them work, you're not gonna work."

Brody said flatly, "You can have my job anytime you want it."

A buzzer sounded on Vaughan's desk. He stood up angrily and picked up the phone. There was a moment's silence, then he said to Brody, "There's a call for you. Janet says it's urgent. You can take it here or outside."

"I'll take it outside," Brody said, wondering what could be urgent enough to call him out of a meeting with the selectmen. Another attack? He left the room and closed the door behind him. Janet handed him the phone on her desk, but before she could release the "hold" button Brody said, "Tell me, did Larry call Albert Morris and Fred Potter this morning?"

Janet looked away from him. "I was told not to say anything."

"Tell me, Janet. I need to know."

"The only ones I called were the four in there."

"Press the button." Janet did, and Brody said, "Brody."

Inside his office Vaughan saw the light stop flashing and he gently eased his finger off the circuit button and placed his hand over the mouthpiece. He looked around the room, searching each face for a challenge. No one returned his gaze.

"It's Harry, Martin," said Meadows. "I know you're in a meeting so I'll be brief. Larry Vaughan is up to his tail in hock."

"I don't believe it."

"A long time ago, maybe twenty-five years, before Larry had any money, his wife got sick. It was serious. And expensive. My memory's a little hazy on this, but I remember him saying afterward that he had been helped out by a friend, gotten a loan to pull him through. It must have been for several thousand dollars. Larry told me the man's name. It was Tino Russo."

"Get to the point, Harry."

"I am. Now jump to the present. A couple of months ago, before this shark thing ever began, a company was formed called Caskata Estates. It's a holding company. The first thing it bought was a big potato field just north of Scotch Road. When the summer didn't shape up well, Caskata began to buy a few more properties at low prices. It was all perfectly legitimate. But then—as soon as the first newspaper reports about the shark thing came out—Caskata really started buying. The lower the real estate prices fell, the more they bought—with very little money down. All short-term promissory notes. Signed by Larry Vaughan, who is listed as the president of Caskata. The executive vice-president is Tino Russo, whom the *Times* has been naming for years as a second-echelon crumb in one of the five Mafia families in New York."

Brody whistled through his teeth. "And Vaughan has been moaning about how nobody's been buying anything from him. I still don't understand why he's being pressured to open the beaches."

"I'm not sure. He may be arguing out of personal desperation. I imagine he's way overextended. The only way he can get out without being ruined is if the market turns around and the prices go up. Then he can sell what he's bought and get the profit. Or Russo can get the profit, however the deal's worked out. If prices keep going down—in other words, if the beaches are still officially unsafe—he can't possibly meet his notes when they come due. He'll lose his cash, and the properties will either revert to the original owners or else get picked up by Russo if he can raise the cash. My guess is that Russo still has hopes of big profits, but the only way he has a chance of getting them is if Vaughan forces the beaches open. As far as I can tell, Russo doesn't have a nickel in cash in this outfit. It's all—"

"You're a damned liar, Meadows!" Vaughan's voice shrieked into the phone. "You print one word of that and I'll sue you to death!" There was a click as he slammed down the phone.

"So much for the integrity of our elected officials," said Meadows.

"What do you think I ought to do, Harry? I offered them my job before I came out to talk to you."

"Don't quit, Martin. We need you. If you quit, Russo will get together with Vaughan and handpick your successor. If I were you, I'd open the beaches. You're going to have to open them sometime. You might as well do it now."

"And let the mob take their money and run."

"What else *can* you do? You keep them closed, and Vaughan'll get rid of you and open them himself. Then you'll be no use to anybody. This way, if you open the beaches and nothing happens, the town might have a chance. Then, maybe later, we can find a way to pin something on Vaughan."

"All right, Harry, I'll think about it," said Brody. "But if I open them, I'm gonna do it my way."

When Brody went back into Vaughan's office Vaughan said, "The meeting's over."

"What do you mean, over?" said Catsoulis. "We ain't decided anything."

Vaughan said, "Don't give me any trouble, Tony! It'll work out all right. Just let me have a private chat with the chief. Okay?"

Hooper and the four selectmen left the office. Vaughan shut the door, walked over to the couch and sat down heavily. He rested his elbows on his knees and rubbed his temples with his fingertips. He said, "I swear to you, Martin, if I had any idea how far this would go, I'd never have gotten into it."

"How much are you into him for?"

"The original amount was ten thousand. I've tried to pay it back, but I could never get them to cash my checks. When they came to me a couple of months ago, I offered them a hundred thousand dollars—cash. They said it wasn't enough. They didn't want the money. They wanted me to make a few investments. Everybody'd be a winner, they said."

"And how much are you out now?"

"Every cent I had. More than every cent. Close to a million." Vaughan took a deep breath. "Can you help me, Martin?"

"The only thing I can do for you is put you in touch with the DA. If you'd testify, you might be able to slap a loansharking rap on these guys."

"I'd be dead before I got home from the DA's office, and Eleanor would be left without anything. That's not the kind of help I meant."

Brody looked down at Vaughan, a huddled, wounded animal, and felt compassion. He began to doubt his own opposition to opening the beaches. How much was self-protection, and how much was concern for the town? "I'll tell you what, Larry. I'll open the beaches. Not to help you, because I'm sure if I didn't open them you'd find a way to get rid of me and open them yourself. I'll do it because I'm not sure I'm right anymore."

"Thanks, Martin. I appreciate that."

"I'm not finished. Like I said, I'll open them. But I'm going to post men on the beaches. And I'm going to have Hooper patrol in the boat. And I'm going to make sure every person who comes down there knows the danger."

"You can't do that!" Vaughan said. "You might as well leave the damn things closed. Nobody's going to the beach if it's crawling with cops."

"I can do it, Larry, and I will. I'm not going to make believe nothing ever happened."

"All right, Martin." Vaughan rose. "You don't leave me much choice. If I got rid of you, you'd probably go down to the beach as a private citizen and run up and down yelling '*Shark!*' So all right. But be subtle—if not for my sake, for the town's."

BRODY ARRIVED HOME that afternoon at 5:10. As he pulled into the driveway the back door to the house opened and Ellen ran toward him. She had been crying, and she was still visibly upset.

"Thank God you're home!" she said. "Come here. Quick!" She led him to the shed where they kept the garbage cans. "In there." She pointed to a can. "Look."

Lying in a twisted heap atop a bag of garbage was Sean's cat— a big, husky tom named Frisky. The cat's head had been twisted completely around, and the yellow eyes overlooked its back.

"How the hell did that happen?" said Brody. "A car?"

"No, a man." Ellen's breath came in sobs. "Sean was right there when it happened. A man got out of a car over by the curb. He picked up the cat and broke its neck. Then he dropped it on the lawn, got back in his car and drove away."

"Did he say anything?"

"I don't know. Sean's inside. He's hysterical, and I don't blame him. Martin, what's *happening?*"

Brody slammed the top back on the can. "Son of a *bitch!*" he said. He clenched his teeth. "Let's go inside."

Five minutes later Brody marched out the back door. He tore the lid off the garbage can and pulled out the cat's corpse. He took it to his car, pitched it through the open window and climbed in. He backed out of the driveway and screeched away.

It took him only a couple of minutes to reach Vaughan's Tudor-style mansion just off Scotch Road. He got out of the car, dragging the dead cat by one of its hind legs, mounted the front steps and rang the bell.

The door opened, and Vaughan said, "Hello, Martin. I—"

Brody raised the cat and pushed it toward Vaughan's face. "What about this, you bastard? One of your friends did this. Right in front of my kid. They murdered my cat! Did you tell them to do that?"

"Don't be crazy, Martin." Vaughan seemed genuinely shocked. "I'd never do anything like that. Never."

Brody lowered the cat and said, "Did you call your friends after I left?"

"Well . . . yes. But just to say that the beaches would be open tomorrow."

"That's all you said?"

"Yes. Why?"

"You damned liar!" Brody hit Vaughan in the chest with the cat and let it fall to the floor. "You know what the guy said after he strangled my cat? You know what he told my eight-year-old boy?"

"No, of course I don't know. How would I know?"

"He said the same thing you did. He said, 'Tell your old man this—be subtle.'"

Brody turned and walked down the steps, leaving Vaughan standing over the gnarled bundle of fur.

7

FRIDAY was cloudy, with scattered light showers, and the only people who swam were a young couple who took a quick dip early in the morning just as Brody's man arrived at the beach. Hooper patrolled for six hours and saw nothing. On Friday night Brody called the Coast Guard for a weather report. He wasn't sure what he hoped to hear. He knew he should wish for beautiful weather for the holiday weekend, but privately he would have welcomed a three-day blow that would keep the beaches empty. The report was for clear and sunny skies, with light southwest winds. Well, Brody thought, maybe that's for the best. If we have a good weekend and nobody gets hurt, maybe I can believe the shark is gone. And Hooper's sure to leave.

He wanted Hooper to go back to Woods Hole. It was not just that Hooper was always there, the expert voice to contradict his caution. Brody sensed that somehow Hooper had come into his home. He knew Ellen had talked to Hooper since the party: young Martin had mentioned the possibility of Hooper taking them on a beach picnic to look for shells. Then there was that business on Wednesday. Ellen had said she was sick, and she certainly had looked worn-out when he came home. But where had Hooper been that day? Why had he been so evasive when Brody had asked him about it? For the first time in his married life Brody was wondering.

He went to the kitchen phone to call Hooper at the Abelard Arms. Ellen was washing the supper dishes. Brody saw the phone book buried beneath a pile of bills and comic books on the counter. He started to reach for it, then stopped. "I have to call Hooper," he said. "You know where the phone book is?"

"The number is six five four three," said Ellen.

"How do you know?"

"I have a memory for phone numbers. You know that."

He did know it, and he cursed himself for playing stupid tricks. He dialed the number and asked for Hooper's room.

"This is Brody," he said when Hooper answered.

"Yeah. Hi."

"I guess we're on for tomorrow," Brody said. "The weather report is good."

"Yeah, I know."

"Then I'll see you down at the dock at nine thirty. Nobody's going swimming before then."

"Okay. Nine thirty."

"By the way," Brody said, "did things work out with Daisy Wicker?"

"What?"

Brody wished he hadn't asked the question. "I was just curious. You know, about whether you two hit it off."

"Well . . . yeah, now that you mention it. Is that part of your job, to check up on people's sex life?"

"Forget it. Forget I ever mentioned it." He hung up the phone and turned to Ellen. "I meant to ask you. Martin said something about a beach picnic. When's that?"

"No special time," she said. "It was just a thought."

"Oh." He looked at her, but she didn't return the glance. "I think it's time you got some sleep."

"Why do you say that?"

"You haven't been feeling well. And that's the second time you've washed that glass."

93

SATURDAY NOON, BRODY stood on a dune overlooking the Scotch Road beach, feeling half secret agent, half fool. He was wearing a polo shirt and swim trunks. In a beach bag by his side were binoculars, a walkie-talkie, two beers and a sandwich. Offshore the *Flicka* moved slowly eastward. Brody watched the boat and said to himself, At least I know where *he* is today.

The Coast Guard had been right: the day was cloudless and warm, with a light onshore breeze. The section of beach below him was not crowded. A few couples lay dozing, and a dozen or so teenagers were scattered about in their ritual rows. A family was gathered around a charcoal fire, and the scent of grilling hamburger drifted to Brody's nose.

Brody reached into the beach bag and took out the walkie-talkie. He pressed a button and said, "You there, Leonard?"

In a moment the reply came rasping through the speaker. "I read you, Chief. Over." Hendricks had volunteered to spend the weekend on the beach, as the third point in the triangle of watch.

"Anything happening on your part of the beach?" said Brody.

"Nothing we can't handle, but there are some TV guys here interviewing people. Over."

"How long have they been there?"

"Most of the morning. I don't know how long they'll hang around, especially since no one's going in the water. Over."

"As long as they're not causing any trouble."

"Nope. Over."

"Okay. Hey, Leonard, you don't have to say over all the time. I can tell when you're finished speaking."

"Just procedure, Chief. Keeps things clear. Over and out."

Brody waited a moment, then pressed the button again and said, "Hooper, this is Brody. Anything out there?" There was no answer. "This is Brody calling Hooper. Can you hear me?" He was about to call a third time when Hooper answered.

"Sorry. I was out on the stern. I thought I saw something."

"What did you think you saw?"

"I can't really describe it. A shadow, maybe. Nothing more."

"You haven't seen anything else?"

"Not a thing. All morning."

"Let's keep it that way. I'll check with you later."

"Fine. I'll be near the beach in a minute or two."

Brody put the walkie-talkie back in the bag, sat down and unwrapped his sandwich.

By 2:30 Brody's section of the beach was almost empty. People had gone to play tennis, to sail, to have their hair done. The only ones left were half a dozen teenagers.

Brody's legs had begun to sunburn, so he covered them with his towel. He took the walkie-talkie out of the beach bag and called Hendricks. "Anything happening, Leonard?"

"Not a thing, Chief. Over."

"Anybody go swimming?"

"Nope. Wading, but that's about it. Over."

"Same here. What about the TV people?"

"They're gone. They left a few minutes ago. They wanted to know where you were. Over."

"Did you tell them?"

"Sure. I didn't see why not. Over."

"Okay. I'll talk to you later." Brody stood up, wrapped his towel around his waist to keep the sun from his legs and, carrying the walkie-talkie, strolled toward the water.

Hearing a car engine, he turned and walked to the top of the dune. A white panel truck was parked on Scotch Road. The lettering on its side said WNBC-TV NEWS. The driver's door opened, and a man got out and trudged through the sand toward Brody. He was young, with long hair and a handlebar mustache.

"Chief Brody?" he said when he was a few steps away.

"That's right."

"Bob Middleton, Channel Four News. I'd like to interview you."

"About what?"

"The whole shark business. How you decided to open the beaches."

Brody thought, What the hell; a little publicity can't hurt the town, now that the chances of anything happening—today, at least—are pretty slim. "All right," he said. "Where?"

"Down on the beach. It'll take a few minutes to set up, so I'll give a yell when we're ready." He went back to the truck.

Brody walked down toward the water. As he passed the group of teenagers he heard a boy say, "What about it? Anybody got the guts? Ten bucks is ten bucks."

A girl said, "Come on, Limbo, lay off."

Brody stopped, feigning interest in something offshore.

Another boy said, "If you're such hot stuff, why don't *you* go?"

"I'm the one making the offer," said the first boy. "Nobody's gonna pay *me* to go in the water. Well, what do you say?"

There was a moment's silence, and then the other boy said, "How far out do I have to go?"

"Let's see. A hundred yards. Okay?"

"You've got a deal." The boy stood up.

The girl said, "You're crazy, Jimmy. Why do you want to go in the water? You don't need ten dollars."

"You think I'm scared?"

The boy turned and began to jog toward the water. Brody said, "Hey!" and he stopped.

Brody walked over to the boy. "What are you doing?"

"Going swimming."

Brody showed the boy his badge. "Do you want to go swimming?" he said.

"Sure. Why not? It's legal, isn't it?"

Brody nodded. Then he lowered his voice and said, "Do you want me to order you not to?"

The boy looked past him at his friends. He hesitated, then shook his head. "No, man. I can use the ten bucks."

"Don't stay in too long," said Brody.

"I won't." He scampered into the water and began to swim.

Brody heard running footsteps behind him. Bob Middleton dashed past him and called out to the boy, "Hey! Come back!"

The boy stopped swimming and stood up. "What's the matter?"

"I want some shots of you going into the water. Okay?"

"Sure, I guess so," said the boy. He started back toward shore.

Two men came up beside Brody. One was carrying a camera

and a tripod. The other carried a rectangular box covered with dials and knobs. Around his neck was a pair of earphones.

"Right there's okay, Walter," said Middleton. He took a notebook from his pocket and began to ask the boy some questions.

The sound man handed a microphone to Middleton, who looked into the camera and said, "We have been here on the Amity beach since early morning, and no one has yet ventured into the water, although there has been no sign of the shark. I'm standing here with Jim Prescott, a young man who has just decided to take a swim. Tell me, Jim, do you have any worries about what might be swimming out there with you?"

"No," said the boy. "I don't think there's anything out there."

"So you're not scared."

"No."

Middleton held out his hand. "Well, good luck, Jim. Thanks for talking to us."

The boy ran into the water and began swimming.

"How much do you want of this?" said the cameraman, tracking the boy as he swam.

"A hundred feet or so," said Middleton. "But let's stay here till he comes out. Be ready, just in case."

Brody had become so accustomed to the far-off, barely audible hum of the *Flicka*'s engine that his mind no longer registered it as a sound. But suddenly the engine's pitch changed from a low murmur to an urgent growl. Brody looked beyond the swimming boy and saw the boat in a tight, fast turn, nothing like the slow, ambling sweeps it had been making. He put the walkie-talkie to his mouth, pressed the button and said, "You see something, Hooper?" The boat slowed, then stopped.

"Yes," said Hooper's voice. "It was that shadow again. But I can't see it now. Maybe my eyes are getting tired."

Middleton called to the cameraman, "Get this, Walter." He walked to Brody and said, "Something going on, Chief?"

"I don't know," said Brody. "I'm trying to find out." He said into the walkie-talkie, "There's a kid swimming out there."

"Where?" said Hooper.

Middleton shoved the microphone at Brody, sliding it between his mouth and the walkie-talkie. Brody brushed it aside, but Middleton quickly jammed it back.

"Thirty, maybe forty yards out. I better tell him to come in." Brody tucked the walkie-talkie into the towel at his waist, cupped his hands around his mouth and called, "Hey, come on in!"

The boy did not hear the call. He was swimming straight away from the beach.

Brody grabbed the walkie-talkie and called Hooper. "He doesn't hear me. You want to toot in here and tell him to come ashore?"

"Sure," said Hooper. "I'll be there in a minute."

THE fish had sounded now, and was meandering a few feet above the sandy bottom, eighty feet below the *Flicka*. For hours its sensory system had been tracking the strange noise above. It had not felt compelled either to attack the "creature" passing overhead or to move away.

Brody saw the boat, which had been heading west, swing toward shore and kick up a shower of spray from the bow.

"Get the boat, Walter," Middleton said to the cameraman.

Below, the fish sensed a change in the noise, which grew louder, then faded as the boat moved away. The fish turned, banking smoothly, and followed the sound toward the beach.

The boy stopped swimming and looked toward shore, treading water. Brody waved his arms and yelled, "Come in!" The boy waved back and started swimming. He swam well, rolling his head to catch a breath, kicking in rhythm with his arm strokes. Brody guessed he was sixty yards away and that it would take him another minute to reach shore.

It took Hooper only thirty seconds to cover the couple of hundred yards and draw near the boy. He stopped just beyond the surf line, letting the engine idle. He didn't dare go closer for fear of being caught in the waves.

The boy heard the engine and raised his head. "What's the matter?" he called to Hooper.

"Nothing," Hooper answered. "Keep swimming."

The boy lowered his head and swam. A swell moved him faster, and with two or three more strokes he was able to stand.

"Come on!" said Brody.

Middleton spoke into the microphone. "Something is going on, ladies and gentlemen, but we don't know exactly what. All we know for sure is that Jim Prescott went swimming, and then suddenly a man on a boat out there saw something. Now Police Chief Brody is trying to get Jim to come ashore. It could be the shark; we just don't know."

Hooper put the boat in reverse, to back away from the surf. As he looked off the stern he saw a silver streak moving in the gray-blue water. For a second Hooper did not realize what he was seeing. When the realization struck he cried, "Look out!"

"What is it?" yelled Brody.

"The fish! Get the kid out! Quick!"

The boy heard Hooper, and he tried to run. But in the chest-deep water his movements were slow and labored.

Brody ran into the water and reached out. A wave hit him in the knees and pushed him back.

Middleton said into the microphone, "The man on the boat just said something about a fish. I don't know if he means a shark."

The boy was pushing through the water faster now. He did not see the fin rise behind him, a sharp blade of brownish gray.

"There it is, Walter!" said Middleton. "See it?"

"I'm zooming," said the cameraman. "Yeah, I've got it."

"Hurry!" said Brody. He reached for the boy. The boy's eyes were wide and panicked. Brody's hand touched the boy's, and he pulled. He grabbed the boy around the chest, and together they staggered out of the water.

The fin dropped beneath the surface, and, following the slope of the ocean floor, the fish moved into the deep.

Brody stood with his arm around the boy. "Are you okay?"

"I want to go home." The boy shivered.

"I bet you do," Brody said.

Middleton came up. "Can you repeat that for me?"

"Repeat what?"

"Whatever you said to the boy. Can we do that again?"

"Get out of my way!" Brody snapped. He took the boy to his friends, and said to the one who had offered the money, "Take him home. And give him his ten dollars." The other boy nodded, pale and scared.

Brody saw his walkie-talkie in the wave wash and retrieved it. He pressed the "talk" button. "Leonard, can you hear me?"

"I read you, Chief. Over."

"The fish has been here. If anybody's in the water down there, get them out. Right away. The beach is officially closed."

As Brody went to pick up his beach bag Middleton called to him, "Hey, Chief, can we do that interview now?"

Brody sighed and returned to where Middleton stood with his camera crew. "All right," he said. "Go ahead."

"Well, Chief Brody," said Middleton, "that was a lucky break, wouldn't you say?"

"It was very lucky. The boy might have died."

"So where do you go from here?"

"The beaches are closed. For the time being that's all I can do."

"I guess it isn't yet safe to swim here in Amity."

"I'd have to say that, yes."

"What does that mean for Amity?"

"Trouble, Mr. Middleton. We are in big trouble."

"Chief, how do you feel about having opened the beaches?"

"How do I *feel?* What kind of question is that? Angry, annoyed, confused. Thankful that nobody got hurt. Is that enough?"

"That's just fine, Chief," Middleton said with a smile. "Thank you, Chief Brody." He paused, then said, "Okay, Walter, that'll wrap it. Let's get home and start editing this mess."

AT SIX o'clock Brody sat in his office with Hooper and Meadows. He had already talked to Larry Vaughan, who had called—drunk and in tears—and muttered about the ruination of his life. Brody's buzzer sounded, and he picked up the phone.

"Fellow named Bill Whitman to see you, Chief," said Bixby. "Says he's from *The New York Times*."

"Oh, for . . . Okay. Send him in."

The door opened, and Whitman stood there. He said, "Am I interrupting something?"

"Nothing much," said Brody. "What can we do for you?"

"I was wondering," said Whitman, "if you're sure this is the same fish that killed the others."

Brody gestured toward Hooper, who said, "I can't be positive. But in all probability it's the same fish. It's too farfetched—for me, anyway—to believe that there are two big man-eating sharks off the south shore of Long Island at the same time."

Whitman said to Brody, "What are you going to do, Chief? I mean, beyond closing the beaches."

"I'd be happy to hear any suggestions. Personally, I think we're going to be lucky if there's a town left after this summer."

"Isn't that a bit of an exaggeration?"

"I don't think so. Do you, Harry?"

"Not really," said Meadows. "At the least—the very least—next winter is going to be the worst in our history, we're going to have so many people on the dole."

"I still don't see why the shark can't be caught," said Whitman.

"Maybe it can be," said Hooper. "But I don't think by us. At least not with the equipment we have here."

"Do you know anything about some fellow named Quint?" said Whitman.

"I've heard the name," Brody said. "Did you ever look into the guy, Harry?"

"I read what little there was. As far as I know, he's never done anything illegal."

"Well," said Brody, "maybe it's worth a call."

"You're joking," said Hooper. "You'd do business with him?"

"You got any better ideas?" Brody took a phone book from his desk and opened it to the Q's. He ran his finger down the page. "Here it is. Quint. That's all it says. No first name. But it's the only one on the page. Must be him." He dialed the number.

"Quint," said a voice.

"Mr. Quint, this is Martin Brody. I'm the chief of police in Amity. We have a problem."

"I've heard. I thought you might call."

"Can you help us?"

"That depends."

"On what?"

"On how much you're willing to spend, for one thing."

"We'll pay whatever you charge by the day."

"I don't think so," said Quint. "I think this is a premium job."

"What does that mean?"

"My usual rate's two hundred. But I think you'll pay double."

"Not a chance."

"Good-by."

"Wait a minute! Come on. Why are you holding me up?"

"You got no place else to go."

"There are other fishermen."

Brody heard Quint laugh—a short, derisive bark. "Sure there are," said Quint. "You already sent one. Send another one. Send half a dozen more. Then when you come back to me again, maybe you'll even pay triple. I got nothing to lose by waiting."

"I'm not asking for any favors," Brody said. "But can't you at least treat me the way you treat regular clients?"

"You're breaking my heart," said Quint. "You got a fish needs killing, I'll try to kill it for you. No guarantees, but I'll do my best. And my best is worth four hundred dollars a day."

Brody sighed. "I don't know that the selectmen will give me the money."

"You'll find it somewhere."

Brody paused. "Okay," he said. "Can you start tomorrow?"

"Nope. Monday's the earliest. I got a charter party tomorrow."

"Can't you cancel them?" Brody asked.

"Nope. They're regular customers. You're just a one-shot deal. And there's one more thing," said Quint. "I'm gonna need a man with me. My mate's quitting, and I wouldn't feel comfortable taking on that big a fish without an extra pair of hands."

103

"Why is your mate quitting?"

"Nerves. Happens to most people after a while in this work."

"But it doesn't happen to you."

"No. I know I'm smarter'n the fish."

"And that's enough, just being smarter?"

"Has been so far. I'm still alive. What about it? You got a man for me?"

"Who are you going to use tomorrow?"

"Some kid. But I won't take him out after a big white."

Brody said casually, "I'll be there." He was shocked by the words as soon as he said them.

"You? Ha!"

Brody smarted. "I can handle myself," he said.

"Maybe. But I still need a man who knows something about fishing. Or at least about boats."

Brody looked across his desk at Hooper. The last thing he wanted was to spend days on a boat with Hooper, especially in a situation in which Hooper would outrank him in knowledge, if not authority. He could send Hooper alone and stay ashore himself. But that, he felt, would be admitting his inability to conquer the strange enemy that was waging war on his town.

Besides, maybe—over the course of a long day on a boat—Hooper might make a slip that would reveal what he had been doing last Wednesday. Brody was becoming obsessed with finding out where Hooper was that day it rained. He wanted to *know* that Hooper had not been with Ellen.

He cupped his hand over the mouthpiece and said to Hooper, "Do you want to come along? He needs a mate."

"Yes," said Hooper. "I'll probably live to regret it, but I want to see that fish, and I guess this is my only chance."

Brody said to Quint, "Okay, I've got your man."

"Does he know boats?"

"He knows boats."

"Monday morning, six o'clock. You know how to get here?"

"Route Twenty-seven to Cranberry Hole Road, right?"

"Yeah. About a hundred yards past the last houses take a left on a dirt road. Leads right to my dock. Mine's the only boat there. It's called the *Orca*."

"All right. See you Monday."

"One more thing," said Quint. "Cash. Every day. In advance."

"All right," said Brody. "You'll have it." He hung up and said to Hooper, "Monday, six a.m., okay?"

"Okay. What's the name of his boat?"

"I think he said *Orca*," said Brody. "I don't know what it means."

"It doesn't *mean* anything. It *is* something. It's a killer whale."

Meadows, Hooper and Whitman rose to go. At the door Hooper turned and said, "Thinking of orca reminds me of something. You know what Australians call great white sharks?"

"No," said Brody, not really interested. "What?"

"White death."

"You had to tell me, didn't you?" Brody said as he closed the door behind them.

PART THREE

8

THE sea was as flat as gelatin. There was no whisper of wind to ripple the surface. The boat sat still in the water, drifting impercep- tibly in the tide. Two fishing rods, in rod holders at the stern, trailed wire lines baited with squid into the oily slick that spread westward behind the boat. Hooper sat at the stern, a twenty-gallon garbage pail at his side. Every few seconds he dipped a ladle into the pail and spilled chum overboard into the slick.

Forward, in two rows that peaked at the bow, lay ten red wooden barrels the size of quarter kegs. Around each was wrapped several thicknesses of three-quarter-inch hemp, which continued in a hundred-foot coil beside the barrel. Tied to the end of each rope was the dart-shaped steel head of a harpoon.

Brody sat in the swivel fighting chair bolted to the deck, try- ing to stay awake. He was hot and sticky. They had been sitting for six hours, and the back of his neck was badly sunburned.

Brody looked up at the figure on the flying bridge: Quint. He wore a white T-shirt, faded blue-jean trousers, white socks and a pair of graying Top-Sider sneakers. Brody guessed Quint was about fifty. He was six feet four and very lean—perhaps a hundred and eighty or a hundred and ninety pounds. When, as now, the sun was high and hot, he wore a Marine Corps fatigue cap. His face, like the rest of him, was hard and sharp. It was ruled by a long, straight nose. When he looked down from the flying bridge, he seemed to aim his eyes—the darkest eyes Brody had ever seen—along the nose as if it were a rifle barrel. His skin was permanently browned and creased by wind and salt and sun. He gazed off the stern, rarely blinking, his eyes fixed on the slick.

Brody tried to stare at the slick, but the reflection of the sun on the water hurt his eyes, and he turned away. "I don't see how you do it, Quint," he said. "Don't you ever wear sunglasses?"

"Never." Quint's tone did not invite conversation.

Brody looked at his watch. It was a little after two o'clock; three or four more hours before they would give up for the day and go home. "Do you have a lot of days like this, when you just sit and nothing happens?"

"Some."

"And people pay you even though they never get a bite?"

Quint nodded. "That doesn't happen too often. There's generally something that'll take a bait." He stopped. "Something's taking one of them now."

Brody and Hooper watched as the wire on the starboard fishing rod began to feed overboard with a soft metallic hiss.

"Take the rod," Quint said to Brody. "And when I tell you, throw the brake and hit him."

"Is it the shark?" said Brody. The possibility that at last he was going to confront the beast, the monster, the nightmare, made his heart pound. He wiped his hands on his trousers, took the rod out of the holder and stuck it in the swivel between his legs.

Quint laughed—a short, sour yip. "That thing? No. That's just a little fella. Give you some practice for when your fish finds us." He watched the line for a few seconds, then said, "Hit it!"

Brody pushed the small lever on the reel forward, then pulled back on the rod. It bent into an arc. Brody began to turn the crank to reel in the fish, but the line kept speeding out.

"Don't waste your energy," said Quint.

Brody held on to the rod with both hands. The fish had gone deep and was moving slowly from side to side, but it was no longer taking line. Brody cranked quickly as he picked up slack, then hauled backward. "What the hell have I got here?" he said.

"A blue," said Quint.

"He must weigh half a ton."

Quint laughed. "Maybe a hundred 'n' fifty pounds."

Brody hauled, until finally Quint said, "You're getting there. Hold it." Brody stopped reeling.

With a smooth, unhurried motion Quint swung down the ladder from the flying bridge. He had a rifle in his hand, an old army M1. He stood at the gunwale and looked down. "You want to see the fish?" he said. "Come look."

In the dark water the shark was indigo blue. It was about eight feet long, slender, with long pectoral fins. It swam slowly from side to side, no longer struggling.

"He's beautiful, isn't he?" said Hooper.

Quint flicked the rifle's safety to "off" and when the shark came within a few inches of the surface he squeezed off three quick shots. The bullets made clean round holes in the shark's head, drawing no blood. The shark shuddered and stopped moving.

"He's dead," said Brody.

"He's stunned, maybe, but that's all," said Quint. He took a glove from one of his hip pockets, slipped his hand into it, and grabbed the wire line. From a sheath at his belt he took a knife. He hoisted most of the shark out of the water, and with a single, swift motion slit its belly. Then he cut the leader with a pair of wire cutters, and the fish slid overboard.

"Now watch," said Quint. "If we're lucky, in a minute other blues'll come around, and there'll be a real feeding frenzy. That's quite a show. The folks like that."

Brody saw a flash of blue rise from below. A small shark—no more than four feet long—snapped at the body of the disemboweled fish. Its jaws closed on a bit of flesh, and its head shook violently from side to side. Soon another shark appeared, and another, and the water began to roil. Fins crisscrossed on the surface, tails whipped the water. Amid the sounds of splashes came an occasional grunt as fish slammed into fish.

The frenzy continued for several minutes, until only three large sharks remained, cruising back and forth beneath the surface.

"My God!" said Hooper.

"You don't approve," said Quint.

"I don't like to see things die for people's amusement. Do you?"

"It ain't a question of liking it or not," said Quint. "It's what feeds me." He reached into an ice chest and took out a baited hook and another leader. Using pliers, he attached the leader to the end of the wire line, then dropped the bait overboard.

Hooper resumed his routine of ladling the chum into the water. Brody said, "Anybody want a beer?" Both Quint and Hooper nodded, so he went below and got three cans from a cooler. As he left the cabin Brody noticed two old, cracked and curling photographs thumbtacked to the bulkhead. One showed Quint standing hip-deep in a pile of big, strange-looking fish. The other was a picture of a dead shark lying on a beach. There was nothing else in the photograph to compare the shark to, so Brody couldn't determine its size.

Brody left the cabin, gave the others their beers and sat down in the fighting chair. "I saw your pictures down there," he said to Quint. "What are all those fish you're standing in?"

"Tarpon," said Quint. "That was a while back, in Florida. I never seen anything like it. We must have got thirty, forty big tarpon in four nights' fishing."

"And you kept them?" said Hooper. "You're supposed to throw them back."

"Customers wanted 'em. For pictures, I guess. Anyway, they don't make bad chum, chopped up."

"What you're saying is, they're more use dead than alive."

"Sure. Same with most fish. And a lot of animals, too. I never did try to eat a live steer." Quint laughed.

"What's the other picture?" said Brody. "Just a shark?"

"Well, not *just* a shark. It was a big white—about fourteen, fifteen feet. Weighed over three thousand pounds."

"How did you catch it?"

"Ironed it. But I tell you"—Quint chuckled—"for a while there it was a question of who was gonna catch who."

"What do you mean?"

"Damn thing attacked the boat. No provocation, no nothing. My mate and a customer and I were sitting out here minding our own business, when whammo! It felt like we was hit by a freight train. Knocked my mate right on his ass, and the customer started screaming bloody murder that we were sinking. Then the bastard hit us again. I put an iron in him and we chased him—we must have chased him halfway across the Atlantic."

"Why didn't he go deep?" asked Brody.

"Couldn't. Not with that barrel following him. They float. He dragged it down for a while, but before too long the strain got to him, and he came to the surface. So we just kept following the barrel. After a couple of hours we got another two irons in him, and he finally came up, real quiet, and we threwed a rope around his tail and towed him to shore."

"You wouldn't try to catch the fish we're after on a hook and line, would you?" asked Brody.

"Hell, no. From what I hear, the fish that's been bothering you makes the one we got look like a pup."

"Then how come the lines are out?"

"Two reasons. First, a big white might just take a little squid bait like that. It'd cut the line pretty quick, but at least we'd know he was around. The other reason is, we might run into something else that'll take the bait. If you're paying four hundred bucks, you might as well have some fun for your money."

"Suppose the big white did come around," said Brody. "What would be the first thing you'd do?"

"Try to keep him interested enough so he'd stick around till we could start pumping irons into him. And that's where we'll have a little trouble. The squid isn't enough to keep him interested. Fish that size'll suck a squid right down and not even know he's et it. So we'll have to give him something special that he can't turn down, something with a big ol' hook in it that'll hold him at least until we can stick him once or twice."

From the stern, Hooper said, "What's something special, Quint?"

Quint pointed to a green plastic garbage can nestled in a corner amidships. "Take a look for yourself. It's in that can."

Hooper walked over to the can, flipped the metal clasps and lifted the top. He gasped at what he saw. Floating in the can full of water was a tiny bottle-nosed dolphin, no more than two feet long. Sticking out from a puncture on the underside of the jaw was the eye of a huge shark hook, and from a hole in the belly the barbed hook itself curled forward. Hooper clutched the sides of the can and said, "A baby."

"Even better," Quint said with a grin. "Unborn. I got it from the mother."

Hooper gazed into the can again, then slammed the top back on and said, "Where did you get the mother?"

"Oh, I guess about six miles from here, due east. Why?"

"You killed her."

"No." Quint laughed. "She jumped into the boat and swallowed a bunch of sleeping pills." He paused, waiting for a laugh, and when none came he said, "Sure I killed her. You can't rightly buy them, you know."

Hooper stared at Quint. He was furious, outraged. "You know they're protected by law."

"What's your line of work, Hooper?"

"I'm an ichthyologist. I study fish. That's why I'm here."

"Okay, you study fish for a living. If you had to work for a living—I mean the kind of work where the amount of money you make depends on the amount of sweat you put in—you'd know more about what laws really mean. That law wasn't put in to stop Quint from taking one or two porpoise for bait. It was meant to stop big-time fishing for them, to stop nuts from shooting them for sport. So you can moan all you want, Hooper, but don't tell Quint he can't catch a few fish to help him make a living."

"I get your message," said Hooper. "Take it while you can, and if after a while there's nothing left, why, we'll just start taking something else. It's so stupid!"

"Don't overstep, son," said Quint. His voice was flat, toneless, and he stared into Hooper's eyes. "Don't go calling me stupid."

"I didn't mean that, for God's sake. I just meant—"

On his perch midway between the two men Brody decided it was time to stop the argument. "Let's drop it, Hooper, okay?" he said. "We're not out here to have a debate on ecology."

"What do you know about ecology, Brody?" said Hooper. "I bet all it means to you is someone telling you you can't burn leaves in your backyard."

"Listen, damn you! We're out here to stop a fish from killing people, and if using one porpoise will help us save God knows how many lives, that seems to me a pretty good bargain."

Hooper smirked and said to Brody, "So now you're an expert on saving lives, are you? Let's see. How many could have been saved if you'd closed the beaches after the—"

Brody was on his feet moving at Hooper before he consciously knew he had left his chair. "You shut your mouth!" he said. Then he stopped short.

A quick, sharp laugh from Quint broke the tension. "I seen that coming since you came aboard this morning," he said.

THE second day of the hunt was as still as the first. The boat lay motionless on the glassy sea, like a paper cup in a puddle.

Brody had brought a book along to pass the time, a sex mystery borrowed from Hendricks. He did not want to have to fill time with conversation, which might lead to a repeat of yesterday's scene with Hooper. It had embarrassed him—Hooper, too, he thought. Today they seldom spoke to one another, directing most of their comments at Quint.

By noon the lines had been in the chum slick for over four hours. The men ate lunch—sandwiches and beer—and when they were finished Quint loaded his M1. For the next hour they sat in silence—Brody dozing in the fighting chair, a hat protecting his face; Hooper at the stern, ladling chum and occasionally shaking his head to keep awake, and Quint on the flying bridge, watching the slick, his Marine Corps cap tilted back on his head.

Suddenly Quint said, his voice soft, "We've got a visitor."

Brody snapped awake. Hooper stood up. The starboard line was running out, smoothly and very fast.

"Take the rod," Quint said. He removed his cap and dropped it onto the bench.

Brody took the rod, fitted it into the swivel and held on.

"When I tell you," said Quint, "you throw that brake and hit him." The line stopped running. "Wait. He's turning. He'll start again." But the line lay dead in the water, limp and unmoving. After several moments Quint said, "Reel it in."

The line came clear of the water and hung at the tip of the rod. There was no hook, no bait, no leader. The wire had been neatly severed. Quint hopped down from the bridge and looked at it. "I think we've just met your friend," he said. "This wire's been bit clean through. The fish probably didn't even know he had it in his mouth. He just sucked the bait in and closed his mouth."

"So what do we do now?" said Brody.

"We wait and see if he takes the other one, or if he surfaces."

"What about using the porpoise?"

"When I know it's him," said Quint, "then I'll give him the porpoise. I don't want to waste a prize bait on some little runt."

They waited. The only sound was the liquid plop of the chum Hooper ladled overboard. Then the port line began to run.

Brody was both excited and afraid, awed by the thought of a creature swimming below them whose power he could not imagine. Hooper stood at the gunwale, transfixed by the running line.

The line stopped and went limp.

"He done it again," said Quint. He took the rod out of the holder and began to reel. The severed line came aboard exactly as the other one had. "We'll give him one more chance," said Quint, "and I'll put on a tougher leader. Not that that'll stop him, if it's the fish

I think it is." From a drawer in the cockpit he took a four-foot length of three-eighth-inch chain.

"That looks like a dog's leash," said Brody.

"Used to be," said Quint.

"What's next if this doesn't work?"

"Don't know yet. I could take a four-inch shark hook and a length of chain and drop it overboard with a bunch of bait on it. But if he took it, I wouldn't know what to do with him. He'd tear out any cleat I've got on board." Quint flipped the baited hook overboard and fed out a few yards of line. "Come on, you bastard," he said. "Let's have a look at you."

The three men watched the port line. Hooper bent down, filled his ladle with chum and tossed it into the slick. Something caught his eye and made him turn to the left. What he saw sucked from him a throaty grunt that made the others turn to look.

"My God!" said Brody.

No more than ten feet off the stern, slightly to starboard, was the conical snout of the fish. It stuck out of the water perhaps two feet. The top of the head was sooty gray, pocked with two black eyes. The mouth was open not quite halfway, a dim cavern guarded by huge, triangular teeth.

Fish and men confronted each other for perhaps ten seconds. Then Quint yelled, "Get an iron!" and, obeying himself, he dashed forward for a harpoon. Just then the fish slid quietly backward into the water. The long, scythed tail flicked once, and the fish disappeared.

"He's gone," said Brody.

"Fantastic!" said Hooper. "That fish is everything I thought. And more. He's fantastic! That head must have been four feet across."

"Could be," said Quint, walking aft to deposit in the stern two harpoon heads and two barrels with their coils of rope.

"Have you ever seen a fish like that, Quint?" Hooper asked.

"Not quite," said Quint.

"How long was he, would you say?"

"Twenty feet. Maybe more. With them things, it don't make much difference. Once they get to six feet, they're trouble."

"I hope he comes back," said Hooper.

Brody felt a chill. "He looked like he was grinning," he said.

"Don't make him out to be more than he is," said Quint. "He's just a dumb garbage bucket."

"How can you say that?" said Hooper. "That fish is a beauty. It's the kind of thing that makes you believe in a god."

A noise behind Hooper made him turn. Knifing the water thirty feet away was a triangular dorsal fin over a foot high, followed by a towering tail that swatted left and right in cadence.

"It's attacking the boat!" cried Brody. Involuntarily he backed into the seat of the fighting chair.

"Hand me that iron," said Quint.

The fish was almost at the boat. It raised its head, gazed vacantly at Hooper with one of its black eyes, and passed under the boat. Quint raised the harpoon and turned back to the port side. The throwing pole struck the fighting chair, and the dart dislodged and fell to the deck.

"Damn!" shouted Quint. "Is he still there?" He reached down, grabbed the dart and stuck it back on the end of the pole.

"Your side!" yelled Hooper. "He's passed this side already."

Quint turned as the gray-brown shape of the fish pulled away and began to dive. He dropped the harpoon, snatched up the rifle and emptied the clip into the water behind the fish. "Bastard!" he said. "Give me some warning next time." Then he put the rifle down and laughed. "At least he didn't attack the boat," he said. He looked at Brody. "Gave you a bit of a start."

"More'n a bit," said Brody. He shook his head, as if to reassemble his thoughts. "I'm still not sure I believe it." His mind was full of images of a torpedo shape streaking upward in the blackness and tearing Christine Watkins to pieces; of the boy on the raft, unknowing, unsuspecting, until suddenly seized by a nightmare creature. "You think he'll come back?"

"I don't know," said Quint. "You never know what they're going to do." From a pocket he took a note pad and a pencil. He extended his left arm and pointed it toward shore. He closed his right eye and sighted down the index finger of his left hand, then scribbled on the pad. He moved his hand a couple of inches to the left, sighted again and made another note. Anticipating a question from Brody, Quint said, "Taking bearings so if he doesn't show up for the rest of today, I'll know where to come tomorrow."

Brody looked toward shore. "What are you taking them on?"

"Lighthouse on the point and the water tower in town. They line up different ways depending where you are."

Hooper smiled. "Do you really think he'll stay in one place?"

"He sure as hell stayed around Amity," said Brody.

"That's because he had food," said Hooper. There was no irony in his voice, no taunt. But the remark was like a needle stabbing into Brody's brain.

They waited, but the fish never returned. At a little after five o'clock Quint said, "We might as well go in."

"You don't think we should spend the night, to keep the slick going?" said Brody.

Quint thought for a moment. "Nope. First, the slick would be big and confusing, and that would foul us up for the next day. Second, I like to get this boat in at night."

"I guess I can't blame you," said Brody. "Your wife must like it better, too."

Quint said flatly, "Got no wife."

"Oh. I'm sorry."

"Don't be. I never saw the need for one." Quint turned and climbed the ladder to the flying bridge.

ELLEN was fixing the children's supper when the doorbell rang. She heard the screen door open, heard Billy's voice, and a moment later saw Larry Vaughan standing at the kitchen door. It had been less than two weeks since she had last seen him, yet the change in his appearance was startling. As always he was dressed perfectly, but he had lost weight, and the loss showed in his face. His skin looked gray, and appeared to droop at the cheekbones.

Embarrassed when she found herself staring, Ellen lowered her eyes and said, "Larry. Hello."

"Hello, Ellen. I stopped by to say farewell."

115

Ellen said, "You're going away? For how long?"

"Perhaps for good. There's nothing here for me anymore."

"What about your business?"

"That's gone. Or it soon will be. What few assets there are will belong to my . . . partners." He spat the word and then he said, "Has Martin told you about . . ."

"Yes." Ellen looked down at the chicken she was cooking.

"I imagine you don't think very highly of me anymore."

"It's not up to me to judge you, Larry. How much does Eleanor know?"

"Nothing, poor dear. I want to spare her, if I can. That's one reason I want to move away." Vaughan leaned against the sink. "You know something? Sometimes I've thought that you and I would have made a wonderful couple."

Ellen reddened. "What do you mean?"

"You're from a good family. You know all the people I had to fight to get to know. We would have fit in Amity. You're lovely and good and strong. You would have been a real asset to me. And I could have given you a life you would have loved."

Ellen smiled. "I'm not as strong as you think, Larry."

"Don't belittle yourself. I only hope Martin appreciates the treasure he has. Anyway, no point in dreaming." He walked across the kitchen and kissed the top of Ellen's head. "Good-by, dear," he said. "Think of me once in a while."

Ellen looked at him. "I will." She kissed his cheek. "Where are you going?"

"I don't know. Vermont, maybe, or New Hampshire. I might sell land to the skiing crowd."

"Send us a card so we'll know where you are."

"I will. Good-by." Vaughan left the room, and Ellen heard the screen door close behind him.

When she had served the children their supper Ellen went upstairs and sat on her bed. "A life you would have loved," Vaughan had said. What would it have been like? There would have been money and acceptance. She would never have missed the life she led as a girl, for it would never have ended. There would have been no craving for renewal and self-confidence and confirmation of her femininity, no need for a fling with someone like Hooper. But it would have been a life without challenge, a life of cheap satisfactions.

As she pondered what Vaughan had said she began to recognize the richness of her relationship with Brody. It was more rewarding than any Larry Vaughan would ever experience, an amalgam of minor trials and tiny triumphs that added up to something akin to joy. And as her recognition grew so did a regret that it had taken her so long to see the waste of time and emotion in trying to cling to her past. Suddenly she felt fear—fear that she was growing up too late, that something might happen to Brody before she could savor her awareness. She looked at her watch: 6:20. He should have been home by now.

She heard the front door open. She ran down the stairs, wrapped her arms around Brody and kissed him hard on the mouth.

"My God!" he said when she let him go. "That's some welcome."

9

"You're not putting that thing on my boat," said Quint.

They stood on the dock in the brightening light. The sun had cleared the horizon, but it lay behind a low bank of clouds. The boat was ready to go. The engine chugged quietly, sputtering bubbles as tiny waves washed against the exhaust pipe.

Quint, with his back to the boat, faced Brody and Hooper, who stood on either side of an aluminum cage slightly over six feet tall, six feet wide and four feet deep. Inside it were a scuba tank, an airflow regulator, a face mask and a neoprene wet suit.

"What the hell is it, anyway?" said Quint.

"It's a shark cage," said Hooper. "Divers use them to protect themselves when they're swimming in the open ocean. I phoned last night and my friends brought it down from Woods Hole."

"And what do you plan to do with it?"

"When we find the fish I want to go down in the cage and take some pictures."

"Not a chance," said Quint. "A fish that big could eat that cage for breakfast."

"But *would* he? I think he might bump it, might even mouth it, but I don't think he'd seriously try to eat it."

"Well, forget it."

"Look, Quint, this a chance of a lifetime. I never thought of doing it until I saw the fish yesterday. Even though people have filmed great whites before, no one's ever filmed a twenty-foot white swimming in the open ocean. Never."

"He said forget it," said Brody. "So forget it. We're out here to kill that fish, not make a home movie about it."

Hooper said to Quint, "I'll pay you."

Quint smiled. "Oh, yeah? How much?"

"A hundred dollars. Cash. In advance, the way you like it." He reached into his back pocket for his wallet.

"I said no!" said Brody.

"I don't know," said Quint. Then he said, "Hell, I don't guess it's my business to keep a man from killing himself if he wants to."

"You put that cage on the boat," Brody said to Quint, "and you don't get your four hundred." If Hooper wants to kill himself, Brody thought, let him do it on his own time.

"And if the cage doesn't go," said Hooper, "I don't go."

"We'll find another man," said Brody.

"Can't do it," said Quint. "Not on this short notice."

"Then the hell with it!" said Brody. "We'll go tomorrow. Hooper can go back to Woods Hole and play with his fish."

Hooper was angry—angrier, in fact, than he knew, for before he could stop himself, he had said, "That's not all I might . . . Oh, forget it."

A leaden silence fell over the three men. Brody stared at Hooper, unwilling to believe what he had heard. Then suddenly he was overcome by rage. He reached Hooper in two steps, grabbed both sides of his collar and rammed his fists alongside Hooper's neck. "What was that?" he said. "What did you say?"

Hooper clawed at Brody's fingers. "Nothing!" he said, choking.

"Where were you last Wednesday afternoon?"

"Nowhere!" Hooper's temples were throbbing. "Let me go!"

"Where were you?" Brody twisted his fists tighter.

"In a motel! Now let me go!"

Brody eased his grip. "With who?" he said.

"Daisy Wicker." Hooper knew it was a weak lie. Brody could check it out with no trouble. But it was all he could think of. He could stop on the way home and phone Daisy Wicker, beg her to corroborate his story.

"I'll check," said Brody. "You can count on it."

"Well, what do you say?" said Quint. "We going today or not? Either way, Brody, it'll cost you."

Brody was tempted to cancel the trip, to return to Amity and discover the truth. But he said to Quint, "We'll go."

"With the cage?"

"With the cage. If this ass wants to kill himself, let him."

"Okay by me," said Quint. "Let's get this circus on the road."

"I'll get in the boat," Hooper said hoarsely. "You two can lean the cage over toward me, then one of you come down and help me stow it."

Brody and Quint slid the cage across the wooden dock, and Brody was surprised at how light it was. Even with the diving gear inside, it couldn't have weighed more than two hundred pounds. They tipped it toward Hooper, who held it until Quint joined him in the cockpit. The two men loaded the cage on deck and secured it under the overhang of the flying bridge.

"Uncleat the stern line, will you?" Quint called to Brody. Then, as Brody jumped aboard, Quint pushed the throttle forward and headed the boat toward the open sea.

Gradually, as the *Orca* fell into the rhythm of the long ocean swells, Brody's fury dulled. Maybe Hooper was telling the truth. He was sure Ellen had never cheated on him before. But, he told himself, there's always a first time. And once again the thought made his throat tighten. He climbed up to the flying bridge and sat on the bench next to Quint.

Quint chuckled. "What is it, you think Hooper's been fooling around with your wife?"

"None of your damn business," Brody said.

"Whatever you say. But if you ask me, he ain't got it in him."

"Nobody asked you." Anxious to change the subject, Brody said, "Are we going back to the same place?"

"Same place. Won't be too long now."

"What are the chances the fish will still be there?"

"Who knows? But it's the only thing we can do."

"You said something the other day about being smarter than the fish. Is that all there is to it?"

"That's all there is. It's no trick. They're stupid as sin."

"But there are fish you can't catch, aren't there?"

"Oh, sure, but that only means they're not hungry, or they're too fast for you, or you're using the wrong bait."

Quint fell silent for a moment, then spoke again. "Once," he said, "a shark almost caught *me*. It was about twenty years ago, I gaffed a fair-sized blue, and he gave a big yank and hauled me overboard."

"What did you do?"

"I come up over that transom so fast I don't think my feet touched anything between water and deck."

Quint pulled back on the throttle, and the boat slowed. He took a piece of paper from his pocket, read the notes and, sighting along his outstretched arm, checked his bearings. "Okay, Hooper," he said. "Start chuckin' the stuff overboard."

Hooper mounted the transom and began to ladle the chum into the sea.

By ten o'clock a breeze had come up—not strong, but fresh enough to ripple the water and cool the men, who sat and watched and said nothing. Brody was again in the fighting chair, struggling to stay awake. He yawned, then he stood, stretched and went down the three steps into the cabin. "I'm going to have a beer," he called. "Anybody want one?"

"Sure," said Quint.

Brody took out two beers, and had started to climb the stairs when he heard Quint's flat, calm voice say, "There he is."

Hooper jumped off the transom. "Wow! He sure is!"

Brody stepped quickly onto the deck. It took his eyes a moment to adjust, but then, off the stern, he saw the fin—a brownish gray triangle that sliced through the water, followed by the tail sweeping left and right. The fish was at least thirty yards away, Brody guessed. Maybe forty.

Quint walked forward and fastened a harpoon head to the wooden shaft. He set a barrel on the transom to the left of Hooper's bucket and arranged the coiled rope beside it. Then he climbed up on the transom and stood, his right arm cocked, holding the harpoon. "Come on, fish," he said. "Come on in here."

The fish cruised slowly back and forth, but he would come no closer than fifty feet.

"I don't get it," said Quint. "He should come in and take a look at us. Brody, throw those squid bait overboard. And make a big splash. Let him know something's there."

Brody did as he was told. But still the fish stayed away.

Hooper said, "What about the porpoise?"

"Why, Mr. Hooper," said Quint. "I thought you didn't approve."

"Never mind that," Hooper said excitedly. "I want to see that fish!"

"We'll see," said Quint. "If I have to use it, I will."

They waited—Hooper ladling, Quint poised on the transom, Brody standing by one of the rods.

"Hell," said Quint. "I guess I got no choice." He set the harpoon down and jumped off the transom. He flipped the top off the garbage can next to Brody, and Brody saw the lifeless eyes of the tiny porpoise as it swayed in the briny water. The sight repelled him, and he turned away.

"Well, little fella," said Quint. "The time has come." He took out a dog-leash chain and snapped one end of it into the hook eye protruding from beneath the porpoise's jaw. To the other end of the chain he tied several yards of three-quarter-inch hemp. Then he made the rope fast to a cleat on the starboard gunwale.

"You said the shark could pull out a cleat," said Brody.

"It might just," said Quint. "But I'm betting I can get an iron in him and cut the rope before he pulls it taut enough to yank the cleat." Quint carried the porpoise over to the transom and cut a series of shallow slashes in its belly before tossing it into the water. He let out six feet of line, then put the rope under his foot on the transom.

"Why are you standing on the rope?" asked Brody.

"To keep the little fella where I can get a shot at the shark. But I don't want to cleat it down that close. If the shark took it and didn't have any running room, he could thrash around and beat us to pieces."

The shark was still cruising back and forth, but coming closer to the boat with every passage. Then it stopped, twenty or twenty-five feet away. The tail dropped beneath the surface; the dorsal fin slid backward and vanished; and the great head reared up, mouth open in a slack, savage grin, eyes black and abysmal. Brody stared in mute horror.

"Hey, fish!" Quint called. He stood on the transom, legs spread, his hand curled around the shaft of the harpoon that rested on his shoulder. "Come see what we've got for you!"

For another moment the fish hung in the water, watching. Then soundlessly the head slid down and disappeared.

"He'll be coming now," said Quint.

Suddenly the boat lurched violently to the side. Quint's legs skidded out from under him, and he fell backward on the transom. The harpoon dart separated from the shaft and clattered to the deck. Brody tumbled sideways, grabbed the back of the chair as it swiveled around. Hooper slammed into the port gunwale.

The rope attached to the porpoise tautened and shivered. Then it snapped backward and lay slack in the water.

"I'll be damned!" said Quint. "I never have seen a fish do that before. He either bit right through the chain, or else . . ." He walked over to the starboard gunwale and grabbed the chain. It was intact, but the hook it was attached to was nearly straight.

"He did that with his mouth?" said Brody.

"Bent it out nice as you please," said Quint. "Probably didn't slow him down for more than a second or two."

Brody felt light-headed. He sat down in the chair and drew several deep breaths, trying to stifle his mounting fear.

"Where do you suppose he's gone?" said Hooper.

"He's around here somewhere," said Quint. "That porpoise wasn't any more to him than an anchovy is to a bluefish. He'll be looking for more food." He reassembled the harpoon and re-coiled the rope. "I'll tie up some more squid and hang 'em overboard."

Brody watched Quint as he wrapped twine around each squid and dropped it overboard. When a dozen squid had been placed around the boat, Quint climbed to the flying bridge and sat down.

Brody looked at his watch: 11:05. At 11:30 he was startled by a sharp, resonant *snap*. Quint leaped down the ladder and across the deck, and picked up the harpoon. "He's back," he said. "He took one of the squid." A few inches of limp twine hung from a cleat amidships.

As Brody looked at the remnant he saw another piece of twine— a few feet farther up the gunwale—go limp. "He must be right underneath us," he said.

"Let's put the cage overboard," said Hooper.

"You're kidding," said Brody.

"No, I'm not. It might bring him out."

"With you in it?"

"Not at first. Let's see what he does. What do you say, Quint?"

"Might as well," said Quint. "Can't hurt just to put it in the water." He laid the harpoon down.

He and Hooper tipped the cage onto its side, and Hooper opened the top hatch and removed the scuba gear, face mask and wet suit. They stood the cage upright again, slid it across the deck and secured it with two lines to cleats on the starboard gunwale.

"Okay," said Hooper. "Let's put her over." They lifted the cage overboard, and it sank until the ropes stopped it, a few feet beneath the surface.

"What makes you think this'll bring him out?" said Brody.

"I think he'll come and have a look at it, to see whether he wants to eat it," said Hooper.

But the cage lay quietly in the water, unmolested.

"There goes another squid," said Quint. "He's there, all right."

Hooper said, "Oh, well," and went below. He reappeared moments later, carrying an underwater movie camera and a stick with a thong at one end.

"What are you doing?" Brody said.

"I'm going down there. Maybe that'll bring him out."

"You're out of your mind. What are you going to do if he does come out?"

"First, I'm going to take some pictures of him. Then I'm going to try to kill him."

"With what, may I ask?"

"This." Hooper held up the stick. "It's called a bang stick or a power head. Basically it's an underwater gun." He pulled both ends of the stick, and it came apart in two pieces. "In here," he said, pointing to a chamber, "you put a twelve-gauge shotgun shell." He took one from his pocket and pushed it into the chamber. "Then you jab it at the fish and the shell goes off. If you hit him right—the brain's the only sure place—you kill him."

"Even a fish that big?"

"I think so. If I hit him right."

"And if you don't? Suppose you miss by just a hair."

"What concerns me is that if I miss, I might drive him off," said Hooper. "He'd probably sound, and we'd never know if he died or not."

"Until he ate someone else," said Brody.

"That's right."

"You're plain crazy," said Quint.

"Am I, Quint? You're not having much success with this fish. I think he's more than you can handle."

"That right, boy? You think you can do better'n Quint? Fine and dandy. You're gonna get your chance."

Brody said, "Come on. We can't let him go in that thing."

"What are *you* bitchin' about?" said Quint. "From what I seen, you just as soon he went down there and never come up. At least that'd stop him from—"

"Shut your mouth!" Brody's emotions were jumbled. Could he really wish a man dead? No. Not yet.

"Go on," Quint said to Hooper. "Get in that thing."

"Right away." Hooper removed his shirt, sneakers and trousers and began to pull the neoprene suit over his legs. "When I'm inside the cage," he said, forcing his arms into the rubber sleeves of the jacket, "stand up here and keep an eye out. Maybe you can use the rifle if he gets close enough to the surface."

When he was dressed, Hooper fitted the airflow regulator onto the neck of the air tank and opened the valve. He sucked two breaths from the tank to make sure it was feeding air. "Help me put this on, will you?" he said to Brody.

Brody held the tank while Hooper slipped his arms through the straps and fastened a third strap around his middle. He put the face mask on his head. "I should have brought weights," he said.

Quint said, "You should have brought brains."

Hooper put his right wrist through the thong at the end of the power head, picked up the camera and walked to the gunwale. "If you'll each take a rope and pull the cage to the surface, I'll open the hatch and go in through the top."

Quint and Brody pulled on the ropes, and the cage rose in the water. When the hatch broke the surface Hooper said, "Okay, right there." He spat in the face mask, rubbed the saliva around on the glass and fitted the mask over his face. He reached for the regulator tube, put the mouthpiece in his mouth and took a breath. He unlatched the hatch and flipped it open, put a knee on the gunwale, then stopped and took the mouthpiece out of his mouth. "I forgot something." He walked across the deck and picked up his trousers. He rummaged through the pockets. Then he unzipped his wet-suit jacket.

"What's that?" said Brody.

Hooper held up a shark's tooth, a duplicate of the one he had given Ellen. He dropped it inside his wet suit. "Can't be too careful," he said, smiling. He replaced his mouthpiece, took a final breath and jumped overboard, passing through the open hatch as he hit the water.

Before his feet touched the bottom of the cage he curled around and pulled the hatch closed. Then he stood, looked up at Brody and put his thumb and index finger together in the okay sign.

Brody and Quint let the cage descend until the top was about four feet beneath the surface.

"Get the rifle," said Quint. He climbed onto the transom and lifted the harpoon to his shoulder.

Brody went below, found the rifle and hurried back on deck.

In the cage Hooper waited for the bubbly froth of his descent to dissipate, then checked his watch. He felt serene. He was alone in blue silence speckled with shafts of sunlight that danced through the water. He looked up at the gray hull of the boat. Even with the bright sunlight, the visibility in the murky water was poor—no more than forty feet. Hooper turned slowly around, trying to pierce the edge of gloom and grasp any sliver of color or movement. Nothing. He looked at his watch again, calculating that if he controlled his breathing, he could stay down for half an hour more.

Carried by the tide, one of the small white squid slipped between the bars and, tethered by twine, fluttered in Hooper's face. He pushed it out of the cage. He glanced downward, started to look away, then snapped his eyes down again. Rising at him from the darkling blue—slowly, smoothly—was the shark.

Hooper stared, impelled to flee but unable to move. As the fish drew nearer he marveled at its colors: the top of the immense body was a hard ferrous gray, bluish where dappled with streaks of sun. Beneath the lateral line all was creamy white. Hooper wanted to raise his camera, but his arm would not obey.

The fish came closer, silent as a shadow, and Hooper drew back. The head was only a few feet from the cage when the fish turned and began to pass before Hooper's eyes, as if in proud display of its mass and power. The snout passed first, then the jaw, slack and smiling. And then the black, fathomless eye, seemingly riveted upon him. The gills rippled—bloodless wounds in the steely skin.

Tentatively, Hooper stuck a hand through the bars and touched the flank. It felt cold and hard. He let his fingertips caress the pectoral fins, the pelvic fin, the genital claspers—until finally they were slapped away by the sweeping tail.

Hooper heard faint popping noises, and he saw three straight spirals of angry bubbles speed from the surface, then slow and stop, well above the fish. Bullets. Not yet, he told himself. One more pass for pictures.

"What the hell is he doing down there?" said Brody. "Why didn't he jab him?"

Quint stood on the transom, harpoon clutched in his fist, peering into the water. "Come up, fish," he said. "Come to Quint."

The fish had circled off to the limit of Hooper's vision—a spectral blur. Hooper raised his camera and pressed the trigger. He wanted to catch the beast as it emerged from the darkness.

Through the viewfinder he saw the fish turn toward him. It moved fast, tail thrusting vigorously, mouth opening and closing. Hooper changed the focus. Remember to change it again, he told himself, when it turns.

But the fish did not turn. It struck the cage head-on, the snout ramming between two bars and spreading them. The snout hit Hooper in the chest and knocked him backward. The camera flew from his hands, and the mouthpiece shot from his mouth. The fish turned on its side, and the pounding tail forced the great body farther into the cage. Hooper groped for his mouthpiece but couldn't find it. His chest was convulsed with the need for air.

"It's attacking!" screamed Brody. He grabbed one of the tether ropes and pulled, desperately trying to raise the cage.

"Damn your soul!" Quint shouted.

"Throw the iron!" Brody yelled. "Throw it!"

"I can't throw it! I gotta get him on the surface! Come up, you devil!"

The fish slid backward out of the cage and turned sharply to the right in a tight circle. Hooper reached behind his head and located the mouthpiece. He put it in his mouth and drew an agonized breath. It was then that he saw the wide gap in the bars, and saw the giant head lunging through it again. He raised his hands above his head, grasping at the escape hatch.

The fish rammed through the space between the bars, spreading them still farther. Hooper, flattened against the back of the cage, saw the mouth reaching, straining for him. He tried to lower his arm and grab the power head. The fish thrust again, and its jaws

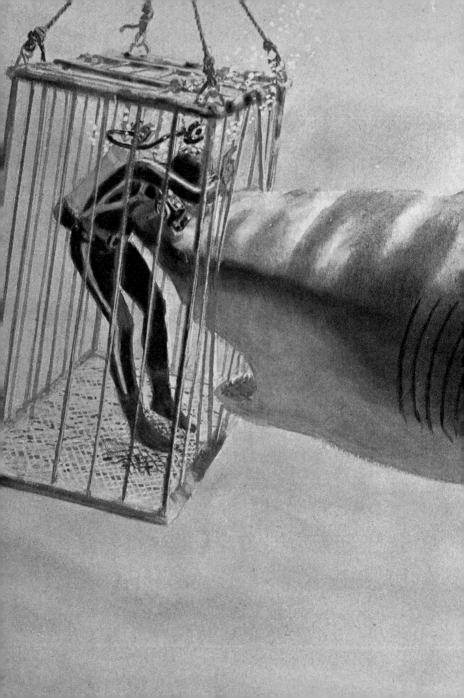

closed around his torso. Hooper felt a terrible pressure, as if his guts were being compacted. He jabbed his fist into the black eye. The fish bit down, and the last thing Hooper saw before he died was the eye gazing at him through a cloud of his own blood.

"He's got him!" cried Brody. "Do something!"

"The man is dead," Quint said.

"How do you know? We may be able to save him."

"He's dead."

Holding Hooper in its mouth, the fish backed out of the cage. Then, with a thrust of its tail, it drove itself upward.

"He's coming up!" said Brody.

"Grab the rifle!" Quint cocked his hand for the throw.

The fish broke water fifteen feet from the boat, surging upward in a shower of spray. Hooper's body hung from each side of the mouth. For a few seconds Brody thought he saw Hooper's glazed, dead eyes staring through his face mask.

Simultaneously, Brody reached for the rifle and Quint cast the harpoon. The target was huge, a field of white belly, and the distance was not too great for a successful throw above-water. But as Quint threw, the fish slid downward and the iron went high.

Brody fired without aiming, and the bullets hit the water in front of the fish.

"Here, give me the damned thing!" Quint grabbed the rifle and in a single, quick motion raised it to his shoulder and squeezed off two shots. But the fish had already begun to slip beneath the surface. The bullets plopped harmlessly into the swirl.

The fish might never have been there. There was no noise save the whisper of a breeze. From the surface the cage seemed undamaged. The water was calm. The only difference was that Hooper was gone.

"What do we do now?" said Brody. "What in the name of God can we do now? There's nothing left. We might as well go back."

"We'll go back," said Quint. "For now."

"For now? What do you mean? There's nothing we can do. The fish is too much for us. It's not real, not natural."

"Are you beaten?"

"I'm beaten. All we can do is wait until God or nature or whatever the hell is doing this to us decides we've had enough. It's out of man's hands."

"Not mine," said Quint. "I am going to kill that thing."

"I'm not sure I can get any more money after what happened today."

"Keep your money. This is no longer a matter of money."

"What do you mean?"

Quint said, "I am going to kill that fish. Come if you want. Stay home if you want. But I am going to kill that fish." His eyes seemed as dark and bottomless as the eye of the fish.

"I'll come," said Brody. "I don't guess I have any choice."

"No," said Quint. "We got no choice."

When the boat was tied up, Brody walked toward his car. At the end of the dock there was a phone booth, and he stopped beside it, prompted by his earlier resolve to call Daisy Wicker. But what's the point? he thought. If there was anything, it's over now.

Still, as he drove toward Amity, Brody wondered what Ellen's reaction had been to the news of Hooper's death. Quint had radioed the Coast Guard before they started in, and Brody had asked the duty officer to phone Ellen.

By the time Brody arrived home Ellen had long since finished crying. She had wept angrily, grieving not so much for Hooper as in hopelessness and bitterness at yet another death. Hooper had been her lover in only the most shallow sense of the word. She had not *loved* him, she had used him.

She heard Brody's car pull into the driveway, and she opened the back door. Lord, he looks whipped, she thought. His eyes were red and sunken, and he seemed slightly hunched as he walked toward the house. At the door she kissed him and said, "You look like you could use a drink."

"That I could." He went into the living room and flopped into a chair.

"What would you like?"

"Anything. Just so long as it's strong."

She went into the kitchen, filled a glass with equal portions of vodka and orange juice, and brought it to him. She sat on the arm of his chair and said, "Well, it's over now, isn't it? There's nothing more you can do."

"We're going out tomorrow. Six o'clock."

"Why?" Ellen was stunned. "What do you think you can do?"

"Catch the fish. And kill it."

"Do you believe that?"

"I'm not sure. But Quint believes it. God, how he believes it."

"Then let him go. Let him get killed."

"I can't."

"Why not?"

Brody thought for a moment and said, "I don't think I can explain it. But giving up isn't an answer."

Tears spilled out of Ellen's eyes. "What about me and the children? Do you want to get killed?"

"No, God, no. It's just . . ."

"You think it's all your fault. You think you're responsible for that little boy and the old man. You think killing the shark will make everything all right again. You want revenge."

Brody sighed. "Maybe. I don't know. I feel . . . I believe the only way this town can be alive again is if we kill that thing."

"And you're willing to get killed trying to—"

"Don't be stupid! I'm not even willing—if that's the word you want to use—to go out in that goddam boat. I'm so scared every minute I'm out there I want to puke."

"Then *why go?*" She was pleading with him, begging. "Can't you ever think of anybody but yourself?"

Brody was shocked at the suggestion of selfishness. "I love you," he said. "You know that . . . no matter what."

"Sure you do," she said bitterly. "Oh, sure you do."

AROUND midnight the wind began to blow hard from the northeast, whistling through the screens and soon bringing a driving rain. Brody got out of bed and shut the window. He tried to go back to sleep, but his mind refused to rest.

At five o'clock he got up and dressed quietly. Before he left the bedroom he looked at Ellen, who had a frown on her sleeping face. "I do love you, you know," he whispered, and he kissed her brow. He started down the stairs and then, impulsively, went and looked in the boys' bedrooms. They were all asleep.

10

WHEN he got to the dock Quint was waiting for him—a tall, impassive figure whose yellow oilskins shone under the dark sky.

"I almost called you," Brody said as he pulled on his slicker. "What does this weather mean?"

"Nothing," said Quint. "It'll let up after a while. Or even if it doesn't, he'll be there." He hopped aboard the boat.

"Is it just us? I thought you liked an extra pair of hands."

"You know this fish as well as any man, and more hands won't make no difference now. Besides, it's nobody else's business."

Brody undid the stern line, and was about to jump down to the deck when he noticed a canvas tarpaulin covering something in a corner. "What's that?" he said, pointing.

"Sheep." Quint turned the ignition key. The engine coughed once, caught, and began to chug evenly.

"What for?" Brody stepped down into the boat. "You going to sacrifice it?"

Quint barked a brief, grim laugh. "Might, at that," he said. "No, it's bait." He walked forward and cast off the bow line. Then he pushed the throttle forward, and the boat eased out of the slip.

The water off Montauk was rough, for the wind was at odds with the tide. The pounding bow cast a mantle of spray.

They had been around the point only fifteen minutes when Quint pulled back on the throttle and slowed the engine.

"We're not as far out as usual," Brody said. "We can't be more than a couple of miles offshore."

"Just about."

"So why are you stopping?"

Quint pointed to the left, to a cluster of lights farther down the shore. "That's Amity there. I think he'll be somewhere between here and Amity."

"Why?"

"I got a feeling. There's not always a why to these things."

"Two days in a row we found him farther out."

"Or he found us." Quint's tone was sly.

Brody bristled. "What kind of game are you playing?"

"No game. If I'm wrong, I'm wrong."

"And we try somewhere else tomorrow." Brody half hoped Quint would be wrong, that there would be a day's reprieve.

"Or later today. But I don't think we'll have to wait that long." Quint went to the stern and lifted a bucket of chum onto the transom. "Start chummin'," he said, handing Brody the ladle. He uncovered the sheep, tied a rope around its neck and laid it on the gunwale. He slashed its stomach and flung the animal over-board, letting it drift twenty feet from the boat before securing the rope to an after cleat. Then he went forward, unlashed two barrels and carried them and their coils of ropes and harpoon darts back to the stern. "Okay," he said. "Now let's see how long it takes."

The sky had lightened to full, gray daylight, and in ones and twos the lights on the shore flicked off. The stench of the mess Brody was ladling overboard made his stomach turn.

Suddenly he saw the monstrous head of the fish—not five feet away, so close he could have touched it with the ladle—black eyes staring at him, silver-gray snout pointing at him, gaping jaw grin-ning. "Quint!" Brody said. "There he is!"

Quint was at the stern in an instant. As he jumped onto the transom the fish's head slipped back into the water, and a second later it slammed into the transom. The jaws closed on the wood and the head shook violently from side to side. Brody grabbed a cleat and held on, unable to look away from the eyes. Quint fell to his knees. The fish let go and dropped beneath the surface, and the boat lay still again.

"He was waiting for us!" yelled Brody.

"I know," said Quint. "We've got him now."

"*We've* got *him?* Did you see what he did to the boat?"

133

"Give it a mighty good shake, didn't he?"

The rope holding the sheep tightened, shook, then went slack. Quint stood and picked up the harpoon. "He's took the sheep. It'll be a minute before he comes back."

Brody saw fever in Quint's face—an anticipation that strummed the sinews in his neck and whitened his knuckles.

The boat shuddered again, and there was a dull, hollow thump. "What's he doing?" said Brody.

"He's trying to chew a hole in the bottom of the boat, that's what! Look in the bilge." Quint raised high his harpoon. "Come out, you son of a bitch!"

Brody raised the hatch cover over the engine room and peered into the dark, oily hole. There was water in the bilges, but there always was, and he saw no new hole. "Looks okay to me," he said.

The dorsal fin and tail surfaced ten yards to the right of the stern and began to move again toward the boat. "There you come," said Quint, cooing. "There you come." He stood, right hand extended to the sky, grasping the harpoon. When the fish was a few feet from the boat, Quint cast his iron.

The harpoon struck the fish near the dorsal fin. Then the fish hit the boat, and Quint tumbled backward. His head struck the fighting chair, and a trickle of blood ran down his neck. He jumped up and cried, "I got you! I got you, you miserable bastard!"

The rope attached to the iron dart snaked overboard as the fish sounded. Then the barrel popped off the transom and vanished.

"He took it down with him!" said Brody.

"Not for long," said Quint. "He'll be back, and we'll throw another into him, and another, and another, until he quits." Quint pulled the twine attached to the wooden harpoon shaft and brought it back aboard. He fixed the shaft to a new dart.

His confidence was contagious, and Brody now felt ebullient, gleeful, relieved—free from the mist of death. Then he noticed the blood on Quint's neck, and he said, "Your head's bleeding."

"Get another barrel," said Quint, "and bring it back here."

Brody ran forward, unlashed a barrel, slipped the coiled rope over his arm and carried the gear to Quint.

"There he comes," said Quint, pointing to the left. The first barrel had come to the surface and bobbed in the water. Quint raised the harpoon above his head. "He's coming up!"

The fish broke water like a rocket lifting off. Snout, jaw and pectoral fins rose straight up, and Quint leaned into the throw. The second iron hit the fish in the belly, just as the great body began to fall. The belly smacked the water with a thunderous boom, and a blinding spray covered the boat.

The boat lurched once, and again, and there was the distant sound of crunching.

"Attack me, will you?" said Quint. He ran to push the throttle forward, and the boat moved away from the bobbing barrels.

"Has he done any damage?" said Brody.

"Some. We're riding a little heavy aft. He probably poked a hole in us. But we'll pump her out."

"That's it, then," Brody said happily.

"What's what?"

"The fish is as good as dead."

"Not quite. Look."

Following the boat, keeping pace, were the two red wooden barrels. They did not bob. Dragged by the great force of the fish, each cut through the water, pushing a wave before it.

"He's chasing us?" said Brody. "He can't still think we're food."

"No. He means to make a fight of it."

For the first time Brody saw a frown of disquiet on Quint's face. "Hell," Quint said, "if it's a fight he wants, it's a fight he'll get." He throttled down to idling speed, jumped to the deck and up onto the transom. He picked up another harpoon. Excitement had returned to his face. "Okay," he called. "Come and get it!"

The barrels kept coming—thirty yards away, twenty-five, twenty. Brody saw the flat plane of gray pass along the starboard side of the boat. "He's here!" he cried. "Heading forward."

Quint detached the harpoon dart from the shaft, snapped the twine that held the shaft to a cleat, hopped down from the transom and ran forward. When he reached the bow he bent down and tied the twine to a forward cleat, unlashed a barrel and slipped its dart onto the harpoon shaft. Then he stood, harpoon raised.

Thirty yards in front of the boat the fish turned. The head lifted out of the water, then dipped back in. The tail, standing like a sail, began to thrash back and forth. "Here he comes!" said Quint.

The fish hit the bow head-on with a noise like a muffled explosion. Quint cast his iron. It struck the fish atop the head, over the right eye, and it held fast. The rope fed slowly overboard as the fish backed off.

"Perfect!" said Quint. "Got him in the head that time."

There were three barrels in the water now, and they skated across the surface. Then they disappeared.

"*Damn!*" said Quint. "That's no normal fish that can sound with three irons in him and three barrels to hold him up."

The boat trembled, seeming to rise up, then dropped back. The barrels reappeared twenty yards from the boat.

"Go below," Quint told Brody, as he readied another harpoon. "See if he done us any dirt up forward."

Brody swung down into the cabin. He pulled back the threadbare carpet and opened a hatch. A stream of water was flowing aft. He went topside and said to Quint, "It doesn't look good. There's a lot of water under the cabin floor."

"I better go take a look. Here." Quint handed Brody the harpoon. "If he comes back, stick this in him for good measure."

Brody stood near the bow, holding the harpoon. The barrels twitched as the fish moved about below. How do you die? Brody said silently to the fish. He heard an electric motor start.

"No sweat," said Quint, walking forward. He took the harpoon from Brody. "The pumps should take care of it. When he dies we'll tow him in."

Brody dried his palms on the seat of his pants. "And until then?"

"We wait."

FOR three hours they waited. At first the barrels would disappear every ten or fifteen minutes, then their submergences grew rarer until, by eleven o'clock, they had not gone under for nearly an hour. By 11:30 the barrels were wallowing in the water.

"What do you think?" said Brody. "Is he dead?"

"I doubt it. But he may be close enough to it for us to throw a rope around his tail and drag him till he drowns."

Quint switched on the electric winch to make sure it was working, then turned it off again. He gunned the engine and moved the boat cautiously toward the barrels.

When he came alongside the barrels Quint reached overboard with a gaff, snagged a rope and pulled one of them aboard. He unsheathed his knife and cut the rope from the barrel. Then he stabbed the knife into the gunwale, freeing both hands to hold the rope and shove the barrel to the deck. He climbed onto the gunwale, ran the rope through a pulley and down to the winch. He took a few turns around the winch, then flipped the starter switch. As soon as the slack in the rope was taken up, the boat heeled hard to starboard, dragged down by the weight of the fish.

The winch turned slowly. The rope quivered under the strain, scattering drops of water on Quint's shirt.

Suddenly the rope started coming too fast. It fouled on the winch, coiling in snarls. The boat snapped upright.

"Rope break?" said Brody.

"Hell, no!" said Quint, and now Brody saw fear in his face. "The son of a bitch is coming up!"

The fish rose vertically beside the boat, with a great rushing *whoosh*, and Brody gasped at the size of the body. Towering overhead, it blocked out the light. The pectoral fins hovered like wings, stiff and straight, as the fish fell forward.

It landed on the stern with a shattering crash, driving the boat beneath the waves. Water poured in over the transom. In seconds Quint and Brody were standing in water up to their hips.

The fish's jaws were not three feet from Brody's chest. In the black eye, as big as a baseball, Brody thought he saw his own image.

"Damn your black soul!" screamed Quint. "You sunk my boat!" A barrel floated into the cockpit, the rope writhing like a worm. Quint grabbed the harpoon dart at the end of the rope and plunged it into the soft white belly of the fish. Blood poured from

137

the wound and bathed Quint's hands. The boat was sinking. The
stern was completely submerged, and the bow was rising. The
fish rolled off the stern and slid beneath the waves. The rope,
attached to the dart Quint had stuck into the fish, followed.

Suddenly Quint lost his footing and fell into the water. "The
knife!" he cried. His left leg lifted above the surface, and Brody
saw the rope coiled around Quint's foot.

Brody lunged for the knife stuck in the starboard gunwale,
wrenched it free, and turned back, struggling to run in the deepen-
ing water. He could not move fast enough. He watched helplessly
as Quint, arms reaching toward him, eyes wide and pleading, was
pulled slowly down into the dark water.

For a moment there was silence, except for the sucking sound
of the boat slipping gradually down. The water was up to Brody's
shoulders when a seat cushion popped to the surface next to him.
"They'd hold you up all right," Brody remembered Hendricks saying, "if you were an eight-year-old boy." But Brody grabbed the
cushion.

He saw the shark's tail and dorsal fin break the surface twenty
yards away. The tail waved once left, once right, and the dorsal
fin moved closer. "Get away, damn you!" Brody yelled.

The fish kept coming, barely moving, closing in.

Brody tried to swim to the bow of the boat, which was almost
vertical now. Before he could reach it, the bow slid beneath the

surface. He clutched the cushion, and he found that by putting his forearms across it and kicking constantly he could stay afloat without exhausting himself.

The fish came closer. It was only a few feet away, and Brody screamed and closed his eyes, waiting for an agony he could not imagine.

Nothing happened. He opened his eyes. The fish was only a foot or two away, but it had stopped. And then, as Brody watched, the steel-gray body began to fall downward into the gloom.

Brody put his face into the water and opened his eyes. He saw the fish sink in a graceful spiral, trailing behind it the body of Quint—arms out, head thrown back, mouth open in mute protest.

The fish faded from view. But, kept from sinking further by the bobbing barrels, it stopped somewhere beyond the reach of light, and Quint's body hung suspended, a shadow twirling slowly in the twilight.

Brody raised his head, cleared his eyes, and began to kick toward shore.

"My interest in sharks," says Peter Benchley, "began during summers spent on Nantucket, when my parents and I would charter boats and go shark fishing." His grandfather, the humorist Robert Benchley, started summering on that lovely island off Massachusetts in the 1920s; and his parents, the novelist Nathaniel Benchley and his wife, have for some time been year-round residents.

Peter Benchley thus represents the third generation of a writing family. After graduating from Harvard in 1961, he worked as a reporter for the Washington *Post,* and then joined the staff of *Newsweek,* where he spent three years as TV-Radio editor. From March 1967 until the end of Lyndon Johnson's presidency, Mr. Benchley was a speech-writer in the White House.

Since then he has been free-lancing: as a television commentator and as a contributor to magazines as diverse as *The New Yorker, National Geographic, Vogue* and *TV Guide.* He has written the screenplay for *Jaws,* which will be produced for Universal Studios by Richard Zanuck and David Brown.

Peter
Benchley

Mr. Benchley, whose hobbies include scuba diving, tennis and the guitar, lives with his wife, Wendy, their daughter, Tracy, seven, and son, Clayton, five, in Pennington, New Jersey. He is now at work on his second novel, about diving for sunken treasure.

The Dogs of War

A CONDENSATION OF THE BOOK BY

Frederick Forsyth

Action and terror
in a new classic as enthralling as
The Day of the Jackal

ILLUSTRATED BY DAVID BLOSSOM

The smell of cordite, the heart-stopping
excitement of battle, the freedom to fight
where he chose—these were the breath
of life to "Cat" Shannon. For Shannon
was a mercenary. In his shadowy and
supremely dangerous profession men
fought on contract for the people and
causes that appealed to them, and
Sir James Manson's scheme appealed
to Shannon. Only a piratical tycoon
like Sir James could possibly have
conceived it, and only a man with Cat's
knowledge and daring could carry it out.
One hundred days, Shannon was given.
One hundred days to steal a republic.

Forsyth's fascinating new thriller moves
at breakneck pace from the financial
capitals of Europe to the heart of Africa
for its shattering—and startling—
conclusion.

PART ONE

The Crystal Mountain

CHAPTER ONE

THERE were no stars that night on the bush airstrip, nor any moon; just the West African darkness wrapping around the scattered groups like warm, wet velvet. The cloud cover was lying off the tops of the iroko trees, and the waiting men prayed it would stay to shield them from the bombers.

At the end of the tarmac the old DC-4, which had slipped in by runway lights that stayed alight for just fifteen seconds, turned and coughed its way blindly toward the palm-thatch huts.

Between two of the huts five white men sat crouched in a Land-Rover, staring at the unexpected arrival with silent attention. The same thought was in each man's mind. If they did not get out of this crumbling enclave before the federal forces overran these few miles, they would not get out alive. They were the last of the mercenaries who had fought on contract for the side that had lost.

The pilot brought his plane to a halt twenty yards from a Constellation already parked on the apron, and climbed down to the concrete. An African ran over to him. There was a muttered conversation, and the two walked toward a group of men standing at the edge of the palm forest. The group parted until the pilot was face-to-face with the one who stood in the center. Even in the darkness, dimly illumined by a few cigarettes, the pilot recognized him as the man he had come to see.

"I am Captain Van Cleef," the pilot said in English accented in the Afrikaner manner.

The African nodded acknowledgment, his beard brushing the front of his camouflage uniform. "It's a hazardous night for flying, Captain," he remarked dryly, "and a little late to be bringing more supplies. Or did you perhaps come for the children?"

His voice was deep and slow, the accent more like that of an English public-school man, which he was, than an African.

"I came to collect you, sir. If you want to come, that is."

"I see. Did your government instruct you to do this?"

"No," said Van Cleef. "It was my idea."

The bearded head nodded slowly. "I am very grateful. It must have been quite a trip. Actually I have my own transport. The Constellation. Which I hope will take me away to exile."

Van Cleef felt relieved. He had no idea what he would have been in for if he had flown back to Libreville with the general. "I'll wait till you're off the ground and gone," he said. He felt like shaking the general's hand, but did not know whether he ought. So he turned and walked back to his aircraft.

There was silence among the black men after he left. "Why does an Afrikaner do a thing like that, General?" one finally asked.

The general smiled briefly. "I don't think we shall ever understand that." As he spoke he lit a cigarette. The glow set into sharp relief a face that half the world now recognized.

On the threshold of an exile he knew would be lonely and humiliating, the general still commanded. For two and a half years, sometimes by sheer force of personality, he had kept his millions of people together—surrounded, besieged, starving, but still fighting. His enemies had refuted his leadership, but few who had been there had any doubts. Even in defeat, as his car passed through the last village before the airstrip, the villagers had lined the mud road to chant their loyalty. He was leaving now, this man the federal government wanted dead by sunrise, because his people feared the reprisals would be so much worse if he stayed.

At his side, dwarfed by his height, stood his confidant, Dr. Okoye. The professor had decided to remain behind, hiding in the bush until the first wave of reprisals had ended. The two men had agreed to wait six months before attempting any contact.

The white mercenaries in the Land-Rover watched the pilot return to his plane. "It must be the South African," said the leader, who was sitting beside the driver, a young black with second lieutenant's tabs. He turned to one of the four men in the back. "Janni, go and ask if he'll make room for us."

A tall, rawboned man in a jungle-camouflage uniform climbed out of the rear of the vehicle and adjusted his beret.

"And make it good, huh?" the leader called. "Because if we don't get out of here in that crate, we could get chopped up."

Janni ambled toward the DC-4. Captain Van Cleef heard no sound behind him. *"Naand, meneer."*

Van Cleef spun around at the sound of the Afrikaans. Taking in the size of the man and the skull-and-crossbones motif on his left shoulder, he asked warily, *"Naand. Jy Afrikaans?"*

The man nodded. "Jan Dupree," he said, and held out his hand. *"Waar gaan-jy nou?"*

"To Libreville. As soon as they finish loading. And you?"

Janni grinned. "Me and my mates are a bit stuck. We'll get the chop for sure if the federals find us. Can you help us out?"

"How many of you?" asked Van Cleef.

"Five in all."

As a fellow mercenary, Van Cleef did not hesitate. "Get aboard. But hurry up. As soon as that Connie is off, so are we."

Dupree nodded his thanks and jogtrotted back to the Land-Rover. "It's okay," he reported, "but we have to get aboard."

"Right. Dump the hardware in the back." The leader turned to the black officer at the wheel. "We have to go now, Patrick. Take the Land-Rover and dump it. Bury the guns and mark the spot. Then you go for the bush. Don't go on fighting. Understand?"

The young lieutenant nodded somberly.

"I'm afraid it's over now, Patrick," the mercenary said gently.

"Perhaps," the lieutenant said, nodding toward the Constellation, where the general and his group were saying good-by. "But while he lives we will not forget. He's only leaving for safety. He's still the leader. We will say nothing, but we will remember."

As he swung the Land-Rover into a turn, the white mercenaries called their good-bys and headed for the DC-4.

The leader was about to follow them when two nuns fluttered out of the bush. "Major."

The mercenary turned and recognized one as the head nurse of a hospital he had helped evacuate a few months earlier.

"Sister Mary Joseph! What are you doing here?"

She began talking earnestly, clutching his sleeve.

He nodded. "I'll try. I can do no more than that."

He walked across and spoke to the South African pilot, then came back to the nuns. "He says yes, but you must hurry, Sister."

"God bless you," said Sister Mary Joseph, and gave hurried orders to her companion, who ran to the rear of the aircraft and climbed the steps to the passenger door. Sister Mary Joseph scurried back to the palm forest. A file of men soon emerged, each carrying a bundle in his arms, which he handed up to the young nun in the DC-4. The copilot watched her lay the first three side by side in the aircraft's hull, then gruffly began to help.

"God bless you," the young nun whispered.

One of the bundles deposited liquid excrement onto the copilot's sleeve. "Bloody hell," he muttered, and went on working.

Left alone, the mercenary leader approached the Constellation, where the general was mounting the steps. "Major Shannon come," someone called.

The general turned. Even at this hour he managed a grin. "So, Shannon, do you want to come along?"

Shannon brought up a salute. The general acknowledged it. "No thanks, sir. We have transport. I wanted to say good-by."

"Yes. It's over, I'm afraid. For some years, at any rate. I find it hard to believe my people will live in servitude forever. By the way, have you been paid up to the contract?"

"Yes, thank you, sir. We're all up to date."

"Well, good-by then. And thank you for all you were able to do." The African held out his hand and Shannon gripped it.

"We've been talking things over, sir, the boys and I," said Shannon. "If . . . if you should ever need us, we'll all come."

"This night is full of surprises," the general said slowly. "Half my senior advisers, and all the wealthy ones, are crossing the lines to ingratiate themselves with the enemy. Thank you for your offer, Mr. Shannon. What do you mercenaries do now?"

"We'll have to look around for more work."

"Another fight, Major Shannon?"

"Another fight, sir."

The general laughed softly. " 'Cry "Havoc!" and let slip the dogs of war,' " he murmured.

"Sir?"

"Just a bit of Shakespeare, Mr. Shannon. Well, now, I must go. The pilot is waiting. Good-by again, and good luck."

Shannon stepped back and gave a last salute. "Good luck to you," he called; then, half to himself, "You'll need it."

When Shannon climbed into the DC-4, Van Cleef had his engines turning. As soon as the Connie had vanished into the clouds, he eased the DC-4 forward. For an hour after takeoff Van Cleef kept the cabin dark, jinking from cloud bank to cloud bank to avoid being caught out in the moonlight by a roving MIG. Only when he was far out over the gulf did he allow the lights on.

Behind him they lit up a weird spectacle. The floor of the aircraft was carpeted with sodden blankets. Their previous contents lay writhing in rows down both sides of the cargo space—forty small children, shrunken, wizened, deformed by malnutrition, the nuns moving among them. The mercenaries glanced at their fellow passengers. They had seen it all before. In the Congo, Yemen, Katanga, the Sudan. Always the same story, always the starved kids. And always nothing you could do about it.

The cabin lights allowed them to see each other clearly for the first time since sundown. Their uniforms were stained with sweat and red earth, and their faces were drawn with fatigue.

The leader lay against the side of the plane. Carlo Alfred Thomas Shannon, thirty-three, blond hair cropped to a ragged crew cut. "Cat" Shannon came from county Tyrone in Ulster, but he'd been sent to a public school in England and no longer carried the distinctive accent of Northern Ireland. He had been in the Royal Marines before he had signed on as a mercenary in Mike Hoare's Fifth Commando at Stanleyville. He had seen Hoare depart, had then joined Robert Denard. Two years later he had been in the Stanleyville mutiny, had been with "Black Jack" Schramme on the long march to Bukavu. After repatriation by the Red Cross he had promptly volunteered for another African war, the one just over, in which he had had his own battalion. But too late to win.

As the DC-4 droned on he brooded over the past year and a half. Thinking of the future was harder, for he had no idea where the next job would come from.

To his left sat what was arguably the best mortarman north of the Zambezi. Jan Dupree, aged twenty-eight, came from Paarl in Cape Province, South Africa. His hatchet face, dominated by a curved beak of a nose, looked even more haggard than usual.

Beside Jan sprawled Marc Vlaminck, "Tiny Marc," so called because of his vast bulk. A Fleming from Ostend, he stood six feet three in his socks, when he wore any, and weighed two hundred and fifty. He was regarded with trepidation by the Ostend police. They said you could tell a bar where Tiny Marc had become playful by the number of artisans it took to put it together again. Marc was extremely useful with a bazooka, which he handled with the easy nonchalance of a boy with a peashooter.

Across the way sat Jean-Baptiste Langarotti, the Corsican—short, lean, olive-skinned. At eighteen he had been called up by France to fight in the Algerian war. By the time he was twenty-two he was fighting on the other side, and after the failure of the 1961 putsch he went underground for three years. He was caught finally, and spent four years in French prisons. He was a bad prisoner, and two guards would carry the marks to prove it until they died. He emerged in 1968 with only one fear in the world, the fear of small enclosed spaces.

He had flown to Africa, talked himself into another war, and joined Shannon's battalion. He had also taken to practicing steadily with the knife he had learned to use as a boy. On his left wrist he wore a broad leather razor strop held in place by two studs. In idle moments he would take it off, turn it over, wrap it around his fist. All the way to Libreville the six-inch blade moved backward and forward across the strop.

Alongside Langarotti was the oldest man in the party, a German. Kurt Semmler was forty, and it was he who had designed the skull-and-crossbones motif that Shannon's unit wore. It was also Semmler who had cleared a five-mile sector of federal soldiers by marking out the front line with stakes, each bearing the head of one of the previous day's enemy casualties. For a month after that, his was the quietest sector of the campaign.

A Hitler Youth graduate, Kurt had run away and joined the French Foreign Legion at seventeen. Eight years later he became a top sergeant in the elite 1er Régiment Étranger de Parachutiste, serving in Indochina and Algeria with one of the few men he had ever revered, the legendary Commandant le Bras. After Algerian independence he joined a former comrade in a smuggling operation in the Mediterranean. Semmler had become an expert navigator and made a fortune, then lost it when his partner double-crossed him. So he booked passage to the new African war he had read about in the papers, and Shannon had taken him on.

It was still two hours before dawn when the DC-4 began to circle the airport. Above the mewling of the children another sound could be made out, the sound of a man whistling. It was Shannon. His colleagues knew he always whistled when going into action or coming out of it. And always a tune called "Spanish Harlem."

As the DC-4 rolled to a halt at the end of a runway, two French officers drove up in a jeep and beckoned Van Cleef to follow them, then signaled him to stop the plane near a cluster of huts on the far side of the airport. Within seconds a kepi, an officer's peaked cap, poked inside, the nose beneath the visor wrinkling in distaste at the smell. The French officer indicated that the mercenaries were to come with him. As soon as they were down the ladder, the DC-4 moved on to the main buildings, where Red Cross nurses and doctors were waiting for the children.

The five mercenaries waited an hour, perched on uncomfortable chairs, in one of the huts. When finally the door opened it was to admit a tanned, hard-faced senior officer in a tropical fawn uniform and a kepi with gold braid ringing the peak. Shannon took in the keen, darting eyes, the rows of campaign ribbons, and the sight of Semmler leaping to ramrod attention. He needed no more to tell him that the visitor was the great le Bras himself, who commanded the Garde Républicaine of the Gabon Republic.

Le Bras shook hands with each, smiled and chatted briefly with Semmler, then addressed them all. "I will have you quartered comfortably. No doubt you will appreciate a bath and some food. Also some civilian clothes. But you will have to remain in your quarters until we can fly you to Paris. There are a lot of newspapermen in town, and any contact with them must be avoided."

An hour later the men were comfortably settled on the top floor of the Gamba Hotel. And there they spent four weeks while press interest in them died down. Then one evening a captain on the staff of Commandant le Bras came to see them.

"Messieurs, I have news for you. You are flying out tonight. To Paris. On the Air Afrique flight at twenty-three thirty hours."

The five men, bored to distraction by this time, cheered.

Just before ten the following morning they emerged into the February cold of Le Bourget. They said their good-bys. Dupree was off to Cape Town, Semmler to Munich, Vlaminck back to Ostend, and Langarotti to Marseilles.

They agreed to stay in touch, and looked to Shannon. He was

their leader. It was up to him to find work, another contract, another war. "I'll stay in Paris for a while," he said. "There's more chance of a job here than in London."

So they exchanged addresses, either general delivery or cafés where the barman would take a message, and went their ways.

When Shannon came out of the terminal building, he heard a voice calling his name. The tone was not friendly. He turned, and his eyes narrowed as he saw who it was. "Roux," he said.

"So, Shannon, you're back," snarled the Frenchman.

"Yes. I'm back."

"A word of advice," snapped Roux. "Do not stay here. This is my city. If there is any contract to be found here, I will conclude it. And select those who share in it."

For answer Shannon walked to the nearest taxi and humped his bag into the back. Roux walked after him, his face mottling with anger. "Listen to me, Shannon. I'm warning you—"

The Irishman turned to face him. "No, you listen to me, Roux. I'll stay in Paris just as long as I want. I was never impressed by you in the Congo, and I'm not now. So get stuffed."

CHAPTER TWO

ON THAT mid-February afternoon Sir James Manson, chairman and director of Manson Consolidated Mining Company Limited, sat back in a leather chair in his lush tenth-floor office and stared at the report on his desk. It was signed by Dr. Gordon Chalmers, the head of ManCon's Department of Research. It was the analyst's report on the rock samples Jack Mulrooney had brought back from the African republic of Zangaro three weeks earlier.

Dr. Chalmers did not waste words. Mulrooney had found a mountain some eighteen hundred feet high and close to a thousand yards across the base. It was called the Crystal Mountain and was set slightly apart from a range of mountains of the same name. He had returned with a ton and a half of gray country rock shot through with quartz stringers, and shingle from the beds of the streams surrounding the hill. The stringers, half-inch-wide veins of quartz, contained small quantities of tin. But it was the country rock that was interesting. Repeated and varied tests showed that both rock and gravel samples contained remarkable quantities of platinum. It was present in all the samples and was fairly evenly distributed. The richest platinum-bearing rock known in the world was in the Rustenberg mines in South Africa, where concentrations, or grades, ran at about .25, or a quarter of a troy ounce, per rock ton. The average concentration in the Mulrooney samples was .81.

Sir James knew that platinum stood at a market price of $130 a troy ounce. He was also aware that, with the growing world hunger for the stuff, it had to rise to $150 an ounce, even to $200. He did some calculations: the mountain contained probably 250 million cubic yards of rock. At two tons per cubic yard it would weigh 500 million tons. At even half an ounce per rock ton, that was 250 million ounces. If the revelation of a new world source dragged the price down to $90 an ounce, and even if the inaccessibility of the place meant a cost of $50 an ounce to get it out and refined, that still meant . . .

Sir James Manson leaned back and whistled softly.

"Good God. A ten-billion-dollar mountain."

THE price of platinum is controlled by two factors: its indispensability in certain industrial processes and its rarity. Total world production, apart from what is secretly stockpiled, is over 1.5 million troy ounces per year. Most of that comes from three sources: South Africa, Canada, and Russia. Russia is the uncooperative member of the group. The producers of platinum would like to keep the world price fairly steady so they can plan long-term investments in new mines and equipment, in the confidence that the bottom will not drop out of the market should a large quantity of the metal suddenly be released. The Russians, by stockpiling unknown quantities which they can release at any time, keep tremors running through the market.

Although James Manson was not into platinum when the Chalmers report hit his desk, he knew its world position. He also knew why American corporations were buying into South African platinum. It was because, by the mid-1970s, America would need much more than Canada could supply. With little likelihood that any nonprecious-metal device for exhaust control would be marketed before 1980, there was a strong probability that every American car would soon require enough pure platinum to add up to perhaps 1.5 million ounces every year—or double current world production. The Americans would not know where to get it. James Manson thought he had an idea where. They could always buy it from him. And with world demand far outstripping supply, the price would be nice, very nice indeed.

There was only one problem. He had to be absolutely certain that he, and no one else, would control all mining rights to this Crystal Mountain. The question was, how?

The normal way would be to show the president of the republic the survey report and propose a deal whereby ManCon secured the mining rights, the government a profit-participation clause that would fill its coffers, and the president a fat regular payment into his Swiss account.

But if advised of what lay inside the Crystal Mountain, there were three parties who, above all others, would want to take control, either to begin production or stop it forever. The South Africans, the Canadians, most of all the Russians. For the advent on the world market of a massive new supply source would cut the Soviet slice of the market back to the level of the unnecessary.

Manson had heard the name of Zangaro, but he knew nothing about it. He must learn more. He pressed a button on his intercom.

"Miss Cooke, would you come in, please?"

Miss Cooke, tailored, efficient, and severe, did so.

"Miss Cooke, it has come to my attention that we have recently made a small survey in Africa—in Zangaro."

"Yes, Sir James. That's right."

"Oh, you know about it. Good. Then please find out for me who secured that government's permission for us to conduct it."

"Mr. Bryant did, Sir James. Richard Bryant, of Overseas Contracts." Miss Cooke never forgot a thing she had heard.

"He submitted a report, I suppose?" asked Sir James.

"He must have, under normal company procedure."

"Send it in to me, would you, Miss Cooke?"

Richard Bryant's report, dated six months earlier, recorded that he had flown to Clarence, the capital of Zangaro, where he had an interview with the Minister of Natural Resources. After a good deal of haggling over the minister's personal fee, an agreement had been reached that a single representative of ManCon might conduct a survey for minerals in the Crystal Mountains.

That was all. The only indication of the character of the place was in the reference to a "personal fee" for a corrupt minister.

Manson finished reading and pressed the intercom again. "Tell Mr. Bryant to come up and see me, would you, Miss Cooke?"

He pressed another button. "Martin, come up here, please."

It took Martin Thorpe two minutes to run up from his office on the floor below. He did not look like a financial whiz kid, protégé of one of the most ruthless go-getters in a traditionally ruthless industry. He looked more like the captain of the rugby team of one of the best schools—charming, boyish, clean-cut. Thorpe had not gone to a good school, and he knew nothing and cared less about batting averages; but he could retain in his head throughout the day the hourly movement of share prices across the range of ManCon's subsidiary companies. At twenty-nine he had ambitions and the intent to carry them out. His loyalty to Manson depended on his exceptionally high salary and the knowledge that he was well placed for spotting what he called "the big one."

By the time he entered, Sir James had slipped the Chalmers report into a drawer and only Bryant's lay on his blotter. "Martin, I've got a job I need done in a hurry and with discretion. It may take half the night." He did not ask whether Thorpe had an engagement.

"Okay, Sir James. I've nothing on that a phone call can't kill."

"Good. Look, I've just come across this report. Six months ago Bryant, from Overseas Contracts, was sent out to a place called Zangaro. He secured a go-ahead for us to survey for possible mineral deposits in a range called the Crystal Mountains. Now, what I want to know is, was this survey ever mentioned to the board of directors? You'll have to look at the minutes. And in case it got a passing mention under 'any other business,' check through the documents of all board meetings over the past twelve months. I want to know who authorized Bryant's trip and who sent out the survey engineer, a man called Mulrooney. I also want to know what Personnel has on Mulrooney. Got it?"

"Yes, Sir James. But Miss Cooke could do that in half—"

"Yes, she could. But I want you to do it. If you look at boardroom documents or a personnel file, it will be assumed it has something to do with finance. Therefore it will remain discreet."

The light began to dawn on Martin Thorpe. "You mean . . . they found something down there, Sir James?"

"Never mind," Manson said gruffly. "Just do it."

Martin Thorpe grinned as he left. Cunning bastard, he thought.

"Mr. Bryant is here, Sir James," Miss Cooke announced.

From the center of the office Sir James walked toward his employee with a smile. "Ah, come in, Bryant. Sit down." He gestured to an easy chair. Bryant, wondering what it was all about and relieved at the boss's tone, sank into the suede cushions.

"Take a drink, Bryant? Sun's well down, I think."

"Thank you, sir. Er—Scotch, please."

"Good man. My own favorite poison. I'll join you."

Bryant recalled an office party at which Sir James had spent the evening on Scotch. It pays to watch things like that, Bryant reflected, as his chief opened the bar cabinet and poured two glasses of his special Glenlivet.

"Water? Dash of soda, Bryant?"

"Is that a single malt, Sir James? Straight as it comes, please." They raised their glasses, then savored the whisky.

"I was just going through a sheaf of old reports," Manson said, "and came across one of yours. The one you filed about—what's it called—Zangaro?"

"Oh, yes, sir. Zangaro. That was six months ago."

"And you had a bit of a rough time with the minister fellow."

Bryant smiled at the memory. "But I got the survey permission."

"Damn right you did!" Sir James smiled. "I used to do that in the old days. I envy you young chaps going off to clinch deals in the old way. Tell me about it. Rough place, Zangaro?"

His head tilted back into the shadows, and Bryant was too comfortable to notice his concentration. "Too right, Sir James. It's a shambles, moving steadily backward since independence five years ago." He recalled something else he had heard his chief say. "Most of these new republics have thrown up power groups whose performance wouldn't entitle them to run a town dump."

Sir James, as capable as the next man of recognizing a playback of his own words, smiled again. "So who runs the show out there?"

"The president. Dictator, rather. A man called Jean Kimba. He won the first and only election, some said by using terrorism and voodoo on the voters. Most of them didn't know what a vote was. Now they don't need to know."

"Tough guy, is he, this Kimba?" asked Sir James.

"Not so tough, sir, as downright mad. A raving megalomaniac. Surrounded by political yes-men. If they fall out with him, they go into the old colonial police cells. Rumor has it that Kimba supervises the torture himself. No one has ever come out alive."

"Hm, what a world we live in, Bryant. And they've got the same vote in the UN General Assembly as Britain or America. Whose advice does Kimba listen to in government?"

"No one of his own people. He claims he is guided by divine voices. The people think he has a powerful juju. He holds them in abject terror."

"What about the foreign embassies?"

"Well, sir, except for the Russians, they are as terrified of this maniac as his own people are. The Russians have an enormous embassy. Zangaro sells most of its produce to Russian trawlers, and most of what it makes from the sales goes into Kimba's pocket. The trawlers, of course, are electronic spy ships or supply ships for submarines."

"So the Russians are strong there. Another whisky, Bryant?"

"They are, Sir James," Bryant replied, accepting another Glenlivet. "Kimba consults them when dealing with outside concerns.

A trader in the hotel told me the Russian ambassador or a counselor was at the palace almost every day."

Manson had learned what he needed to know. When Bryant had finished his drink, he ushered him out as smoothly as he had welcomed him. At five twenty he called Miss Cooke in. "We employ an engineer named Jack Mulrooney," he said. "I'd like to see him at ten tomorrow morning. And I'd like Dr. Gordon Chalmers here at twelve. Leave me time to take him out for a spot of lunch. Book a table at Wilton's. That's all, thank you. Have the car round front in ten minutes."

When Miss Cooke withdrew, Manson pressed another button and murmured, "Come up for a minute, would you, Simon?"

Simon Endean came from an impeccable background. He was polished and clever, but he had the morals of a thug. He needed a Manson to serve. His ambitions were more modest than Thorpe's, but not by much. For now, the shadow of Manson would suffice. It paid for the six-room pad, the Corvette, the girls.

"Sir James?"

"Simon, tomorrow I'm having lunch with a fellow called Gordon Chalmers. The head of the laboratory out at Watford. I want a rundown on him. The personnel file, of course, but anything else you can find. What his homelife is like, any failings—above all, if he has any pressing need of money over and above his salary. Phone me here not later than eleven forty-five."

Sir James Manson never faced any man, friend or foe, without a personal rundown. He had beaten more than one opponent into submission by being better prepared. Endean nodded and left.

As his Rolls-Royce slid away from ManCon House, Sir James leaned back and lit his first cigar of the evening. The chauffeur handed him a late *Evening Standard*, and they were abreast of Charing Cross Station when a paragraph caught his eye. As he stared at it a germ of an idea began to form in his mind. Another man would have dismissed it, but not Manson. He was a twentieth-century pirate and proud of it. The paragraph referred to an African republic. Not Zangaro, but as obscure. The headline said: NEW COUP D'ETAT IN AFRICAN STATE.

CHAPTER THREE

MARTIN Thorpe was waiting in his chief's outer office when Manson arrived at five past nine.

"What have you got?" demanded Sir James while he was hanging up his topcoat. Thorpe flicked open a notebook and began.

"One year ago we had a survey team in the republic lying to the north of Zangaro. It was accompanied by an aerial reconnaissance unit we hired from a French firm. One day, when there was a following wind stronger than forecast, the pilot flew several times up and down the entire strip to be covered by the aerial survey. No one knew until the film was developed that on each downwind leg he had overshot by forty miles into Zangaro."

"Who first realized it? The French company?" asked Manson.

"No, sir. The French simply developed the film. Then a bright spark on our own team had a close look at the pictures and noticed a hilly area which had a variation in the density and type of its plant life. The sort of thing you can't see on the ground but which an aerial photo will show up."

"I know how it's done," growled Sir James. "Go on."

"The spark passed the films to Photo-Geology, and a blowup confirmed that there the plant life was different over an area involving a hill about eighteen hundred feet high. He identified the range as the Crystal Mountains and the hill as probably the original Crystal Mountain. He sent his file to Overseas Contracts. It was Willoughby, head of OC, who sent Bryant down there."

"He didn't tell me," said Manson, now seated behind his desk.

"He sent a memo, Sir James. You were in Canada at the time. As soon as Bryant got Zangaro's permission, Ground Survey agreed to detach a prospector, Jack Mulrooney, from Ghana and send him in to look the place over. He got back three weeks ago with samples, which are now at the Watford laboratory."

"Now," said Sir James, "did the board hear about all this?"

"No, sir." Thorpe was adamant. "I've checked every meeting for twelve months. It never reached board level."

Manson's satisfaction was evident. "How bright is Mulrooney?"
For answer Thorpe tendered a file from Personnel.

Manson flicked through it. "He's experienced, anyway," he
grunted. "An old Africa hand. Such people can be perceptive."

He dismissed Martin Thorpe and muttered to himself, "Now
we'll see how perceptive Mr. Mulrooney can be."

When the prospector was ushered in Manson greeted him
warmly. Miss Cooke was asked to produce coffee. Mulrooney's
coffee habit was on file.

Jack Mulrooney looked out of place in the penthouse suite of a
London office building. He did not seem to know where to put his
hands. It was the first time he had ever met the man he called the
gaffer. Sir James used all his efforts to put him at ease.

"That's just the point, man," Miss Cooke heard her employer
say when she came in with the coffee. "You've got twenty-five
years' hard-won experience getting the damn stuff out of the
ground." Jack Mulrooney was beaming.

When Miss Cooke had gone Sir James gestured at the porcelain
cups. "Look at these poofy things. Used to drink out of a good mug.
Now they give me thimbles. I remember back on the Rand . . ."

Mulrooney stayed for an hour. When he left he felt the gaffer
was a damn good man despite all they said. Sir James Manson
thought Mulrooney was damn good, too—at chipping bits of rock
off hills and asking no questions.

"Stake my life on it, there's tin down there, Sir James," Mulrooney had said. "Only thing, can it be got out economically?"

Sir James had slapped him on the shoulder. "Don't you worry
about that. We'll know as soon as the report comes through from
Watford. Now how about you? What's your next adventure?"

"I don't know, sir. I have three more days' leave yet—"

"You like the wild places, I hear," said Sir James expansively.

"Yes, I do. You can be your own man out there."

"You can indeed." Manson smiled. "I almost envy you. No, dam-
mit, I *do* envy you. We'll see what we can do."

What Manson did was to instruct Accounts to send Mulrooney a
thousand-pound bonus. Then he rang Ground Survey. "What

surveys have you got pending?" There was one in a remote part of Kenya, a year's job. "Send Mulrooney," said Sir James.

He glanced at the clock. It was eleven. He picked up the report on Dr. Chalmers that Endean had left for him. Graduate with honors from the London School of Mining. Degree in geology and, later, chemistry. Doctorate in his mid-twenties. Head of ManCon's Department of Research at Watford for the last four years.

At eleven thirty-five the private phone rang. It was Endean. He spoke for two minutes from Watford station. Manson grunted approval. "Useful," he said. "Now get back to London. I want a complete rundown on the Republic of Zangaro." He spelled it out. "History, geography, economy, crops, mineralogy, politics, state of development. Three things are crucially important. First, I want to know about Russian or Chinese involvement, or local Communist influence on the president. Second, no one remotely connected with the place is to know any questions are being asked, so don't go there yourself. Third, under no circumstances are you to announce that you come from ManCon. So use a different name. Got it? Report back within twenty days."

Manson then called Thorpe. Within minutes Thorpe was there with the paper the chief wanted. It was a copy of a letter.

DR. GORDON Chalmers stepped out of his taxi and paid it off. As he walked the last few yards toward ManCon House, his eye caught an *Evening Standard* poster on the news kiosk. THALIDOMIDE PARENTS URGE SETTLEMENT. He bought the paper. The story recorded that after another marathon of talks, between representatives of the parents of the four hundred-odd children in Britain who had been born deformed because of the drug thalidomide and the company that had marketed it, a further impasse had been reached. Talks would resume at a later date.

Gordon Chalmers' thoughts went back to the house he had left that morning; to Peggy, his wife, just turned thirty and looking forty; and to Margaret, legless, one-armed Margaret, nine years old, in need of a pair of legs—and a specially built house, the mortgage on which was costing him a fortune. After nearly ten years of watching unmoneyed parents try to face down a giant corporation, Gordon Chalmers harbored bitter thoughts about bigtime capitalists. Ten minutes later he was facing one of the biggest.

Manson came right to the point. "I suppose you can guess what I want to see you about, Dr. Chalmers."

"I can guess, Sir James. The report on the Crystal Mountain."

"That's it. Incidentally, you were quite right to send it to me personally in a sealed envelope. Quite right."

Chalmers shrugged. It was routine, as soon as he had realized what the samples contained.

"Let me ask you two things, and I need specific answers," said Sir James. "Are you absolutely certain of these results?"

"Absolutely. For one thing, there are a variety of tests to establish the presence of platinum, and these samples passed them all. For another, I not only did every known test on every one of the samples, I did the whole thing twice. The summary of my report is accurate beyond dispute."

Sir James nodded in admiration. "How many other people in your lab know the results of your analysis?"

"No one," said Chalmers with finality. "When the samples came in they were crated as usual and placed in store. Mulrooney's report predicated the presence of tin. As it was a minor survey I put an assistant onto it. He assumed tin or nothing and did the appropriate tests. When they failed to show up positive I had him do some more tests. These, too, were negative. The laboratory closed for the night, but I stayed on late, doing further tests. By midnight I knew the shingle sample contained platinum.

"The next day I put the assistant onto another job. I went on by myself. There were six hundred bags of shingle and fifteen hundred pounds of rocks from all over the mountain. Deposits are present in all parts of the formation."

Sir James stared at the scientist with well-feigned awe. "It's incredible. I know you scientists like to remain detached, but I think even you must have been excited. This could create a whole new world source of platinum. You know how often that happens with a rare metal? Once in a lifetime."

Chalmers had been excited by his discovery, but he merely shrugged. "Well, it'll certainly be profitable for ManCon."

"Not necessarily," said Manson. This shook Chalmers.

"No?" queried the analyst. "But surely it's a fortune?"

"A fortune in the ground, yes," replied Sir James. "But it depends upon who gets it. You see . . . Let me put you in the picture, my dear doctor. . . ." He put him in the picture for thirty minutes. "So there you are. The chances are it will be handed on a plate to the Russians if we announce it."

"I can't change the facts, Sir James," Dr. Chalmers said.

Manson's eyebrows shot up in horror. "Good gracious, Doctor! Of course you can't." He glanced at his watch. "Close to one," he exclaimed. "Let's go and have a spot of lunch."

Two bottles of Côtes du Rhône with lunch encouraged Chalmers to talk about his work, his family, his views.

It was when he touched on his family that Sir James, looking suitably sorrowful, recalled a recent TV interview with Chalmers. "Do forgive me," he said. "I hadn't realized before—I mean, about your little girl. What a tragedy."

Slowly Chalmers began to tell his superior about Margaret. "You wouldn't understand," he said at one point.

"I can try," replied Sir James quietly. "I have a daughter myself, you know. Of course, she's older." He drew a folded piece of paper from his inside pocket. "I don't know how to put this," he said with some embarrassment, "but—well, I am aware how much time and trouble you put in for the company. So I issued this instruction to my bank this morning."

He passed Chalmers the copy of a letter instructing the manager of Coutts bank to remit by registered mail, each month on the first day, fifteen banknotes, each to the value of £10, to Dr. Gordon Chalmers at his home address.

"Thank you," Chalmers said softly, seeing concern tinged with embarrassment on his employer's face.

Sir James's hand rested on his forearm. "Now come on, that's enough of this matter. Have a brandy."

In the taxi Manson suggested he drop Chalmers off at the station. "I have to go back to the office and get on with this Zangaro business and your report," he said.

"What *are* you going to do about it?" Chalmers asked.

"Don't know, really. Pity to see all that going into foreign hands, which is what must happen when your report gets to Zangaro. But I've got to send them something."

There was a long pause as the taxi swung into the station.

"Is there anything I can do?" asked the scientist.

"Yes," said Sir James in measured tones. "Junk the Mulrooney samples. Destroy your notes. Make an exact copy of the report with one difference—let it show the tests prove there exist marginal quantities of low-grade tin which could not be economically mined. Burn your original. And never mention a word of it.

"You have my solemn word," murmured Sir James Manson as the taxi stopped, "that when the political situation changes, Man-Con will put in a tender for the mining concession in accordance with normal procedures."

Chalmers got out of the taxi and looked back at his employer. "I'm not sure I can do that, sir. I'll have to think it over."

Manson nodded. "Of course you will. I know it's asking a lot. Look, why don't you discuss it with your wife?"

Sir James dined at his club with an official of the Foreign Office that Friday evening. Adrian Goole had been the FO's liaison with the West Africa Committee, of which Manson was a key member, during the Nigerian civil war. The committee's advice to the FO had been that the federal side could win quickly, given British support, and that a quick victory was essential for British business in Nigeria. Instead the war lasted thirty disrupting months, and ManCon, like Shell-BP and others, had taken tremendous losses.

Manson despised Adrian Goole, whom he reckoned for a pedantic fool. That was why he had invited him to dinner. That, and the fact that the man was in FO economic intelligence.

Across the table now, Goole was earnestly intent as Manson told him some of the truth about the Crystal Mountain. He stuck to a tale of tin. It would have been viable to mine this tin, of course, but quite frankly he'd been scared off by the dependence of Zangaro's president on Russian advisers. It might be dangerous to increase Kimba's power through wealth. Who knew what problems he'd then make for the West?

Goole took it all in. "You're right. A real dilemma. You have to send Zangaro the analysis. If they show it to the Russians, the trade counselor is bound to realize the tin deposits are viable."

"The question is, what do I do about it?" grunted Manson.

Goole thought it over. "What would happen if you halved the figures showing the quantity of tin per rock ton in the report?"

"Well, it would be shown to be economically unviable."

"And the rock samples could have come from another area? If your man had taken his samples a mile from where he actually operated, the tin content *could* be down by fifty percent?"

"It probably would be. But he operated where he did."

"Under supervision?" asked Goole.

"No. Alone."

"And there are no real traces of where he worked?"

"Just a few rock chippings. Besides, no one goes up there." Manson paused. "You know, Goole, you're a damnably clever fellow. Steward, another brandy, if you please."

They parted with mutual jocularity on the steps of the club. "One last thing," said the FO man. "Not a word to anyone else about this. I'll have to file it, well classified, at the department, but otherwise it remains between you and us at the FO."

"Of course," said Manson.

"I'm very grateful you saw fit to tell me all this. I'll keep a quiet eye on Zangaro, and if there should be any change in the political scene, you'll be the first to know."

Sir James signaled to his chauffeur. "The first to know," he mimicked as he sat back in his Rolls-Royce on the way to Gloucestershire. "Too bloody right I will, boy. I'm going to start it."

AN HOUR later Gordon Chalmers lay beside his wife, tired and angry. "I can't do it," he said. "I can't falsify a mining report to help the likes of Manson make more money."

"What does it *matter?*" Peggy Chalmers pleaded. "Whether he gets the concession, or the Russians. Whether the price rises or falls. What does it matter? We need that money, Gordon. Please, darling, please do what he wants."

"All right," Gordon Chalmers said at length. "Yes, I'll do it."

She pillowed her head on his chest. "Thank you, darling. Please don't worry. You'll forget it in a month. You'll see."

Ten minutes later she was asleep, exhausted by the nightly struggle to get Margaret bathed and into bed, and by the unaccustomed quarrel with her husband. Gordon Chalmers continued to stare into the darkness.

"They always win," he said softly. "The bastards always win."

The following day, Saturday, he wrote out a new report for the Republic of Zangaro. Then he burned his notes and trundled the core samples to the scrap heap.

On Monday the report was received by Sir James Manson and sent down to Overseas Contracts. Bryant was told to leave the next day, to deliver it to the Minister of Natural Resources in Clarence, the capital of Zangaro. A letter from the company would be attached, expressing the appropriate regret.

On Tuesday, Jack Mulrooney also flew to Africa, happy to leave London. Ahead lay Kenya, the bush, the chance of a lion.

Only two men had in their heads the knowledge of what really lay inside the Crystal Mountain. One had given his word to remain silent forever, and the other was plotting his next move.

CHAPTER FOUR

Simon Endean entered Sir James Manson's office with a bulky file on Zangaro. "No one learned who you were or what you were doing?" Manson asked as he lit a cigar.

"No, Sir James. I used a pseudonym. No one questioned me. I claimed I was doing a graduate thesis on postcolonial Africa."

"Good. I'll read the report later. Give me the main facts."

Endean spread out a large-scale map of a section of the West African coast. "As you see, Zangaro's bordered on the north and east by this republic and on the southern border by this one. The western side is the sea. It's shaped like a matchbox, the short edge seventy miles of coastline, the longer sides stretching a hundred miles inland. The capital, the port of Clarence, is here, on the seaward end of this stubby peninsula, midway down the coast.

"Behind the capital lies a coastal plain, which is the only cultivated area in the country. Behind that, running north and south, is the Zangaro River, which cuts the country in two, with the plain on one side and the mountains on the other."

Manson stared intently at the map. "What about roads?"

Endean warmed to his explanation. "There is one road here, which runs along the spine of the peninsula for six miles inland, going straight east. Then there is the junction—here—with the other main road. You turn left there to go to the northern border. To the south it becomes a dirt road and just peters out."

"Surely there must be a road to the mountains?"

"Too small to be marked. There's a right turn off the northbound road that takes you to a rickety wooden bridge over the river."

"Is that the only way to get from one half of the country to the other?" Manson asked in wonderment.

"The only way for wheeled traffic. The natives go by canoe."

"Who *are* the natives? What tribes live there?"

"There are two," said Endean. "East of the river is the country of the Vindu. They are practically in the Stone Age, and most of them stay in the bush. The plain, including the peninsula, is Caja country. The Caja hate the Vindu and vice versa. The Caja were in favor with the colonial power, but they're a shiftless bunch. President Kimba is Vindu, and he won the election by organizing tough squads of his tribe, who saw to it that he got the vote."

"Population?"

"Almost uncountable, but officially thirty thousand Caja and a hundred and ninety thousand Vindu."

"What about the economy?"

"Disaster," replied Endean. "Bankrupt. Worthless paper money. Exports down to nothing, and nobody letting them have any imports. There's one hospital, run by the UN, and there have been gifts of medical supplies, insecticides, and so on, from the UN, the Russians, and the colonial power, but as the government always just sells the stuff elsewhere and pockets the cash, even these three have given up."

"A real banana republic, eh?" murmured Sir James.

"In every sense. Corrupt, vicious government. People diseased and undernourished. There are resources—like timber and fish— and under the colonial power there were coffee and cacao, cotton and bananas. It was enough, with a guaranteed buyer, to make some hard currency and pay for necessary imports. Now nobody works. They grow enough to subsist on. That's it."

"They can't always have been so idle. Who worked the plantations in colonial days?"

"Ah, the colonial power brought in some black workers from elsewhere. They settled, and live there still. With their families they must be about fifty thousand. But they were never enfranchised by the colonial power, so they never voted in that single election at independence. If there is any work done, they still do it."

"Where do they live?"

"About fifteen thousand still live in huts on the estates, even though there's hardly any work, with all the machinery broken down. But most live in shantytowns scattered down the road back of the capital. They grub a living as best they can."

"How many Europeans are still there?"

"About forty diplomats and a handful of UN technicians. Kimba's fanatically antiwhite. There was a ruckus in Clarence about six weeks ago, and one UN man was beaten half to death."

"Has the country any friends, diplomatically speaking?"

Endean shook his head. "Even the Organization of African Unity is embarrassed by the place. No one wants to invest anything, not because there isn't any potential, but because nothing is safe from confiscation by anyone wearing a Kimba party badge—their methods of intimidation are mind-boggling! The Russians have the biggest mission and probably a bit of say over foreign policy, about which the president knows nothing except what he's told by a couple of Moscow-trained Zangaran advisers."

"And who precisely has produced this paradise on earth?"

Sir James Manson found himself looking at a photograph of a middle-aged African in a silk top hat and black frock coat. It was evidently the inauguration, for several colonial officials stood in the background. The face beneath the shining black silk was long and gaunt. But the eyes held the attention. There was a glazed fixity about them, such as one sees in the eyes of fanatics.

"Africa's 'Papa Doc,'" said Endean. "Mad as a hatter. Liberator from the white man's yoke, communicant with spirits, swindler, police chief, torturer: His Excellency, President Jean Kimba."

Sir James Manson stared at the face of the man who, all unknowing, was sitting on ten billion dollars' worth of platinum. He wondered if the world would really notice his passing on.

THE next morning Endean found his presence again desired on the tenth floor. "One thing I need to know more about, Simon," Sir James said without preamble. "You spoke of a ruckus in Clarence. What was it all about?"

"The president is known to have a psychotic fear of assassination. Sometimes he invents the rumor of an attempt on his life if he wants to arrest and execute somebody. In this case it was the commander of the army, Colonel Bobi. I was told that the quarrel was about Kimba's not getting a big enough rake-off from a deal Bobi put through. A shipment of drugs and medicines had arrived for the UN hospital. The army stole half, and Bobi sold it on the black market. But when the head of the UN hospital protested to Kimba and quoted the true value of the missing stuff, Kimba found out that it was a lot more than Bobi had split with him. So he went mad and sent his private thugs after Bobi. They missed Bobi, but they got their hands on the unfortunate UN man."

"What happened to Bobi?" asked Manson.

"He had already fled over the border."

"What's he like?"

"A human gorilla. No brains, but a certain animal cunning."

"But Western-trained? Not Communist?" insisted Manson.

"No, sir. Not a Communist. Not anything politically."

"Bribable? Cooperate for money?"

"Certainly. He must be living pretty humbly outside Zangaro."

"Find him for me, wherever he is."

Endean nodded. "Am I to visit him?"

"Not yet," said Manson. "What I want now is a complete breakdown of the military security situation in the capital and around the president's palace. How many troops, where they are quartered, how experienced they are, what fight they would put up if under attack, what weapons they carry—in fact, the lot."

Endean stared at his chief in amazement. If under attack? What on earth was the old man up to? "I couldn't furnish that information myself, Sir James. It requires a sound judgment of military matters. And of African troops."

Manson stood at the window, staring out over the City, the financial heart of London. "I know," he said softly. "It would need a soldier to produce that report."

"Well, Sir James, you would hardly get an army man to go and do that sort of mission. Not for any money."

"There is a kind of military man who would," said Manson. "A mercenary. I'm prepared to pay well. Go and find me a mercenary with initiative and brains. The best in Europe."

Cat Shannon lay on his bed in the small hotel in Montmartre. He was bored. In the weeks that had passed since his return from Africa, he had spent most of his money traveling around Europe trying to set up another job.

There was little being offered. Rumors abounded that the CIA was hiring mercenaries for training anticommunist Meos in Cambodia, and that some Persian Gulf sheikhs were getting fed up with their British military advisers and were looking for mercenaries to fight for them or take charge of palace security. Shannon wouldn't trust the CIA as far as he could spit. The Arabs were not much better. And since there appeared to be no good wars, that left the chance of working as a bodyguard for a European arms dealer, and he had had one approach from such a man in Paris.

Without actually turning it down, the Cat was not keen on the proposition. The dealer was in trouble because he had double-crossed the Provisional IRA, having tipped off the British as to where some arms he had sold them would be landed. There was sure to be a gunfight, and the French police would take a dim view of having their streets littered with bleeding Fenians. Moreover, as Shannon was an Ulster Protestant, they would never believe he had just been doing his job.

He lay staring at the ceiling, thinking of the wild sweep of turf and stunted trees that sprawls across the border of Tyrone and Donegal. He still thought of it as home, though he had hardly been there since he was sent away to school at eight. Eleven years ago, when he was twenty-two and still a sergeant in the Royal Marines, his parents had died in a car crash. He had gone home for the funeral; then he had closed up the house.

As a civilian his first job had been in a London merchant house with African interests. He had learned the intricacies of company structure, trading and banking, setting up holding companies, and the value of a discrete Swiss account. After a year in London he had been posted as assistant manager of the Uganda branch office, from which he had walked out without a word and driven into the Congo. For six years now he had lived as a mercenary, at best regarded as a soldier for hire, at worst a paid killer. The trouble was, once he was known as a mercenary there was no going back. Not that he couldn't get a job. The problem was being able to stick it. To sit in an office, to go back to the ledgers and the commuter train, then to look out the window and recall the bush country, the waving palms, the rivers, the smell of sweat and cordite, the copper-tasting fear just before an attack, and the wild, cruel joy of being alive afterward—that was what was impossible. He knew he would eat his heart out if it ever came to that.

So he lay on his bed and smoked and wondered where the next job was coming from.

SIMON Endean was aware that in London it was possible to find out anything known to man, including the name and address of a first-class mercenary. The only problem was where to start looking.

After a reflective hour drinking coffee in his office, he took a taxi to Fleet Street. Through a friend on one of London's biggest newspapers he got access to virtually every press clipping about mercenaries for the past ten years. He read them all and paid special attention to the by-lines. At this stage he was not looking for the name of a mercenary. There were too many pseudonyms, *noms de guerre,* and nicknames. He was looking for a reporter who knew what he was talking about. At the end of two hours he had found one. A phone call to his newspaper friend eventually produced the writer's address. It was a small flat in North London.

Simon Endean pressed the bell next to the writer's name just after eight the following morning, and a minute later a voice answered "Yes?" from the metal grille set in the woodwork.

"Good morning," said Endean into the grille. "My name is Harris. Walter Harris. I wonder if I might have a word with you?"

Upstairs, he came straight to the point. "I represent a business consortium with interests in a state in West Africa."

The writer nodded warily and sipped at a mug of coffee.

"We have reports of the possibility of a coup d'etat in this republic which could well be communist-backed. You follow me?"

"Yes. Go on."

"For the coup to succeed, it would be necessary for the plotters first to assassinate the president. Therefore the question of palace security is vital. The Foreign Office says it is out of the question to send a professional British officer to check on such matters."

"So?" The writer finished his coffee and lit a cigarette.

"So the president would consider accepting the services of a professional soldier, on contract, to advise on all matters regarding

173

the safety of his person. What he is seeking is a man who could make a thorough survey of the palace and plug any loopholes."

The reporter had strong doubts about the truth of Harris' story. If palace security were really what was sought, the British government would not be against providing the expert to advise on improving it. Furthermore, there was a firm at 22 Sloane Street, London, called Watchguard International, whose speciality was precisely that. He pointed this out to his visitor.

"Evidently," Endean said, "I must be a little more candid."

"It would help," said the writer.

"The point is, you see, that the government might agree to send an expert merely to advise, but if further training of the palace guards were needed, a Britisher sent by the government could not do that. As for Watchguard, if one of their men were on the staff of the palace guard and despite his presence a coup were tried, you know what the rest of Africa would think about that. To them, Watchguard is the FO."

"So what do you want from me?" asked the writer.

"The name of a good mercenary soldier," said Endean. "One with brains and initiative who'll do a good job for his money."

"I write for my living," said the reporter.

Endean gently withdrew £200 in ten-pound notes from his pocket and laid them on the table. "Then write for me," he said. "Names and track records. Or talk if you like."

"I'll write." The reporter consulted a set of files, and typed for twenty minutes. Then he handed Endean three sheets of paper. "These are the best around today, the older generation of the Congo six years ago, and some up-and-comers from Nigeria."

Endean took the sheets and studied them intently.

ROBERT DENARD: Frenchman. Police background. Was in Katanga secession 1961–62. Left after failure of secession and exile of Tshombe. Commanded French mercenary operation in Yemen. Returned Congo 1964. Headed the 6th Commando. Took part in second Stanleyville revolt (the mercenaries' mutiny) 1967. Wounded badly. Living in Paris.

JACQUES SCHRAMME: Belgian. Nicknamed "Black Jacques." Formed own unit of Katangese in 1961. Prominent in secession attempt. Launched 1967 Stanleyville mutiny in which Denard and his unit joined. Took joint command after wounding of Denard and led march to Bukavu.

MIKE HOARE: British-turned-South African. Adviser in Katanga secession. Close friend of Tshombe. Formed English-speaking 5th Commando unit 1964. Retired December 1965.

CHARLES ROUX: French. Fought under Hoare in 1964. Quarreled with Hoare, joined Denard. Took part in first Stanleyville revolt in 1966, in which his unit was nearly wiped out. Smuggled out of Congo. Returned to join Schramme 1967. Wounded at Bukavu. Not in action since, but lives in Paris and claims leadership over all French mercenaries.

CARLO SHANNON: British. Served under Hoare in 5th. With Schramme at Bukavu throughout siege. Repatriated April 1968. Commanded own unit throughout Nigerian civil war. Believed staying in Paris.

There were others—Belgian, German, South African, French—some, like Shannon and Roux, the "up-and-comers" from Nigeria.

When he had finished reading, Endean looked up. "These men would all be available for such a job?" he asked.

The writer shook his head. "I doubt it. I included all those who could. Whether they would is another matter."

"Tell me," Endean said. "Which man would you choose?"

"Cat Shannon," the writer said without hesitation. "He can think unconventionally and has a lot of audacity. I'd pick the Cat."

"Where is he?" asked Endean.

The writer mentioned a hotel and a bar in Paris he could try.

"And if this Shannon's not available, who's your second?"

The writer thought for a while. "The only other one who'd almost certainly be available and has the experience would be Roux."

CAT Shannon walked pensively up a side street toward his hotel, which was near the summit of Montmartre. It was just after five o'clock on a mid-March evening, with a cold wind blowing. The weather matched Shannon's mood. He was thinking about Dr.

Dunois, who had just given him a thorough checkup. A former paratrooper and army doctor, Dunois had gone on expeditions to the Himalayas and Andes as team medico and later had volunteered for several tough missions in Africa. He had become known as the mercenaries' doctor. If they had a medical problem, they usually went to his Paris office.

Shannon turned into his hotel and crossed to the desk for his key. The old man who was on duty said, "Ah, monsieur, one has been calling you from London. He left this message." In the old man's scrawl the message said simply, "Careful Harris," and was signed by an English writer Shannon knew.

The old man gestured toward the small room across the lobby. "There is another, monsieur. He is waiting in the salon."

The visitor rose as Shannon approached. "Mr. Shannon?"

"Yes."

"My name is Harris, Walter Harris. I've been waiting to see you. Can we talk here?"

"We can. The old man won't hear us. Sit down."

"I understand you are a mercenary, Mr. Shannon."

"Yes."

"You have been recommended to me. I represent a group of London businessmen. We need a job done. It requires a man who has some knowledge of military matters and who can travel to a foreign country without exciting any suspicion. One who can analyze a military situation and then keep his mouth shut."

"I don't kill on contract," said Shannon briefly.

"We don't want you to," said the man called Harris.

"All right, what's the mission? And what's the fee?"

"First, you would have to come to London for briefing." Endean drew a wad of notes from his pocket. "We'll pay you a hundred and twenty pounds for air fare and overnight stay," he said. "If you decline the proposition, you get another hundred for your trouble in coming. If you accept, we discuss it further."

Shannon nodded. "All right. When?"

"Tomorrow. Arrive anytime during the day and stay at the Post House Hotel on Haverstock Hill. At nine the day after tomorrow

I'll phone and make a rendezvous for later that morning. Clear?"

Shannon picked up the money. "Book the hotel room in the name of Keith Brown," he said.

Endean left the hotel and headed downhill, looking for a taxi. He had not seen any reason to mention to Shannon that he had talked earlier with another mercenary, a man by the name of Charles Roux. Nor that he had decided, despite the Frenchman's evident eagerness, that Roux was not the man for the job.

TWENTY-FOUR hours later Shannon was in his room at the Post House Hotel. He had come in on the first plane, using his false Keith Brown passport, which he had acquired long ago.

On arrival in London he had phoned the writer and been given a rundown on the Harris visit. He had then gone to see an agency of private investigators and paid a deposit of £20, promising to phone them the next morning with instructions.

Harris rang on the dot of nine the following morning. "There's a block of flats on Sloane Avenue called Chelsea Cloisters. I have booked flat three seventeen. Please be in the lobby at eleven sharp."

Shannon noted the address and rang the detective agency. "I want a man in the lobby of Chelsea Cloisters on Sloane Avenue at ten fifteen. He'd better have his own transport."

"He'll have a motorbike," said the head of the agency.

The agency's man, when Shannon met him at the designated spot, turned out to be a youth in his late teens, with long hair. Shannon surveyed him suspiciously. "Do you know your job?" he asked. The boy nodded. He seemed full of enthusiasm, and Shannon only hoped it was matched by a bit of skill.

Shannon gave him a newspaper he'd brought along. "Sit over there and read this," he said. "At about eleven a man will come in, and we'll go into the lift together. He should come out about an hour later. By then you must be across the road, astride your bike, pretending to be busy with a breakdown. Got it?"

"Yes. I've got it."

"The man will take either his own car or a taxi. Follow him."

The youth grinned and sat down, hidden behind the newspaper.

Forty minutes later the man called Harris walked in. Shannon noticed that he dismissed a taxi and hoped the youth had noticed it, too. He strolled to the lift and Shannon joined him.

In flat 317 Harris opened his briefcase and took out a map, which he handed to Shannon. In three minutes Shannon had taken in all the map could tell him. Then came the briefing, a judicious mixture of fact and fiction. The men he represented, Harris claimed, did business with Zangaro. All had suffered as a result of President Kimba. He went on to describe, truthfully, conditions in the republic. The punch line came at the end.

"A group of army officers got in touch with some local businessmen. The officers are considering toppling Kimba in a coup, and one of the businessmen put their problem to us. It is that the officers are virtually untrained in military terms, despite their status, and do not know how to topple the man, because he spends so much time hiding in the palace, surrounded by his guards. Frankly, we would not be sorry to see this Kimba fall. Nor would his people. We want a complete report on Kimba's military strength."

If the officers on the spot couldn't assess that, they were incompetent to carry out a coup, Shannon thought in disbelief. But he said only, "I'd have to go in as a tourist, and there can't be many of those. Could I go as a company visitor to one of your friends' business houses?"

"Not possible," said Harris. "If anything went wrong, there'd be hell to pay. But you'll do it, will you?"

"If the money's right, yes."

"Very well. Tomorrow morning a round-trip plane ticket from London to the capital of the neighboring republic will be at your hotel," said Harris. "You have to stop in Paris to get a visa, then fly down by Air Afrique and take the connecting plane service to Clarence. With your tickets will be five hundred pounds in French francs for expenses, plus five hundred for yourself."

"A thousand for me," said Shannon.

"Dollars? I understand you people deal in U.S. dollars."

"Pounds," said Shannon. "That's twenty-five hundred dollars, or two months at flat salary if I were on a normal contract."

"But you'll only be away ten days," protested Harris.

"Ten days of high risk. If the place is half what you say it is, anyone caught on this job will be very dead, very painfully."

"Okay. Five hundred down, five hundred when you return."

Ten minutes later Endean was gone.

At three that afternoon Shannon rang the detective agency.

"Ah, yes, Mr. Brown," said the voice on the phone. "My man followed him to the City, where he entered ManCon House. Headquarters of Manson Consolidated Mining."

"Do you know if he works there?" asked Shannon.

"It would seem he does," said the agency chief. "My man noticed that the doorman touched his cap to the subject and held the door for him. He did not do that for a stream of secretaries and junior executives who were emerging for lunch."

The youth had done a good job, Shannon conceded. He gave several further instructions and that afternoon mailed £50 more to the agency. The next morning he opened a bank account and deposited £500 in it. Then he flew to Paris.

As SHANNON was taking off for West Africa, Dr. Gordon Chalmers was dining with an old college friend, now also a scientist. Fifteen years earlier, when they had both been working hard on their degrees, they had joined thousands of other concerned young people marching for the Campaign for Nuclear Disarmament. In their indignation over the state of the world, they had dabbled with the Young Communist movement. Chalmers had grown out of it, married, merged into the salaried middle class.

The combination of worries that had come his way over the previous two weeks caused him to take more than his usual single glass of wine with dinner. It was over the brandy that he felt he had to confide his worries to someone, someone who, unlike his wife, was a fellow scientist and would understand. Of course it was highly confidential. The friend was solicitous, and when he heard about the crippled daughter his eyes clouded over with sympathy.

"Don't worry about it, Gordon. Anyone would have done the same thing." Chalmers felt better, his problem somehow shared.

Though he had asked his friend how he had fared over the years, the man had been slightly evasive. Chalmers had not pressed him. Even had he done so, it was unlikely the friend would have told him he was now a committed member of the Communist Party.

CHAPTER FIVE

THE Convair 440 coming into Zangaro from the neighboring republic banked steeply over Clarence. Shannon looked down and saw the capital of Zangaro occupying the end of the peninsula, surrounded on three sides by the palm-fringed waters of the gulf. The spit of land was three miles wide at its base and a mile wide where the town was situated near the tip. The coastline was composed of mangrove swamps. At the end of the peninsula was a small port with two long, curving, sandy spits running out into the sea. Outside the arms of the bay, Shannon could see the water ruffled by the breeze, while inside, the water was a flat calm.

On the ground the heat was overpowering. About a dozen soldiers with rifles lounged about the small airport building, and Shannon kept half an eye on them as he filled in an immensely long form. It was at customs that the trouble started. A civilian instructed him curtly to go into a side room. As he did so, four soldiers swaggered in after him. Then he remembered something. Long ago in the Congo, just before the worst of the massacres of that war, he had noticed this same menacing mindlessness, the sense of power without reason, that can suddenly turn to frenetic violence.

The civilian customs officer dumped the contents of Shannon's bag on the rickety table. He picked up the electronic shaver, tried the switch, and, being fully charged, it buzzed furiously. Without a trace of expression he put it in his desk and gestured to Shannon to empty his pockets onto the table. He grunted at the traveler's checks and handed them back. The coins he pocketed. There were two French-African 5000-franc notes and several 100s. He scooped up the 5000s. One of the soldiers grabbed the rest.

The customs man lifted his shirt and tapped the butt of a Browning 9-mm. short, jammed into his trouser band. "Police," he said.

Shannon itched to smash him in the face. Instead he gestured to what remained of his belongings on the table. The man nodded, and Shannon began to repack. Behind him he felt the soldiers back off. It seemed an age before the customs officer motioned toward the door and Shannon left. Sweat was running down his spine.

Outside in the small square there was no transportation. Shannon heard a soft Irish-American voice behind him. "Can I give you a lift into town, my son?"

The invitation came from a Catholic priest who was there to meet the only other white on the plane, an American girl.

As they all drove off in a Volkswagen Beetle, the priest glanced across at Shannon with understanding. "They shook you down."

"The lot," said Shannon. The losses were not important, but both men had recognized the mood of the soldiery.

"One has to be very careful here. Have you a hotel?"

When Shannon told him he had not, the priest drove him to the Independence. "Gomez is the manager. He's a good enough sort."

Usually, when a new face arrives in an African city, there are invitations from other Europeans to come for drinks, but the priest made no such gesture. The mood of Zangaro, Shannon learned, affected the whites as well. He would learn more of this from Jules Gomez, beginning that same evening in the hotel bar.

Gomez had bought the hotel five years before independence. After independence he had been brusquely informed that it was to be nationalized and he would be paid in local currency. He never was—it was worthless paper, in any case—but he hung on as manager, hoping that one day things might improve.

After the bar closed, Shannon asked Gomez to join him for a drink in his room. The soldiers had left him a bottle of whisky he had had in his bag, and when Gomez had sunk half of it, Shannon probed gently for information. Gomez confirmed, lowering his voice in fear, that President Kimba was in residence in his palace and that he rarely left it except for an occasional trip, under massive guard, to his home village in Vindu country.

By the time Gomez weaved his way back to his own room, further nuggets of information had been culled. The three units known as the civilian police force, the gendarmerie, and the customs force, although all carried side arms, had, Gomez swore, no ammunition in their weapons. Being Caja, they were not trusted to have any. The side arms were just for show. The power in the city was exclusively in the hands of Kimba's Vindu. The dreaded secret police wore civilian clothes and carried automatics. The soldiers of the army had bolt-action rifles such as Shannon had seen at the airport. The president's own guards had submachine guns. The latter, ultra-loyal to Kimba, lived in the palace grounds.

The next morning Shannon went out to explore. Within seconds he found a small boy scampering by his side. Only later did he learn why. It was a service Gomez supplied to all his guests. If the tourist were arrested and carted off, the boy would speed back with the news. Gomez would then slip the information to the Swiss or West German embassy so someone could begin to negotiate the tourist's release before he was beaten half dead.

From Gomez, Shannon had obtained a small map. Heading first for the outskirts of Clarence, he walked mile after mile, always with the boy at his heels. Back in town, he found the bank, the post office, half a dozen ministries, the port, and the UN hospital, each guarded by half a dozen shabby, lounging soldiers carrying old Mauser 7.92 bolt-action rifles. He figured there were about a hundred soldiers and estimated their fighting capacity at nil. In a fire-fight they would almost certainly quit and run. The most interesting thing he observed was the state of their ammunition pouches. Flat, empty of magazines. Each Mauser had its fixed magazine, of course, but Mausers hold only five shells.

That afternoon Shannon patrolled the port. The two spits of sand which formed the natural harbor were about twenty feet high where they left the shoreline and six feet above the water at the tip. From the tip of one spit the palace was hidden behind a warehouse, but from the other the top story of the palace was plainly visible. To the south of the warehouse was a beach where fishing canoes lay. A good place for a landing, Shannon thought.

Behind the warehouse numerous footpaths and one road ran back toward the palace. Shannon took the road. As he breasted the

top of the rise, the full façade of what once must have been a colonial governor's mansion came into view two hundred yards away
across a flat space. He continued another hundred yards and
reached a lateral road which ran along the seashore. At the junction
four soldiers waited, smarter, better dressed than the others, armed
with Kalashnikov AK 47 assault rifles. They watched him as he
turned toward his hotel. The palace guards. Evidently no closer
access to the palace was allowed than the junction.

As he walked he noted details of the palace. Thirty yards wide,
its ground-floor windows bricked up, the main building was dominated at ground level by an archway with a tall, wide, bolt-studded
timber door. On the floor above there were seven windows, on
the top floor ten, much smaller, below the tiled roof.

Before the sun went down he had made a complete tour of the
palace from afar. He saw that a new wall, eight feet high, topped
with broken bottles, ran from each side of the mansion inland for
eighty yards, another wall joining them together at the rear to form
a courtyard. Interestingly, there was no entrance other than the
front one to the entire compound.

Shannon grinned at the uncomprehending boy. "You know, kid,
that fool thinks he has protected himself with a big wall and only
one entrance. All he's done is pin himself inside a big brick trap."

That night Gomez invited Shannon to his room. Shannon stuck
to his cover as a tourist, so he collected his information in dribs
and drabs. He learned that Kimba kept both the national treasury
and the national armory under his own lock and key. The national
radio station was also in the palace. Apart from the hundred soldiers
scattered around the capital, there were another hundred outside
the town. This was half the army. The other half were in the barracks, rows of low tin shanties four hundred yards from the palace.
These, and the sixty-odd palace guards, constituted Kimba's entire
defense force. There were no artillery, no armored cars.

It was on his third evening that Shannon met his soldier. He had
managed a close look at the back and sides of the palace. Trying
at the front, he had been intercepted by two of the palace guards,
who had brusquely ordered him on his way. He had established

that there was always a group of them sitting at the road junction, where he had seen them the day before. He had also established that they could not see the harbor from where they stood.

On the road back to the Independence he passed several bars. Just beyond them the soldier stopped him. Evidently drunk, he swayed up to Shannon, gripping his Mauser and grunting what Shannon assumed to be a demand for money. Before Shannon could reach for his money the man snarled and jabbed the gun at him. From then on it was quick and silent. A stab of pain went up Shannon's arm and shoulder as he heard the neck crack. The Zangaran went down like a sack, his gun falling to the ground.

Shannon looked up and down the road, but no one was coming. He rolled the body into a ditch and examined the rifle. He pumped the cartridges out of the magazine; at three they stopped coming. And there had been none in the breech. He removed the bolt and held the gun to the moon, looking down the barrel. Several months of dirt and rust met his eye. He replaced the cartridges, tossed the rifle onto the corpse, and walked home.

"Better and better," he murmured as he slipped into bed. He doubted there would be a police inquiry. The broken neck would be put down to a drunken fall into the ditch.

Nevertheless, the next day he pleaded a headache, stayed in, and talked to Gomez. The following morning he took the Convair north again to the neighboring republic. As he watched the land disappear something Gomez had mentioned in passing ran like a current through his head. There were not, and never had been, any mining operations in Zangaro.

Forty hours later he was back in London.

AMBASSADOR Leonid Dobrovolsky always felt slightly uneasy when he had his weekly interview with President Kimba. Like others who had met the dictator, he had few doubts of the man's insanity. Unlike others, he had orders from Moscow to do his utmost to establish a working relationship with the unpredictable African. Behind his mahogany desk President Kimba seemed to be holding himself immobile. Dobrovolsky knew the interview would begin in one of two ways. Either the man who ruled Zangaro would speak lucidly, or scream like someone possessed.

Kimba nodded slowly. "Please proceed," he said.

Dobrovolsky breathed a sigh of relief. But he had bad news to give. That could change things. "I am informed by my government, Mr. President, that they have received information that a mining survey report recently sent to Zangaro by a British company may not be accurate. I am referring to the survey carried out several weeks ago by a firm called Manson Consolidated, of London."

The ambassador went on to describe the report that had been delivered by a Mr. Bryant to the Minister of Natural Resources. "In essence, your Excellency, I am instructed to inform you that my government believes the report was not a true representation of what was found in the Crystal Mountain."

"In what way was this report inaccurate?" whispered Kimba.

"It would appear, your Excellency, that there was more in the mineral samples than the British were prepared to inform you."

The ambassador waited for the explosion. It did not come.

"They cheated me," whispered Kimba.

"Of course, your Excellency," cut in Dobrovolsky, "the only way of being sure is for another survey party to examine the area. I am instructed to ask your Excellency to grant permission for a team from the Institute of Mining of Sverdlovsk to come to Zangaro."

Kimba digested the proposal. Finally he nodded. "Granted."

Dobrovolsky bowed. By his side, Volkov, ostensibly Second Secretary at the embassy, but also a member of the KGB, shot him a glance.

"The second matter that concerns us is your personal security," said Dobrovolsky.

At last the dictator reacted. His head jerked up, and he shot suspicious glances around the room. "My security?"

"To guarantee the continued security of the invaluable person of your Excellency and in view of the recent treason by one of your army officers, we would respectfully propose that a member of my embassy staff be permitted to reside in the palace and lend his assistance to your Excellency's own personal guard."

The reference to Bobi's "treason" brought Kimba out of his trance. He began to talk fast, his voice rising as he glared at the Russians. He spoke Vindu, but the Russians understood the gist: the ever-present danger of treachery, the warnings he had received from the spirits about plots, his complete awareness of the identity of all those who were not loyal.

When they emerged into the sunlight both men were sweating.

"I'll install my man tomorrow," muttered Volkov.

"And I'll get the mining engineers sent in," said Dobrovolsky. "Let's hope there really is something fishy about that British report. If there isn't, I don't know how I'll explain that to the president."

Volkov grunted. "Rather you than me," he said.

SHANNON checked into the Lowndes Hotel, as agreed upon with Harris before he left London. After ten days Harris was to phone that hotel and ask for Mr. Keith Brown each morning at nine. Shannon arrived at noon, so he had till the next day to himself.

After lunch he called the detective agency. He asked the head of it to read his findings over the phone. The man cleared his throat. "On the morning following the client's request, my operative waited close to the entrance of the underground parking lot of ManCon House. The operative got a clear view of the subject as he swung a Corvette into the lot. The vehicle is registered in the name of Simon Endean, of South Kensington. Endean is the personal aide and right-hand man of Sir James Manson, chairman and director of Manson Consolidated."

"Thank you," said Shannon, and put the phone down.

SIMON Endean had been busy while Shannon was away. He was imparting the results of his labors to Sir James that afternoon.

"I've found the man Bobi," he told his chief.

"Where is he?" Manson asked.

"In Dahomey," said Endean. "Place called Cotonou. In a rented villa. He lives quietly, probably because it is the safest way of ensuring the Dahomey government doesn't hand him back to Kimba."

"And Shannon, the mercenary?" asked Manson.

"Due any day. He hadn't arrived this morning at nine."

"Try him now," said Manson.

Endean found that Mr. Brown had indeed arrived but was out.

"Leave a message," Manson growled at Endean. "That you'll ring him tonight at seven. I want his report as soon as possible."

Shannon was in his room to take the call at seven. He spent the evening making up his notes, and in the morning he wrote his report. He began with a straight narrative of his visit and a detailed description of the capital, accompanied by diagrams. He then gave an equally detailed description of the military situation, including the fact that he had seen no signs of an air force or a navy. The one thing he did not mention was his stroll among the shanties of the thousands of immigrant workers, chattering to each other in their native tongues, brought with them from miles away.

He finished the report with a summary:

The problem of toppling Kimba has been simplified by the man himself. If he should lose control of the coastal plain, producing the bulk of the nation's resources, he must lose the country. His men could not hold this area in the face of the hatred of the entire Caja population. And he has no strength within the capital if he should lose the palace. In short, his policy of centralization has reduced the number of targets to one—his palace complex. The means of taking it have also been reduced to one, by virtue of the wall surrounding it and its single door. It has to be stormed.

The palace and grounds could be taken with little loss of life after being first pulverized with mortar fire. Against mortars the encircling wall, far from being a protection, becomes a death trap to those inside. The door could be taken apart by a bazooka rocket. I saw no signs of either of these weapons, or of any one single person capable of using them.

Conclusion: any faction within the republic seeking to take over must destroy Kimba and his guards inside the palace compound. To achieve this they would require expert assistance at a technical level they have not achieved, and such assistance would have to arrive, complete with all necessary equipment, from outside the country. With these conditions fulfilled Kimba could be toppled in a firefight lasting no longer than one hour.

"Is SHANNON AWARE THAT there is no faction inside Zangaro that wants to topple Kimba?" Sir James asked Endean the next day.

"I told him there was an army faction inside and that the businessmen I represented wanted a military assessment of their chances of success. But he's no fool. He'll have seen there's no one there capable of doing the job."

"I like the sound of this Shannon," said Manson. "He's obviously got nerve. Question is, could he do the whole job himself?"

"He did say, when I was questioning him, that the caliber of the Zangaran army was so low that any assisting force would have to do the whole job and hand over to the new men when it was done."

"Did he now? Did he?" mused Manson. "Then he already suspects the reason for his going down there was not the stated one."

Endean said, "May I put a question, Sir James? Why do you need a military report on how Kimba could be toppled and killed?"

Manson stared out of the window for some time. Finally he said, "Get Thorpe up here."

Manson knew why he had promoted Endean and Thorpe to positions beyond their years. It was because he recognized an unscrupulousness in each of them that matched his own. But could he trust them with this one, the big one? As Thorpe entered the office he decided how to guarantee their loyalty. "I want you two to think this over carefully," he said. "How far would you be prepared to go for five million pounds each, in a Swiss bank?"

Endean stared. "A very, very long way," he said softly.

Thorpe made no reply. He knew this was what he had joined Manson for. The big one, the grand slam. He nodded assent.

Manson talked steadily for the next hour. He ended with Chalmers' findings on the samples from the Crystal Mountain.

For Thorpe's benefit Manson read much of Endean's and Shannon's reports. He stressed the Russian influence, also the recent exiling of Bobi, who could be returned as a plausible alternative in the seat of power. "If it is to work at all, it must be a question of mounting two parallel, highly secret operations," Manson said finally. "In one, Shannon, stage-managed throughout by Simon, mounts a project to destroy the president's palace and make Bobi the new president. In the other, Martin would have to buy a shell company without revealing who had gained control or why."

Endean furrowed his brow. "Why the second operation?"

"Tell him, Martin," said Manson.

"A shell company, Simon, is a company, usually old and with few assets, whose shares are cheap—say a shilling each. Now, say this company is bought secretly through a Swiss bank, and it has a million shares, valued at one shilling each. Unknown to the other shareholders or to the Stock Exchange, Sir James, via the Swiss bank, owns six hundred thousand of these shares. Then President Bobi sells to that company—Company X—an exclusive ten-year mining franchise in Zangaro. A survey team from Company X goes out and discovers the Crystal Mountain. What happens to the shares of Company X when the news hits the stock market?"

"They go right up," said Endean.

"With a bit of help they go from a shilling to well over a hundred pounds a share. Six hundred thousand shares at a shilling each cost thirty thousand pounds to buy. Sell six hundred thousand shares at a hundred pounds each—the minimum you'd get—and you have a cool sixty million, in a Swiss bank. Right, Sir James?"

"That's right. And rather than selling the shares in small packets, a larger company might put in a bid for the whole block of six hundred thousand shares."

Thorpe nodded thoughtfully. "Whose bid would you accept?"

"My own," said Manson. "ManCon's bid would be the only acceptable one. That way the concession would remain firmly British, and ManCon would have gained a fine asset."

"Paying *yourself* sixty million quid?" queried Endean.

"No," said Thorpe quietly. "ManCon's shareholders would be paying Sir James sixty million quid, without knowing it."

Sir James Manson tendered them each a glass of whisky. "Are you on, gentlemen?" he asked.

Both young men nodded.

"Then here's to the Crystal Mountain." And they drank.

"Report to me here tomorrow morning at nine sharp," Manson told them, and they rose to go. At the door Thorpe turned.

"You know, Sir James, it's going to be bloody dangerous. If one word gets out . . ."

Sir James Manson stood with his back to the window.

"Knocking off a bank," he said, "is merely crude. Knocking off an entire republic has, I feel, a certain style."

CHAPTER SIX

"WHAT you are saying is that there is no faction within the army that has ever thought of toppling President Kimba?" Cat Shannon and Simon Endean were in Shannon's hotel room.

Endean nodded. "The information has changed in that one detail. What difference does that make? You said the technical assistants would have to do all the work themselves in any case."

"It makes a hell of a difference. Capturing the palace is one thing. Keeping it is another. Who's going to take over?"

"We have a man in view," Endean said cautiously. "He's in exile. In Dahomey."

"He would have to be installed in the palace and broadcasting that he has conducted a coup d'etat and taken over the country by noon of the day following the night attack."

"That could be arranged."

"One more thing. Troops loyal to the new regime must be visibly present by sunrise of that day. Otherwise we'd be stuck—a group of white mercenaries holed up inside the palace, unable to show ourselves for political reasons, and cut off from retreat in the event of a counterattack. Does your exile have such a backup force?"

"You have to let us take care of that," said Endean stiffly. "What we are asking you for is a plan of attack, right through to the death of Kimba. Fortunately Kimba has long since destroyed anyone with enough initiative or brains to become a rival. So there will be no one to lead a counterattack."

"Yeah. And the people believe he has a juju, a powerful protection, given him by the spirits, ensuring him against death. No one will support your new man unless Kimba is known to be dead. Once they see his corpse, the man who killed him becomes the leader, for he has the stronger juju. That means we have absolutely to guarantee Kimba's in the palace when we strike. There's one day he never misses. Independence Day."

"When is Independence Day?"

"Three and a half months away."

"Could a project be mounted in that time?" asked Endean.

"With luck, just. Do you want me to prepare a project from start to finish, with estimated costs and time schedule?"

"Yes. The cost is very important to my—er—associates."

"The report will cost you five hundred pounds," said Shannon.

"Five hundred is a bit steep," said Endean coldly.

"Rubbish. I'm an expert in war. I know where to get the best men, the best arms, how to ship them. That knowledge would cost you double five hundred pounds if you tried to research it yourself—which you couldn't anyway—you haven't the contacts."

Endean rose. "All right. The money will be here this afternoon. I'll come for your complete report tomorrow at three."

Not for the first time did Shannon thank his stars for the garrulous Gomez. Gomez had mentioned the affair of the exiled Bobi. He had also mentioned that, without Kimba, Bobi was nothing, being hated by the Caja and not able to command the Vindu. Which left Shannon with the problem of a backup force with black faces to take over on the morning after.

He spread out his maps and diagrams of Zangaro. The classical military approach would have been to land a force on the coast, march inland, and cover the junction of the road from Clarence. That would have sealed off the peninsula and the capital from reinforcement. It would also have lost the element of surprise.

Shannon understood Africa, and his thinking was unconventional. Therein lay his talent. He based his plan on three facts about war in Africa that he had learned the hard way. One was that, in darkness, the African soldier is sometimes reduced to near helplessness by his fear of the hidden enemy. The second was that the speed of recovery of the disoriented African is slower than a European soldier's—thereby exaggerating the normal effects of surprise. The third was that noisy firepower can bring African soldiers to panic and headlong flight, without consideration of the actual numbers of their opponents.

So Shannon based his plan on a night attack of total surprise in conditions of deafening noise.

As he worked he whistled a plaintive little tune. Anyone who knew him well would have recognized "Spanish Harlem."

MARTIN Thorpe was awake late that night. He knew he had a long weekend ahead, a weekend of poring over cards describing in detail 4500 of the public companies registered at Companies House in the City of London.

There are two agencies in London who provide information about British companies. These are Moodies and the Exchange Telegraph, known as Extel. ManCon took the Extel service, and Thorpe had their cards in his office. But for the business of finding a shell company, he decided to buy the Moodies service and have it sent to his home. For security reasons, he had a firm of lawyers order a complete set of these cards for him, keeping his name out of it. He also engaged a van to pick up the three filing cabinets containing the cards on Friday afternoon.

As he lay in bed in his elegant house in Hampstead, Thorpe, like Shannon, was planning a campaign, using shareholders and parcels of voting stock as Shannon used bazookas and mortars. Thorpe had never met the mercenary. But he would have understood him.

SHANNON handed his fourteen-page report to Endean at three on the Friday afternoon. He had been tempted to put "For Sir James Manson's Eyes Only" on the cover, but had resisted. Sniffing a good contract, he also continued to refer to Endean as Harris.

Partly from curiosity, partly from the feeling that one day he might need the information, Shannon had an urge to learn something about Sir James Manson—and why he had hired a mercenary to make war in Zangaro on his behalf. A copy of *Who's Who* gave the basic facts about the self-made tycoon. It mentioned a daughter, a girl who now would be about twenty. He phoned the detective agency that had traced Endean for him.

"I need information about a young lady to whom there have probably been references in gossip columns in the London press. I need to know—quickly—what she does and where she lives. She is Julie Manson, daughter of Sir James Manson."

By five o'clock Shannon had what he wanted and was phoning the writer who had recommended him to Mr. Harris.

"Hi," he said gruffly. "It's Cat Shannon."

"Cat!" came the surprised reply. "Where have you been?"

"Around," said Shannon. "I just wanted to say thanks for recommending me to that fellow Harris."

"Not at all. Did he offer you a job?"

Shannon was cautious. "Yeah, a few days' worth. It's over now. But I'm in funds. How about a spot of dinner?"

"Why not?" said the writer.

"Tell me," said Shannon, "are you still going out with that girl—a model, wasn't she?"

"Yeah. The same one. Why?"

"Look, I want to meet a girl who's also a model. Name of Julie Manson. Could you ask your girl if she knows her?"

"Sure. I'll call Carrie and ask her."

Shannon was lucky. The two girls were handled by the same agency. A dinner date, a foursome with Carrie and her boy friend, was fixed for the evening.

They ate at a small restaurant called the Baker and Oven, and the meal was the kind Shannon liked: enormous portions of English roast meats, washed down with Beaujolais. He liked the food, and he liked Julie. She was amusing and pretty, with dark brown hair that fell to her waist. She also seemed intrigued by him.

Carrie had let it slip that Shannon was a mercenary. But he managed to avoid the subject during dinner. When they left the restaurant the writer asked Shannon to take Julie home. "I think you're on," he whispered.

Outside her Mayfair flat Julie invited Shannon to come in for coffee. Only when they were seated, drinking the appalling brew she'd prepared, did Julie refer to the way he earned his living. "Have you killed people?"

"Yes."

"How many?"

"I don't know. I never counted."

She savored it. "I've never known a man who has killed."

"You don't know that," countered Shannon. "Anyone who has been in a war has probably killed people."

"Have you many scars?" It was another of the usual questions. Shannon nodded. "Some." He had a score of them.

"Show me," she said.

He grinned. "I'll show you mine, if you'll show me yours."

"I haven't got any," Julie said indignantly.

"Prove it," said Shannon shortly, and turned to place his empty coffee cup on a table behind the sofa. When he turned back he nearly choked. It had taken her less than a second to unzip her dress and let it slip to a pool of cloth around her ankles. Beneath it she wore only a thin gold waist chain.

"See," she said softly, "not a mark anywhere."

Shannon swallowed. "I thought you were supposed to be Daddy's sweet little girl," he said.

She giggled. "That's what they all think, especially Daddy," she said. "Now it's your turn."

At that moment Sir James Manson sat in the library of his Gloucestershire mansion, Shannon's file open on his knee and a brandy and soda at his elbow. He started to read.

Object of the Exercise. To storm and capture the president's palace at Clarence, capital of Zangaro, and to liquidate the president and his personal guards living inside. Also, to take possession of the weapons and armory of the republic, its national treasury and radio station—all inside the palace.

Method of Attack. There is no doubt the attack must be launched directly from the sea. A landing at the airport is not feasible. The necessary quantity of arms and men could not be transported by air without causing suspicions as to the nature of the flight. Similarly, a land attack offers no advantages. Men and arms would have to be smuggled into and through the neighboring republic, which has an efficient security system. The risk of premature discovery and arrest would be extremely high.

It is felt the only realistic plan must be for an attack by light boats, departing from a larger vessel moored out at sea.

Requirements for the Attack. The force should be not less than a dozen men, armed with mortars, bazookas, and grenades, and all carrying submachine guns for close-quarters use. The men should come off the sea between two and three in the morning, when all in Clarence are asleep, but sufficiently before dawn for no traces of white mercenaries to be visible by sunrise.

The report continued for six more pages to describe how Shannon proposed to engage personnel; what arms and ammunition he needed; what assault craft, uniforms, food, and supplies; how much all this would cost; and how he planned to storm the palace. On the question of the ship to carry the attacking force he said:

Apart from the arms the acquisition of the ship will prove the most difficult part. I would be against chartering, since this involves a crew and a captain who may turn out to be unreliable. I advocate buying a small freighter, crewed with men paid by and loyal to the patrons.

He stressed the need for tight security.

It is recommended that Mr. Harris remain the sole link between the patrons and me. Payments of the necessary money should be made to me by Mr. Harris, and my accounting of expenditure returned the same way. Similarly, although I would need four subordinate operatives, none would know the nature of the project until all were well out to sea. The equipment would be bought separately in different countries by different operatives. Only myself, Mr. Harris, and the patrons would know the whole plan.

Manson picked up the cost sheet. From Shannon's trip to Zangaro, for which he had already been paid, through to the final strike, the mercenary projected a total expenditure of £100,000. Then he turned to a sheet which bore the estimated timings.

Preparatory Stage: Recruitment of personnel.   20 days
Setting up bank account. Setting up of
foreign-based company to cover purchases.

Purchasing Stage: Purchase of all items.   40 days

Assembly Stage: Assembly of equipment and   20 days
personnel onto the vessel.

Shipment Stage: Transporting entire project   20 days
by sea to Clarence.

Strike day would be Zangaran Independence Day, which, if the project is set in motion by next Wednesday, would be Day 100.

Sir James Manson read the report twice, then locked it in his wall safe and went upstairs to bed.

CAT Shannon ran his hand idly over the girl's body that lay half across his own. It was a small but highly erotic body, as he had discovered during the previous hour. "Funny," he said reflectively, "here we are like this, and I don't know a thing about you."

She said, "Like what?"

"Like where's home, apart from this pad?"

"Gloucestershire," she mumbled.

"What does your old man do?" There was no answer. He took a handful of her hair and pulled her face around to him.

"Ow, you're hurting. He runs some company to do with mining. That's his specialty, and this is mine. Now watch—"

Shannon laughed. "Now wait. Tell me about your old man."

"Daddy? Oh, he's just a boring old businessman in the City."

SIR James Manson was enjoying his midmorning coffee on the terrace of his country mansion that Saturday when a call came from Adrian Goole that jerked him out of his weekend ease.

"That mining survey of yours, Sir James," the FO man began. "You remember—"

"Yes. The report went off. The figures were changed as you suggested. I've heard no more about it."

"Actually, we have," Goole said. "Nothing really disturbing, but odd all the same. I heard a rumor late yesterday that the Soviets have secured permission to send in a mining survey team of their own. Of course . . ."

Sir James Manson stared at the telephone as Goole's voice twittered on.

"I was only thinking, Sir James, that if they should go over the same area your man went over, their findings might be somewhat different. Fortunately it's only a question of minor quantities of tin. Still, I thought you ought to know. Hello? Are you there?"

With a massive effort Manson jerked himself out of his reverie. "Yes indeed. Sorry, my dear fellow. I was just thinking. Very good of you to call. I don't suppose they'll hit the same area. Damn useful to know, all the same."

He walked slowly back to the terrace, his mind racing. Coincidence? It could be. On the other hand, if they went straight to the Crystal Mountain, that would be no coincidence. That would be bloody sabotage. Could Chalmers have talked? The man he was convinced he had silenced with money? He ground his teeth. He had half a mind to let Endean take care of Dr. Chalmers. But that would change nothing.

He sat down and thought hard. He intended to go forward as planned, but there was now a new element, a time limit. He had, he figured, three months. If the Russians learned the content of the Crystal Mountain, a "technical aid" team would be there in a flash, half of them from the KGB. Shannon's shortest schedule had been a hundred days. They might not have a hundred days.

He returned to the telephone and called Simon Endean.

On Monday morning Endean called Shannon and set up a rendezvous for two p.m. at a flat in St. John's Wood. He had hired this flat for a month on the instructions of Sir James Manson. The reason: its telephone did not go through a switchboard.

Shannon arrived on time and found the man he called Harris already there. The telephone was hung in a desk microphone set that would allow a conference between the people in the room and the person on the other end of the line.

"The chief of the consortium has read your report," he told Shannon, "and wants to have a word with you." The phone rang. Endean threw the "speak" switch, and Shannon heard Manson's voice for the first time.

"I approve your judgment and conclusions, Mr. Shannon. If offered this contract, would you go through with it?"

"Yes, sir, I would," said Shannon.

"I notice in the budget you award yourself the sum of ten thousands pounds. What does this salary buy me?"

"It buys you my knowledge, my contacts with the world of arms dealers, smugglers, gunrunners, and mercenaries. It buys my silence in case anything goes wrong. It pays me for three months' damned hard work and the constant risk of arrest and imprisonment. Last, it buys the risk of my getting killed in the attack."

"Fair enough. Now as regards financing. The sum of one hundred thousand pounds will be transferred into a Swiss account which Mr. Harris will open this week. He will pay you the necessary money in slices, as and when you need it. When the money is spent he will either have to be present or to receive receipts."

"That will not always be possible, sir. There are no receipts in the arms business, least of all in the black market, and most of the men I shall be dealing with would not have Mr. Harris present. I would suggest the use of traveler's checks and credit transfers by banks. Further, I cannot have Mr. Harris follow me around, on grounds of my own security. I don't know Mr. Harris. You have taken your security precautions. I have to take mine. These are that I travel and work alone and unsupervised."

"You're a cautious man, Mr. Shannon."

"I have to be. I'm still alive."

There was a grim chuckle. "Fair enough, Mr. Shannon. You have the job. You have one hundred days to steal a republic. One hundred days."

PART TWO

The Hundred Days

CHAPTER SEVEN

FOR several minutes after Manson had rung off, Endean and Shannon stared at one another. Shannon recovered first. "Okay," he said. "I'll fly to Belgium tomorrow and open a bank account. I'll be back by evening and tell you which bank. And I'll need a transfer of credit of ten thousand pounds. Mainly for salaries."

"Where do I contact you?" asked Endean.

"That's my next point," said Shannon. "I'll need a base secure for telephone calls and letters. What about this flat?"

"It's hired for one month, cash in advance," said Endean.

"Then I'll take it over and take up the payments. Since I assume you won't want to give me your phone number, set up a post office address in London and check twice daily for telegrams. If I need you, I'll telegraph the phone number of where I am and a time to call. Understand?"

"Yes. I'll have the money by tomorrow. Anything else?"

"Only that I'll be using the name of Keith Brown throughout the operation. Anything signed Keith is from me. When ringing a hotel ask for me as Keith Brown. If ever I reply, 'This is Mr. Brown,' get off the line fast. It means trouble."

Endean left. Shannon booked a flight to Brussels for the following morning. Then he sent four identical telegrams—one to Paarl, Cape Province, South Africa; one to Ostend; one to Marseilles; one to Munich: URGENT. PHONE ME LONDON 507-0041 ANY MIDNIGHT OVER NEXT THREE DAYS. SHANNON. Finally he took a cab to the Lowndes and checked out. He left no forwarding address.

THOUGH IT WAS DARK early in London that evening, it was still light on a warm, sunny summer evening in Cape Province. Janni Dupree was on his way home after a day of swimming. He always liked to come back to Paarl after a contract, but inevitably it bored him quickly. He wished he were heading for another war.

MARC Vlaminck leaned on the bar and downed another foaming schooner of ale. Outside the front windows of the place his girl friend, Anna, managed for him, the streets of Ostend's red-light district were almost empty. It was still too early for summer tourists. He was bored already.

For the first month it had been good to be back, to take hot baths, to chat with his friends. But inactivity palled. He could hear *thump thump* from upstairs, where Anna was cleaning their flat. As he heaved himself off his barstool and lumbered up the back stairs the door opened and a telegram was tossed in.

IT WAS a clear spring evening and the water of the Old Port of Marseilles was like glass. In the caldron of seething humanity that called itself Le Panier, where only a policeman is illegal, Jean-Baptiste Langarotti sat at a corner table in a small bar. With a sigh he glanced at his watch and finished his drink. It was about time to drop in at the all-night post office to see if there were word of a contract from Shannon.

The Corsican was not as bored as the South African or the Belgian. Years in prison had taught Jean-Baptiste to survive long periods of inactivity. And he had had an offer of sorts. Charles Roux had contacted him from Paris, proposing that the Corsican sign on with him exclusively. But Langarotti had checked and found that Roux was mostly talk, for he had set up no projects of his own since his return from Bukavu in '67 with a hole in his arm.

IN MUNICH it was cold, and Kurt Semmler shivered in his leather coat as he headed for the post office. He made a regular check every evening. Like most army veterans, he disliked civilian life, despised politics, and longed again for some sort of routine combined with action. He had drunk too much, smoked too much, whored a bit, and become thoroughly disgruntled.

At the post office that evening there was nothing for him.

AT MIDNIGHT Marc Vlaminck phoned in from Ostend. Shannon told him to be at the Brussels airport with a car at ten a.m.

Belgium has, for those wishing to operate a secret but legal bank account, many advantages that outweigh those offered by the Swiss banking system. It permits unlimited quantities of money to pass in and out without government interference. Also, Belgian bankers are just as discreet as Swiss.

It was to the Kredietbank in Bruges that Shannon had himself driven by Tiny Marc. The big Belgian kept his curiosity to himself. On the road, Shannon mentioned briefly that he had a contract and could use four helpers. Was Vlaminck interested?

Vlaminck was. It was a job, Shannon said, that had not merely to be fought, but set up from scratch.

"I'm not knocking off banks," Marc said.

"Nor I. I need some guns put on board a boat. We have to do it ourselves. Then it's Africa and a nice little firefight."

Marc grinned. "A long campaign, or a quick in-and-out job?"

"An attack," said Shannon. "Mind you, if it works, there could be a long contract in the offing, though. And a fat success bonus."

"Okay, I'm on," said Marc as they drove into Bruges.

Inside the Kredietbank, Shannon introduced himself to the head of the foreign accounts section and proved his identity as Keith Brown by tendering his passport. Within forty minutes he had opened an account with £100 sterling, stated that £10,000 could be expected any day, and left instructions that of this sum £5000 was to be transferred at once to his bank in London. He left examples of his Keith Brown signature and agreed on a method of establishing his identity over the phone by reeling off the twelve numbers of his account in reverse order, followed by the previous day's date. This way oral instructions for transfers and withdrawals could be made without his coming to Bruges.

By half past twelve he was finished and joined Vlaminck outside.

They ate lunch, and then Marc drove him back to the Brussels airport. Before parting, Shannon gave him £50 in cash and told him to be at the London flat at six on the following evening.

Simon Endean had also had a busy day. He had caught the first flight to Zurich and landed at Kloten airport as Shannon was landing in Brussels. Within an hour he had opened an account at Zurich's Handelsbank. He informed the bank that the sum of £100,000 would be transferred into the account within the week. The bank was then to remit £10,000 to an account in Belgium, of which he would advise them by letter.

Endean was back in London just before six.

That same Tuesday afternoon Martin Thorpe was exhausted when he came into the office. He had spent three days going through 4500 Moodies cards, looking for a small company, preferably founded many years ago and now largely run-down, with a market capitalization of under £200,000. He had come up with two dozen companies that fitted the bill, but he needed more information. By midafternoon he was at London's Companies House.

He sent up to the archivists a list of his first eight companies and paid the fee for the right to examine the full company documents. As he waited for the folders he glanced at the Stock Exchange list and noted that none was quoted at over three shillings a share.

By the time Companies House closed for the evening, Thorpe's search was over. He would brief the boss on his chosen company in the morning. On paper the company looked great—so good, there had to be a flaw somewhere.

At eleven forty-five p.m. Shannon's phone rang. It was Semmler. Shannon told him he had work and that Semmler should be in London by six p.m. the next day. Expenses paid.

Ten minutes later Langarotti was on the line from Marseilles. He, too, agreed to be in London at six and would report to the flat.

Janni Dupree's call was the last. It came through at half past midnight. He would be at Shannon's flat on Thursday evening.

With the last call taken, Shannon read *Small Arms of the World* for an hour. Then he slept. It was the end of Day One.

SIR JAMES MANSON, first class on the Trident-3 to Zurich, ate a hearty breakfast that Wednesday morning. Shortly before noon he was ushered into the office of Dr. Martin Steinhofer at the Zwingli Bank. The bank had several times acted on Manson's behalf when he had needed a nominee to buy shares which, if purchased in his own name, would have trebled in value. Coffee and cigars were brought, and Sir James broached his business.

"I shall presently be seeking to acquire a controlling interest in a small British company, a public company. At the start it will involve relatively little money. Later I have reason to believe news will hit the Stock Exchange that will have an interesting effect on the value of that company's stock."

There was no need for him to explain to the Swiss banker the rules of the London Stock Exchange. Under British company law any person acquiring ten percent or more of the shares of a public company must identify himself to the directors. One way to get around this rule and gain secret control is to use nominee buyers. However, any reputable brokerage house will soon spot it if the real buyer of a big block of shares is in fact one man operating through nominees, and will obey the law.

But a Swiss bank, not bound by the laws of Britain, simply refuses to answer questions about who stands behind the names it presents as its clients. Nor will it reveal anything else, even if it suspects the front men do not exist at all. Both men in Dr. Steinhofer's office were aware of all the finer points involved as Sir James went on. "In order to make the necessary acquisition of shares," he said, "I have entered into association with six partners. They all agree to open small accounts with the Zwingli Bank and ask you to be so kind as to make the purchases on their behalf."

"That presents no problem," Dr. Steinhofer said carefully. "These gentlemen will be coming here to open their accounts?"

"They may find themselves too busy to come personally. I have appointed my financial assistant, Mr. Martin Thorpe, to stand in for me. The other six partners may wish to avail themselves of the same procedure. You have no objection to that?"

"Of course not," murmured Dr. Steinhofer.

"Here, then, is my power of attorney, signed by me, and duly notarized. You have my signature for comparison, of course. Mr. Thorpe will be in Zurich within ten days to finalize arrangements."

Dr. Steinhofer nodded. "I see no problem, Sir James."

Manson stubbed out his cigar. "Then I'll bid you good-by, Dr. Steinhofer."

They shook hands and Sir James Manson was ushered to the street. As the solid oak door clicked quietly shut behind him, he stepped into the waiting limousine.

ASSISTANT Under Secretary Sergei Golon was not in a good humor that morning. His chronic indigestion had elected to ensure him a day of unrelenting misery, and his secretary was out sick.

Beyond the windows of his office in the West Africa section of the Foreign Ministry, Moscow's windswept boulevards were covered with slush, a grimy gray in the dim morning light. Golon took a file that had been marked for his attention by the Under Secretary: "Assess and Instigate Necessary Action." He perused it gloomily. He noted that the file began with a memorandum from foreign intelligence and that the latest cable from Ambassador Dobrovolsky had urged prompt action.

"As if we had nothing else to bother about," Golon snorted. He could not see why it mattered whether there was, or was not, tin in Zangaro. The Soviet Union had enough tin.

Nevertheless, action had been authorized from above, and as a good civil servant he took it. To a stenographer borrowed from the typing pool he dictated a letter to the director of the Sverdlovsk Institute of Mining requiring him to select a team of geologists and engineers to study a suspected tin deposit in West Africa.

AFTER lunch on Wednesday, Cat Shannon rang his friend the writer. "I thought you'd left town," the writer said. "Carrie says Julie has been looking for you. She hasn't stopped talking about you. She rang the Lowndes Hotel, and they said you had left, address unknown."

Shannon promised he'd call her. He gave his friend the flat's

phone number, but no address. With the small talk over, he re-
quested the information he wanted.

"I suppose I could," said the friend dubiously. "But honestly, I
ought to ring him first and see if it's okay."

"Well, do that. Tell him it's me, that I need to see him, and am
prepared to go down there for a few hours with him. Tell him I
wouldn't trouble him if it wasn't important, in my opinion."

The writer agreed to put through the call and ring him back with
an address if the man agreed to speak to Shannon.

THE first of the mercenaries to arrive in London was Marc
Vlaminck, who phoned Shannon just after five p.m. The Cat
glanced down the list of three hotels in his neighborhood and read
the name of one. Kurt Semmler was ten minutes after Vlaminck.
He wrote down the name of the hotel Shannon gave him and took
a cab. Langarotti was the last. He, too, hired a taxi to his hotel.

At seven Shannon rang them all and bade them to his flat.

When they greeted each other it was the first indication any of
them had that the others had been invited. Their broad grins came
partly from the pleasure of meeting old friends, partly from the
knowledge that Shannon's bringing them all to London could only
mean he had money. When he told them Dupree was flying in
from South Africa, they knew he was not playing games.

"The job I've been given," he told them, "has to be organized
from scratch. The object is to mount a commando-style attack on
a town on the west coast of Africa. We have to capture one building, knock off everyone in it, and pull back out again."

Vlaminck grinned; Semmler muttered, *"Klasse."* Langarotti
moved his knife blade across the black leather around his left fist.

Shannon spread a map out on the floor and outlined the kind
of attack he had proposed to his patron. The three men concurred.
Not one asked the destination. They knew he would not tell. It was
not a question of lack of trust, simply of security. "So that's it," he
said. "The terms are twelve hundred and fifty dollars a month from
tomorrow for three months. Plus expenses and a five-thousand-dollar success bonus. Two of the tasks that have to be done in the

preparation stages are illegal—a border crossing from Belgium to France and a problem of loading some cases onto a ship somewhere in southern Europe. We'll all be involved in both jobs. So what do you say?"

Langarotti stropped his knife. "Is it against French interests?"

"You have my word it is not."

The four of them shook on it, and that was enough.

"All right, then," Shannon said. "Kurt, start looking for a boat. I need a small and inconspicuous freighter with a clean record, all papers in order. I don't want speed, but reliability. Price not over twenty-five thousand pounds. Sailing date, fully fueled and supplied for Cape Town, sixty days from now. Got it?"

Semmler nodded and began to think at once of his contacts in the Mediterranean shipping world.

"Jean-Baptiste, you go back to Marseilles and find me three large rubberized inflatable semirigid craft. The sort developed for water sports from the basic design of marine commando assault craft. I want them black. Buy them at separate suppliers, book them into the warehouse of a respectable shipping agent for export to Morocco. Also three outboard engines, battery-started, about sixty horsepower. They must be fitted with underwater exhausts for silent running. Open a bank account and mail me its name and number. I'll send money by credit transfer. Okay?"

Langarotti nodded and resumed his knife stropping.

"Marc. You mentioned once that you knew a man in Belgium who had knocked off a large German store of brand-new Schmeisser submachine guns in 1945. If he still has some, I want a hundred in first-class working order. Write me, here at this flat, when you have found him and can set up a meeting for me. Got it?"

By nine thirty they were through, and Shannon took them to the Paprika for a meal. They were all elated at the prospect of going to war again under Cat Shannon.

Across the Channel another man was thinking hard about Carlo Alfred Thomas Shannon. He paced the floor of his flat and considered information that had just reached him from Marseilles.

If the writer who had recommended Charles Roux to Simon Endean as a second possible mercenary had known more about the Frenchman's character, his description would have been less complimentary. Also, he did not know of the vitriolic hatred that Roux bore for the first man he had recommended.

After Endean had left Roux, the Frenchman had waited a fortnight for a second contact from the man called Harris. When it never came he concluded either that the project had been abandoned or that someone else had gotten the job. He made inquiries and learned that Shannon had been in Paris. This had shaken him. He thought Shannon had left after their parting at Le Bourget. At this point he had briefed a henchman called Henri Alain to trace the hated man. Alain had reported back that Shannon had been living at a Montmartre hotel and had left it, address unknown, the morning after he had had a visitor from London. Roux had no doubt who the visitor was. So Mr. Harris had seen two mercenaries in Paris. And he, Roux, was the one who was left on the shelf.

He had Alain stake out the hotel for four days, but Shannon had not come back. Then he recalled that newspaper reports had linked Shannon with Langarotti in the recent fighting in West Africa. He had sent Alain to Marseilles. Alain had just informed him that Langarotti had left Marseilles for London.

When Alain had gone Roux thought things over. Shannon was recruiting, no doubt for Walter Harris' contract—a contract Roux felt he personally should have had. His hold over the French mercenary community was likely to slip unless he could produce some form of work. If Shannon were to disappear—permanently—Mr. Harris would presumably have to come back to Roux.

Without further delay he made a local phone call.

Roux's next visitor, Raymond Thomard, was a killer by instinct and profession. He, too, had been in the Congo and Roux had used him as a hatchet man. In the mistaken view that Roux was a big shot, he was as loyal as a paid man can be.

"I've got a contract for you," Roux said. "Five thousand dollars."
Thomard grinned. "Who's the buzzard you want knocked off?"

"Cat Shannon."

Thomard's face dropped. Roux went on before he could reply. "I know he's good. But you're better. Does he know you?"

Thomard shook his head. "We never met," he said.

Roux clapped him on the back. "Then you've got nothing to worry about. Stay in touch. I'll let you know where to find him."

BACK in London the dinner was nearing its end, and Tiny Marc was proposing the Congo toast.

> *Vive la mort, vive la guerre,*
> *Vive le sacré mercenaire.*

Clearheaded while the rest got drunk, Cat Shannon wondered idly what havoc would be wreaked when he let slip this group of dogs on Kimba's palace. Silently he drank to the dogs of war.

CHAPTER EIGHT

SHORTLY after nine on Thursday morning Martin Thorpe presented himself in Sir James Manson's office with his findings.

"There's no doubt you are right about Bormac, Martin," Manson said when he had studied the documents. "But why hasn't the major stockholder been bought out long ago?"

The Bormac Trading Company had been founded to exploit the output of vast rubber plantations in Borneo, using Chinese laborers. The founder had been a ruthless Scot by the name of Ian Macallister. In 1904 Macallister and a group of London businessmen created Bormac with an issue of half a million shares. The Scot received 150,000 shares, a place on the board, and managership of the rubber estates. Ten years later, thanks to lucrative war contracts, the price per share had climbed from four shillings to over two pounds. The war profiteers' boom lasted until 1918. There was a slump just after the First World War; then the motorcar craze of the 1920s boosted the need for rubber tires. There was a one-for-one new stock issue, raising the total number of shares to a million and Sir Ian's block to 300,000.

The Depression of the 1930s sent prices down again. In 1937 they were recovering when one of the Chinese coolies ran amok and performed an unpleasantness on the sleeping Sir Ian with a heavy-bladed parang. The assistant manager took over, but lacked the drive of his dead master, and production fell. The company had staggered on, its assets unrecoverable after the Second World War and Indonesian nationalism. By the time Martin Thorpe went over the company's books, the shares stood at a shilling each.

The Bormac board was composed of five directors, who controlled no more than eighteen percent of the million shares. Fifty-two percent of the rest were distributed among 6500 shareholders. But what interested Thorpe and Manson was one single block of 300,000 shares held by the widowed Lady Macallister.

The puzzle was why someone had not long since bought the entire block from her and taken on the shell of this once flourishing company. It was ideal, set up as it was to permit the company to exploit any country's natural assets outside the United Kingdom.

"She must be eighty-five if she's a day," said Thorpe. "Lives in a dreary flat in Kensington, guarded by a lady companion."

"She *must* have been approached," mused Sir James. "Martin, find out about her. She has to have a weak spot that would persuade her to sell. Whatever it is, find it." Then from his desk drawer Manson drew six printed forms, applications for numbered accounts at the Zwingli Bank in Zurich. He explained briefly and concisely what he wanted done.

ENDEAN rang Shannon just after two and was given a precise report on his arrangements.

Shannon put forward his next requirements. "I want five thousand pounds telexed from your Swiss bank to my credit as Keith Brown at the Banque de Crédit in Luxembourg by next Monday noon, and another five thousand at the Landesbank in Hamburg."

He explained that the money was needed mainly so that he could prove his credit before entering into purchasing negotiations. Later most of it would be remitted to Bruges.

Endean promised to get the instructions off to Zurich at once.

JANNI DUPREE CHECKED IN from Cape Town on Thursday, and there was a second reunion celebration. When he heard Shannon's terms Janni's face cracked into a grin. "Count me in, Cat."

"Good man. I want you to stay in London and buy the clothing we'll need. I'll give you a full list."

Dupree nodded. "Okay. How much will it cost?"

"About a thousand pounds. Get the things at different shops. Pay cash and take the purchases away with you. Give no one a real name or address. Store the stuff in a warehouse, have it crated for export, and contact four separate freight agents. Pay each to send his consignment to a freight agent in Marseilles for collection by Mr. Jean-Baptiste Langarotti."

"To which agent in Marseilles?" asked Dupree.

"We don't know yet," said Shannon. He turned to the Corsican. "Jean, when you have the name of the agent you intend to use for the export of the boats and engines, mail us the name and address, one copy to me here and a second copy to Jan Dupree, General Delivery, Trafalgar Square Post Office. Now for money."

From his desk Shannon took four letters addressed to the Krediet-bank in Bruges. Each mercenary dictated the name of his bank as Shannon filled in the blanks. The letters bade the Kredietbank transmit 1250 in U.S. dollars to each of the men in the named banks on the day of receipt of the letter; again on May 5; again on June 5. Last, he gave them each the money to cover hotels and air fares, and told them to meet him outside the door of his London bank at eleven the following morning.

When they had gone he sat down and wrote a long letter to a man in Africa, having checked by phone with the writer that it was in order to do so. That evening Shannon dined alone.

IN ZURICH, Friday morning, Martin Thorpe handed to Dr. Stein-hofer of the Zwingli Bank six application forms for numbered accounts. They were in the names of Messrs. Adams, Ball, Carter, Davies, Edwards, and Frost. Attached to each form were two letters. One gave power of attorney to Mr. Martin Thorpe to operate their accounts. The other was a letter signed by Sir James Manson, requesting Dr. Steinhofer to transfer to the accounts of each of his business associates the sum of £50,000.

Dr. Steinhofer took the application forms without comment. If a wealthy Englishman chose to get around the tiresome rules of his own country, that was his business.

"The company we have our eye on is called Bormac Trading Company," Thorpe told Steinhofer. "We'll try to persuade Lady Macallister to sell her thirty percent of Bormac," he went on. "As you know, it is not possible for one purchaser to buy more than ten percent of a company without declaring his identity. Therefore the four buyers will be Mr. Adams, Mr. Ball, Mr. Carter, and Mr. Davies—who will each acquire seven and a half percent. We will wish you to act on their behalf."

The banker nodded. It was standard practice.

"I shall attempt to persuade the old lady to sign the transfer certificates with the name of the buyer left out," Thorpe said.

"I completely understand," said Dr. Steinhofer smoothly. "When you have had your interview with the lady, we will see how best it can be arranged. Tell Sir James to have no fear."

Thorpe was back in London by nightfall to begin his weekend.

SHANNON came out of his bank carrying four brown envelopes containing money and instructions. The four mercenaries, waiting on the sidewalk, took their envelopes and went their separate ways.

At his flat, Shannon wrote out a statement for Endean and mailed it that evening. With his weekend free, he called Julie Manson and suggested taking her out to dinner. She came to collect him, looking pert at the wheel of her red MGB.

"Let's go and eat at one of my places," she suggested. "Then I can introduce you to some of my friends."

Shannon shook his head. "Forget it. I am not spending the whole evening being asked damn fool questions about killing people."

She pouted. "Please, Cat darling. I won't say what you are."

Shannon weakened. "One condition. My name is Keith Brown. Nothing else do you say about me or what I do. Understood?"

She giggled. "Great! Come on, then, Mr. Keith Brown."

She took him to Tramp's, where she was greeted with a kiss by the manager. He shook Shannon's hand.

From their table Shannon glanced around at the diners. Long hair, casual dress. Show business or its fringes, he guessed. But some were young businessmen trying to be trendy, and among these he spotted a face he knew. After the lobster cocktail he excused himself and strolled out to the lobby as if on his way to the men's room. Within seconds a hand fell on his shoulder, and he turned to face Simon Endean.

"Are you out of your mind?" grated Endean.

Shannon looked at him in mock surprise, a wide-eyed innocent.

"No. I don't think so. Why?" he asked.

Endean's face was white with fury. He knew how Manson doted on his "innocent" little girl. But to bawl the man out for dining with a girl called Manson would blow his own cover and his boss's. "What are you doing here?" he asked lamely.

"Having dinner," said Shannon, appearing puzzled. "Look, Harris, if I want to go out and have dinner, that's my affair."

"Who's the girl?" Endean asked.

Shannon shrugged. "Name's Julie. Met her in a café."

"Picked her up?" asked Endean in horror.

"Yes, you might say that. Why?"

"Oh, nothing. But be careful about girls, all girls. It would be better if you left them alone for a while, that's all."

"Harris, don't worry. There won't be any indiscretions, in bed or out. Besides, I told her my name was Keith Brown."

Endean departed before Julie Manson saw him.

Shannon and Julie had their first row on the way back to his flat. He had told her she shouldn't tell her father she was going out with a mercenary, or even mention his name. "He'd send you away somewhere."

Her response had been to tease, saying she could handle her father. Besides, Shannon could rescue her. "Anyway, I'm not being told what to do," she said as they entered the flat.

"You will by me," growled Shannon. "You'll just keep damn silent about me when you're with your father."

"I'll do what I damn well like," she insisted. Shannon picked her up, sat down in a chair, and turned her over his knee. For five minutes there were two sounds in the sitting room, the girl's protesting squeals and the crack of Shannon's hand. Then he let her up and she scuttled into the bedroom, sobbing loudly.

Shannon made some coffee and drank it slowly by the window. When he entered the bedroom it was dark. In the far corner of the bed was a small hump, but no sound. He sat on the edge of the bed.

"You're rotten," she whispered.

He stroked her neck. "You're a spoiled little girl."

"I'm not." There was a pause. "Yes, I am."

He went on caressing her.

"Cat," she said. "Did you really think Daddy might take me away from you if I told him?"

"Yes. I still do."

"Tell me something—"

"What?"

"Why do you live the way you do? Why be a mercenary and go around making wars on people?"

"I don't make wars. The world we live in makes wars—governed by men who pretend they are moral, whereas most of them are self-seeking bastards. I just fight the wars, because it's the way I like to live. It's not only the money. Most of us fight for the same reason: we enjoy the life, the hard living, the combat."

"But why do there have to be wars?"

"Because there are only two kinds of people in this world: the predators and the grazers. And the predators always get to the top, because they're prepared to fight to get there and consume people that get in their way. The predators become the potentates. And the potentates are never satisfied. They must go on and on seeking more of the currency they worship. In the communist world the currency is power. Power and more power. In the capitalist world the currency is money. More and more money. Which in the end is power, too. If it needs a war to grab it, you get a war. The rest, the so-called idealism, is a lot of bull."

"Some people fight for idealism."

"Yeah. They do. And ninety-nine out of a hundred of them are being conned. Those GIs in Vietnam, do you think they die for life, liberty, and the pursuit of happiness? They die for the Dow Jones index. And the British soldiers who died in Kenya, Cyprus? They were in those lands because their colonel was ordered by the War Office, and that was ordered by the Cabinet, to keep British control over the economies. It's a big con, Julie. The difference with me is that no one tells me when to fight. Or which side to fight on. That's why the politicians, the establishments, hate mercenaries. They can't control us. We pick our own contracts."

"You're a rebel, Cat," she murmured.

"Sure. Always have been. No, not always. Since I was in the marines and buried six of my mates in Cyprus. That's when I began to question the wisdom and integrity of our leaders."

"But you could get killed in one of these futile wars."

"Yes, and I could earn a futile salary in a futile office until a futile retirement. I prefer to live my way. And die my way, with a bullet in my chest, and a gun in my hand. Now go to sleep, love. It's dawn already."

IN LUXEMBOURG the following Monday, Shannon identified himself at the Banque de Crédit as Keith Brown and asked for the £5000 in his name. The credit had just come through. He took £1000 in Luxembourg francs and had the balance transferred to Keith Brown's account in Bruges.

He had time for a quick lunch before making his way to the firm of accountants, Lang and Stein. His appointment was with Mr. Emil Stein, one of the partners in this highly respectable firm.

"Over the next few months," he told the gray-haired Luxembourger, "a group of British associates wish to engage in commercial activities in the Mediterranean area. For this purpose we would like to establish a holding company in Luxembourg."

Mr. Stein received such requests every day. "That should present no problem, Mr. Brown. You are aware, of course, that all the procedures required by the Grand Duchy of Luxembourg must be complied with. There must be a minimum of seven shareholders,

and normally, shares and the names of the shareholders are registered. But there is a provision for the issuance of bearer shares,
which do not require registration of the identity of the majority
holder. The snag is that bearer shares are exactly what they sound
like. The bearer of the majority of them controls the company without needing a vestige of proof as to how he acquired them. Do you
follow me, Mr. Brown?"

Shannon did. A company called Tyrone Holdings SA would be
set up. Shannon paid a deposit of £500 in cash. In a week or so
there would be a general meeting to float it. Semmler could then
buy the boat behind the cover of an uncheckable company.

It was to Hamburg that Shannon flew the next morning. This
time he was looking for arms.

THE trade in lethal weapons is the world's most lucrative, after
narcotics. All the major powers operate teams of salesmen to trot
the globe, persuading potentates that they do not have enough
weapons or should replace what they do possess. What the arms
are used for is of no concern to the sellers. But profit desirability
and political durability sometimes conflict, and so countries will
cooperate to a degree on arms sales, and an application for an
arms purchase made to any of them habitually undergoes close
scrutiny.

A licensed dealer, usually a resident of his own country, sells
only after consulting his government to make sure that the sale is
acceptable. This is the highest level of the private-enterprise arms
business. Lower in the pond is the more dubious fish—the licensed
dealer who keeps no stocks, but holds franchises to negotiate sales.
And in the mud at the bottom sits the black-market dealer. He holds
no license and remains in business by being of value to secret buyers who cannot clinch intergovernmental deals.

The vital document in an arms deal is called the end-user certificate. This certifies that the weapons purchase is being made by,
or on behalf of, the end user, who almost without exception in
the Western world has to be a sovereign government. The crucial
point about end-user certificates is that some countries carry out the

most rigorous checks to ensure their authenticity, while others come under the heading of "no questions asked" suppliers. End-user certificates, like anything else, can be forged. It was into this world that Shannon carefully entered when he flew to Hamburg.

Two countries had earned a reputation of asking few questions about where the presented end-user certificates really came from. One was Spain, whose CETME factories produced a wide range of weapons. The other, a newcomer in arms manufacture, was Yugoslavia. She produced a good light company mortar and a useful bazooka. Because her goods were new, Shannon estimated that a dealer could persuade Belgrade to sell a tiny quantity of these arms, as few as two 60-mm. mortar tubes and three hundred bombs, plus two bazooka tubes and forty rockets. The excuse could well be that such a customer might wish to make some tests before placing a larger order.

Shannon knew that he was in no position to apply to governments or to the big legitimate dealers. The trouble with the packet of arms he sought was that it looked like what it was: a single packet of arms for a single job, just such a job as the taking of one building in a short period. He had decided it would be less of a giveaway to split the packet even smaller and to buy only one kind of item from each dealer.

From one of the men he was going to see he wanted 400,000 rounds of standard 9-mm. ammunition, the sort that fits into automatic pistols and also submachine guns. This could well be the kind of consignment needed by the police force of any small country. It would not raise questions, because there were no matching guns in the packet. It could pass as an order designed simply to replenish stock. To get it he needed a licensed arms dealer who could slip such a small order through among a batch of bigger orders. Although licensed, the dealer must be prepared to do a "bent" deal with a forged end-user certificate, which he could present to a supplier government that asked few questions.

Shannon had flown to Hamburg to place his orders, the first with one Johann Schlinker, who was licensed to trade with CETME in Madrid, but who was known not to be above putting through a phony end-user certificate. For the second he would see an acquaintance, Alan Baker, who had established good relations with the Yugoslavs, although he was unlicensed.

Shannon's first stop was the Landesbank. His £5000 was there. He took the whole sum in a banker's check made out to himself.

Johann Schlinker, whom Shannon met in his modest office, was round and jovial. "What brings you here, Mr. Brown?" he asked.

"You were recommended to me, Herr Schlinker, as having a high reputation for reliability in the business of military hardware."

Schlinker smiled and nodded. "By whom, may I ask?"

Shannon mentioned a man in Paris, closely associated with African affairs on behalf of a certain French governmental service. Shannon had told the man he would be using the name Brown.

Schlinker raised his eyebrows. "Would you excuse me a minute?" he asked. When he came back he was smiling brightly. "I had to call a friend in Paris. Please go on."

"I want a quantity of nine-millimeter ammunition," Shannon said bluntly, "for a group of people in Africa to whom I am technical adviser. The delivery is to be by ship."

"How much would the order be?" asked the German.

"Four hundred thousand rounds."

"That is not very much," Schlinker said simply.

"A small investment now might lead to more later."

"And have you an end-user certificate?" the German asked.

"No, I'm afraid not. I hoped that could be arranged."

"Oh, yes, it can. I can offer you nine-millimeter standard ball at sixty-five dollars per thousand, plus a surcharge of ten percent for the certificate and ten percent free on board."

Free on board meant a cargo complete with export license, cleared through customs, and loaded onto the ship, with the ship itself clearing the harbor. Shannon calculated hastily: $26,000 for ammunition, plus $5200. Steep. "How would payment be made?"

"Fifty-two hundred dollars at once. When I have the certificate, the full purchase price. I also need the name of the vessel, in order to get an export permit. It must be a scheduled ship, or one owned by a registered shipping company."

Shannon nodded. "How long from when I pay until shipment?"

"Madrid is quite slow. About forty days at the outside."

Shannon rose. He left, and came back in an hour with the cash. While Schlinker was writing the receipt for the money, Shannon glanced at a brochure put out by a company which made non-military pyrotechnic goods, such things as flares and rockets. "Are you associated with this company, Herr Schlinker?" he asked.

Schlinker smiled broadly. "I own it," he said. "It is what I am best known for to the general public."

And good cover for holding a warehouse full of crates labeled DANGER OF EXPLOSION, thought Shannon. Quickly he wrote out a list of items. "Could you fill this order?" he asked.

Schlinker glanced at the list. It included two rocket-launching tubes, ten magnesium-flare rockets attached to parachutes, two penetrating foghorns, four sets of night binoculars, three walkie-talkie sets, and five wrist compasses.

"Certainly," he said. "I stock all these things. And since they aren't classified as arms, there's no export problem."

"Good," said Shannon. "How much would that lot cost, with freight in bond to an exporting agent in Marseilles?"

"Forty-eight hundred dollars," Schlinker said.

"I'll be in touch with you in twelve days," said Shannon. "I'll send you a banker's check for this lot and the address of the agent in Marseilles. Within thirty days I'll give you the twenty-six thousand dollars for the ammunition deal and the name of the ship."

Shannon met Alan Baker for dinner that night. A wiry man, Baker was a former Royal Engineer who had settled in Germany after the war. He had drifted into running arms to the scores of tiny nationalist or anticommunist bands who still ran resistance movements. He knew Shannon by his real name.

"Yes, it can be done," he said when he had heard what Shannon wanted. "Just at the moment I have one problem, though."

"What's that?"

"End-user certificates. I used to have an East African diplomat in Bonn who would sign anything for a price, but he's been sent home. I'm a bit stuck for a replacement." Not being a licensed dealer, Baker could not obtain a legal certificate, as Schlinker could.

"Are the Yugoslavs particular about end users? If I could get a certificate from an African country, would that work?"

"Sure. As long as the documentation's in order. They don't check further. As for price, a sixty-millimeter mortar tube would run you eleven hundred dollars. Say, twenty-two hundred for the pair. The bombs are twenty-four dollars each."

"All right," said Shannon, "I'll take three hundred."

"So that's seventy-two hundred dollars for the bombs. A pair of bazookas costs you two thousand. With forty rockets at forty-two dollars and fifty cents each, that's . . . let's see—"

"Seventeen hundred dollars," said Shannon. "Thirteen thousand one hundred dollars for the whole packet."

"Plus ten percent for getting the stuff free on board your ship, Cat. Let's face it, it's a tiny order, but even so, there are expenses for me. Let's say fourteen and a half, eh?"

"We'll say fourteen four," said Shannon. "I'll get the certificate and mail it, with a fifty percent deposit. Twenty-five percent more when I see the stuff in Yugoslavia crated and ready to go. The rest as the ship leaves the quay. How long will you take?"

"From the moment I get your end user, say thirty-five days."

Outside the restaurant they shook hands. "Don't worry, Cat. You can trust me," Baker said.

"In a pig's ear I can," Shannon muttered as he walked away.

The next morning—Day Nine—Shannon flew back to London.

CHAPTER NINE

MARTIN Thorpe stepped into Sir James Manson's office that Wednesday morning, and Sir James waved him to a seat.

Thorpe said, "I've been checking on Lady Macallister. She's eighty-six, very tetchy, and she's *such* a dyed-in-the-wool Scot, she has all her affairs handled by a solicitor up in Dundee. She appears to have an obsession in life, and it's not money. She's rich in her own right. She was the daughter of a laird with more land than ready cash. After her old man died she inherited the lot, and the fishing and hunting rights have brought in a small fortune. Two people have tried to buy her holdings in Bormac. I suspect they offered money. That would not interest her."

"Then what in hell would?" asked Sir James.

"She tried to have a statue of her husband erected, but it was refused by the London County Council. She had a memorial put up in his hometown. I think that's her obsession—the memory of the old slave driver she married."

Thorpe outlined his idea, and Manson listened thoughtfully.

Shannon was back in his London flat shortly after twelve. He found a cable from Langarotti in Marseilles, giving the address of a hotel where he had checked in as M. Lavallon. Shannon placed a call to M. Lavallon, who was out. He left a message for M. Lavallon to call Mr. Brown in London. Then he typed a letter to the Corsican asking about a man in Paris he had mentioned who could get end-user certificates from one of the African embassies. Next he telegraphed Walter Harris that he would like to see him the next morning at eleven. He spent the afternoon typing a full account of his Luxembourg and Hamburg trips. He had just finished it when Janni Dupree knocked at the door.

Janni reported that he would have much of the clothing ready for collection by Friday. Next week he would start on such things as sleeping bags, knapsacks, and footwear. Shannon promised to get for him the name of the shipping agent in Marseilles to whom he should consign them. Then he gave Janni the letter to Langarotti, addressed care of the main post office in Marseilles, and ordered him to post it at once, express rate.

He was very hungry at eight, when Langarotti finally called. Shannon asked him, in the guarded terms he'd insisted they use on the phone, how he was getting on.

"I've written to three boat makers for their brochures. When I see what I want I can order from local dealers," said Langarotti.

"Good idea," said Shannon. "Now listen. I need the name of a good shipping agent in Marseilles. There will be a few crates sent from here in the near future, and one from Hamburg."

"I'd prefer to use an agent in Toulon," said Langarotti.

Shannon could guess why. Marseilles police had been tightening up on the port, and the new customs chief was believed to be a holy terror. The aim was to clamp down on the heroin traffic, but a search of a boat for drugs could just as easily turn up arms.

"Fair enough," said Shannon. "Wire me the name when you have it. Also the answer to a letter you'll be getting."

The next morning Shannon booked a seat on a BEA weekend flight to a certain place in Africa, via Paris.

At eleven sharp, Endean arrived at the flat. "You've covered a lot of ground," he said when he had read Shannon's report.

"Yes. I want to get all the orders placed by Day Twenty, which leaves forty days for them to be fulfilled. We must allow twenty days to collect all the components and get them aboard ship. Sailing date should be Day Eighty, if we are to strike on schedule. By the way, I shall need more money soon."

After some initial objections Endean agreed to put another £20,000 into Shannon's Belgian account. Then he left.

THE drawing room in the apartment above Cottesmore Gardens, not far from Kensington High Street, was gloomy in the extreme. Around the walls hung portraits of ancestors, Montroses and Monteagles, Farquhars and Frazers. Bigger than all, in a vast frame above a fireplace that was never used, stood a man in a kilt. The face was framed by ginger muttonchop whiskers. Sir Ian Macallister, Knight of the British Empire.

Martin Thorpe dragged his eyes back to Lady Macallister, who was slumped in a chair. "People have come before, Mr. Thorpe. But I don't see why I should sell my husband's company. It was all his work. I will not sell—"

"But Lady Macallister—"

"You see, the company was my dear husband's legacy to me."

"Lady Macallister—" he began again.

"You'll have to speak directly into the hearing aid. She's deaf as a post," said Lady Macallister's companion.

Thorpe nodded his thanks and noticed her properly for the first time. In her late sixties, she had the look of those who have fallen on hard times and have had to put themselves in bond to others.

Thorpe leaned close to the hearing aid. "Lady Macallister, the people I represent do not want to change the company. Only to make it rich and famous again, like when your husband ran it."

A glimmer of light awoke in her eyes. "Like my husband . . ."

"Yes, Lady Macallister," bawled Thorpe. "We want to re-create his life's work and make the Macallister estates a memorial to him."

"They never put up a memorial to my Ian. They wouldn't."

"If the company was rich, it could insist on a memorial," Thorpe shouted. "It could found a Sir Ian Macallister Trust."

"It would cost a lot of money," she wailed. "I don't know. If only Mr. Dalgleish were here. He signs papers for me. Mrs. Barton, I'd like to go to my room."

"It's time you did," said the housekeeper companion brusquely.

Mrs. Barton helped the old woman to her feet and out of the room. In a few minutes she came back alone.

Thorpe, standing, smiled his most rueful smile. "It looks as if I've failed. And yet, you know, her stock is valueless unless the company is rejuvenated. I'm sorry if I put you to inconvenience."

"I'm quite used to inconvenience," said Mrs. Barton, but her face softened. "Would you care for a cup of tea before you leave?"

Instinct prompted Thorpe to accept. As they sat over a pot of tea in the kitchen, Mrs. Barton told him all about Lady Macallister.

"She can't see all your fine arguments, Mr. Thorpe, not even when you offered to put up a memorial to that old ogre."

Thorpe was surprised. Evidently the tart Mrs. Barton had a mind of her own. "She does what you tell her," he said.

"Would you like another cup of tea?" And as she poured it she said quietly, "Oh, yes, she does what I tell her. She knows if I went, she'd never get another companion."

"It can't be much of a life for you, Mrs. Barton."

"It's not," she said, "but I get by. It's the price one pays."

"For being a widow?" asked Thorpe gently.

"Yes."

There was a picture of a young man in the uniform of an RAF pilot propped on the mantelpiece. "Your son?" questioned Thorpe.

"Yes. Shot down over France in 1943."

"So he won't be able to look after you when she's gone."

"No. I'll get by. She'll no doubt leave me something in her will. I've looked after her for sixteen years."

When Thorpe left an hour later on that Thursday afternoon, he went straight to a phone booth. A West End insurance broker agreed to see him at ten the next morning.

JUST after lunch on Friday, Sir James Manson summoned Endean to his office. He had read Shannon's report and was agreeably surprised at the speed with which the mercenary worked. What pleased him even more was the call he had just had from Thorpe.

"You say Shannon will be abroad next week, Simon. That's good. There's a job I want you to do. Get one of our standard contracts of employment. Paste over the name of ManCon with a strip of white paper and fill in the name of Bormac in its place. Have it photocopied and make it out for one year for the services of Antoine Bobi at a salary of five hundred pounds a month. Specify payable in Dahomean francs so he won't vamoose."

"Bobi?" queried Endean. "You mean Colonel Bobi?"

"That's the one. I don't want the future president of Zangaro running off anywhere. On Monday you are going to Dahomey to persuade him that Bormac would like to engage him as a consultant. Tell him his duties will be communicated to him later, that the sole condition of employment now is that he remain where he is until you visit him again. As for the date on the contract, make sure the last figure for the year is blurred."

THAT same afternoon at four Thorpe emerged from the Kensington apartment with the four stock-transfer deeds he needed, signed by Lady Macallister and witnessed by Mrs. Barton. He also bore a letter instructing Mr. Dalgleish in Dundee to hand over to Mr. Thorpe the stock certificates upon presentation of his check.

The name of the recipient of the shares had not been entered on the transfer deeds, but Lady Macallister had not noticed. She had been too distraught at the very thought of Mrs. Barton's packing her bags and leaving. Before nightfall the name of the Zwingli Bank's nominee company, acting on behalf of Messrs. Adams, Ball, Carter, and Davies, would be written into the vacant spaces.

It had cost Sir James Manson two shillings to buy each of the 300,000 shares, a total of £30,000. It had cost another £30,000 to purchase a life annuity which would assure a worry-free end to her days for one lady housekeeper companion.

BENOIT Lambert, known to friends and to the Paris police as Benny, was a small-fry member of the underworld who cultivated the notion of himself as a mercenary and an arms dealer. The first he certainly was not, but with his variety of contacts he had occasionally been able to provide an item of weaponry here and there, usually handguns for the underworld. He had also come to know an African diplomat who was prepared, for a price, to provide a serviceable end-user certificate. Eighteen months earlier he had mentioned this in a bar to a man called Langarotti.

The Corsican cabled the information to Shannon now, and called Benny to set up a weekend meeting. The arms dealer had been surprised to hear that he was about to be visited by Cat Shannon. He had heard of Shannon. He had heard, too, that Charles Roux would pay for information as to the Irish mercenary's whereabouts.

"Yes, I can get that certificate," Benny Lambert told Shannon. He quoted an exorbitant sum.

"*Merde*," said Shannon. "I'll pay you a thousand pounds."

Lambert calculated. "Okay," he said.

"You let out one word of this, and I'll slit your gizzard," said Shannon. "Even better, I'll get the Corsican to do it."

"Not a word, honest. I'll get you the letter in four days."

When he had gone Benny Lambert thought things over. He decided to get the letter, collect his fee, and tell Roux later.

The following night Shannon flew to Africa.

IT WAS a long drive up-country. The taxi was hot, and rattled abominably. Shannon did not mind. It was good to be back in Africa again, even after a six-hour flight without sleep. Familiar were the village women walking to market, gourds or bundles balanced on their heads, the villagers chattering in the shade of palm-thatch roofs. He sniffed the palms, the woodsmoke, the brown, stagnant river. He arrived at the villa just before noon.

The guards at the gate frisked him thoroughly. Inside, he recognized one of the personal attendants of the man he had come to see. The attendant ushered Shannon into an empty room.

Shannon was staring out the window when he heard the creak of a door. He turned around.

The general was much the same as when they had parted on the darkened airstrip, the same luxuriant beard, the deep bass voice.

"Well, Major Shannon, so soon. Couldn't you stay away?"

Shannon grinned at the familiar banter. "I need something, sir. And I have an idea I think we ought to talk over."

"There's not much that an impoverished exile can offer you," said the general, "but I'll always listen to your ideas. If I remember rightly, you used to have some fairly good ones."

Shannon said, "There's one thing you have that I could use. You still have your people's loyalty. And what I need is men."

They talked and elaborated the plan all afternoon. When darkness fell Shannon was drawing diagrams. Only at three in the morning was the car summoned to drive Shannon to the airport.

"I'll be in touch, sir," said Shannon as they parted.

"And I'll have to send my emissaries immediately," replied the general. "But in sixty days the men will be there."

Shannon was dead tired. The strain of the constant travel was beginning to tell. He reached Le Bourget at six on Tuesday afternoon and settled into a hotel in the heart of Paris' 8th Arrondissement. He had forsaken his Montmartre hideout, where he was known as Shannon. But he had decided it was safe to go to his favorite place for dinner. He called Madame Michèle and ordered a filet mignon. Then he put in two person-to-person calls, the first to M. Lavallon in Marseilles.

"I have the shipping agent in Toulon," said Langarotti. "Agence Maritime Duphot. They have their own bonded warehouse. Send consignments marked as the property of J. B. Langarotti."

"Good," said Shannon, and picked up the phone to talk to Janni. He said he had four crates ready to go. "Well done," said Shannon, and gave him the name and address of the shipping agent in Toulon. Then he placed one more call, to Ostend.

"I'm in Paris," said Shannon when he heard Vlaminck's voice. "That man with the merchandise I wanted to examine . . ."

"Yes. He's prepared to meet you and discuss terms."

"Suggest Friday breakfast in the Brussels airport Holiday Inn."

"Do you want me to come, too?" asked the Belgian.

"Certainly," said Shannon. "Ask for Keith Brown. Have you bought that truck I asked you to get?"

"Yes, why?"

"Has this gentleman seen it yet?"

There was a pause while Vlaminck thought. "No."

"Then don't bring it to Brussels. Hire a car and pick him up on the way. Understand?"

"Yes," said Vlaminck, perplexed. "Anything you say."

While Shannon ate his long-awaited dinner in Paris, Simon Endean boarded the overnight flight to Dahomey. Shannon would not have been surprised if he had known this, for he assumed the exiled Zangaran, Bobi, had to play a part in Manson's scheme. But if Endean had known of Shannon's visit to the general in the same area of Africa, it would, despite the pill he had taken, have ruined his sleep on the UTA DC-8 that night.

At ten the next morning Shannon rang for breakfast, and the coffee and rolls were on the table when he emerged from his shower. He placed a call to Benny Lambert and asked whether the documents were ready.

Benny's voice sounded strained. "Yes. When do you want them?"

"This afternoon," said Shannon.

"All right. Come to my place at four," said Lambert.

"No, I'll meet you here," Shannon said, and gave Lambert the name of his hotel. Better to meet the little crook in a public place. To his surprise Lambert agreed. There was something not quite right about this, but Shannon couldn't put his finger on it.

Next Shannon called Mr. Stein of Lang and Stein in Luxembourg. "About the meeting to launch my holding company, Tyrone Holdings . . ."

They set the meeting for three the next day in Stein's office.

Six thousand miles away Simon Endean sat with Colonel Bobi in his small rented villa in the residential district of Cotonou.

Bobi was a lumbering giant with a brutish face. It was of no consequence to Endean with what disastrous effects Bobi might rule Zangaro. What he had come to find was a man who would sign away the Crystal Mountain mineral rights to Bormac Trading Company for a pittance and a hefty bribe.

The colonel would be delighted to accept the post of West African consultant to Bormac. He pretended to study the contract, but when he turned to a page which Endean had stapled upside down, his expression did not flicker. He was illiterate.

Endean explained the terms of the contract slowly in a mishmash of basic French and pidgin English. Bobi nodded soberly and scrawled what could pass for a signature on the document. Only later would he be told that Bormac was putting him into power in Zangaro in exchange for mining rights.

At dawn Endean was flying north.

THE meeting with Benny Lambert took place in the hotel lounge. Lambert handed over an envelope, from which Shannon took two pieces of paper, both bearing the printed crest of the ambassador of Togo. One of the sheets was blank except for a signature and an embassy seal. The other was a letter in which the signer stated that he had been authorized by his government to engage the services of _____ to apply to the government of _____ for the purchase of the attached list of military weapons.

Shannon handed Lambert £1000 and left. Alan Baker would insert his own name in one blank and Yugoslavia in the other.

Like most weak men Lambert was indecisive. He had for three days been on the verge of telling Charles Roux that Shannon was in town and seeking an end-user certificate. He was afraid of Roux and felt he ought to tell him. But he was afraid of Shannon also. He decided to wait until morning.

When he finally gave Roux the tip-off it was too late. Roux telephoned the hotel at nine a.m. and asked for Mr. Shannon. The desk clerk replied truthfully that they had no Mr. Shannon. Within minutes Roux's man, Henri Alain, was at the hotel desk. He established that a man whose description exactly corresponded to Cat Shannon's had spent the night, registered as Keith Brown, and left for Luxembourg that morning. Alain also received a description of the Frenchman with whom Mr. Brown had been seen speaking in the lounge. All this he reported to Roux at midday.

Roux, Henri Alain, and Raymond Thomard held a conference of war. Roux made the final decision.

"Henri, you stake out that hotel. Get friendly with the staff. If Shannon checks in there again, I want to know. Understand?"

Alain nodded.

Roux turned to Thomard. "When he comes again, Raymond, you take the bastard. In the meantime make sure that Lambert doesn't do any walking for the next six months."

THE floating of the company to be known as Tyrone Holdings was over within five minutes. Shannon was invited into Mr. Stein's office, where Mr. Lang and a junior partner were already seated. Along one wall were the three secretaries of the three partners. With the required seven stockholders present, Shannon handed over the balance of £500 to Mr. Stein, and a thousand shares were issued. Everyone but Shannon received one and signed for it, then passed them to Mr. Stein, who agreed to keep them in the company safe. Shannon received 994 shares in a block represented by one sheet of paper, and signed for them. The memoranda of association were also duly signed, copies to be filed with the Registrar of Companies for the Grand Duchy of Luxembourg. That was it. Tyrone Holdings SA existed in law.

Shannon checked into the Holiday Inn at the Brussels airport just before eight.

The man who accompanied Tiny Marc Vlaminck when they knocked at Shannon's door the following morning was introduced as M. Boucher. The two of them, Shannon thought, were a comic pair. Marc towered over his companion, who was so fat as to seem almost circular. He was carrying a thick briefcase.

Shannon poured coffee and went straight to business. "M. Boucher, I represent a group who would be interested in acquiring about a hundred submachine guns. M. Vlaminck mentioned to me that you might be in a position to supply me with some Schmeissers, nine millimeter, of wartime manufacture, but never used. I understand also that an export license is out of the question. My people accept this."

Boucher nodded. "I might," he said carefully, "be able to make available a quantity of these pieces. But strictly on a cash basis."

M. Boucher, in his younger days, had worked as a cook in the Belgian SS barracks at Namur. In 1944, when the Germans were pulling back, a truck loaded with unused Schmeissers had broken down on the road from Namur. There was no time for repairs, so the cargo was shifted into a nearby bunker and the entrance dynamited. Boucher watched it happen. Later he had returned, shoveled away the rubble, and removed the thousand weapons. Since then they had reposed beneath the floor of the garage of his country cottage. To date he had unloaded half of them.

"If these guns are in good working order," said Shannon, "all reasonable conditions imposed by you would be adhered to in the handing over of the cargo. We expect complete discretion."

"They are all brand-new, monsieur. Still in their maker's grease and each still wrapped in greaseproof paper with seals unbroken. They are possibly the finest submachine gun ever made."

"May I see?" Shannon asked.

Boucher pulled the case he carried onto his knees, twirled the combination lock, and flicked open the catches.

Shannon lifted out the Schmeisser. It was a beautiful piece of weaponry. He slid his hands over the smooth blue-black metal, tried the pistol grip, and felt the lightness of it. He operated the breech mechanism several times and squinted down the barrel. The inside was unmarked.

"The others," wheezed Boucher, "are identical. Unused."

Shannon put it down. "What about magazines?"

"I can supply five with each weapon," said Boucher.

After two hours of bargaining they settled for a hundred Schmeissers at $100 each. They fixed time and place for the following Wednesday evening after dark, and agreed on the method for the handover.

Shannon offered Boucher a lift home, but the fat man chose to call a taxi. He was not prepared to assume that the Irishman, who he was certain was from the IRA, would not take him somewhere and work him over until he had learned the location of the secret hoard. Boucher was right. Trust is a superfluous weakness in the black-market arms business.

Shannon said to Vlaminck, "Do you see what I meant about the truck you bought?"

"No," said the other.

"We have to use it for the pickup. I saw no reason why Boucher should see the real license plates. Have a spare set ready for Wednesday night, will you? If Boucher does want to tip off anyone after delivery, they'll have the wrong truck."

"Okay, Cat, I'll be ready," said Marc.

Shannon had written two letters, one to Schlinker, which included the name and address of the Toulon shipping agent and the money to cover the goods ordered. The second, addressed to Alan Baker, contained the end-user certificate and the payment due for purchases made a week earlier. He mailed the letters, and Marc drove him to Ostend, where Shannon boarded the evening ferry to Dover.

The next evening around dinnertime Shannon presented Endean with his third report. "You'll have to make further transfers of money if we are to move ahead," he concluded. "We are entering the areas of major expenditures now—the arms and the ship."

"How much do you need at once?" Endean asked.

"Two thousand pounds for salaries, four thousand for boats and engines, four thousand for submachine guns, and over ten thousand for nine-millimeter ammunition—make it thirty thousand."

Endean eyed him coldly. "There had better be some purchases being made with all this money," he grated.

Shannon stared him out. "Don't threaten me, Harris. A lot of people have tried it; it costs a fortune in flowers."

He dined alone that Saturday evening. He had found that Julie Manson was already at home with her parents in Gloucestershire.

It was in the middle of Sunday morning that Julie decided to ring her lover's flat. Outside, the spring rain was washing out her hope of riding the handsome new gelding her father had given her. As her mother was within earshot of the telephone in the hallway, she decided to use the one in her father's study.

She had lifted the telephone on the desk when she noticed a folder lying on the blotter. She idly opened it to glance at the first page. A name on it caused her to freeze, the dial tone still buzzing furiously in her ear. The name was Shannon.

She flicked her eyes down the page. Figures, costs, a second reference to Shannon, two references to a man called Clarence. The turning of the door handle interrupted her.

With a start she closed the folder and began to babble into the unhearing telephone. Her father stood in the doorway.

"All right, Christine, that will be marvelous, darling. I'll see you on Monday, then. Bye now," she chattered.

Her father's expression had softened as he saw his daughter. "Now what are you up to?" he said with mock gruffness.

"Just phoning a friend, Daddy," she said in her little-girl voice. "Mummy was fussing about in the hall, so I came in here."

"Humph. Well, you've got a phone in your own room. So please use that for private calls."

"All right, Daddikins. Come on and help me saddle Tamerlane so I can ride as soon as it stops raining."

He smiled. "Give me a few minutes and I'll join you."

Mata Hari, Julie was sure, could not have done better.

CHAPTER TEN

DAY Twenty-three—Wednesday, April 28—began for Shannon with a flight to Brussels and a visit to the Kredietbank at Bruges. He and Marc Vlaminck then had four hours to kill before their scheduled rendezvous with M. Boucher. Just before dusk they set off.

There is a lonely stretch on the road from Bruges to Ghent where the old main road is bypassed by the new motorway E5. Halfway along this old road the two mercenaries found the faded sign for an abandoned farm, which was hidden from view by a clump of trees. Shannon drove the truck on past it and parked, and Marc checked that the farm was indeed deserted. "The house is locked front and back," he said. "No sign of interference. I checked out the barns and stables. No one there."

Shannon glanced at his watch. "Get back there and keep a watch from cover. I'll watch the front entrance from here."

When Marc had gone Shannon taped two false license plates over the truck's real plates. Once they were well away they could rip them off. Inside were six large sacks of potatoes Shannon had ordered Vlaminck to bring. Satisfied, he resumed his vigil.

The truck he was expecting turned up at five to eight. As it swung down the track to the farm, Shannon could make out a blob beside the driver that could only be M. Boucher. The vehicle went down the track and disappeared behind the trees.

Shannon gave Boucher three minutes; then he followed. He parked the nose of his truck ten feet from the rear of Boucher's; he climbed down, leaving his sidelights on.

"M. Boucher," he called, stepping back into darkness.

"M. Brown," he heard Boucher wheeze, and the fat man waddled into view with his helper, a big beefy-looking type, strong but slow-moving. Marc, Shannon knew, could move like a ballet dancer when he wished. He saw no problem if it came to trouble.

"You have the money?" asked Boucher as he came close.

"In the truck. You have the Schmeissers?"

Boucher waved a pudgy hand at his own truck. "In the back."

"I suggest we get both our consignments out onto the ground between the trucks," said Shannon. Boucher said something to his helper in Flemish, and the man moved to the back of their truck. Shannon tensed. If there were to be any surprises, they would come when the doors opened. There were none. The dull glimmer from his own truck's lights showed ten flat crates and an open carton.

233

Shannon whistled and Tiny Marc emerged from behind a barn.

"Let's get the handover done," Shannon said. He reached into the driver's compartment and pulled out a fat envelope. "Ten bundles. Fifty twenty-dollar bills in each."

He stayed close to Boucher as the fat man flicked through each bundle, counting with surprising speed for such plump hands. Then he checked the notes for forgeries. "All in order," he said at last, and his man moved aside from the truck doors.

Shannon nodded at Marc, who went to the truck and heaved the first crate onto the grass. He prised up the lid and counted the ten Schmeissers. One of them he took out and checked for firing-mechanism pin and breech movement. It took him twenty minutes to go through all ten cases. Finally he looked into the open-topped carton. It contained five hundred magazines. He tested one to ensure that it was the right fit for a Schmeisser.

"All in order," he said in his turn.

"Would you ask your friend to help load them up?" Shannon asked Boucher. Within five minutes the sacks of potatoes were removed and the ten flat crates and the carton were loaded in Marc's truck.

Taking a knife, Marc slit the first sack and emptied it into the loaded truck. With a laugh, the other Belgian started to help him, until every trace of the cargo in the truck was covered. Anyone looking in would be confronted with a sea of loose potatoes.

"If you don't mind, we'll leave first," said Shannon to Boucher.

Only after Marc had turned the truck around did he leave Boucher's side and leap aboard. Halfway down the lane there was a pothole over which Marc had to drive slowly. Shannon muttered something and jumped from the truck to hide in the bushes.

Two minutes later Boucher's truck came along. It, too, slowed almost to a halt to negotiate the pothole. Shannon slipped from the bushes as it went past and jammed his knife into the right rear tire. He heard it hiss as it deflated; then he was back in the bushes. He rejoined Tiny Marc on the main road, where the Belgian had just ripped off the false license plates. Shannon had nothing against Boucher, but he wanted a clear half-hour start.

By ten thirty the pair were in Ostend; the truck, loaded with spring potatoes, was garaged. In Marc's bar on the Kleinstraat they toasted each other in foaming steins of ale.

In the morning Marc called for Shannon at his hotel. Over breakfast Shannon explained that the Schmeissers had to be smuggled over the Belgian border into France, for loading onto the ship in a southern French port. For half an hour he told Vlaminck what he wanted done with the submachine guns.

"All right," the Belgian said. "I can work on them mornings in the garage before the bar opens. When do we run them south?"

"About May fifteenth," said Shannon. "We'll use the champagne route."

Shannon was back in London early that evening.

Friday's morning post brought a sheaf of brochures from Langarotti. Three European firms manufactured the kind of rubberized inflatable dinghies he wanted. An Italian firm seemed to be the best for Shannon's purpose. Of their largest model, an eighteen-footer, two were available for immediate delivery—one in a Marseilles shop, one in Cannes. A French manufacturer had a sixteen-foot craft, one of which was available in Nice.

Shannon wrote instructing Langarotti to buy those three models and to buy the three outboard engines for them also, but at separate shops. He told the Corsican he was transferring to his account the equivalent of £4500. He was to pay for these and with the balance buy a serviceable secondhand truck into which he could load the assault craft and the engines, delivering them himself to his freight agent in Toulon to be bonded for export. The whole consignment had to be ready for shipment by May 15. On the morning of that day Langarotti was to rendezvous with Shannon in Paris. He was to bring the truck with him.

Cat Shannon mailed this letter and one to the Kredietbank in Bruges, and then lay down. The strain of the past weeks was taking its toll. He felt flat and tired. Things seemed to be going according to plan, except for the ship. Semmler was still searching.

The telephone rang, and Shannon rolled off his bed to answer. It was Julie. He wished it had been Semmler.

"Are you going to be in town this weekend?" she asked.

"Yes. Should be."

"Good," said the girl. "Let's spend it doing things."

It must have been the tiredness. He was getting slow on the uptake. "What things?" he asked. She began talking in detail until he interrupted and told her to come around and prove it.

In the thrill of seeing her lover again Julie had forgotten the news she had for him. It was not until nearly midnight that she remembered. "Oh, by the way, I saw your name the other day. In a folder on my daddy's desk."

If she had meant to surprise him, she succeeded. Shannon sat up, gripping both her arms hard. The intensity of his stare frightened her. "You're hurting me," she said, on the verge of tears.

"What folder on your father's desk?"

"A folder," she sniffed. "I only wanted to help you."

His expression softened. "Tell me about it," he said. "All of it."

When she had finished she coiled her arms around his neck. "I love you, Mr. Cat. I only did it for that. Was it wrong?"

Shannon thought for a moment. She already knew too much, and there were only two ways of ensuring her silence. "Do you love me? Would you want anything bad to happen to me because of something you did or said?"

She stared deep into his face. This was like schoolgirl dreams. "Never. I'd never talk. No matter what they did to me!"

Shannon blinked. "Nobody's going to do anything to you. Just don't tell your father that you know me or went through his papers. You see, he employs me to gather information about mining prospects in Africa. If he learned we knew each other, he'd fire me. Then I'd have to find another job. Miles away from here."

That struck home. "I won't say anything," she promised.

"A couple of points," said Shannon. "You said you saw the title on the sheets with mineral prices on them. What was the title?"

She furrowed her brow. "What's that stuff they put in expensive fountain pens . . . platinum? Would that be it?"

"Platinum." Shannon looked pensive. "And the title on the outside of the folder. Do you know what that was?"

"Oh, I remember that," she said happily. "Like something out of a fairy tale. The Crystal Mountain."

Shannon sighed. "Go and make some coffee, there's a love."

He leaned against the head of the bed. "You cunning bastard," he breathed. "But it won't be that cheap, Sir James, not that cheap at all." Then he laughed into the darkness.

THAT Saturday night Benny Lambert was ambling home after an evening in his favorite café. He had been buying a lot of rounds for his cronies, celebrating with the money Shannon had paid him. He took no notice of the car that cruised slowly behind him. Nor did he think much of it when the car swept up to him as he came abreast of a vacant lot. By the time he did and started to protest, a giant figure had emerged from the car.

His protests were silenced when the figure slammed a fist into his solar plexus. Benny Lambert slumped to the ground. The big man drew a two-foot iron bar from his belt. The iron bar made a dull *whumph* as it crashed onto Lambert's kneecap, shattering it instantly. Lambert screamed shrilly, like a skewered rat, and fainted. He never felt the second kneecap being broken at all.

Twenty minutes later Thomard was phoning his employer.

Roux listened, and then he said, "Good. Now listen. Alain has just informed me that Shannon's hotel has reserved a room for Mr. Keith Brown the night of the fifteenth. You will be on standby, not far from the hotel, from noon of that day onward. Got it? You will wait until he comes out alone," continued Roux. "And then you will take him. For five thousand dollars."

WHEN the phone rang on Sunday morning, Shannon was lying on his back on the bed while Julie was getting breakfast.

"Carlo?" It was Semmler's voice. "I'm in Genoa. I have the boat. She's good. But there is someone else who would like to buy her. We may have to outbid them. Can you come out and see her?"

"I'll come tomorrow. What hotel are you staying at?"

Semmler told him.

He was grinning when he hung up. Julie came in with the coffee.

If Kurt was right, he could conclude the ship deal over the next twelve days and be in Paris on the fifteenth for his rendezvous with Langarotti.

CHAPTER ELEVEN

The port of Genoa was bathed in late afternoon sunshine when Kurt Semmler led Cat Shannon along the quays to where the motor vessel *Toscana* was moored. Rusty, old, and dowdy, she had the quality Shannon looked for—she was anonymous. There are thousands of such small freighters plying the coastal trade.

On board they found their way down into the crew quarters, where they were met by a muscular, hard-faced man in his mid-forties. "Carl Waldenberg, the first mate," said Semmler.

Waldenberg nodded abruptly and shook hands. "You have come to look her over, our old *Toscana?*" he asked in good if accented English. And without waiting for the Italian captain's return, the first mate showed them over the *Toscana.*

Shannon was interested in three things: the ability of the boat to accommodate twelve men in addition to the crew, the possibility of secreting a few crates below the flooring down in the bilges, and the trustworthiness of the engines. The German seaman answered Shannon's questions civilly and then offered his visitors beer, which they drank under a canvas awning behind the bridge. That was when the negotiations really started. The two Germans rattled away in their own language, until at last Waldenberg looked keenly at Shannon. "Possibly," he said in English.

Semmler explained. "Waldenberg is interested in why a man like yourself, who evidently does not know the charter cargo business, wants to buy a freighter."

Shannon nodded. "Fair enough. Kurt, I want a word with you."

They went aft and leaned over the rail. "How do you reckon this guy?" muttered Shannon.

"He's good," said Semmler. "The captain is also the owner of the boat, and he wants to retire. Waldenberg would like to be captain. He has his master's license, he knows this boat inside out, and he knows the sea. As to whether he would run a cargo with a risk attached, I think he would, if the price is right."

"Then the first thing is to buy the ship. He can decide whether to stay on later. If he quits, we can find another captain."

"No. For one thing, we would have to tell him enough beforehand for him to know roughly what the job is. If he quits then, it would be a breach of security."

"If he learns what the job is and then quits, he only goes out one way," said Shannon, and pointed down at the water.

"There's another point, Cat. The captain trusts him. If he's on our side, he can persuade the captain to let us have the *Toscana*."

The logic appealed to Shannon. He decided to make an ally of Waldenberg, if he could. They strolled back to the awning.

"I'll be straight with you, mister," he told the German. "If I buy the *Toscana*, she will not be used for carrying peanuts. I need a good skipper, and Kurt tells me you're good. So let's get down to basics. If I get this ship, I'll offer you the post of captain, with a six-month guaranteed salary at double your present one. Plus a five-thousand-dollar bonus for the first shipment."

Waldenberg grinned. "Mister, you just got yourself a captain."

"Fine," said Shannon. "First, we have to get the boat."

"No problem," said Waldenberg. "There's been an offer of twenty-five thousand pounds. How much would you spend?"

"I'll go to twenty-six thousand. Will the captain take that?"

"For that, with me as captain, he'll let you have her."

"When can I meet him? Tomorrow morning?" asked Shannon.

"Right. Tomorrow at ten, here on board."

They shook hands again, and the two mercenaries left.

VLAMINCK was at work in the garage he had rented, while the locked truck stood outside in the alley. Along one wall of the garage stood five large green oil drums. That they had once contained lubricating oil was plainly marked on each. From the first in the line Marc had cut a disk out of the bottom, and the barrel stood upended with the gaping hole showing upward.

From the truck Marc had taken two crates of Schmeissers, and the twenty submachine guns were almost ready to enter their new hiding place. Each weapon, with five magazines taped to it, had been carefully mummified in sticky masking tape. Thus wrapped, each had been slipped into a stout polyethylene envelope, which Marc had sucked empty of air, tied securely with twine, and sealed into a second, outer envelope. That, he reckoned, should keep each gun dry. Then with stout webbing he strapped the twenty packages into one bundle, which he put in the drum.

His next job was to reseal the barrel with a fresh tinplate disk. It took half an hour to fit and solder the new piece onto the drum head. When the solder had cooled he spray-painted the area with the exact original green of the oil drums. After the paint had dried he turned the drum right side up and, removing the screw cap, he poured in lubricating oil.

The thick emerald-green liquid filled up the air spaces between the sides of the drum and the bundle of submachine guns inside. When the drum was full to the brim, Marc took a pencil flashlight and scanned the surface of the liquid. Of what lay at the bottom of the drum there was not a sign.

Satisfied, Marc knew he could have the barrels ready by May 15.

Dr. Ivanov was incensed, not for the first time.

"The bureaucracy," he snapped at his wife across the breakfast table, "the sheer, incompetent, stultifying bureaucracy in this country is unbelievable."

"I'm sure you're right," his wife said soothingly.

"If the capitalist world knew how long it takes to get a couple of nuts and bolts in this country, they'd die laughing."

It had been weeks since the director had informed him that he was to lead a survey team to West Africa and that he should take charge of the details himself. It had meant forsaking a project that interested him deeply, but he had done it. His team was ready, his equipment prepared and crated down to the last water-purification tablet. With luck, he had thought, he could do the survey and be back with his samples before the brief Siberian summer was over. The letter in his hand told him it was not to be.

It came from his director personally, and stated that, because of the confidential nature of the survey, the Foreign Ministry had decided that the team could be best transported by a Soviet freighter heading past the coast of West Africa toward the Far East. When they had completed their survey they were to notify Ambassador Dobrovolsky, and a freighter heading back toward home would take the team and its crates of samples on board.

"The whole summer!" shouted Ivanov. "I'm going to miss the whole glorious summer. And it'll be the rainy season down there."

CAT Shannon and Kurt Semmler met the captain, gnarled old Alessandro Spinetti, at the ship the following morning. With Waldenberg translating, Captain Spinetti accepted the deal as Shannon had put it to the first mate the evening before. The rest of the crew, an engineer and a deckhand, might either stay on for six months or part company with severance pay. Shannon had privately decided to persuade the deckhand to leave, but to do all he could to keep the engineer, a surly Siberian who Waldenberg said could coax those engines to hell and back.

For tax reasons the captain had long ago formed a small private company, Spinetti Marittimo Shipping Company. It had one hundred shares, of which ninety-nine were his. The other belonged to his lawyer, a certain Signor Ponti. The sale of the ship MV *Toscana*, the company's only asset, was therefore linked to the sale of the shipping company, which suited Shannon perfectly. What did not suit him so well was that it took days of meetings with Ponti before the details were in order. It was Day Thirty-one of Shannon's calendar of one hundred days before Ponti could start drawing up the contracts. It would take time.

Meanwhile, Cat Shannon dispatched a series of letters from his Genoa hotel. The first was to Johann Schlinker to tell him the ship that would carry the ammunition from Spain would be the MV *Toscana*, owned by Spinetti Marittimo of Genoa. He would need from Schlinker details of where the arms shipment was supposed to be heading, so that the captain could draw up the appropriate manifest.

A similar letter went to Alan Baker, so that he could give the Yugoslav authorities the facts for the export license.

He next wrote to Mr. Stein, instructing him to prepare for a board meeting of Tyrone Holdings on May 14. Agenda: the purchase of Spinetti Marittimo for £26,000, and the issuance of a further 26,000 bearer shares to Mr. Keith Brown.

He dashed off a line to Vlaminck, telling him the pickup of the Ostend cargo would have to be delayed until May 20; another to Langarotti, putting back the Paris rendezvous to the nineteenth; and one to Dupree, asking him to fly to Marseilles.

Last, he wrote to Simon Endean asking that he transfer to his account, by the thirteenth, funds amounting to £26,000.

JANNI Dupree was content with life. Four bulky consignments of clothes and equipment were on their way to Toulon, and he had received a letter from Shannon telling him to get to Marseilles, check into a given hotel, and wait to be contacted. It was good to be going into action again.

On the evening of May 13, Langarotti was driving his truck into Toulon. He, too, was content with life. He had in the truck the last two outboard engines, both equipped with underwater exhaust attachments for silent running. He was delivering them to the warehouse. Already there were three black inflatable dinghies and the third engine; also four large crates from Dupree.

It was a pity he had had to move from his hotel. A chance encounter with an old underworld friend had forced him to clear out fast. He would have informed Shannon of his new address if he had known where Shannon was. It made no matter. In forty-eight hours, on the fifteenth, they would rendezvous in Paris.

AFTER the meeting in Luxembourg on May 14, Tyrone Holdings legally owned Spinetti Marittimo. Ponti dispatched by registered post the one hundred shares of stock to the office of Tyrone Holdings. The lawyer also accepted a package from Shannon and locked it in his vault. He took two sample signatures from Shannon, in the name of Keith Brown, to authenticate any letter from Shannon regarding the disposal of this package. Unknown to Ponti, the package contained the 26,994 bearer shares of Tyrone.

Shannon returned to Genoa. Semmler was told to get the *Toscana* ready for sea—overhauled, fueled, and supplied. "You have to be in Toulon by June first, at the latest. I'll be there with Marc, Jean-Baptiste, and Janni. I'll see you then. Good luck."

JEAN-BAPTISTE Langarotti was alive, in part at least, because of his ability to sense danger. On the fifteenth he sat, at the appointed hour, in the lounge of Shannon's Paris hotel. After two hours he inquired at the reception desk. There was no Mr. Brown from London in the hotel. Assuming Shannon had been delayed, the Corsican decided to make the rendezvous again the next day. So he was sitting in the lounge at the same hour on May 16. There was still no Shannon, but there was something else. Twice the same staff member of the hotel peeked into the room, then vanished. After another two hours he left the hotel again. As he walked down the street he had a glimpse of a man in a doorway showing a bizarre interest in a shopwindow. The window was full of women's corsets.

Over the next twenty-four hours the Corsican began to sniff the wind in the bars of Paris where mercenaries forgather. Each morning he went to the hotel, and on May 19 Shannon was there. He told his colleague over coffee in the lounge that he had bought a ship for their operation.

"No problems?" asked Langarotti. Shannon shook his head.

"But here in Paris we have a problem." Unable to strop his knife in a public place, the small Corsican sat with his hands idle in his lap. Shannon put down his coffee cup. If Langarotti called it a problem, it was trouble.

"Such as?" he asked softly.

"There's a contract on you. Expensive. Five thousand dollars." The two men sat in silence as Shannon considered the news.

"Do you know who placed it?" he asked finally.

"No. The word is, only a good hit man would take a contract on you, or a stupid one. But someone has taken it up."

Shannon cursed silently. Had there been a leak in the present operation? Could it be Manson himself, because of Julie? So far as he knew he hadn't offended anyone like the Mafia or the KGB. It must be someone with a private grudge. But who, for God's sake?

"Do they know I'm here in Paris?"

"I think so. And in this hotel. I was here four days ago—"

"Didn't you get my letter changing the meeting to today?"

"No. I had to move out of my Marseilles hotel a week ago."

"Oh? Go on."

"The second time I came here the place was being watched. It still is. I had asked for you as Brown, so I think the leak came from inside the hotel. Someone knows the Keith Brown name."

Shannon thought quickly. He would like to talk to the man who had placed the contract. The only person who could identify that man was the one who had taken the contract. He put this to the Corsican, who nodded somberly.

"Yes, *mon ami*. We have to lure the hit man out."

They talked, studied a street map, and Langarotti left.

During the day Langarotti parked his truck at a prearranged spot. In the afternoon Shannon asked the desk clerk Langarotti had described if a certain well-known restaurant was within walking distance.

"But certainly, monsieur. Fifteen minutes, maybe twenty."

Shannon thanked him and used the telephone at the desk to book a table in the name of Brown for ten o'clock that night.

At nine forty exactly, he left the hotel and turned up the street in the direction of the restaurant. The route he took was not direct. It led down small streets dimly lit. He dawdled, killing time until the hour of his table reservation was long past. Sometimes, in the quiet, he thought he could hear the soft slap of a moccasin behind him. Whoever was there, it was not Langarotti. The Corsican could move without disturbing the dust.

It was past eleven when he reached the alley he had been told was there. It had no lights at all, and the far end was blocked, making it a cul-de-sac. A truck with its rear doors open was parked there. Shannon walked toward the truck's gaping back and, when he reached it, turned. It was a relief to face the danger. Moving up the alley with his back to the entrance, he had felt the hairs on his neck prickling. If the psychology was wrong, he could be very dead. But it had been right. As long as Shannon kept to empty streets, the man behind him had stayed well back, hoping for just such an opportunity as now presented itself.

Shannon stood and stared at the hulking shadow that suddenly blocked the dim light from the entrance to the alley. He waited, hoping there would be no sound. The shadow moved softly toward him. Shannon could make out the right arm now, holding something forward. The figure stopped, raising his gun. He aimed. Then, straight-armed, he slowly lowered it again. It was almost as if he had changed his mind. Staring at Shannon, he slowly went down on all fours. A Colt .45 clattered on the stones. There was a light splashing sound, and finally the man's arms gave out and he slumped forward into the puddle of his own aortic blood.

Shannon hissed and Langarotti padded down the cobbles.

"I thought you'd waited too long," grunted Shannon.

"*Non*. Never. He could not have squeezed the trigger of that Colt at any time since you emerged from the hotel."

The rear of the truck was already laid with a large sheet of tough polyethylene over a canvas tarpaulin. Cord and bricks were stacked at the far end. The two men swung the body onto the sheet. Langarotti retrieved his knife and shut the doors.

"Do you know him?" Shannon asked as the truck started up.

"Yes. Raymond Thomard. Professional hit man, but not good enough for a big contractor. Works for Charles Roux."

Shannon swore quietly and viciously. Endean must have interviewed Roux, too. He had to be discouraged, and in a way that would keep him out of the Zangaro affair, once and for all. He spoke urgently for several seconds.

Langarotti nodded. "I like it. It should fix him."

CHARLES Roux was tired that day. Ever since Thomard had telephoned about Shannon walking to the restaurant, he had been waiting for word. There had been none by midnight. None by

sunrise. At midmorning, as Langarotti and Shannon were crossing into Belgium in their empty truck, Roux went down to check his mailbox.

The mailbox was some twelve inches tall, nine wide, and nine deep, screwed to the wall along with those of the other tenants. Roux used his key to unlock it; then he stood for about ten seconds without moving. His ruddy face turned a chalky gray. His stomach turned over. With an air of almost sleepy sadness, eyes half closed, lips gummed together, the head of Raymond Thomard gazed back at him from inside the mailbox. Roux closed the door, went back to his flat, and found the brandy. He needed a lot of it.

In Belgrade, Alan Baker emerged from the Yugoslav state arms office feeling well pleased. On receiving Shannon's down payment of $7200 and the Togolese end-user certificate, he had come here to a licensed arms dealer he knew. The man had accepted his argument that this small order might lead to more. From the state warehouse, they had selected the two mortar tubes and two bazookas, and crates of ammunition for both. The goods would be granted an export license and sent by army truck to a bonded warehouse at the port of Ploče northwest of Dubrovnik. No one had questioned the end-user certificate for Togo. Baker should realize a profit of $4000.

The *Toscana* was to take the shipment aboard at Ploče any time after June 10. With a light heart Baker flew to Hamburg.

Johann Schlinker was in Madrid that morning, May 20, with the end-user certificate he had bought from a corrupt diplomat at the Iraqi embassy in London for £1000. The Spanish formalities were more complicated than those Baker had found in Belgrade. Two applications were necessary, one to buy the hardware, the second to export it. The application to buy had been vetted by the three departments in Madrid that concern themselves with such matters, the Finance Ministry, the Foreign Ministry, and the Defense Ministry. It had taken eighteen days for the dossier to be approved. At this point the crates of ammunition were taken from the CETME factory and stored in an army warehouse on the outskirts of Madrid.

Schlinker had come to Madrid to present personally the application for an export license. He had been in possession of the full details of the *Toscana* on his arrival, and the seven-page questionnaire had been filled out. He expected no problems. The *Toscana* was a clean ship. She would berth in Valencia between June 16 and June 20, take the shipment on board, and, according to the application, proceed to Latakia, in Syria. From there the Iraqis would truck it to Baghdad. The export license should take no longer than two weeks, and then a movement order would be issued, permitting the crates to be taken from the warehouse and detailing an army officer to mount escort with ten soldiers as far as Valencia quayside.

Schlinker left for Hamburg, satisfied that the crates would be in Valencia in time for the arrival of the *Toscana*.

IN THE small South Belgian town of Dinant, Shannon and Langarotti were shaken from their slumbers shortly after dark by Marc Vlaminck. Both were stretched out in the back of the empty French truck. "Time to be going," said the Belgian.

"I thought you said just before sunrise," Shannon grumbled.

"That's when we go over," said Marc. "But we ought to get these trucks out of town before they become too noticeable. We can park by the roadside for the rest of the night."

There is no great technical difficulty in running an illegal consignment across the Belgian-French border in either direction. The border sprawls for miles and is crossed by scores of side roads and tracks through the forest. By no means all of them are manned. Both governments seek to establish some kind of control, using flying customs squads who pick a side road at random and set up a border post. If the flying customs on either side happen to be posted on one of the unmanned roads for the day, every vehicle going through gets a check. The smugglers of French champagne see no reason why this drink, connected with mirth, should receive the attentions of the very unhumorous Belgian import duty. They therefore have developed a system for finding a road where there is definitely no customs post set up.

As a bar owner, Marc Vlaminck knew about this. It is called the champagne run and requires two vehicles. Shortly before dawn Marc got out his maps and briefed Shannon and Langarotti on the drill. Their truck, being empty and clean, would go through on the route Marc indicated. Marc, with the cargo, was to wait exactly twenty minutes one mile inside the border. If either the Belgian or French customs men had set up a flying barricade, Langarotti would stop to be searched, then, being clean, proceed south to the main road. There he'd double back and return via the fixed customs post to Belgium. If the flying customs were in operation, the first truck could not turn back up the road within twenty minutes. The loaded vehicle—in this case, Marc's—would have taken warning and returned to Dinant to try another day.

"The border is down there." Marc pointed. "If you're not back in twenty minutes, I'll meet you at the café in Dinant."

Langarotti nodded and let in the clutch. At exactly one mile Shannon spotted a small booth. Empty. The French border was also unmanned. They had been gone five minutes. They checked around two more corners, but no one was in sight.

"Turn her around," snapped Shannon. "*Allez.*" Now time was precious.

Langarotti was off to the main road like a cork from a bottle of the best champagne. When they came in sight of Marc's gun-laden truck, Langarotti flashed his lights. A second later Marc was racing toward France. He could be through the danger area within four minutes. If any customs men hove in sight in those vital minutes, he would just have to hope the oil barrels stood up to a thorough check.

There were no officials there, even on the second run. Langarotti followed Marc through back roads until he finally emerged onto a sizable road, where a signpost pointed ahead with the word REIMS. They allowed themselves a cheer.

They did the changeover in a parking lot next to a truckers' café south of Soissons. The two trucks, open-doored, were backed up tight against each other. The big Belgian eased the five heavy oil barrels into the French truck. Langarotti should have no trouble.

The truck was legally his. His cargo would not be searched.

Marc's truck, being old and slow, was soon driven into a gravel pit and abandoned, its license plates thrown into a stream. After that the three mercenaries proceeded together. Just south of Paris they dropped Shannon off for Orly airport.

"The *Toscana* is due in by June first at the latest," Shannon said in parting. "I'll be with you before then. Good luck."

He was home in St. John's Wood by sundown. Of his hundred days he had used up forty-six.

WHEN Endean came to the flat two days later, it took Shannon an hour to explain all that had happened since they last met.

"I have to return to France within five days and supervise the loading of the first section of the cargo onto the *Toscana*," said Shannon. "Everything about the shipment is legal except what's in those oil barrels. They will have to go aboard as ship's stores. The quantity is rather excessive, but that shouldn't be a problem."

"And if it is? If Toulon customs examines those barrels?"

"We're busted," said Shannon simply. "The ship impounded. The exporter arrested. The operation wrecked."

"Bloody expensively," said Endean. "You could have bought the guns legally, through Spain."

"I could," Shannon conceded, "but if I'd bought the guns and the ammo together, it would have looked like a special order to outfit one company of men. Which Madrid might have turned down. Or I could have bought the guns in Spain and the ammo in the 'black.' But smuggling ammo is riskier. Either way, there's risk. And it's me and my men who go down, not you. You're protected."

"I still don't like it," snapped Endean.

"What's the matter?" Shannon mocked. "Losing your nerve?"

"No."

"So cool it. All you have to lose is a bit of money."

Endean was on the verge of telling Shannon just how much he and his employer stood to lose, but thought better of it.

They talked finance for another hour. Shannon explained why he wanted the balance of the agreed budget now. "Also," he added, "I want the second half of my salary in my Swiss account before the weekend, and the rest transferred to Bruges."

"Why now?" asked Endean.

"Because the risks of arrest start next week, and I won't return to London after that. The ship sails for Brindisi while I arrange the pickup of the Yugoslav arms. Then Valencia and the Spanish ammo, and we head for the target. If I'm ahead of schedule, we'll kill time safely at sea. From the moment that ship has hardware on board, I want her in port as little as possible."

Endean digested the argument. It seemed sound. The next day he called to say that both transfers had been authorized.

Shannon booked a ticket to Brussels for May 26.

He spent that night and the next with Julie, and then he packed his bags, mailed the flat keys to the estate agents, and left. Julie drove him to the airport.

"When are you coming back?" she asked him as they stood outside the Departing Passengers Only entrance.

"I won't be coming back," he said, and gave her a kiss.

"You will come back. You must."

"I won't be," he said quietly. "Find someone else, Julie."

She began to sniffle. "I don't want anybody else. I love you. You've got another woman, that's what it is—"

"There's no other woman," he said, stroking her hair. There would be, Shannon knew, no other woman in his arms. Just a gun, the cool comforting caress of the blued steel against his chest at night. She was still crying when he kissed her at the gate.

As the jet headed for Brussels a passenger complained to the stewardess that someone was whistling a monotonous little tune.

It took Cat Shannon two hours in Bruges to close his account. He took half of the money in two certified bank checks and the rest in traveler's checks.

The next morning he flew to Marseilles and took a taxi to the hotel on the outskirts where Langarotti had once lived under the name of Lavallon, and where Janni Dupree was now waiting. Shannon and Dupree drove to Toulon together. It was the end of Day Fifty-two, and the French naval port was bathed in sunshine.

THE RENDEZVOUS spot was the pavement in front of the shipping agent's office, and here Shannon and Dupree met Vlaminck and Langarotti on the dot of nine a.m. The *Toscana* should now be steaming along the coast with Semmler aboard. At Shannon's suggestion Langarotti telephoned the harbor master's office and ascertained that the *Toscana* was due in the following morning and that her berth was reserved.

There was nothing more to do that day, so they spent the time swimming and soaking up the sunshine. Shannon could not relax. If any inspector insisted on peering deep into those oil barrels, someone would spend months, maybe years, sweating in Les Baumettes, the great forbidding fortress prison he had passed between Marseilles and Toulon. The waiting was always the worst.

The *Toscana* slipped quietly into her berth on schedule. From his seat on a mooring post a hundred and fifty feet away Shannon could see Semmler and Waldenberg moving about the decks. There was no sign of the engineer, but two other figures were on deck, making fast and coiling lines. Two new crewmen recruited by Waldenberg, no doubt.

A Renault drew up to the gangway and a rotund Frenchman emerged. The representative of Agence Maritime Duphot. Soon Waldenberg joined him and they walked over to the customs shed. In an hour they came out and the shipping agent drove off.

Shannon waited thirty minutes; then he strolled up the gangway onto the *Toscana*. Semmler beckoned him into the cabin. "All smooth and easy so far," he said. "I had a complete engine service done and bought an unnecessarily large number of blankets and foam-rubber mattresses. No one asked any questions. The captain thinks we are going to run immigrants into Britain."

"What about the engine-lubricating oil?"

"Waldenberg wanted to order it in Genoa, but I vetoed that and said we would get it here in Toulon."

"Fine," said Shannon. "Tell him you've ordered it. Then when the fuel-company truck arrives he'll be expecting it. Langarotti will be driving. Make sure no one bangs those barrels about, or the quay could be waist-deep in Schmeissers."

"When do the men come aboard?"

"Tonight after dark. Just Marc and Janni. Jean-Baptiste has one more job to do. When can you sail?"

"Anytime. Tonight. Incidentally, where are we going?"

"Brindisi. Know it?"

"Sure I know it. What do we pick up there?"

"Nothing. I'll be in Germany. Wait for my telegram telling you your next destination and when to arrive. Then get a local agent to cable the Yugoslav port in question and reserve a berth."

Semmler said, "You know, Waldenberg will have to realize what we are taking on board in Yugoslavia. He accepts the boats and the engines, the walkie-talkies, and the clothing as quite normal, but arms are something else again."

"I know," said Shannon. "It will cost a bit of money. But you and Marc and Janni and I will all be on board. He'll go along. And by then we can tell him what's in the oil drums. What are the two new crewmen like?"

"Italians. Hard boys, but good. I think they're both wanted for something. They were so pleased to get on board."

In midafternoon two trucks from Agence Maritime Duphot, accompanied by the same man who had appeared that morning, rolled to a stop by the *Toscana*. A French customs officer, clipboard in hand, emerged from the customhouse and ticked off the crates as they were swung aboard. He didn't even look inside them. He knew the agency well. When he stamped the cargo manifest, Waldenberg said something in German, which Semmler translated, explaining to the agent that Waldenberg needed lubricating oil for his engines. "Five drums," he said.

"That's a lot," said the agent.

Semmler laughed. "This old tub burns up the oil."

"When do you need it?" asked the agent.

"Five o'clock this afternoon be all right?" asked Semmler.

"Make it six," said the agent, and departed.

At five o'clock Semmler went to a phone on the waterfront, rang the agency, and canceled the order. The skipper, he said, had discovered a full barrel in the stores locker.

At six a truck drove along the quay and stopped opposite the *Toscana*. It was driven by Jean-Baptiste Langarotti in a bright green uniform with the name of the oil company on it. Opening the back of the truck, he carefully rolled five large oil drums down a plank. From the customhouse the officer peered out.

Waldenberg caught his eye and waved. He pointed to the barrels and back to his ship. "Okay?" he called.

The customs officer nodded and withdrew. At Waldenberg's orders the two crewmen slipped cradles under the barrels and one by one winched them aboard. They slid out of sight into the hold of the *Toscana*, and soon the hatch was clamped back in place.

Langarotti had long since left in his truck. From a distance Shannon had watched the loading with bated breath. When it was over, Semmler joined him, grinning. "I told you. No problems."

Shannon grinned back with relief. "Now you get back there and guard that cargo like a mother hen!"

Just after midnight Janni Dupree and Marc Vlaminck quietly boarded the boat. At five, watched from the quay by Shannon and Langarotti, the *Toscana* slipped back to the sea.

Langarotti ran Shannon to the airport to catch a midmorning flight to Hamburg. Over breakfast Shannon had given the Corsican his last set of instructions and money to carry them out.

"I'd prefer to be going with you," Jean-Baptiste said.

"I know," said Shannon. "But I need someone reliable to do this. And you have the added advantage of being French. Janni couldn't get in with a South African passport. I need Marc to intimidate the crew if they cut up, and Semmler to check on Waldenberg. So it depends on you to do it right, Jean-Baptiste. It can all fall through if we get there and have no backup force. I'll see you in a month."

CHAPTER TWELVE

"You can pick up the mortars and bazookas any time after June tenth," Alan Baker told Shannon, "at a small port called Ploče, halfway between Split and Dubrovnik."

"How small?"

"Half a dozen wharves and two large warehouses. Very discreet. The customs unit is probably only one man. If he gets his present, he'll see everything on board within a few hours."

"Okay, Ploče. On June eleventh. Any problems at your end?"

Baker shifted slightly. "One," he said. "The price. I know I quoted you fixed prices, totaling fourteen thousand, four hundred dollars. But I had to engage a Yugoslav partner. At least, that's what he is called. He's the brother-in-law of the official in the Trade Ministry. They've wised up to kickbacks."

"So?" asked Shannon.

"So he has to get a fee for getting the paperwork through the Belgrade office. I supposed it was worth it to you to have the shipment ready on time and no bureaucratic hang-ups."

"How much extra will he cost?"

"A thousand pounds sterling. In dollars. Cash, not checks."

Shannon thought it over. It might be the truth, or it might not. If it was, refusing to pay would force Baker to pay out of his own cut. That would so reduce his margin as to make him cease caring whether the deal went through. And Shannon still needed him.

"All right," he said. "Who is this partner?"

"Fellow called Ziljak. He's out there now, getting the shipment to Ploče and into the warehouse. Then when the ship comes in he'll get the stuff through customs and onto the boat."

"All right. I'll pay him in dollars. But you get yours in checks."

"Fine by me," said Baker. "When do you want to go?"

"Day after tomorrow," Shannon said. "We'll fly to Dubrovnik and have a week in the sun. I could do with a rest. Or you can join me on the eighth or ninth, but not a day later. We can motor up to Ploče on the tenth. I'll have the *Toscana* come in that night."

"I'll join you in a week," said Baker. "I have work to do."

"If you don't turn up," said Shannon, "I'll come looking."

JOHANN Schlinker was as confident as Baker that he could fulfill his arms deal. "The port is likely to be Valencia, though it has yet to be fixed," he told Shannon. "Madrid tells me that the loading will have to take place between the sixteenth and twentieth of June."

"I'd prefer the twentieth," said Shannon. "The *Toscana* should berth on the night of the nineteenth and load in the morning."

"I'll tell my Madrid partner. There should be no problem."

"There must be no problem," growled Shannon. "The ship has already been delayed once, and I have no margin of time."

It was not true, but he wanted Schlinker to believe it was true. "I also want to board the ship at Valencia."

"That's difficult," said Schlinker. "The port is sealed off. Entry is by authority only. You'd have to go through passport control."

"Could the captain engage another crewman locally?"

Schlinker thought it over. "If the captain informed the agent that he had permitted a man to leave the vessel at the last port to fly home for his mother's funeral, and that he would be rejoining the vessel at Valencia, I suppose there would be no objection. But you would need a merchant seaman's card."

"Okay. I can fix that."

Schlinker consulted his diary. "I'll be in Madrid on the nineteenth and twentieth on other business. I shall be at the Mindanao Hotel if you want to contact me. If loading is for the twentieth, the chances are an army convoy will run the shipment down to the coast during the night of the nineteenth. If you *are* going to board the ship, you should do so before the military convoy arrives."

"I could be in Madrid on the nineteenth," said Shannon. "Then I could check with you that the convoy had indeed left on time. By driving fast, I could be in Valencia well ahead of it."

"That is up to you," said Schlinker. "I will have my agents arrange the freighting, transportation, and loading. That is what I contracted to do. If there is risk attached to your boarding the vessel, that is your affair. I can only point out that ships carrying arms are subject to scrutiny. They must leave Spanish waters six hours after loading. And the cargo manifest must be in perfect order."

"It will be. I'll see you in Madrid on the nineteenth."

Shannon wrote to Semmler, in care of the port office in Brindisi. He told him to be in the port of Ploče, Yugoslavia, on June 10. He also told him to acquire a merchant seaman's card for a deckhand by the name of Keith Brown, stamped and up to date.

The last letter he posted before leaving Hamburg was to Simon Endean, making a rendezvous in Rome on June 16, to which he should bring certain maritime charts.

CAT Shannon spent a week in Dubrovnik behaving like any other tourist. When Alan Baker arrived, Shannon looked fit and tanned, though thinner. Over drinks on the hotel terrace they exchanged news. The *Toscana* was on schedule, and so was Baker's partner, Ziljak. The crates were in the Ploče warehouse, under guard. Shannon felt suddenly optimistic.

The following morning they hired a taxi and drove to Ploče. They were established in a hotel by lunchtime and waited until the port office opened again at four. As they approached the office a small and battered Volkswagen squealed to a halt a few yards away and hooted noisily. Shannon froze. His first instinct said trouble. The man who climbed out of the small car might be a policeman. But Shannon glanced at Baker and saw his shoulders sag with relief.

"Ziljak," Baker muttered, and went to meet the Yugoslav. The latter was a big, shaggy man, and he embraced Baker with both arms. Introduced by Baker, he shook hands with Shannon, muttering something in what Shannon took to be Serbo-Croatian. Baker and Ziljak communicated in German.

Ziljak roused the head of the customs office, and they were taken off to the warehouse. The customs man jabbered a few words at the guard, and in a corner of the building they found the crates. There were thirteen, not marked with any description of contents, but stenciled with serial numbers and the word *Toscana*. Ziljak and the customs chief babbled away. Then Ziljak said something in his halting German to Baker. Baker replied, and Ziljak translated for the customs man, who smiled and departed.

"What was all that about?" asked Shannon.

"The customs man just asked if there was a little present in it for him," explained Baker. "Ziljak said yes, if the paperwork was kept trouble-free and the ship loaded on time."

Shannon had already given Baker the first half of Ziljak's bonus for helping the deal go through, and Baker drew the Yugoslav to one side to give it to him. The man's all-embracing bonhomie became even more embracing, and they adjourned to the hotel to celebrate with a little slivovitz. "A little" was Baker's word, but happy Yugoslavs never drink a little of the fiery plum liquor. The sun went down and the Adriatic evening slipped through the streets, and Baker was hard put to it to translate as the exuberant Ziljak relived his years of hunting and hiding in the Bosnian hills with Tito's partisans.

Shannon asked if he was now a committed Communist.

"*Guter Kommunist,*" Ziljak exclaimed, pointing at himself. Then he ruined the effect with a broad wink and a roar of laughter as he tossed another slivovitz down the hatch. Shannon laughed, too, and wished the giant were coming along to Zangaro. Unsteadily they wandered back to the quay to watch the *Toscana* come in.

After Baker had headed for the hotel with Ziljak, Shannon slipped up the gangplank and into the captain's tiny cabin. Semmler brought Waldenberg in and they locked the door. Carefully, Shannon told Waldenberg what the *Toscana* was about to take on board. The German captain kept his face expressionless.

"I never carried arms before," he said when Shannon had finished. "You say this cargo is legal. How legal?"

"Perfectly legal," said Shannon. "It's a perfectly legal shipment under the laws of Yugoslavia."

"And the laws of the country it's going to?" asked Waldenberg.

"The *Toscana* never enters the waters of the country where these arms are to be used," said Shannon. "After Ploče, there are two more ports of call. In each case only to take on cargoes. You know ships are never searched when they arrive in port to take on cargo unless the authorities have been tipped off."

"It has happened, all the same," said Waldenberg. "And if these things are discovered, the ship gets impounded and I get imprisoned. I didn't bargain on arms. With the Black September and the IRA around, everyone's looking for arms."

"You bargained for illegal immigrants to Britain."

"They're not illegal until their feet touch British soil," the captain pointed out. "And the *Toscana* would be outside territorial waters. They could go inshore in fast boats. Arms are different. They are illegal on this ship if the manifest says there aren't any. Why not put it on the manifest?"

"Because if there are arms already on board, the Spanish authorities will not allow the ship to stay in any Spanish port."

"Supposing the Spanish police search the boat?"

"They won't. But if they do, the crates will be belowdecks."

"And if the police find them there, we'd be inside forever," Waldenberg said. "They'd think we were bringing the stuff to the Basques."

The talk went on till three in the morning and cost Shannon £5000, half before, half after Valencia.

"You'll take care of the crew?" Shannon asked.

"I'll take care of the crew," said Waldenberg with finality.

Back in his hotel, Shannon paid Baker the third quarter of his bill for the arms and tried to get some sleep. The sweat rolled off him, and he imagined the *Toscana* lying in the port, the arms in the customs shed, and prayed there would be no problems. He was so close now, just three short steps from the point where no one could stop him, whatever was tried.

The loading started at seven. By nine it was over.

As he watched the *Toscana* chugging out of the port, Shannon slipped Baker and Ziljak the rest of their fees. Unbeknown to either, he had had Vlaminck prise up the lids on five of the crates, taken at random, to verify the contents. Just in case the crates contained only scrap iron. It has been known to happen, quite frequently, in the arms world.

On Shannon's calendar of a hundred days, given him by Sir James Manson to bring off his coup, it was Day Sixty-seven.

No sooner was the *Toscana* out to sea than Captain Waldenberg ordered the three other crewmen into his cabin for a quiet interview. Had they refused to continue to serve, there would have been some unfortunate accidents aboard the *Toscana*. Few places are quite as well suited for a complete disappearing act as a ship on a dark night at sea. In any case, no one objected, especially when Waldenberg dispensed a thousand pounds.

With this done, the new crates were broken open and the contents stowed deep in the bilges, below the floor of the hold. The planks were replaced and covered with the innocent cargo of clothing, dinghies, and outboard engines.

Then Semmler told Waldenberg he had better put the oil drums in the back of the stores locker, and why. This time Waldenberg lost his temper and used some expressions that could best be described as regrettable. But in a while Semmler calmed him down. They sat having beer as the *Toscana* plowed her way south.

Finally Waldenberg began to laugh. "Schmeissers," he said. "Bloody Schmeissers. *Mensch,* it's a long time since they've been heard in the world."

"Well, they're going to be heard again," said Semmler.

Waldenberg looked wistful. "You know," he said at length, "I wish I was going ashore with you."

CHAPTER THIRTEEN

WHEN Shannon arrived, Simon Endean was reading a copy of *The Times,* bought that morning in London before he left for Rome. The lounge of the Excelsior was almost empty, for most of those taking late morning coffee were on the outside terrace watching the chaotic traffic of Rome inch past and trying to make themselves heard above the noise.

Shannon eased himself into a chair beside the man from London.

Endean eyed him. "You've been out of touch a long time."

"It takes time to get a ship from Toulon to Yugoslavia," said Shannon. "By the way, did you bring the charts?"

"Of course." Endean pointed to his bulging briefcase. On receiving Shannon's letter, he had acquired inshore charts for the entire African coast from Casablanca to Cape Town. "Why the hell do you need so many?" he asked in annoyance.

"Security," said Shannon briefly. "If the ship were boarded and searched in port, one single chart showing the ship's destination would be a giveaway. As it is, no one, including the captain and crew, can discover which section of the coast really interests me. Do you have the slides as well?"

"Yes."

Another of Endean's jobs had been to get slides made of the photographs Shannon had taken in Zangaro, and of the maps and sketches he had made of Clarence and the shoreline.

Shannon himself had already sent a slide projector, bought duty-free at London airport, to the *Toscana* in Toulon.

Endean listened in silence, making notes for Manson, as Shannon brought him up to date and went on to tell him what was planned for the coming days: the loading of the 9-mm. ammunition in Valencia, and then departure for the target. He made no mention of the fact that one of his men was already in Africa.

"Now I need to know from you," he told Endean, "what happens after the attack. We can't, as I've said, hold on for long before a new regime takes over and broadcasts news of the coup."

"That," said Endean smoothly, "is the whole point of the exercise." From his briefcase he withdrew three sheets of paper. "These are your instructions, starting the moment you have possession of the palace. Read, memorize, and destroy these sheets before we part company here."

Shannon ran his eyes quickly over the first page. There were few surprises. He had already guessed that Manson's new man had to be Colonel Bobi. The rest of the plan was simple, from his point of view. He glanced up at Endean. "Where will you be?"

"A hundred miles north of you," said Endean.

Meaning, Shannon knew, in the capital of the republic north of Zangaro. "Are you sure you'll pick up my message?" he asked.

"I shall have the best portable radio set they make. It will pick up anything within range of your ship's radio."

"Let's get one thing clear," Shannon said. "I'll broadcast on the stated frequency at the agreed hours from the *Toscana*, and she'll be somewhere off the coast, probably at five or six miles. But if you don't hear me, if there's too much static, I can't be responsible for that."

"The frequency has been tested," said Endean. "From the *Toscana's* radio it must be picked up by my set at a hundred miles. If you repeat for thirty minutes, I have to hear it."

"All right," said Shannon. "One last thing. The news of what has happened at Clarence should not have reached the Zangaran border post. That means it will be manned by Vindu. It's your business to get past them. Nearer Clarence, there may be scattered Vindu on the roads, running for the bush but still dangerous. Supposing you don't get through?"

"We'll get through," said Endean. "We'll have help."

Shannon supposed, rightly, that this would be provided by the small mining operation ManCon had going in the neighboring republic. For a company executive they could provide a jeep and maybe a couple of hunting rifles. For the first time he considered that Endean might have some guts to back up his nastiness.

Shannon read the instruction sheets and memorized the code words and the radio frequency he needed and, with Endean, burned the sheets in the men's room. Then they parted. There was nothing else to say.

FIVE floors above the streets of Madrid, Colonel Antonio Almela, head of the exporting office of the Spanish Army Ministry (Foreign Arms Sales), perused the file of papers in front of him. He was a simple man whose loyalties were uncompromising. His fidelity was to his beloved Spain, and he was trusted, therefore, with one of the jobs that is unmentionable and top secret. No Spaniard ever learns that Spain exports arms to almost all comers. Almela could be counted on to grant, or refuse, export licenses and keep his mouth shut.

The file in front of him had been in his hands for four weeks and had been thoroughly checked out. The top paper was an application for a movement order to shift crates from Madrid to Valencia and export them on the MV *Toscana*. The export license carried his own signature.

Then he noticed something and glanced up at the civil servant in front of him. "Why the change of port?" he asked.

"Colonel, it is simply that there is no berth available in Valencia for two weeks. The port is crowded to capacity."

Colonel Almela grunted. The explanation was plausible. In the summer months Valencia was always crowded. But he did not like changes. Nor did he like this order. It was too small. And he did not trust Herr Schlinker. But there was nothing wrong with any of the papers, including the end-user certificate. If only he could find one discrepancy. But everything was clean. Finally the colonel scrawled his signature on the movement order.

"All right," he growled. "They go to Castellón, not Valencia."

"WE'VE had to change the port of embarkation to Castellón," said Schlinker two nights later. "There was no choice. Valencia was full up for weeks. As soon as the *Toscana* checks in by radio she will be advised of the change."

Cat Shannon was sitting in the German arms dealer's room in the Mindanao Hotel. "Where's Castellón?" he asked.

"Forty miles up the coast. Small. Better for you."

"What about my going aboard?"

"Well, I've informed the cargo agent that a seaman named Keith Brown is due to rejoin the *Toscana*. How are your papers?"

"Fine," said Shannon. "They're all in order."

"The agent in Castellón is Senor Moscar. The truck will set off from Madrid with an escort at midnight tomorrow, timing its arrival at Castellón harbor gates at six a.m., the hour they open. I have given the transport manager instructions to phone me here when the convoy actually departs."

That afternoon Shannon hired a powerful Mercedes.

At half past ten the following evening he was back in the Mindanao with Schlinker, and they waited for the telephone call. Both men were nervous, as men must be when a carefully laid plan rests in the hands of others. Schlinker knew that if anything went wrong, a complete investigation into his end-user certificate could be ordered, and that must include a check with the Interior

Ministry in Baghdad. If he were exposed, all his lucrative deals with Madrid would be forfeit.

Midnight came. Half past midnight. Shannon paced the room, snarling his frustration at the fat German. At twelve forty the phone rang. Schlinker leaped at it.

"What is it?" snapped Shannon.

Schlinker waved his hand for silence. Finally he grinned and put the phone down. But Shannon was gone.

The Mercedes was more than a match for the convoy. Shannon kept a careful eye open as he sped past hundreds of trucks roaring toward the coast. West of Valencia his lights picked up the army jeeps holding station on a covered eight-ton truck, and as he swept by he noted the name on the truck's side. It was the name of the trucking company Schlinker had given him.

He drove into Castellón just after four. As usual with Mediterranean ports, there are three separate harbors, one for freighters, one for pleasure craft, and one for fishing vessels. The commercial port of Castellón is ringed by a chain link fence, its gates manned day and night by armed sentries. The gates were locked at this hour, and the sentry was dozing in his box, but Shannon peered through the fence and with a surge of relief spotted the *Toscana* already berthed.

At six o'clock he was back at the gate where the jeeps and the truck were now parked. At ten after six a civilian car arrived and a small, dapper Spaniard climbed out.

Shannon approached him. "Senor Moscar?"

"*Sí.*"

"My name's Brown. I've got to join my ship here."

The Spaniard puckered his brows.

"Brown," insisted Shannon. "*Toscana.*"

"*Ah, sí. El marinero.* Come, please."

The gate had been opened, and Moscar showed his pass. He babbled at the guard, pointing at Shannon. Cat's passport and merchant seaman's card were examined. Then he followed Moscar to the customs office. An hour later he was on board the *Toscana.*

The search started at nine. There was no warning. The captain's manifest had been presented and checked out. The army escort captain consulted with two customs officers. Then the latter came aboard. Moscar followed. They checked the cargo to make sure it was what the manifest said and no more. They looked in the stores locker, gazed at the tangle of chains, oil drums, and paint cans, and closed the door. It all took an hour. The main thing that interested them was why Captain Waldenberg needed seven men on such a small ship. It was explained that Dupree and Vlaminck were company employees who had missed their ship in Brindisi and were being dropped off at Malta. Asked for a name, Waldenberg gave the name of a ship he had seen in Brindisi harbor. The customs men left the ship. Twenty minutes later, loading began.

At half past noon the *Toscana* slipped out of Castellón harbor and turned her helm south to Cape San Antonio. Cat Shannon, feeling sick now that it was all over, was leaning against the after rail when Waldenberg came up behind him. "That's the last stop?" he asked.

"The last where we have to open our hatches," said Shannon. "We have to pick up some men on the coast of Africa, but they'll come out by launch. Deck-cargo native workers. At least, that's what they'll be shipped as."

"I've got no charts beyond Gibraltar," objected Waldenberg.

Shannon reached into his Windbreaker and pulled out a sheaf of them. "These will get us to Freetown, Sierra Leone. That's where we pick up the men. They'll come out by launch. On July second."

The captain left to plot his course, and Shannon was alone with the sea gulls. Anyone listening would have heard another sound amid their screaming, the sound of a man whistling "Spanish Harlem."

FAR away to the north the motor vessel *Komarov* was easing her way out of the harbor of Archangel.

In the stern Dr. Ivanov and one of his technicians leaned over the rail beneath the hammer-and-sickle flag.

"Comrade Doctor," the younger man began. "Have you been to Africa before?"

"To Ghana, yes."

"What is it like?"

"Full of jungle, swamps, mosquitoes, snakes, and people who don't understand a damn thing you say."

"The captain told me that we should arrive at Clarence in twenty-two days. That will be their Independence Day."

"Bully for them," said Ivanov, and walked away.

PAST Cape Spartel, nosing her way from the Mediterranean into the Atlantic, the MV *Toscana* radioed a ship-to-shore telegram to Gibraltar for onpassing to Mr. Walter Harris in London. It said simply: PLEASED ANNOUNCE YOUR BROTHER COMPLETELY RECOVERED. This meant the *Toscana* was on her way and on schedule.

"Good," said Sir James when Endean broke the news. "How much time does Shannon have to reach target?"

"Twenty-two days. He's ahead of schedule."

"Will he strike early?"

"No, sir. Strike Day is still Day One Hundred."

"All right. You fly down there and get our new employee, Colonel Bobi, settled into this place next to Zangaro. When you receive Shannon's signal that he is going in for the attack, break the news to Bobi. Then get him to sign that mining concession as President Bobi, date it one month later, and send me three copies in three different envelopes. Keep Bobi virtually under lock and key until Shannon's second signal to say he has succeeded. Then in you go. By the way, that bodyguard you are taking with you. Is he ready?"

"For the kind of money he's getting, good and ready."

"Shannon could prove troublesome, you know."

Endean grinned. "I can handle him. Like all mercenaries, he's got his price."

ON THE voyage from Spain, Shannon had insisted that the cargo remain untouched in case of a search at Freetown. Only one job had he allowed to be done. The bundles of knapsacks Dupree had bought in London were opened and transformed into backpacks fitted with narrow pouches, each capable of taking one bazooka rocket. The smaller knapsacks had been altered to carry twenty mortar bombs apiece.

The *Toscana* announced her presence, from six miles offshore, to the harbor master's office at Freetown, and was given permission to anchor in the bay. Having no cargo to load or unload, she did not need the quay. She had only come to take on deck crew. Since coastal steamers regularly do this, it caused no surprise.

When the anchor cable rattled down, Shannon's eyes scanned the waterfront for the hotel where, if anywhere, Langarotti would be waiting.

As Shannon watched, a small pinnace came out from the custom-house, with a uniformed man standing in the back. Shannon met him, shook hands profusely, and led him to the captain's cabin. Three bottles of whisky and two cartons of cigarettes were waiting. The officer sighed gustily with pleasure and cast an incurious eye over the new manifest, which said the *Toscana* had picked up machine parts and supplies at Brindisi for an oil-drilling company on the Cameroon coast. He stamped it and an hour later was gone.

It wasn't until just after six that Shannon saw the longshore boat moving away from the beach. The two Freetown men who ran passengers out to waiting vessels heaved at their oars. Aft sat seven other Africans, clutching bundles. In the prow sat a lone European. As the craft swung expertly into the side of the *Toscana*, Jean-Baptiste Langarotti came nimbly up the ladder that hung to the water.

The seven Africans followed. Six of them young, one a dignified older man. Although it was indiscreet to do so in sight of land, Vlaminck, Dupree, and Semmler clapped the grinning young Africans on the back, and Shannon signed to the captain to take the *Toscana* back to sea.

Later, as the *Toscana* rolled on to the south, Shannon introduced his recruits to a puzzled Waldenberg. First there was Patrick, then Johnny, Jinja (nicknamed "Ginger"), Sunday, Bartholomew, and Timothy. Each of them had been personally trained by one of the mercenaries; each of them had been tried and tested in battle many times and would stick it out however hard the fight. And each of them was loyal to his leader. The seventh, the older man, Shannon introduced as Dr. Okoye. He, too, was loyal to his leader and his people.

"How are things at home?" Shannon asked him.

Dr. Okoye shook his head sadly. "Not well."

"Tomorrow we start preparing," Shannon told him.

PART THREE

The Big Killing

CHAPTER FOURTEEN

FOR the remainder of the sea voyage Cat Shannon worked his men without pause. Only the man he called "Doctor" was exempt. The rest were divided into parties, each with separate jobs.

Vlaminck and Semmler broke open the five oil drums and plucked out the Schmeissers. The six African soldiers helped unwrap the submachine guns and wipe them clean of grease, thereby becoming thoroughly familiar with their operating mechanisms. Breaking open the boxes of 9-mm. ammunition, the eight of them sat on the deck slotting shells into magazines, until the first fifteen hundred rounds had gone into the five hundred magazines at their disposal. Meanwhile, Langarotti prepared sets of uniforms from the bales of clothing Dupree had provided. When each set was wrapped in a bundle, it was stuffed into a sleeping bag, with one Schmeisser and five full magazines wrapped in an oily cloth and tied into a polyethylene bag. Each sleeping bag then comprised the necessary clothing and weaponry for one soldier.

Dupree had stripped down three of the ammunition crates, tailored them to fit neatly over the tops of the outboard engines. Lined with foam rubber, these boxes would muffle engine noise.

Then Vlaminck and Dupree turned their attention to the weapons they would use for the strike. Janni familiarized himself with the aiming mechanisms of his two mortar tubes, and prepared the mortar bombs. Marc concentrated on bazookas. He had picked Patrick as his backup man, for they had worked together before. The African would carry a Schmeisser and ten bazooka rockets. Marc would carry twelve, plus a bazooka.

Shannon had the *Toscana* heave to well out at sea while the men tested their Schmeissers. The whites had each in their time used enough different submachine guns to find no problem, but the Africans had used only bolt-action 7.92-mm. Mausers or the standard 7.62 NATO self-loading rifle. Each man fired off nine hundred rounds, until he was accustomed to the feel of the gun. Next, the empty oil drums were streamed astern for bazooka practice. Before they had finished, all of the men could riddle a barrel at a hundred yards. Four barrels were sunk in this manner. The fifth was Vlaminck's own target. He let it stream to two hundred yards, then planted himself in the stern. His first rocket screamed over the top of the barrel and exploded with a spout of spray. His second took the barrel in the center. A cheer came from the watchers. Grinning, Marc turned to Shannon. "You say you want a door taken off, Cat?"

"That's right, a bloody great wooden gate, Tiny."

"I'll give it to you in matchsticks, and that's a promise."

Because of the noise they had made, Shannon ordered the *Toscana* to move on. Their next halt was to test the assault craft. With muffling boxes in place and the engines throttled back to quarter power, there was hardly a sound at thirty yards. The walkie-talkies were tested up to four miles. All ten men, black and white, Shannon put through night exercises at sea to accustom their vision to the blackness of sky and ocean, in which they would have to operate when they struck.

Waldenberg watched the exercises curiously. "Even listening hard, I can't hear you out there," he said to Shannon. "Unless they have very alert guards, you should be able to make the beach, wherever you're going. Incidentally, where *are* you going?"

"I think you'd all better know," said Shannon. And until dawn the whole company listened while Shannon went through the entire plan of attack, using his projector and slides.

When he had finished there was dead silence.

Finally Waldenberg said, "*Gott im Himmel.*" Then the questions started. Waldenberg wanted reassurance that if anything went wrong the survivors would be back on board and the *Toscana* well over the horizon before sunrise. Shannon gave it to him.

"We have only your word for it that they have no gunboats."

"Then my word will have to do," snapped Shannon.

The young Africans had no questions. The doctor asked where he would be, and accepted that he would remain on the *Toscana*.

Sitting together on deck after the briefing, the five mercenaries talked until the sun was high. They all approved of the attack plan although they knew they were very few, dangerously few, for such a job, and there was no margin for error. They accepted that either they had to win within twenty minutes or they would have to get back to their boats and leave in a hurry, those that could leave. They knew that anyone finding a colleague badly wounded would be expected to give him one mercenary's last gift to another, the quick, clean way out. It was one of the rules.

THEY all awoke early on the morning of Day Ninety-nine. Shannon had been up half the night, watching beside Waldenberg as the coastline loomed up on the tiny radar screen.

"I want you to come within visual range of the coast just south of Clarence," he had told the captain, "and spend the morning steaming northward, parallel to the shore, so that at noon we are off the coast here." His finger jabbed at the capital of the republic north of Zangaro.

The first message to Endean was timed for noon.

The morning passed slowly. Through the ship's telescope Shannon watched the estuary of the Zangaro River, a long, low line of mangrove trees on the horizon. At midmorning he could make out the break in the green line where the town of Clarence lay, and he handed the telescope in turn to Vlaminck, Langarotti,

Dupree, and Semmler. Each studied the coast in silence. They smoked and mooched around the deck, tense and bored.

At noon Shannon began to transmit. His message was one word, "Plantain," which meant that he was in position.

Twenty-two miles away Simon Endean heard the word. Then he began, painstakingly, to explain to the ex-colonel in his custody that within twenty-four hours he, Antoine Bobi, would be president of Zangaro. Chuckling at the thought of the reprisals he would take, Bobi struck his deal with Endean. He signed the document granting Bormac Trading Company a ten-year exclusive mining concession in the Crystal Mountains, and watched Endean seal in an envelope a certified check for half a million dollars.

Meanwhile, in Clarence, preparations went ahead for Independence Day. Six prisoners, lying badly beaten in the cells beneath the police station, knew they would be battered to death in the main square as part of the celebrations Kimba had prepared.

In the palace, surrounded by guards, Jean Kimba sat at his desk, contemplating the advent of his sixth year of office.

DURING the afternoon the *Toscana* and her lethal cargo put about and began to cruise slowly back down the coast.

"Hold her just north of the border until dark," Shannon told his captain. "At nine p.m. move diagonally toward the coast. At two a.m. we end up four miles out and one mile north of the peninsula."

"When does the first craft set free and move inshore?"

"At two. That will be Dupree and his mortar crew. The other two boats head for the beach one hour later. Okay?"

"Okay," said Waldenberg. "I'll have you there."

He knew the rest. After the firefight began, he would ease the *Toscana* across the mouth of the harbor, still four miles out, and heave to again two miles south of the tip of the peninsula. He would listen on his walkie-talkie, and if all went well, he would stay where he was until sunup. If things went badly, he would turn on the ship's lights to guide the men back to the *Toscana*.

When darkness fell Shannon began organizing the assault craft. First over the side was Dupree's. Semmler and Dupree hoisted the heavy outboard engine into place, screwed it tight to the back-board, and placed the muffler on top of it.

Semmler climbed out, and the equipment was lowered to Janni's waiting hands. Baseplates and sighting gear for both mortars, then the two mortar tubes and sixty bombs, all primed and fused. Janni also took the flares and the flare-launching rockets, a gas-powered foghorn, and one walkie-talkie. His Schmeisser was slung over his shoulder. Then the Africans who were going with him, Timo-thy and Sunday, slid down the ladder to join Dupree.

Shannon stared at the three faces looking up at him in the dim glow from the flashlight. "Good luck," he called softly. For an-swer Dupree raised one thumb and nodded. When the assault craft was streamed astern of the *Toscana*, Semmler tied her line to the after rail.

The second boat was for Vlaminck and Semmler, with their backup men, Patrick and Jinja. When their craft was streamed astern of the ship, Dupree's line was passed to Semmler, who made it fast to his own dinghy.

Langarotti and Shannon took the last boat with Johnny, who had worked with Shannon before, and Bartholomew.

Just as Shannon, who was the last man into the boats, was about to descend the ladder, Captain Waldenberg appeared from the bridge. "We may have a problem," he muttered quietly. "There's a ship. Lying off Clarence, farther out than us."

Shannon froze. "When did you first see it?"

"Some time ago," said Waldenberg. "I thought she must be cruis-ing south down the coast. But she's riding to."

"Any indication of what she is, who she belongs to?"

"She's the size of a freighter. No indication who she is."

"If you've seen her, presumably she's seen you?"

"Bound to," said Waldenberg. "We're on her radar, all right."

"Could her radar pick up the dinghies?"

"Unlikely," said the captain. "They're too low in the water."

"We go ahead," said Shannon. "It's too late now. We have to assume she's a freighter waiting out the night."

"She's bound to hear the firefight," said Waldenberg.

"What can she do about it?"

"Not much," said the German. "But if you fail and we're not out of here before sunrise, she'll see the *Toscana* through binoculars."

"We mustn't fail, then. Carry on as ordered."

Waldenberg went back to his bridge. The middle-aged African, who had watched the proceedings in silence, stepped forward.

"Good luck, Major," he said. "God go with you."

Shannon nodded, said, "Sure," and went over the side.

Out in the darkness there was complete silence but for the slap of the water against the rubberized hulls of the boats. They were out of earshot of the shore, and by the time they came close enough to hear landward sounds it would be well past midnight and, with luck, everyone would be asleep.

At nine the *Toscana* emitted a low rumble, and the water beneath her stern began to churn and bubble, the phosphorescent white wake slapping against the snub nose of Shannon's assault craft. Then they were under way. The next five hours went by like a nightmare, building tension in every man in the operation.

Shannon's watch said five past two when the *Toscana* slowed to idle in the water. From above the after rail a low whistle came through the darkness—Waldenberg's signal for cast off. Dupree's engine coughed into life and began to move.

At the helm of his assault craft big Janni checked his power setting and held the compass as steady as he could under his eyes. He was trying to make landfall on the outer side of the northern arm that curved around the harbor. He should make it in thirty minutes. If the others gave him one hour to set up his mortars and flare rockets, they should be landing just about the time he was ready. But for that one hour he and Timothy and Sunday would be alone in Zangaro.

Twenty-two minutes on his way, Dupree heard a low *psst* from Timothy in the bow. He glanced up from his compass, and what he saw caused him to throttle back quickly. They were already close to shore, and the starlight revealed a line of deeper darkness right ahead. Mangrove. Dupree could hear the water chuckling among the roots. He had made landfall north of the harbor.

He brought his boat about, keeping the throttle very low, and headed back to sea. At the point of the peninsula he again moved slowly inshore. At two hundred yards he could make out the long, low spit of sand and shingle he was seeking. He cut the engine and let the craft drift until it grounded with a soft grating sound.

Dupree swung his legs over the prow and stood listening. When he was sure they had caused no alarm, he slipped a marlin spike out of his belt and rammed it into the shingle, tying the line to it. Then he ran up the hummock ahead of him. It was barely fifteen feet above sea level at its top. To his left the spit of land widened into the darkness. Ahead lay the mirror calm of the protected harbor. The end of the point was ten yards to his right.

Silently, Dupree and the two Africans unloaded and set up their equipment. The main mortar was to go at the far end of the spit. If Shannon's measurements were accurate, and Janni trusted they would be, the range from there to the center of the palace courtyard was 781 yards. He adjusted the elevation of his first mortar to drop a range-finding bomb as near to that spot as possible.

He set up the second mortar pointing at the barracks. Accuracy here was less vital, since the intent was to drop bombs at random and scatter the army through panic. Timothy would handle this.

Between the two mortars he established the two flare-launching rockets and jammed one rocket down each launcher, leaving the other eight lying handy. Each flare had a life of twenty seconds, so if he was to operate both his own mortar and the illuminations he would have to work fast. Sunday would pass him the mortar bombs from the stack he had built beside the emplacement. He looked at his watch. Three twenty-two. The other two boats must be heading for the harbor. He switched on his walkie-talkie and pressed the blip button three times at one-second intervals.

A mile offshore, Shannon's eyes were straining into the darkness ahead. On his left Semmler kept the second craft in formation order and listened for Dupree's signal. He hissed to let Shannon know that he had heard it. Two minutes later Shannon caught the quick glimmer of Dupree's flashlight. It was off to his right, so he swung to starboard, aiming for a point a hundred yards to the right of the light. He knew that would be the harbor entrance.

Shut down to less than quarter power and making no noise louder than a bumblebee's, the two assault craft went by the spit where Dupree crouched. The South African caught the glitter of their wake; then they were gone into the harbor entrance.

There was still no sound from the shore when Shannon's straining eyes made out the warehouse against the skyline. He steered to the right and grounded on the fishing beach among dugout canoes and fishnets. Semmler came in beside him, and both engines died together. All eight men remained motionless for several minutes waiting for an alarm to be called. Then Shannon and Semmler stepped out, jabbed in their marlin spikes, and tethered the boats. The others followed. With a muttered, "Come on, let's go," Shannon led the way up the slope toward the two-hundred-yard-wide plateau between the harbor and the sleeping palace.

The eight men ran in a low crouch up the slope and out onto the plain at the top. It was after half past three, and no lights were burning in the palace. Shannon knew that ahead lay the coast road, and standing at the junction would be at least two palace guards. He expected he would not be able to take them both silently and that, after the firing started, they would have to crawl the last hundred yards to the palace wall. He was right.

Out on his gravel spit big Janni Dupree waited for the shot that would send him into action—the first shot, whoever fired it.

Shannon and Langarotti were out ahead of the other six when they made the road junction. Their faces, darkened with sepia dye, were already streaked with sweat. Shannon could make out the line of the roof against the sky, but he missed the guards until he stumbled over one. The man was on the ground, snoozing.

After stumbling, Shannon recovered, but the Vindu guard jumped up with a yell of surprise. The call aroused his partner, who rose up from his lair in the uncut grass, gurgled once as the Corsican's knife opened his throat, and went back down again, choking out his last seconds. Shannon's man took a swipe in the shoulder from his bowie knife, let out another scream, and ran.

It was never certain who fired first. A wild shot from the palace gate, and the snarl of Shannon's half-second burst, that sliced the running man in two, blended with each other. Behind them the sky exploded in blistering white light. Shannon caught a brief impression of the palace, two figures in front of its gate, and the feeling of his men fanning out to right and left of him. Then they were all face down in the long grass and crawling forward.

Janni Dupree slipped his mortar bomb down the tube as the first flare screamed upward. The *smack thump* of the mortar bomb departing on its parabola toward the palace coincided with the crash of the flare. Squinting into the light, he waited to watch the bomb fall. It hit the front right cornice of the palace roof, blowing off tiles. Dupree twirled the traverse knob of the aiming mechanism a few mils to the left and slipped in his second bomb just as the first flare fizzled out. The second flare burst into light above the palace, and four seconds later the second bomb landed. This one fell onto the tiles directly above the main door. Dupree adjusted the nose of the mortar a whisker. His third bomb went clean over the palace roof and into the courtyard behind. He saw the glow for a split second; then it was gone. He knew he had his range. There would be no shortfalls to endanger his own men.

Between the second and third explosions, Shannon heard screams from inside the fortress. These were the only sounds the defenders made before the roar of explosive blotted out all else.

When Janni's main barrage began to hit the palace there was no more need for flares; the roaring crash of the mortar bombs going into the flagstone-covered courtyard behind the palace threw up gobbets of red light every two seconds.

Tiny Marc Vlaminck was the only one of the eight men who had anything to do. He was at the left of the line, almost exactly in front of the main gate. Standing foursquare to the palace, he took careful aim and sent off his first rocket. A twenty-foot tongue of flame whirled out of the rear of the bazooka as the warhead sped forward. It exploded high on the right-hand edge of the double doors, ripping a hinge out of the masonry and leaving a yard-square hole in the woodwork.

Kneeling by his side, Patrick passed rockets to him. The second shot exploded against the arch above the door. The third hit the center lock. The doors sagged and fell apart, revealing a fiery furnace beyond the archway, which apparently was a through passage to the courtyard behind. When Dupree's barrage stopped, Shannon leaped to his feet, screaming, "Come on!" He was firing as he ran, sensing more than seeing Langarotti on his left and Semmler closing up on his right. Through the gate the scene was enough to stop anybody in his tracks.

Dupree's first sighting shots had brought Kimba's guards out of their huts and into the center of the paved area. That was where the bombs had found them. There were piles of bodies, some still half alive, most very dead. Two army trucks and three civilian cars, one the presidential Mercedes, were shredded against a wall.

To right and left were archways leading to stairs to the upper floors. Without waiting to be asked, Semmler took the right, Langarotti the left. Soon there were bursts of Schmeisser fire as the two mercenaries laundered the upper floor. Shannon shouted at the Africans to take the ground floor. He did not have to tell them to shoot everything that moved.

Slowly, cautiously, Shannon moved through the archway that led into the rear courtyard. If there was still any opposition, it would come from there. Suddenly a figure with a rifle ran screaming at him from his left. Shannon whirled and fired, and the man jackknifed in a froth of blood. The whole place smelled of blood and fear.

He sensed footsteps behind him and swung around. From one of the side doors a man had emerged. The man saw Shannon as Shannon saw him, and snapped off a shot. Shannon felt the slug blow softly on his cheek as it passed. He fired a second later, but the man was agile. He went to the ground, rolled, and came up in fire position a second time. Shannon's Schmeisser had let off five shots, but they'd gone above the gunman's body as he hit the flagstones; then the magazine ran out. Shannon stepped behind a pillar to slap in a new one, then came around the corner firing. The man was gone.

It was only then he became fully conscious that the gunman, stripped to the waist and barefoot, had not been an African. He swore and ran back to the main gate. He was too late.

As the gunman ran out of the shattered palace, Tiny Marc was walking toward the archway, his bazooka cradled in both hands. Still running flat out, the gunman loosed two fast shots. They found the gun later in the long grass. It was a Makarov 9 mm.

The Belgian took both shots in the chest, one in the lungs. The gunman was past him, dashing for safety out of reach of the flares Dupree was still sending up. Shannon watched Vlaminck, moving in a kind of slow motion, raise his bazooka, aim, and fire.

Not often does one see a bazooka the size of a warhead hit a man in the small of the back. Afterward they could find nothing more than a few pieces of cloth from his trousers.

Shannon had to throw himself flat to avoid the backlash of flame from Tiny Marc's last shot. He was still on the ground, eight yards away, when the big Belgian crashed forward, arms outspread, across the hard earth before the gate.

JANNI Dupree straightened up after dispatching the last of his flares, and shouted to Sunday to stay and keep watch over the mortars and the boat. Then signaling to Timothy to follow him, he began to jogtrot along the spit of land toward Clarence. He still had the job of silencing the army barracks. It took them ten minutes to reach the road that ran across the end of the peninsula. From there it was, Janni knew, a left turn to the barracks.

The trouble was around that bend. Scattered by Timothy's mortar bombs, Kimba's army had fled into the night. But about a dozen of the men had regrouped in the darkness and were standing at the edge of the road. Dupree and Timothy were almost on the group before they saw them. Ten of the men were naked, having been roused from sleep. The other two had been on guard duty and were clothed and armed. One had a hand grenade.

When Dupree saw the soldiers he screamed, "Fire!" and opened up. Four of them were cut apart by the stream of slugs from the Schmeisser. The rest ran, two more falling as Dupree's fire pursued them. But one, as he ran, turned and hurled the thing he had in his hand. It was his pride and joy. He had always wanted to throw it.

The grenade went high in the air, and when it fell it hit Timothy full in the chest. The African veteran clutched at the object as he went over backward and, sitting on the ground, recognized it for what it was. He saw that the fool who had thrown it had forgotten to take out the pin. Rising to his feet, Timothy promptly did so and threw it as far as he could after the retreating Vindu soldiers. But this time it hit a tree and fell to the ground. At that moment Janni Dupree started in pursuit. Timothy shouted a warning, but Dupree ran on, firing from the hip, and was two yards from the grenade when it exploded.

He came to, lying on the road, and there was someone kneeling beside him, cradling his head. He had a comfortable, drowsy feeling. He could hear a voice saying something urgently, but he couldn't make out the words. "Sorry Janni, so sorry, sorry . . ." He could see the moon glistening like a giant pearl, like the Paarl rock after the rain at home. It was good to be back home. He closed his eyes and died.

At half past five enough daylight filtered over the horizon for the men at the palace to switch off their flashlights.

Vlaminck's body lay in a room on the ground floor. Beside him lay Dupree, brought in by Timothy, and Johnny, who had evidently been shot by the white bodyguard with the Makarov.

Semmler summoned Shannon to the bedroom upstairs to show him the figure he had gunned down clambering out of the window.

"That's him," said Shannon. "Kimba."

Six survivors from the domestic staff Shannon used as forced labor to dump the bodies in the back courtyard. He had a large carpet hung over the ruined entrance to mask the grisly view.

At five o'clock Semmler had gone out to the *Toscana* in one of the boats, towing the other two behind him. He was back at six thirty with the African doctor, and the boats, now loaded with stores, the remaining Schmeissers, and nearly a ton of ammunition.

At six, acting on Shannon's instructions, Waldenberg had begun to broadcast three words on the frequency to which Endean was listening—paw-paw, cassave, and mango—meaning the operation went as planned, was successful, Kimba is dead.

When the African doctor viewed the carnage in the palace, he sighed and said, "I suppose it was necessary."

"It was," affirmed Shannon, and asked Okoye to set about the task he had been brought to do.

By nine the clearing-up process was almost complete. The burial of the Vindu would have to wait for more manpower. Two of the dinghies were back on the *Toscana;* the third was hidden in a creek nearby. All traces of mortars and rocket launchers had been removed from the point. Everything else had been put inside the palace, which, apart from the destroyed door and three broken windows, did not show the beating it had taken.

At ten Semmler and Langarotti joined Shannon in the upstairs dining room. Both men reported on the result of their searches. The transmitter was intact. The treasury was in a safe in the cellar. The armory contained plenty of guns and ammo.

"So what now?" asked Semmler.

"So now we wait," said Shannon, thinking of Janni Dupree and Tiny Marc and Johnny.

"Wait for what?" Langarotti said, slowly stropping his knife on the band around his fist.

"We wait for the new government," Shannon said.

A one-ton truck carrying Simon Endean arrived just after one in the afternoon. At the wheel was a hulking strong-armer from East London, Ernie Locke, who was being paid a handsome fee to keep Endean alive and well. Cowering under canvas in the back was Bobi, who had evidently not won his colonelcy by personal courage. He had yet to be persuaded that Kimba was dead.

Shannon leaned out the window as Endean climbed suspiciously down, looked at the carpet hanging in the doorway, and examined the eight black guards at attention before the gate. "Everything okay?" Endean called up to Shannon.

"Sure," said Shannon. "But get out of sight. No one has moved yet, but someone is bound to start snooping soon."

Endean led Bobi and Locke upstairs and asked Shannon for a

report on the battle. For answer Shannon led him to the rear window and pointed into the courtyard from which a ferocious buzzing of flies mounted. Endean looked out and drew back.

"And the army?"

"Twenty dead, the rest scattered. Their arms and the presidential armory are here in the cellar, under our control. The national radio is intact."

Endean nodded, satisfied. "Then there's nothing left but for the new president to announce the success of his coup and the formation of a new government. By the way, let me introduce him." He gestured toward the Zangaran colonel whose face now wore a broad grin.

"Former commander of the Zangaran army, successful operator of a coup d'etat, as far as the world knows. Colonel Antoine Bobi."

Shannon bowed. "Perhaps the president would like to examine the presidential office," he said, moving to open a door at the end of the room. Endean translated.

Bobi nodded and lumbered across the floor and through the door, followed by Shannon. It closed behind them. There was the crash of a single shot.

After Shannon reappeared, Endean sat staring at him. "What was that?" he asked unnecessarily.

"A shot," said Shannon.

Endean was on his feet, across the room, and standing in the open doorway to the study. He turned around, ashen-faced.

"You shot him," he whispered. "All this bloody way, and you shot him. You're mad, Shannon, you bloody mercenary idiot."

Shannon sat back in his chair. From the corner of his eye he saw Locke's hand move under his shirt. The second crash seemed louder to Endean, for it was nearer. Ernie Locke went into a backward somersault and sprawled across the floor. He was quite dead. Shannon brought his hand out from under the table and laid the Makarov automatic on the table. A wisp of blue smoke wriggled out of the end of the barrel.

Endean seemed to sag at the shoulders, as if the knowledge of the certain loss of his personal fortune was compounded by the

sudden realization that Shannon was the most completely dangerous man he had ever met.

Semmler appeared in the office doorway, and Langarotti slipped
quietly in from the corridor. Both held Schmeissers.

Shannon rose. "Come on," he said. "I'll drive you back to the
border. From there you can walk."

In the hallway they met a middle-aged African in civilian
clothes. "Everything okay, Doctor?" Shannon asked.

"Yes, so far. I have arranged with my people to send a hundred
volunteer workers to clean up. Another fifty soldiers will be here
this afternoon. Seven Zangaran notables have agreed to serve."

"Good. Perhaps you had better take time off to broadcast the
first bulletin. Ask Mr. Semmler to help with the radio."

"I have just spoken to Mr. Semmler," said the doctor. "He has
been in touch with the *Toscana* by walkie-talkie. Captain Waldenberg reports there is a ship out there trying to raise Clarence port
authorities with a request for permission to enter."

"Any identification?" asked Shannon.

"She identifies herself as the Russian freighter *Komarov*."

"Tell Mr. Semmler to man the port radio at once. Tell him to
reply to the *Komarov*, 'Permission refused. Permanently.'"

The vehicle that had brought Endean stood in the courtyard.
Three African soldiers crouched in the back with submachine
guns. Another twenty, fully uniformed and equipped, were being
marshaled into a line outside the palace. Shannon took the wheel
of the truck himself.

"Who was that man?" asked Endean sourly as they sped past the
shantytown of the immigrant workers, where all seemed to be
bustle and activity. At the crossroads, well-dressed soldiers were
on duty, carrying Schmeissers.

"Dr. Okoye," said Shannon. "He's an Oxford Ph.D."

"All right," said Endean after a long silence. "You've ruined one
of the biggest and richest coups that has ever been attempted.
What I'd like to know is, why? In God's name, why?"

"You made two mistakes, Endean," Shannon said. Endean
started at the sound of his real name. "You assumed that be-

cause I'm a mercenary I'm stupid. It never seemed to occur to you that you, too, are a mercenary, along with Sir James Manson. Your second mistake was to assume that all people who are black are alike."

"I don't follow you."

"You did a lot of research on Zangaro; you even found out about the thousands of immigrant workers who virtually keep this place running. Those workers form a community of their own, the most intelligent and hardworking one in the country. Given half a chance, they can play a part in the political life of the country. You failed to recognize that. Or that the new army of Zangaro might be recruited, not from Vindu or Caja, but from that community. In fact, it just has been. In five days there will be over four hundred new soldiers in Clarence—untrained, of course, but efficient enough to keep law and order. They'll be the real power in this country from now on. There was a coup last night, all right, but it wasn't conducted on behalf of your Colonel Bobi."

"For whom, then?"

"For the general. For whom Dr. Okoye is acting."

"Which general?"

Shannon told him the name. Endean's mouth opened in horror. "Not him. He was defeated. Exiled."

"For the moment. Not necessarily forever. Those immigrant workers are his people. They call them the Jews of Africa. There are one and a half million of them scattered over this continent."

"That stupid great idealistic bastard—"

"Careful," warned Shannon. "We have three of his soldiers with us, and they all speak English."

Endean turned and looked in the back at three impassive faces above three Schmeisser barrels. "What happens now?" he asked.

"The Committee of National Reconciliation takes over. Four Vindu members, four Caja, and two from the immigrant community. But the army will be made up of the people behind you. And this country will be used as a base from which they may one day avenge what was done to their people. Maybe the general will come and set up residence here."

"You expect to get away with that?"

"You expected to impose that slobbering ape Bobi and get away with it. At least the new government will be moderately fair. No doubt they will eventually find that mineral deposit or whatever you were after. And no doubt it will be exploited. But if you want it, you will have to pay a fair price for it."

Around the corner they came within view of the border post. Shannon stopped the truck. "You can walk the rest of the way."

Endean climbed down. He looked back at Shannon with undiluted hatred. "You still haven't explained *why*."

Shannon stared ahead up the road. "For nearly two years," he said, "I watched between half a million and a million small kids starved to death. It was done so that people like you and Manson could make bigger profits, and it was done in the name of law and order. I may be a fighter, I may be a killer, but I am not a bloody sadist. I worked out for myself how it was done, and why, and who were the men behind it. Profiteers like your precious Manson. That's why I did it. Tell Manson when you get back home. I'd like him to know. Personally. From me. Now walk."

Ten yards on, Endean turned around.

"Don't ever come back to London, Shannon," he called. "We can deal with people like you there."

"I won't," yelled Shannon. And under his breath he murmured, "I won't ever have to."

EPILOGUE

THE new government was duly installed and at the last count was ruling humanely and well. There was hardly a mention of the coup in the European newspapers, just a brief piece in *Le Monde* to say that dissident units of the Zangaran army had toppled the president on the eve of Independence Day.

Janni Dupree and Marc Vlaminck were buried down on the point, beneath the palm trees where the wind blows off the gulf. The graves were left unmarked at Shannon's request. Johnny was taken by his own people, who keened over him in their own way.

Simon Endean and Sir James Manson kept quiet. There was really nothing they could say publicly.

Shannon gave Jean-Baptiste Langarotti the £5000 remaining in his money belt from the operation's budget, and the Corsican went back to Europe. As he told Shannon when they parted on the shore, "It's not really the money. It was never for the money." In a matter of months he was back in Africa, training partisans in another civil war.

Shannon wrote letters to Signor Ponti in Genoa in the name of Keith Brown, ordering him to hand over the bearer shares controlling the ownership of the *Toscana* in equal parts to Captain Waldenberg and Kurt Semmler. A year later Semmler, hankering once more for the soldier's life, sold Waldenberg his shares. Semmler died laying a mine in South Sudan.

The last thing Shannon did was to order his bank in Switzerland to make a credit transfer of £5000 to the parents of Janni Dupree in Paarl, Cape Province, and another in the same sum to a woman called Anna, who ran a bar in the Kleinstraat in Ostend.

He died a month after the coup, the way he had told Julie Manson he wanted to go, with a gun in his hand and blood in his mouth and a bullet in the chest. His own gun and his own bullet. It was not the fighting that destroyed him, but the little black mole on the back of his neck. That was what he had learned from Dr. Dunois in his Paris office. Less than six months if he pushed himself, and the last month would be bad. So when he judged the time had come he walked alone into the jungle with his gun and an envelope of typescript addressed to a friend in London.

The natives who saw him go, and later brought him back for burial, said he was whistling when he went. They did not know what the whistling was. It was a tune called "Spanish Harlem."

Whether fighting bulls in Spain, flying bomber planes for the RAF, or visiting far-flung corners of the world as a foreign correspondent, Frederick Forsyth brings a passionate intensity to everything he does. A born adventurer, the British journalist-turned-novelist has visited more than forty countries. Now, at the age of thirty-six, Forsyth is an acknowledged master of fiction so ingeniously blended with reality that each book reads like firsthand experience.

Frederick Forsyth

Forsyth's first two thrillers, *The Day of the Jackal* and *The Odessa File*, grew directly out of what he learned as a reporter in the Paris and Berlin bureaus of Reuters. *The Dogs of War* was born of eighteen months in Africa covering the Nigerian-Biafran war, where he came to know mercenaries like the legendary Schramme and Hoare, on whom he based the character of "Cat" Shannon.

Forsyth writes novels in record time. June 1973, a month of self-imposed isolation, produced this one. But first, of course, had come weeks of research done more often than not, as he says, "among people rather than archives." His journalistic background has given him a wealth of contacts and a key to undercover operations and secret organizations. It also, he says, "gave me the training to ferret out facts that some of the pertinent authorities would prefer did not emerge. It taught me, too, how to draw people out and how to sift information."

The author and his Irish-born bride, Carrie, live on their farm near Valencia, Spain. As for future plans, Forsyth intimates that a return to active journalism, the seedbed of his novels, has a strong appeal.

ACKNOWLEDGMENT

Page 5: *The Fox Hunt,* an oil painting on canvas by Winslow Homer, is used by courtesy of the Pennsylvania Academy of the Fine Arts, Philadelphia.